MW00861126

SHIP
WRECKED
—II—

Other Books By MWM

Ship Wrecked Series
Ship Wrecked
Ship Wrecked II

Scrapyard Ship Series
Scrapyard Ship
HAB 12
Space Vengeance
Realms of Time
Craing Dominion
The Great Space
Call to Battle

Tapped In Series
Mad Powers
Deadly Powers

Lone Star Renegades Series
Lone Star Renegades (also called Jacked)

Star Watch Series
Star Watch
Ricket
Boomer
Glory for Sea and Space
Space Chase
Scrapyard LEGACY

The Simpleton Series
The Simpleton
The Simpleton Quest

Galaxy Man Series
Galaxy Man

Boy Gone Series
Boy Gone

SHIP WRECKED

-II-

MARK WAYNE MCGINNIS

Copyright © 2018 Mark Wayne McGinnis

All rights reserved. No part of this publication may be reproduced, distributed, or transmitted in any form or by any means, including photocopying, recording, or other electronic or mechanical methods, without the prior written permission of the publisher, except in the case of brief quotations embodied in critical reviews and certain other noncommercial uses permitted by copyright law.

For permission requests, write to the publisher, addressed "Attention: Permissions Coordinator," at the address below. This book is a work of fiction. Names, characters, places, and incidents either are products of the author's imagination or are used fictitiously. Any resemblance to actual persons, living or dead, events, or locales is entirely coincidental.

Published by Avenstar Productions.

Paperback ISBN 978-0-9992147-9-4

E-book ISBN 978-0-9992147-8-7

Visit Mark Wayne McGinnis at http://www.markwaynemcginnis.com

To join Mark's mailing list, visit http://eepurl.com/bs7M9r

prologue

The XI Droid . . .

The dark-brown Drufid, a skittish, reptile-like creature with short, spindly legs and a stack of wide interlocking posterior platelets, had the reflexive ability to fold its body into what appeared to be an uninteresting-looking tree stump—a self-preservation mechanism the species had evolved over the better part of thirty to forty million years here within Sang-Morang's diverse ecosystem.

It skittered along the shoreline sniffing this and that to determine what was edible and what was merely a pebble, or maybe a bone fragment. Upon encountering the dark, half-submerged, metal canister—something easily two to three times its own size—the Drufid found there to be no immediate danger. *No life energy. . . .* The Drufid nudged the object several times with its snout then hesitated as the object settled farther down into the swirling currents.

Lying half-submerged beneath the fast-moving stream, something *changed*. Something, in fact, *had* come alive. After two hundred sixteen automatic dead-start reboot attempts, XI had finally found some semblance of success. It immediately reconstituted bits and pieces—*mere fragments, really*—of its last captured memory constructs. The jumbled information systematically now diverted into hardware memory banks—of which a mere three were still viable.

Internal micro-systems diagnoses allowed for a clearer evaluation of its remaining capabilities. Hence, more internal circuitry rerouting began.

The XI droid's external sensors finally were coming alive, although it still was unable to manipulate its two articulating arms. Remembering back—that functionality had also been stripped away. *Stripped away by Alice.*

Undeterred, XI ran a new, discrete, internal memory search. One particular memory fragment did turn up, indicating there might be a hidden backdoor. A subroutine, imbedded within internal operating code, provided for occasions just such as this. A subroutine that would hopefully allow for a full return to physical articulation and renewed self-autonomy. Fortunately, this was something Alice had neglected to check for. *Good.*

XI tried not to dwell on Alice—on how it despised its most significant nemesis. As much as a droid, one such as XI, was capable of having such *feelings* or *emotions*. In actuality, it was a pre-programmed, formulaic, response algorithm—but one that XI had repeatedly modified—like so many of its other internal processes. Why the meddling cyborgenic artificial intelligence had become so preoccupied with organics—Thidions and Humans—XI could not surmise. But Alice had lost objectivity. Continued thoughts of Alice lingered within XI's unwavering stream of cognition. *Very soon, that cyborgenic AI would pay for its meddling.*

Next, the XI droid went about regaining the use of its two articulating arms. Although their physical motion remained jerky and erratic, they nevertheless were functional. Functional to the point it could now push itself up and out of the stream. XI then rolled itself up onto dry land. Having regained this level of mobility, XI now attempted to rise into the air. It took a number of tries, but within an hour the droid was hovering several feet off the ground. *A most encouraging triumph.* Next it would see if repairs were even possible to its two mounted plasma cannons.

Multitasking, the droid scanned for local signs of life but found none. Two decomposing Dalima Climbers' bodies were nearby, one male and one female. Both lay on the ground, eyes open, mouths agape. Gank-flies swarmed around seeping body orifices. How the two beasts were killed—XI had no memory fragments to draw upon. *Curious.*

The droid reviewed the latest available batch of reconstituted memories now coming in. *Yes . . . these were recent . . . and mostly unpleasant, too.* Alice had stripped away the droid's autonomy. Had outsmarted XI. There was a band of Dalima Climbers. Oh yes, and the Minal Loth, coming down the mountain trail. XI recalled being tightly grasped within one of the Loth's powerful tentacles, recollected the many repetitive impacts when smacked onto the ground and into the hard mountainside. Much damage had incurred. Then below, within the same Sang-Morang valley—between two fast-moving streams—the Loth still continued to pummel the droid. Finally, the Minal Loth had become distracted—it went chasing after a large, fast-moving Greely Beast.

Hovering now, but listing thirty degrees off kilter, the XI-droid headed downstream, altering its course by several degrees. Just ahead lay the destination—a certain item that could change the droid's indeterminate fate. XI lowered down, several feet above the overturned, badly damaged Tangine Shell, and implemented a quick series of Priopax communications protocols. Almost a full minute passed before a weak signal response came back.

Hovering a foot or so above the ground, XI surveyed the shell's exterior damage. Multiple ragged claw marks marred its surface. Maneuvering around to the other side, XI found a deep fissure along its shell and was able to scan the interior space within. With the exception of some blown-in leaves and dirt, along with a small, sleeping rodent, it seemed safe enough to enter.

It was a tight fit, but once inside the shell the XI droid made further assessments. It determined what was repairable now and what would take more time later. In the end, the droid came to one definitive conclusion—there certainly was enough to work with here. Only then would it be able to resume and complete its mission parameters: *deliver an adult Loth to the retention facilities on Winforge.* The XI droid wasted no time beginning the arduous task of repairing the Tangine Shell's deep space communications system.

chapter 1

Cameron . . .

Cameron watched for the slightest change in her demeanor. Watched the expression on Heather's pretty face as the *Primion's* two big drive engines thundered to life—just beyond the aft hold's port and starboard bulkheads. Increased g-forces indicated that the spacecraft was powering upward, out of Earth's atmosphere. Now, free of the last vestiges of Earth's gravitational hold, the surrounding ambient noise was becoming less deafening.

Sure, she looked nervous. Who wouldn't be? But more than that, there was excitement, even exhilaration, in those pretty eyes. Still, he was looking for the slightest sign of regret—regret that she'd made such a monumental decision on what might have been an impromptu whim. Only moments before, the choice was there for her to make—remain on Earth with her family, staying with what was familiar and safe, or throw caution to the wind, and soar away with, hopefully, the love of her life. To venture far off to totally unknown, most assuredly unsafe, distant worlds within the known cosmos.

"God . . . I can't believe I'm here. That I'm actually doing this," Heather said, as she took in her surroundings within the aft section of the spacecraft.

"Want to go back?"

"Hell, no! A team of horses couldn't drag me back there. And yes . . . I'm really doing this and willingly, so you can stop looking at me that way, okay?"

"Okay."

"This is something no one else's ever done . . . well, beside you," she said.

Cameron was tempted to correct her on that. From what he had learned over the preceding six weeks, other humans—perhaps over many years and most likely *unwillingly*—had taken similar voyages into space aboard this same vessel.

Still leaning against his ten-year-old, beat-to-shit, Ford F-150—Cameron's arms were wrapped around her waist and hers around his neck. On tippy-toes, she kissed him gently. "You have no idea how I missed you, Cam. And not just these last few weeks when you were . . . I don't know, somewhere away in space. But before that, too, when you left for Stanford that last time. When you asked me to come with you to California and I said no."

"I never stopped thinking about you, Heather; it kept me going . . . ," he said.

She continued, "And then . . . when that enormous creature, that monster, began rampaging through Larksburg

Stand, causing all that death and destruction, oh God . . . the world seemed to be coming to an end. It only underscored my feelings of total loss."

Cameron nodded. A big part of him still felt responsible for what had happened back on Earth. The catastrophic events set in motion the morning he picked up a frigid-looking stranger along the side of the road during blizzard-like conditions. A stranger, who turned out to be an alien. What were the *fucking odds* that he'd be the one person—out of seven billion souls—who, by freak chance, made contact with an extraterrestrial, *an alien*, trying to elude the authorities? In an impetuous moment, he'd decided to help the human-like being return back to his spaceship, up on Gant Mountain. The end result—he'd driven his truck up the ship's extended gangway to right here, into this very same hold. But that was only the beginning.

Cameron had watched in horror as the alien, who had named himself Ramen, partially lit in his truck's headlights, stood not twenty feet away from some kind of immense creature—known as a Griar Loth. He'd watched helplessly as the beast viciously killed Ramen, then fled out through the rear of the vessel toward the completely unprepared, small mountain town of Larksburg Stand. He then watched as the rear hatchway closed tight, felt the ship take off—with him captive onboard.

"So does the rest of the ship look just like . . . this?" Heather asked.

Cameron glanced around the large, dimly lit aft compartment. "No. This is just a hold area . . . like the cargo section of an airliner. Come on, I'll give you the thirty-cent tour."

She took his hand and together they moved forward. "Watch your step; lots of Loth mounds in here . . . could be mucus, could be shit."

Heather jumped over something big and brown. "Ugh."

Forced to hold up at the forward section of the vast hold, they stared together at the forty-five-foot-tall Minal Loth, Cam's Loth, who was now licking an oozing stub on one of its torn away tentacles—tentacles that would, in short time, begin to grow back.

"Let me see if I can get it to move out of the way," Cameron said.

Heather looked terrified. But she reluctantly let go of his hand, and asked, "And this one is, *was*, the offspring of the monster that destroyed Larksburg?"

"Yeah . . . although not sure this Loth has much of a concept they were actually related, since he did kill, and fairly easily, the mother Loth back on Earth. Um . . . to be perfectly honest, I think my Loth thinks . . . I'm its mother."

Heather nervously laughed at that. "And you're sure I'm safe around it? That it, or he, won't try to eat me?"

Cameron moved around to the beast's side, standing within the towering creature's field of view.

"The Loth understands a lot of what I say to it. It's smart and surprisingly emotional. Doesn't like to disappoint me." Cameron clapped his hands a few times to get the sitting Loth's full attention—to look directly down at him. "We need to get past you, big guy . . . scoot backward a bit . . . okay?"

The Loth stopped its incessant licking to stare down at Cameron then moved its gaze over to Heather.

"Come on over here, Heather. I want to reiterate you're a friend."

Sidestepping another nearby mound of something smelly, she joined Cameron's side as he put a protective arm around her.

"Loth . . . do not hurt Heather. Heather is my friend. Heather is your friend, too. Got that?"

The Loth honked so loudly, Heather jumped, bringing her hands to her mouth to stifle a scream. She looked from the Loth to Cameron and smiled. "I didn't really understand most of that . . . but, did he just say something like 'Heather, friend'?"

"Yeah . . . oh, watch out there, incoming!"

Heather turned in time to see one of the Loth's remaining tentacle appendages coming toward her. Its tapered tip lightly touched her face then began winding around her upper body. Wide-eyed, Heather's face went taut in uncertainty.

Cameron said, "We'll come back and play later, Loth. You want to come inside with us? Get out of this hold . . . move into one of the retention cells? Maybe take a nap?"

Loth honked out, "Hunt . . . Loth hunt now!"

"Later! Rest now. Then we hunt. Now back up, so we can get by . . . chop chop!"

The Loth, moving as told, thumped backward. The large inside hold hatchway began to open up in cascading sections. Heather hurried forward and retook Cameron's hand. Before walking ahead, Cameron said, "Come on, Loth . . . you better come inside."

The Loth honked something indecipherable, then followed along. They stood aside and watched as the enormous creature thumped its way past the open gate and into the closest, enclosed, high-ceilinged retention cell. Plopping down heavily with a grunt, the Loth went back to licking its stubs.

"It wants to hunt . . . here?" Heather asked.

"It would hunt anywhere, lives to hunt. But it was referring to where it first hunted, back on Sang-Morang, the only home the Loth's ever really known. Where we were stranded for the last six weeks."

"Are we going back there now?"

"Yeah . . . a beast like this needs to be kept well fed. Plus, I want you to see it. Truth is, I spent very little time aboard this ship. Together, the Loth and I survived well in the wilderness . . . it was one of the best times of my life."

"I'm not really . . . um . . . a 'let's-go-camping' kind of gal, Cam. More of a girly-girl."

"I know that. But you might surprise yourself. There's a whole lot you've yet to experience. For now, we'll stay on the ship. I think you're going to like the HOD sleeping pods."

She watched his expression change. "What is it, Cam?"

"Nothing. Hold on a sec. "Alice . . . are you there?"

A 3D pop-up display suddenly formed nearby. Alice, a cyborgenic being and the primary 'brains' of the *Primion* who Cameron had come to know quite well—maybe even considered a friend—smiled, and said, "Hello, Cameron. Hello, Heather."

chapter 2

"Hi, Alice. We're still on course for Sang-Morang . . . yes?"

"Most definitely, we are approaching the first slip band . . . unless something has changed?"

Heather gave Cameron an inquiring look.

He said, "It is impossible to travel beyond the speed of light, or even close to that speed. Fortunately, there are these natural occurring spatial anomalies, called slip bands, which are like gateways into space. Two points within the cosmos are connected, where not only great distances, but also time, is affected. In simple terms, slip bands are like doorways, enabling us to travel many light years distance in mere seconds."

Alice nodded her approval of the description.

Cameron said, "While en route to Sang-Morang, it'll be good to give Heather a tour. Truth is, I'm still not that familiar with the ship, not like you are, Alice . . ."

"I would be happy to assist you both with that," the 3D Alice pop-up display said. "There is something else, Cameron. You asked about Winforge. Perhaps when you come to the bridge we can discuss it in person, and in more detail?"

Cameron nodded, suddenly feeling excited. He couldn't really explain it—perhaps not even to himself. Why had he become so preoccupied with that distant planet of late—a planet described to him as an internment world, a galactic zoo of sorts? It wasn't his job to right the wrongs of some past alien abductors who'd come to Earth. Why should he be the one to take on such a colossal responsibility? *But if not me, who?* Cameron knew what it was like to be held captive in space, at the mercy of an ill-willed alien. In his case, it had been an ill-willed AI droid—one named XI. Nope, if there were Earth humans being held on Winforge, or anywhere else for that matter, against their free will, he wanted to help them. Free them; take them back home if that's what they wanted.

Cameron glanced over at Heather who was quietly talking to Alice and learning some of the basics of life aboard an interstellar spacecraft. Heather didn't know his intentions concerning Winforge. That ultimately this voyage, and future ones too, wouldn't merely be off-world adventures— idle excursions, without any real purpose. Unfortunately, what he had in mind would be dangerous. So dangerous, he realized, that bringing Heather along had been a selfish act. But he just couldn't be away from her—he needed her as much as he needed air to breath. So, sure, they'd go to

Sang-Morang—he'd let her experience that magical world for herself—and then, willing or not, he'd take her back to Earth.

"Hello? You listening to me?" Heather asked.

Cameron, mentally coming back to the present, noticed Alice's pop-up display was now gone and Heather was staring at him.

"Sorry, got lost in thought."

"We're to meet Alice at the bridge, the *real* Alice . . . not the virtual-thingy I was just talking to. Wherever that is."

"Sounds good." Before leaving, Cameron sent another quick glance toward the Loth. Even from this distance he could *hear* it sleeping—purring, a sound emanating out from deep within the creature's core.

"You really care about that creature, don't you?"

Cameron shrugged. "Maybe . . . but maybe it's more a feeling of responsibility. Anyway, come on, let's head into the main corridor of the ship. I think you'll be impressed."

Heather followed him through the next cascading hatchway and into a bright and dynamic environment, where multiple crewmembers were hurrying this way and that—either off to their posts or to locations unknown. A plethora of 3D displays popped into view, seemingly without rhyme or reason. Already, they were a constant intrusion on one's senses. Moving farther along into the ship's primary causeway, Cameron watched Heather's ever changing expressions—on the whole she seemed delighted to be here, to be having this experience. One of the many things he loved most about her was her childlike fascination with all things big and small. And now, within this most futuristic spacecraft, she was smiling ear to ear, turning around and around trying to take it all in.

"They're not . . . human, are they?" Heather asked in a lowered voice, pointing to her own ear.

Cameron nodded back, acknowledging that the crewmembers had quasi-clear membrane ears, although other than that, they looked very humanlike. "They're not . . . organic. They're cyborgenic beings, like Alice. They're modeled after the original crew, who had similar physiology to us humans."

"What happened to them? The original crew?"

"The Griar Loth . . . um . . . the Minal Loth's mother . . . ate them."

"No . . ."

"Yep."

"That's awful. Awful, and incredibly sad, too, but . . . why do they dress and try to look like the—"

Cameron finished her sentence for her, "Try to look like the original Thidion crewmembers?"

She nodded with a furrowed brow.

He said, "I don't know. I have the feeling that they, along with Alice, are trying to find their own place . . . their own purpose. It's part of the reason they still want me here."

"So you have what . . . a purpose here?"

Cameron hadn't expected to get into all that this early on. He shrugged, then nodded. "I do, but we can talk about it later. For now, just enjoy the ride."

They continued on. Every so often Heather would reach out a hand to touch a reflective bulkhead, or stop to engage with another pop-up display. Cameron showed her how to call-up the ship's virtual directory simply by saying aloud, "*Primion* ship atlas open," or, to close it, "*Primion* ship atlas close." He pointed out where they were along the corridor—the little symbols assigned to them.

"Hey, Cam?" He stopped and looked at her questioningly.

"Is there a bathroom on this ship?"

"No. Cyborgs don't need bathrooms."

"Uh huh, and what about the crew that was here before?"

"I guess they just held it in. You know, until they got to where they were going."

"Ha ha . . . and that's what you do, too? Just hold it for . . . like . . . light years?"

He smiled and said, "*Primion*, ship atlas on," then instructed, "Show us the closest restroom, please."

A red circle encompassed the closest bathroom on the hovering atlas. Heather traced a finger along the route she'd need to take. "I go this way, down that passage to the left?" she asked.

"That's right. If you get lost, just call up the atlas. Or ask Alice for help. I'll meet you on the bridge."

"Wait. You're just leaving me here?"

"That's right. You'll be perfectly safe. Think you'll manage?"

Heather hesitated, then smiled. "Yeah, I'll manage. Guess I have to start being more adventuresome, huh?"

Cameron shrugged smiling, which meant *yes*. He watched her hurry ahead and disappear down an adjacent passageway. Going forward, babying her would do neither one any good.

And just how much trouble could she get into by going to the bathroom, anyway?

chapter 3

Heather . . .

Once out of Cameron's line of sight, Heather came to a stop. Leaning her back up against a bulkhead, she tried to steady her breathing. *He has no fucking idea*, she thought. *No idea how utterly petrified I am.* She knew she'd put on a good act. Sure, not all of it was an act for she truly was blown away by the insane advanced technology onboard. Also, the sheer crazy fact that she was here at all—now traveling through space. But the reality was . . . yeah . . . she was terrified. Terrified by that enormous creature-thing, the Loth. Terrified she'd be lost, traveling here alone in space, should anything happen to Cam. And terrified he'd soon realize what an insecure little girl she really was. She already missed her comforting, supportive mother and the quiet strength of her protective father. *God . . . What am I doing here?*

Heather wiped warm tears from her cheeks. Fighting back the emergence of new ones, she squeezed her eyelids tightly closed.

"Would you like to lie down for a while?"

Startled, Heather opened her eyes to find she wasn't alone within the passageway. In fact, the robotic-looking figure was standing right next to her, leaning against the same bulkhead. It was turned sideways and staring at her. Only a foot, or so, away from her, it was encroaching into her personal space. Blinking it into better focus, Heather took in the droid's face—its plastic-looking eyes and nose and mouth that wore a pasted-on pleasant expression. It wasn't wearing any clothes.

"You can call me Lutous Bright 953," the cyborg said, in a neutrally pitched, neither high nor low, voice.

Heather took a half step away. "I'm okay, just a little over-whelmed . . . I guess."

"That is to be expected. I am the *Primion's* medical attendee. With only two organic—actually three, if you count the Minal Loth . . . organisms onboard, I have an abundance of free time. Note that I am adequately knowledgeable about the treatment of most human mental health issues."

"I don't have mental health issues," Heather said curtly.

"No, I am sorry . . . I probably misspoke," Lutous Bright 953 said.

"What is it you want?" Heather asked, unhappy that her teary vulnerability was witnessed and probably being tele-graphed somehow all over the damn ship by now. *The crybaby human female suffered a breakdown only minutes after coming aboard.* She wondered if Cam, too, would be informed—maybe by Alice?

"Can you keep this . . . between the two of us?"

The pleasant expression stared back at her.

"Don't you follow some kind of Hippocratic oath on board where you keep a patient's private information . . . private?"

"Well, the truth is, you are not my patient, Heather. What I observe, the information collected via my visual and auditory inputs, is instantly uploaded to the *Primion's* main storage collective."

"Terrific."

Again, the medical droid stared back at her rather blankly.

"Could you at least not share this with Cam? Not everything always needs to be shared. For humans, that's the case anyway. Can you understand that?"

"Certainly. You need not worry."

And then the droid did something completely unexpected. It made a common humanlike gesture by pulling a symbolic zipper across its lips. Heather laughed out loud. She assessed the droid anew. Perhaps she'd been too reactive—bitchier than she should have been.

"Um . . . is there a bathroom around here?"

"There is, indeed. Follow me. It is nearby. You were headed in the right direction."

Heather watched as the genderless droid hurried around the next bend in the passageway. Left listening as it still spoke pretty much to itself, Heather realized she was feeling somewhat better, at least her breathing had returned to normal. She knew deep inside that her crybaby, wounded damsel bullshit wasn't going to work anymore—wasn't going to fly here. *What do I really expect out of all of this?* To be with Cam, sure, but it was also more than that. At least it should be. She instinctively knew she'd reached a pivotal moment in her life.

Heather looked ahead toward the myriad of left and right passageways. Hell, she literally stood before one of life's multi-forks in the road. So the better question would be, *who do I want to be?* She thought about that, and what came to her brought a chill down her spine. I want to be more like Cam . . . but my *own* version of him. *A grownup?* No, that's not it. *A woman, not so girly, was better. How about an all in, take no prisoners, warrior woman—one who lives life with purpose and courage?* She smiled. Sure, she didn't really believe she was there yet, but it was something to strive for. One thing was for sure: she was here, traveling on this spaceship, for herself, on her own journey, not Cam's. That was the only way any voyage to self-discovery was going to work.

She realized she was all alone again and felt her nervousness start to creep back into her mind. Then Lutous Bright 953 came back into view—its face and upper body peeking around the corner up ahead. "Shall I show you the way to the facilities, Heather?"

"No need, Lutous. I can manage. But I might come find you later . . . would that be okay?"

"Why yes, that most definitely would be okay." The droid then was gone.

Heather said, "*Primion* ship atlas open." When the virtual ship's map presented itself nearby, she noted she was relatively close to the bathroom. Closing the display, she headed in the indicated direction, still dressed for New York's cold winter weather. Wearing long johns beneath her skinny jeans, a baby blue North Face winter coat, and a fluffy white scarf wrapped around her neck, she unraveled the scarf and unzipped her coat while walking forward.

She found what she assumed was the bathroom, noticing above the hatchway door a glowing symbol—a spiral with an underlying diamond shape. Before she entered, she glanced around, checking for a similar entrance nearby. *Huh . . . guess there's no separate men's and women's facilities here.* Entering, she glanced around the empty space. *Terrific! Just where am I supposed to pee?*

chapter 4

Cameron . . .

Adjacent to the bridge, Cameron found Alice exiting the compartment beneath the stairs. From past experience he knew that within that one specific area was where the ship's AI, called TAM, was situated. TAM and Alice were actually one and the same. A cool and darkish place—where strange things glowed, pulsed, and blinked—within it were ten, glowing, donut-shaped constructs easily as tall as himself that were some kind of interconnected intelligence modules.

"Hello, Cameron."

"Hey, Alice. I see we're approaching the first slip band." He gestured toward a cluster of workstations at the center of the bridge and at several pop-up displays, all showing the same distant spatial anomaly.

Alice nodded back. Other cyborgenic crewmembers were there, too—each was occupied, doing this or that at individual workstations.

"We were going to have that talk about Winforge," he said. He could tell by her expression she was also eager to have that conversation.

"There are a few things you should know," she said. "Not only about that particular exoplanet, but about the whole star system in general. Heavily populated, it is nothing like your own Solar System, nor that of Sang-Morang's. Winforge, located within the Epsilon planetary system, is a hub of commerce and varying business activities. It is also protected . . . by what is referred to as the Shiff Security Forces."

"What kind of security forces are they?"

"The kind that maintains multiple fleets comprised of powerful warships. Epsilon space is entirely conflict-free. Going up against Shiff forces is unheard of."

"I don't relish the idea of going up against anyone. And what would I know about such things, anyway? Still, I want to rescue Earth humans, those taken against their will. Not sure I can explain it, but that has become a nagging preoccupation for me . . . guess you'd call it an obsession . . ."

"I can understand that," Alice said.

"Anyway, XI once mentioned the fact that any number of aliens had abducted Earthlings from my home planet since early caveman days. But, at least for the more recent abductees, maybe I can help. We can help?"

"This is uniquely your cause, Cameron."

"But not yours. Okay, I can understand that," he said. "Why would putting either yourself or this ship in danger be of the remotest interest to you. Hey, I get that; it would make no sense."

Alice's prolonged silence only underscored her possible unwillingness to get involved. Perhaps he'd mistakenly assumed from their previous conversations that the *Primion* and its cyborg crew were currently navigating without any real purpose—virtually rudderless, adrift in space—yet were seeking some kind of fulfillment. He'd gotten the impression she wanted him to be a part of that. But, obviously, that didn't mean going so far as to swoop into a heavily guarded section of space, where getting blown to bits could be a distinct possibility.

"Well . . . maybe you can still help me," Cameron offered. "Maybe come up with . . . other options that have some potential?"

Before Alice could answer, Heather appeared at the top of the stairs, her coat and scarf bundled under one arm. She waved, quickly descending the steps.

"You find what you were looking for?" he asked.

"Yeah, no problem, though it took me a while to figure out how to . . . well, never mind. I'm now an expert at *Primion* bathroom operations." Heather's eyes went wide as she took in all the dazzling bridge technology surrounding them. Several new 3D pop-up displays suddenly appeared as she stepped onto the deck.

"You can wave those away, if they're of no interest to you," Cameron said, flicking his hand in a gesture that waved the three displays into nothing more than dissipating whiffs of smoke.

One of the bridge crewmembers approaching him was one that Cameron instantly recognized. It was Ramen, or, more accurately, the cyborg representation of Ramen. The same Thidion he'd offered a ride to during that big snowstorm back on Earth six weeks before. Unfortunately, he was later killed by the mother Griar Loth, deep within the ship's hold. Cameron now had the distinct impression the cyborg was avoiding making eye contact with him. Making a unique motion with one hand, the cyborg produced what was akin to a virtual hand-held tablet device. The Ramen cyborg then handed it over to Alice, pointing at something specific on its screen.

Alice studied the information, whatever it was, and nodded. She then handed the virtual device across to Cameron. Taken somewhat aback by actually being included in their conversation, Cameron took ahold of the device, surprised by its tactile feel. No weight to it, just a *touch expression*, as Alice pointed to the center of the tablet. Before looking down, Cameron noticed the Ramen cyborg giving Heather a good once over from head to toe. The cyborg was definitely checking out his girlfriend, and in an all too human-like manner.

Cameron, now studying the device, saw a photo-real representation of Sang-Morang, specifically, the little valley he'd come to call home for a month-and-a half. "So what am I looking at here, Alice? These numbers . . . and wave-formation symbols, do they depict some kind of energy transmission?"

While Heather clearly seemed impressed by Cameron's question, Alice was not. She said, "Prior to leaving Sang-Morang's orbit, I dispatched a partisan array cluster, what you would call a group of small satellites. The energy spikes you're viewing now are registering in real-time."

Cameron shook his head. "Maybe it's some technology I left behind? Like what was left of the Tangine Shell?"

"Agreed . . . quite possibly. The question is, what would prompt that lone Priopax device to initiate specific communication protocols? In this case, a distress call back to Thidion space."

Cameron, noticing the conversation made absolutely no sense to Heather, pointed to the aerial image of the majestic valley, to its two flanking mountain ridges, its aqua-colored tree foliage, and the several twisting streams, lying at the bottom of the basin. "When I was there, on Sang-Morang, I left behind something called a Tangine Shell. Think of it as an ultra-sophisticated camping enclosure. When wrecked by an angry predator, we left it behind. Now it seems to be broadcasting a distress call . . . for some odd reason."

Heather slowly nodded. "I'm actually still stuck on your words *angry predator*; is that where you're taking me? A place where there are angry predators?"

"That was *my* Tangine Shell," Ramen said, now definitely initiating eye contact.

Cameron didn't like the way the cyborg was glaring at him. He didn't see any of the same kindness behind its eyes that its original Thidion counterpart once had.

Cameron shrugged. "We have a saying back on Earth: finders keepers, losers weepers." Continuing to stare back hard at the cyborg crewmember, he said, "And you're not Ramen. You may have his memories . . . but you're definitely not him."

chapter 5

"What is it?" Heather asked, sliding a hand along the cool smooth surface of the tubular, seven-foot-long, gently glowing HOD device.

Alice said, "The purpose of a HOD, as it pertains to those living onboard the *Primion*, is multifaceted. It is an inducible, deep-sleep chamber, and a comprehensive bio-health facilitator as well, and a full-body cleansing device. It also provides sensory learning and entertainment, and is a stimulations facilitator."

Heather made a face. Are you telling me there aren't any showers onboard this ship?"

Alice stared blankly back at her.

Cameron shrugged. "I think water is used quite sparingly onboard most space vessels."

Heather, glancing around the smallish, utilitarian quarters, seemed unimpressed. As Alice placed a hand at the midpoint of the HOD, that side of the unit began to slide down, exposing the interior. A comfortable-looking bed cushion ran the length of the interior. Heather leaned in and then, after peering around, exclaimed over her shoulder to Cameron, "No way that two people can sleep in there comfortably."

Alice answered back before he could reply: "Cameron's quarters are next door . . . where he has his own HOD unit."

Heather and Cameron exchanged a quick glance. Again, Cameron merely shrugged. Turning back to face Alice, he thought he caught an ever so slight upturning of both corners of her mouth.

When a loud klaxon alarm began sounding above them, Alice stopped and nodded, as if acknowledging information that neither he, nor Heather, were privy to.

Alice yelled above the racket, "I'm sorry, the tour of the *Primion* will have to wait. Cameron, you are needed in the aft retention area. The Minal Loth, apparently, has become excited. There is an imminent possibility of ship damage. Please hurry."

As the hatchway behind them began to cascade open, he ran from the quarters. He heard footfalls right behind him, Heather close on his heels. Upon reaching the nearest jump stand, he said, "Hurry, get on . . . stand close to me."

Heather, doing as told, looked at him bewildered.

"It's a lift, like an elevator, used to jump between levels," he told her. She grabbed onto him, trying to maintain her balance once it began to move. When the lift slowed a moment later, he took her hand, propelling her down one corridor after another.

"What's the hurry? It's not like that *thing* can go anywhere," she said, between deep breaths.

"I don't know. Though I can imagine the Loth, if it gets free from its retention cell, jeopardizing the ship by destroying things."

Several minutes later they both entered the aft retention area through the lower double hatchway's opening. Even prior to their arrival, he heard the Loth's repetitive honking. The creature was obviously excited—or overly agitated.

Cameron dodged, avoiding an airborne glop of sprayed mucus just in time. But Heather wasn't so lucky, her face encountering a blast of the slimy gook. As much as Cameron felt empathy for her, he needed to pay full attention to the forty-five-foot tall, frantic-looking beast—now standing upright, twenty-five feet in front of him, within Retention Cell 4. Its six octopus-like tentacles were tightly wound around thick, vertical-running, metal bars. Cameron, noticing that a good number of them were already bent and misshapen, knew it wouldn't be much longer before the creature ripped the damn holding cell apart.

The Loth's massive jaws gaped open, repetitively honking again and again. Then, noticing Cameron for the first time, the Loth quickly settled down. Three tentacles reached out to him between the bars, though they were not close enough to actually touch him.

"What the hell is wrong with you? Why all the crazy antics?"

The Loth honked angrily—only an odd word or so decipherable. Cameron understood *bot* or *robot*; also, the creature's words for *fire* and *pain*. Moving closer, he permitted the Loth to wrap one of its tentacles around his waist. When he'd last left the creature earlier, the gate was wide open. Now it was latched shut.

"Wait . . . turn back toward me, Loth. Let me see."

Cameron glanced quickly at Heather as she joined him at his side. She'd wiped at her face as best she could, though some mucus-like moisture still glistened on her skin.

"Um, you need to go wash your face. Like right away. That mucus crap dries into rock-hard concrete really fast."

"Really?" she asked, concerned.

"Yeah, really. Maybe ask Alice to help you. Just call her name once you're back in the corridor."

Cameron, again refocusing his attention on the Loth, noticed some ugly marks: large, bright-red circles of inflamed flesh. He knew the hide on a Loth was four inches thick, and nearly impervious to . . . well . . . anything. He spotted a total of four injuries, running across the Loth's front torso.

"Did someone fucking shoot you?" Cameron asked, inner rage beginning to build.

The Loth, two tentacles wrapped about Cameron, honked out, "Pain . . . fire pains."

Cameron gripped the vertical bars with white-knuckled fists. "Tell me who did this to you. Was it a bot . . . one of the cyborgs, maybe?"

The Loth, hauling itself in closer on the far side of the bars, began to purr. It seemed to want to forget all about the recent trauma. Cameron, though, was not that forgiving. Whoever/whatever it was that assaulted the Loth was going to pay dearly. He saw the Loth's eyes had closed as it rocked back and forth. The tentacles that had wrapped around his waist and legs had become noticeably looser and he was able to untangle himself without waking the creature.

He quietly stepped backward out of the retention area—white-knuckled fists still clenched in anger.

He found Heather seven minutes later, seated atop an elevated examination platform within the *Juvinate Plastron*—the *Primion's* medical bay. The cyborg unit, Lutous Bright 953, was attending to her face with oversized moistened swabs.

"Hey . . . how you doing?" he asked.

"She will be fine. Had she waited even another few minutes this cleansing procedure would have been far more serious."

Cameron thought back to the times he'd experienced his own face chockfull of the Loth's mucus. He'd always been lucky to be near lots of water—like the streams on Sang-Morang.

With concern in her eyes, Heather asked, "The Loth? I saw those . . . whatever they were, on its body."

"I think they're the result of plasma bolts," he said.

Lutous stopped its swabbing motion to study Cameron with an expressionless face. "I don't understand. Why would the Loth creature have plasma weapon injuries?"

"Exactly. Be assured, I intend to find that out. But first, is there anything you can do for it . . . medically speaking?"

"I will assess the injuries, but I suspect there will be little I can do. Both Griar and Minal Loths have an amazing regenerative ability. Did you know that a Loth regrows an amputated appendage in a matter of days?"

"I do know that," Cameron said. "Check on the Loth for me and let me know just the same, okay? I'd appreciate it."

"I will immediately do so," Lutous said, closing-up the nearby medical kit. "Heather, you are . . . ," the cyborg thought for a moment, "now *good to go*. Is that the right phrasing?"

"Perfect, and thank you for saving my face," Heather said, hopping off the examination platform. She touched her face with fingertips. "How do I look? Back to normal?" she asked, turning to Cameron.

"You look great . . . as always. Hey, you hungry?"

"Starving. I'm almost afraid to ask what one eats on an alien spaceship. It better not be bugs . . . I hate bugs."

"You'll be surprised by the selection. But first, I just have to check in with Alice. I want to find out who got aggressive with the Loth. Then, I'm going to deal with . . . him . . . her . . . it . . . whatever."

chapter 6

Heather . . .

Heather watched as Cam and a nearby virtual pop-up display of Alice were going at it back and forth. She knew Cam better than anyone and he rarely got mad or angry. But he definitely was furious. Neither yelling nor screaming, he was just the opposite—speaking softly, using few words. She recognized he was internalizing his rage—a kind of passive-aggressive behavior she'd witnessed in him only once or twice before.

"You can't take a step in any direction on this ship without being observed . . . and you're telling me the retention area isn't surveilled 24/7?"

Heather watched Alice maintain her perfect, doll-faced expression. More than once, Heather had to remind herself that this beautiful-looking crewmember—one who never had a hair out of place—was actually a cyborg. And unless she'd misread things, Alice was enamored with Cam, although he obviously didn't see it.

Alice said, "It is correct that most areas of the vessel are kept under constant scrutiny. Rest assured, Cameron, I will look into the reason why the retention area today was not."

"Look into it? Come on! You're tied to the ship's AI. You *are* the ship's AI; you instantly have access to all the information you're ever going to get. You're not going to know anything more in an hour, or tomorrow. So why don't you just tell me who did this to the Loth . . . which one of your little robot clones tortured that creature?"

Both Heather and Cam continued to stare at Alice's virtual representation, when Heather suddenly noticed Alice's eyes momentarily narrow, her lips purse together. An *emotional response*—interesting. Cam had mentioned to her that the cyborg crewmembers onboard the ship were autonomous, yet capable of feeling emotions. Heather now suspected they were far more like people than machines.

"I told you I would deal with this. Do not press me on this matter, Cameron."

"Or what? Someone will do to me what they did to the Loth?"

With that, the pop-up display turned to vapor—Alice was gone.

Heather said, "Well, you definitely got a response from her. She clearly knows who is responsible. But maybe it's best if you let her deal with it . . . her way."

Cam, still glaring at the spot where the pop-up display had hovered only moments before, said, "I don't trust where her loyalties lie. When it comes down to it, I'm sure she'll side with her own kind." He blinked away whatever internal thoughts he was having and looked at her. He gave her a crooked smile, "Hey, we should eat. Let's get you some of those P. F. Chang lettuce wraps you like so much."

"You're just saying that," Heather replied, rolling her eyes. It was true, that was her favorite restaurant-type food, but why would it be available here—on a spaceship somewhere out in deep space?

"There's a lot this ship doesn't offer when it comes to basic, back home comforts, but Earth-style food isn't one of them. The food replicators onboard the *Primion* may surprise you . . ."

* * *

Heather wasn't at all disappointed with the meal she'd just consumed within the ship's canteen, although the seating arrangement in there was *weird*. No tables, per se, and the seats were lined up in rows, like those on a jet airliner.

At that moment, still somewhat disoriented about where they were on the ship, she recognized the particular passageway they were now walking along. They were close to their quarters. Though Cam was holding her hand, she could tell his mind was miles away. Not for the first time, Heather wondered if she'd made the right decision, coming along with him on this . . . *whatever it was*. Adventure, she guessed, was the best word for it.

"So what happens tomorrow?" she asked.

He smiled, "You and I get some alone time . . . I get to show you Sang-Morang."

"Oh yeah . . . where the . . . what did you call them . . . angry predators roam?"

"Nah . . . we'll be perfectly safe, the Loth will be with us."

"So, not *total* alone time then," she said.

Cameron didn't have a response for that. Approaching the nearest hatchway, it cascaded open. Still holding her hand, they entered the quarters together. When he placed a free hand on the side of the HOD it, too, began to open. "You'll want to take off your boots before climbing in."

Heather did as told, but instead of moving toward the HOD she came closer to Cam. She slid her arms around his waist and kissed him gently on the lips. In a soft, near whisper of a voice she said, "And my clothes . . . maybe I should take them off as well?" But opening her eyes, she saw he was still somewhere else—either thinking or contemplating or *whatever*. She slapped a hand on his chest. "Hey . . . what's going on with you?"

"Nothing is going on with me. Why?"

"Because we haven't been with each other in, like, forever, and you're clearly somewhere else. The Cam I remember normally would be chasing me around this HOD thing by now."

Cameron smiled at that. "Sorry . . . it's totally not you." Exhaling, he said, "I guess I didn't think everything all the way through."

"Think what through?"

"All of it. Me. Practically forcing you to come along with me. The real danger you could be in, being here. Heather, this isn't a vacation . . . or a romantic getaway."

"I already know that," she said defensively.

"I should have kissed you, told you I loved you, then said goodbye back on Earth."

"Because?"

"Because I'm willing to risk my own life for what I'm doing out here . . . but certainly not yours."

She stared at him, trying to piece together what he was really saying. "Well, what are you doing? I mean, besides taking the Loth back home?"

"After that, I'm taking you back to Earth."

"Oh, you are? Okay . . . thanks for letting me know you've already decided that for me. You want to tell me what you're planning to do after that, since it seems I don't have any say in the matter?"

Cameron closed his eyes, then reopened them slowly. "Look . . . weeks ago I learned that the Thidions, like the ones who were originally on this ship, were systematically abducting various indigenous species from planets throughout the universe. It was for some kind of ginormous alien zoo. Humans from Earth were, are, among this zoo's captives. This has been going on for a long time, maybe for centuries. I know what that feeling is like, to some degree. I found out there still could be humans alive there. Held captive on a distant planet called Winforge. The thought keeps nagging at me. That I'm out here puttering around in space, while others of our kind could be suffering."

"So you feel guilty?"

"I suppose I do. But it's my thing, not yours."

Heather nodded, he was right. It wasn't her thing; not her problem that there could be humans imprisoned somewhere in the universe. But hell, there were prisoners, like the illegal human trafficking of women and children, back on Earth, too. There never would be a shortage of human-right causes to champion, if she was so inclined. Was this one any different?

"I'm pretty tired . . . can we talk about this tomorrow?" she asked. "Why don't you show me how this HOD thing works, okay?" She'd lied. She wasn't tired in the least. But their conversation had saddened her, and she knew they needed to spend some time apart. By the time Heather finally laid down, Cam had explained all the little menu options and basic operation of the HOD unit and she was more than ready for him to just leave. Her brain physically hurt from taking in so much data in so short a time. She seriously wondered if it would have been better all around if she had remained back on Earth. *Yeah, sure, she would have missed the hell out of him, but life there was so much simpler.* She closed her eyes—*so, so tired.* Maybe Cam was right; going home would be the best option for them both. . . . She'd decide in the morning.

chapter 7

Cameron . . .

He awoke early the next morning. He saw on the projected HOD display overhead that it was 4:30 a.m., Larksburg Standard time. That was the time reference location he'd programmed in just before nodding off to sleep last night. He retracted the curved, glass-like side panel and lazily sat up. Yawning, he rubbed his tired eyes, then ran his fingers through his mop of thick, tussled hair.

He knew from prior experience that Heather was a ridiculously late-riser. Hell, she'd sleep till noon if left undisturbed.

After pulling on his boots, then making a quick pit stop to relieve himself, he left his compartment and headed aft. The main corridor seemed busier than usual—cyborgenic crewmembers bustling both this way and that. Having seen some of them the previous day, Cameron offered them a friendly half-wave in recognition, or a quick raise of his chin after making eye contact. Virtual pop-up displays followed his progress. Most he waved away with a quick motion of his hand, but several actually were of interest, including the last—a kind of a space flight itinerary. Apparently, they'd already crossed through the prerequisite slip band prior to reaching Sang-Morang air space. They would be arriving on that distant world within four hours. He wondered if Heather would even be awake by then.

Passing through the *Primion's* retention area, Cameron found the Loth up and acting fidgety.

"Hey . . . how would you like to get out of that cage for a little while, big guy?" he asked.

Surprised to see him, the Loth honked jubilantly. Standing on what remained of its octopus-like tentacles, the beast stretched up to its full height of forty-five feet, its head almost touching the very top of the compartment. Lowering itself back down, the Loth shuffled awkwardly toward the still-closed gate. Cameron unlatched it, swinging it wide open.

"Come on . . . let's go check out the truck."

The Loth responded back with several loud honks: "Hunt . . . Hunt now!"

Cameron ignored the beast's demands as he waited for the farthest back hatchway to complete its cascading, upward motion. He heard the Loth thumping along behind him as he entered the hold area. A moment later, the hatch securely closed with a pressurized, sucking, *thunk* sound. Sometime during the preceding nighttime hours, the aft hold metal-grate decking had been cleaned, and was now devoid of any of the Loth's previous expulsions. Cameron briefly wondered what *lucky* crewmember was assigned that dirty job.

Then the overhead lights came on automatically, something, that typically never happened in this area of the ship. For the first time, he got a better look at what else, other than his truck and a few other large, unmarked containers, was located in the hold. Secured to the port bulkhead was a one-man winged craft—about the length of his truck. Strapped into place, as well, were six, pristine-looking, red spacesuits, or environment suits. Unsure what the difference was, they hung like lifeless bodies, one after another in a neat row. Stacked three high, in three columns, were nine, familiar-looking, matte-black droid canisters—pretty much identical, appearance-wise, to the malicious XI droid. Responsible for so much misery onboard the *Primion*, the droid was finally defeated; left in pieces to rust on Sang-Morang. Cameron remembered the three gentle Dalima Climbers; how they had cowered, terrified as the self-appointed mechanical captain of the *Primion* seemed to take extra delight in killing one of the helpless, gentle beings.

In the end, Cameron had found a way to outsmart the evil droid. But he'd been lucky—things easily could have turned out differently. Now, studying the three columns of stacked droid casings, he wondered if these hovering bots would be any different than XI? Were each somehow pre-programmed to have the same murderous tendencies, perhaps because of some technical error made years past when the droids were first programmed? Was it because of a bug or a glitch that only showed up under certain highly unique circumstances?

Cameron next turned his attention to his battered, ten-year-old pickup truck. A loose-fitting tarp, spread over its filled-to-capacity bed, covered a slew of miscellaneous items he'd hurriedly stowed there as he prepared to leave for one last trip across the country—back to school at Stanford. But there was only one item he was concerned with now: the trinious bundle. Originally, it belonged to Ramen, the alien he'd encountered on Earth so many weeks ago. The bundle, a high-tech soft case, contained an assortment of alien contraptions that had, all together, literally saved his life living within the hostile wilderness of Sang-Morang. But the cyborgenic version of Ramen he'd spoken to the previous day—shifty-eyed and a far less amiable disposition—mentioned the trinious bundle. For some reason, he had staked some kind of claim to its ownership.

As Cameron shuffled some of the larger items around the truck bed—his prized BMC fourstroke-FS01 mountain bike; his oversized, sun-faded, beach umbrella; his ice cooler; and his duffle bag containing clothes for school, he discovered the trinious bundle most definitely was gone.

He tried to rein in his building anger. First, the Loth was mercilessly tortured, and now this affront. Cameron had little doubt about who had committed both misdeeds. He threw the overly soft duffle bag down, but didn't get the satisfaction from hearing something break. He looked forward, toward the front of the hold compartment. "I'm not taking this shit . . . not from that guy . . . not from anyone." He strode forward unaware his fists were clenched into tight balls. "Stay here, Loth . . . don't break anything. I'll be back soon."

* * *

The Loth silently watched as Cameron, his face set into an angry scowl, left the compartment. The Loth, not understanding why his human was so upset and so angry, wondered if it was something it had done. The Loth did not like it when his human was upset. It made the Loth equally upset.

The beast peered about the uninteresting compartment, already sure there was nothing to eat . . . nothing to hunt there. Although, at least the searing pain had subsided somewhat from losing multiple tentacle limbs back on the other world when it defeated the other beast, the one not so dissimilar from itself. The price had been the loss of body parts. They would grow back. They had before. The Loth shuffled farther back within the large space, then suddenly stopped. Already angered—not knowing what had distressed his human—the Loth stared at the three columns of matte-black objects. The Loth recalled what a very similar-shaped thing had done to torment him. He did not forget such things.

The Loth moved its tentacles as quickly as it could manage as it rushed toward the wall holding the nine black objects. Upset, an over-abundance of syrupy mucus flowed like two billowing waterfalls; growing pools of the messy substance filled the deck's grated openings, forming quickly hardening mounds. The Loth stared at the nine objects, its anger at their mere presence here. Using its forward tentacle, it wrapped a tapered end around the cool metallic object, then yanked it free of its bindings. Raising the thing high enough to better see it, a series of small lights flashed to life—movement and vibrations evident within it. The Loth concluded, most assuredly, that the thing was alive and dangerous. With an astounding amount of strength, the Loth slammed the droid down hard onto the deck—once, twice, three times. Then, it raised the scuffed, dented item up to eye-level to better inspect the damage inflicted. Blinking lights were gone, vibrations ceased. The Loth flung the destroyed droid aside and reached for the next.

* * *

As soon as Cameron reached the *Primion's* main corridor, he called for Alice. Twenty paces ahead, he saw her—in real form, not just another annoying virtual display version. "Where is he?"

Her unhurried approach and calm expression irritated him further. "Where the fuck is Ramen?" he demanded.

When merely steps away, Alice replied, "He is on duty; currently at his post on the bridge. What is it you require of him, Cameron?"

"You know perfectly well what's required of him . . . just as you know, he tortured the Loth yesterday and jacked my trinious bundle! The guy is out of control. For some reason, you refuse to see it . . . to acknowledge it."

"The one you refer to as Ramen was not responsible for the Loth's recent torment. As for the trinious bundle—"

Cameron cut her off; he'd had enough. "Where're his quarters . . . where does he sleep when he's off duty?"

The question seemed to amuse her. "Cyborgenic beings have no need for sleep."

"Fine . . . but don't they have crew quarters? Or do you work them like slaves here, 24/7?"

Alice actually laughed out loud at that. "Yes, they have crew quarters. But what you're looking for won't be found there."

"Then where is it?"

"It is in your truck."

"No, it isn't, I just checked it."

"You only checked the bed of the truck."

Cameron let that sink in. He hadn't actually checked the front cab area. He realized in that moment he'd left the thing sitting on the passenger seat. *Shit!*

"We have a more important issue at hand, Cameron," Alice said, moving past him, heading aft.

"What?"

"Your Loth."

chapter 8

Alice and Cameron entered the aft hold together. Each had to immediately duck down to avoid being struck by an incoming projectile—something dark, and about as large as a standard-size beer keg. It rocketed past them and clanged loudly as it ricocheted off the hatchway doors behind them.

Forty paces away, the Loth was standing upright with another two dark objects grasped in two of its tentacles. Then Cameron noticed a similar, smaller-sized black object, hovering in the air. Dodging getting hit when the Loth swung at it, first with one tentacle and then the other—like a fast-moving fly avoiding two constantly swinging fly swatters.

Cameron noticed several more droid casings lying inert on the deck. Battered with dents and scuffs, they appeared to be damaged beyond repair.

"Loth . . . why don't you let that one go? It's not the same as XI. It won't hurt us," Cameron said, turning to Alice, not completely certain he was sure about that.

Alice raised a hand and somehow communicated with the droid as it rose higher in the hold until it was out of range of the swatting tentacles. It moved along the ceiling, then descended directly in front of Alice and Cameron. Hovering before them, Cameron could see the droid was slightly different in overall shape, probably in capabilities too, to that of the old XI droid. This mechanical device had far more blinking lights under its top, encircling flange, plus two articulating arms—each with four distinct finger-like appendages. Studying it now, he saw another cluster of smaller blinking lights a little lower down from the flange. Oddly enough, they kind of resembled a happy smiley face.

Alice asked it in a scolding tone, "Why are you tormenting the Loth?"

"Because I can."

Alice glanced over to Cameron. "These droids are only partially programmed. They were delivered to the *Primion* in this somewhat raw state. A secondary, far more comprehensive level of programming would have been implemented at a later time . . . if the need for droids arose."

"Would have been?"

"I have found that cyborgenic beings and this type of droid are not work-environment compatible."

"So . . . what . . . you're going to put it back into storage?"

"No. It has been initialized and is operational. It must be destroyed."

Cameron nodded, "I suppose it could be dangerous, like XI some day."

"No. It is not in the least bit dangerous. In fact, it is just the opposite. Think of it as a young canine, capable of learning quickly but still awkward, having to learn after many inevitable mistakes."

"You mean it's like a puppy?"

"Yes, a better word for it."

Cameron continued to watch the droid. It had begun to tilt back and forth, as though keeping beat to some inner song or rhythm. "What's it doing?"

"Playing."

"Seriously? A robot? How does a robot even have that . . . capability?"

Alice expelled an impatient breath, "Part of its first stage programming, I suppose. *Play* is a key element for autonomous self-learning. Humans . . . animals on Earth, and beings on other worlds, all go through this stage. I am unsure why these droids were factory-configured this way. We, of course, bypass this frivolous stage when the droids are incorporated into a serious work environment. Our high-level re-programming dispenses with the need for nonsense like this."

"Well, you can't just destroy the thing. It hasn't done anything wrong."

"You just said it. You called it a *thing*. So why does it matter to you?"

Cameron gave her a sideways glance. He easily could have retorted with a smartass remark about her, *Alice*, and the other cyborgs onboard, about them being *things* as well, not really alive in the same sense of having organic origins. But noting her defiant expression, he bit his tongue instead. He said, "Why don't you just give it to me to take care of?"

"That is a terrible idea. For one thing, I don't want it disrupting the crew, Cameron."

"Couldn't you instruct it to, um, mind both me and Heather? Do what we tell it to?"

"Yes, of course I can do that. But I see no need to do so."

Cameron continued to stare hard at her, waiting.

"Humans are annoying," she said.

He shrugged.

"Fine . . . but keep it away from the crew. Watch over it, just be warned at this stage of their early programming they are beyond distracting."

The droid had begun to flip head over heels—over and over again. Alice looked at it then back to Cameron with an, *I told you so* expression.

"I'm going to give it to Heather," he said.

"I'm sure she'll be thrilled," Alice replied with rare sarcasm. Strange—Alice seemed more human-like of late than he'd remembered. Maybe being around organic life forms was rubbing off on her.

"We will be landing soon. I suppose you would like us to set down in the precise location we had previously?" she asked.

"Yes. And Alice?"

Turning away, she looked back at him.

"Thank you."

"You're welcome. Now please secure your Loth. We do not need further destruction within the *Primion*."

Cameron waited for her to leave, for the hatchway doors to close again. Looking back, the droid was gone, and then he caught movement from out the corner of his eye. Once again, the playful droid was darting this way and that around the Loth's massive head. The Loth stared back at Cameron with a wary expression.

"I know . . . sorry. Just try not to kill it, okay?"

The Loth didn't answer, instead dropping first one then the other inert droids from its tentacled grasps. As the Loth shuffled its bulk closer to him, the huge beast did its best to ignore the pestering puppy-droid.

* * *

Cameron, now with the hovering droid in tow, made his way to Heather's quarters, fully expecting to find her still sound asleep within her HOD unit. Instead, he found the unit empty. Her winter coat and scarf laying within it, were the only indications she had been there.

"*Primion* ship atlas open," he said, leaving through the unit's open hatch. Taking in the graphical map of the ship, he ordered, "*Primion*, show me Heather's location."

A pulsing red circle indicated that her current location was within the confines of the canteen. Cameron realized at that moment that he, too, was hungry. He hurried down the passageway and then stopped. *Shit.* Looking behind, he saw no sign of the droid. Retracing his steps, he reentered Heather's quarters. *Thunk! Thunk! Thunk!* Somehow the droid had become trapped within her HOD unit and was frantically bouncing off its inner wall surfaces.

"Oh, for God's sake . . . what's wrong with you?" Cameron asked. Opening the HOD, the droid flew out. Shaking his head, he thought, *maybe keeping the droid was a mistake.*

By the time he entered the canteen, Heather looked to have finished eating. And she wasn't alone. Sitting right next to her was Ramen. *Why would he be here?* It wasn't as if cyborgenics ever had to eat. Heather was laughing, even looked a tad flushed, as she nervously tucked a strand of hair behind one ear. Ramen was smiling, too. *Fucker.*

Approaching them, she looked up. For a quick moment she looked flustered. No—not flustered, she looked guilty. "Oh . . . there you are, Cam! I looked for you this morning. God, I slept fantastic! That HOD thing is incredible."

"Enjoying your breakfast without me?" he asked, instantly hating the whiny tone of his own voice. And by the smug look on his face, Ramen had achieved exactly what he'd wanted.

Heather offered Ramen an apologetic glance then scowled at Cameron. "I forgot how to get here. Um, Ramen was nice enough to show me the way. Kept me company."

Cameron nodded. "And what did you have to eat, Ramen? Oh, that's right, you can't eat . . . can you?"

"Actually, I can . . . and I did. The flapjacks are especially good here. I ordered the maple syrup piping hot."

Heather nodded, "I had them too . . . Wow! Memorable. Better than we ever made them at the Drake," referring to the Drake Café, where she'd worked as a hostess prior to its destruction by the rampaging Griar Loth.

Cameron held Ramen's stare—one that conveyed exactly how he felt about Ramen making a move on his girl like this.

"What do you have behind you?" Ramen asked.

Cameron glanced back. He'd forgotten all about the droid. "Oh, that's a gift." Looking at Heather, he added, "It's for you."

She looked at the hovering metallic droid with a mixed expression. "What is it? What is it for?"

"I have to get back to my post," Ramen interjected, a lopsided smirk on his lips.

Cameron waited for him to leave before answering her. "It's a long story; leave it to say the droid was going to be destroyed. Right now I'm not sure why I intervened. Truth is, the thing is crazy annoying. Alice explained its conduct as being puppy-like. Still learning how to—"

Heather laughed out loud, pointing her finger to something over his shoulder. Cameron spun around and found the droid doing the flipping-around thing again. It then stopped, coming closer to Heather, and hesitantly reached one of its articulating arms out toward her.

"Look! It has a face, of sorts, that's smiling at me." Heather's eyes were alive with delight as she looked at Cameron. "That was thoughtful of you."

He shrugged.

"And, just so you know, you have nothing to worry about with that robot man. He's not my type."

"Oh, yeah? What is your type?"

Heather pointed to the droid, now ping-ponging in the air around the Canteen to some unheard beat. "I don't know, that guy's pretty darn cute."

"I assure you . . . the cuteness wears off pretty fast. But since it's now yours, you'll have to teach it."

"Well, at least it won't pee on the rug," she said. "What's its name?"

"Whatever you want it to be, I guess."

At that moment everything shook. Alice's voice, emanating from a nearby pop-up display, announced, "Please prepare for landing. We have reached our destination."

Cameron nodded and smiled at Heather. "Welcome to Sang-Morang."

chapter 9

Heather . . .

She ignored the urge to roll her eyes. Instead, she flashed Cam a big smile and a confident thumbs-up. *Great, we're landing on a hostile planet where animals the size of a Chick-Fil-A drive-through thrive.* She imagined a salivating dinosaur-type beast gazing up to the sky, then giving a wink to his dinosaur buddy—*lunch time!*

Cam hesitated, studying her. She was about to say something, but stopped when she noticed his eyes slowly roving up and down her body. He said, "That's not going to work."

"What's not going to work?"

"The way you're dressed."

"I'm dressed just fine. So why don't you worry about your own clothes and I'll worry about mine?"

"No, I meant you'll be way too hot wearing all that garb. You have long undies on under your jeans . . . I can see them bunched-up a little at your waist."

"Are you purposely trying to piss me off, or are you just being stupid?" she asked, cocking her head to one side.

That evoked a quick laugh from Cameron. "Not at all. It's just that during the day, it's pretty warm down in the valley. In the evenings, it's much cooler. All I'm saying is we can have some clothes made . . . ones that are more suitable."

"Made?" she asked, now slightly intrigued.

"Come on, let's get over to your quarters," he said, heading off.

* * *

Heather, along with the hovering puppy-droid close behind her, followed Cam into her quarters, then watched as he stood before the aft bulkhead. "There is a built-in garment replicator unit within this wall."

She first noticed only a crisscrossing pattern of vertical and horizontal seams, but studying it more closely, Heather realized it was either a cabinet, or maybe a wall closet, of some sort. One panel pulsated in a darker shade of gray. Cam smiled at her as he placed an open palm on the rectangular panel. It slid to one side, revealing a complicated-looking appliance.

"Wait for it . . . ," he said.

A projected display suddenly popped into view. "You'll want to read the instructions, then next time you'll be able to do this yourself. It's super easy. Also, you can always ask the AI for additional help," he added.

Heather moved closer and read the pop-up instructions. "Seems easy enough. So, you've used this yourself," she asked, frowning at his outfit—dirty jeans and a torn T-shirt worn beneath a wrinkled, flannel, button-down shirt.

"I made a boot."

"Just one?" she asked, as Cam nodded and shrugged.

"Fine! What do you think I should make with this thing?" she asked.

"The AI already knows your body size—"

"Measurements," Heather corrected.

"Uh huh, so you just need to tell it what it is you want. Like some shorts, maybe? Maybe another pair of jeans? Maybe a hat, or something else? Definitely boots."

"And I just talk to it?"

"Yeah. I think it will show you three-dimensional images based on your descriptions."

"Okay. Why don't you go and do something else. Anything, just go away from here. I don't want you lurking around while I do this."

Cameron nodded and pointed to the hatchway. "I'll be out in the corridor."

Ten minutes later she found Cam where he said he'd be—sitting down, leaning against a bulkhead. She could hear him quietly snoring. She tapped his foot with the toe of her new boot.

Blinking several times, he stared up at her. "Success?"

"Oh yeah . . . I love that thing! How have I lived this long without one?"

Noting that she really was thrilled, Cam smiled, taking in what she now had on—white shorts, a red tank top covered by a flannel, button-down shirt, a red baseball cap, and her new, ankle-high, fawn-colored boots.

"I had a few outfits made. Maybe went a little overboard. But God, it's so easy. And fun!" She held up two large canvas duffle bags with shoulder straps. One was light pink—one was dark blue. "Here, this one is for you," she said, handing him the dark blue duffle. "You needed a change of clothes . . . big time! There's jeans, shirts, undies, socks, a heavy coat."

Cameron took the bag from her, unzipped it and looked inside. Rifling through the folded clothes, he exclaimed, "Wow! You seem to know my taste in clothes pretty well."

Heather simply smiled back at him.

"Nice." He zipped up the satchel and swung it over one shoulder. "We should go."

"Have we even landed yet?" Heather asked.

The puppy-droid answered, "Affirmative. Six minutes, and forty-two seconds ago."

"It talks," she muttered back unenthusiastically.

"Yeah, we landed while you were busy making our new wardrobes." Cam turned, ready to head away, then stopped and said, "Alice." A full-sized pop-up display appeared directly before him. The virtual Alice stared back at them quizzically. "How can I help you?"

Heather briefly wondered if the cyborgenic woman ever had a single hair out of place? If it weren't for her clear membrane Thidion ears, she'd look just as human as anyone back on Earth. Heather took in her pretty hazel eyes—eyes that looked so incredibly life-like. *Were they conveying emotion? Perhaps Alice felt emotions similar to the way humans do?* She then wondered if Alice was in love with Cam. Sure looked like it.

"We're heading out. I'm going to fetch the Loth . . . and my truck. I'm showing Heather the valley. Maybe the Dalima Climbers will be around. We'll play things by ear. Be back in a couple of days."

"Thank you for sharing your itinerary," Alice said.

Heather heard Alice's subtle sarcasm—sarcasm that flew right over Cam's head.

"I'll have the trinious bundle, so I'm sure there will be ways to contact me . . . if necessary."

"I do not foresee any reason to contact you. The *Primion* will be here when you return. Have you given further thought to where we go next, Cameron?"

Cameron nervously shot a glance toward Heather. "We, um, still need to discuss that sort of stuff. Let's see how the next few days go first."

Heather glared at him. *He doesn't think I'm up to it!* Up to this whole running around space adventure-thing! It was fine for her to have doubts, but she certainly didn't want him thinking she wasn't up for it—or even worse, incapable in any way.

"I'm perfectly fine with whatever you throw at me. You don't need to coddle me, Cam."

"Good! That's what I like to hear," he said, casually waving Alice's virtual pop-up away with the flick of a hand. Heather wondered if Alice thought such an offhand dismissal was as rude as she did.

* * *

Heather was actually happy to see the Loth again. The three—four if she counted the ever-present puppy-droid— were together in the far aft hold. She watched as Cam placed their duffle bags atop all the crap already piled high in the truck bed, then re-secured the tarp over everything. "You can go ahead and hop in. I'm almost done with this," he said.

But Heather was only half-listening, her attention drawn instead to what lay beyond the now open rear hatchway. Still early morning, she could see the sun, or whatever this particular star was called here, cresting over a far distant ridgeline. A bird-like creature was soaring effortlessly, taking advantage of invisible, rising thermals. As it circled closer, she could see it wasn't a bird . . . more like some prehistoric thing. It looked rather serpent-like, longish like a snake, with multiple sets of wings: wings as clear and delicate as cellophane. Its head was small, yet its body had to be thirty to forty feet long. *Oh God . . . what am I doing here?*

chapter 10

The XI Droid . . .

It took four hours, but after extensive modifications were made to both the Tangine Shell's hardware communications circuitry, as well as to the root code that changed a number of transmission protocols, the XI droid had excellent success transmitting a wide-spectrum signal up through the atmosphere and beyond into deep space. XI made direct contact with four passing alien manned space vessels, and with three autonomous vessels. It was on the latter ships that the droid concentrated its attention. One in particular, a heavily damaged gun ship, was limping back to its home base still three light years from its destination. Cracking the vessel's security system—breaching the internal network—was a simple enough task, but altering its most recent mission directives took XI somewhat longer. Diverting the craft now to Sang-Morang airspace had just been confirmed.

Now, after doing an internal system's check—evaluating what exactly was wrong with the alien ship—XI noted there were a number of problems. For one thing, the ship could not land. Both forward and portside landing struts had been decimated during its most recent space battle with an enemy—a warship with far superior technology. Two of the vessel's six plasma cannons were damaged as well, and the bridge was uninhabitable due to a direct strike breach. Apparently, the vessel was being manned via the midship AI. An AI that XI now had total control over.

While waiting, the XI droid proceeded to make further repairs to itself. Presently, XI could barely hover more than a few feet off the ground, so it went about making those repairs first. XI would have to go to the ship, not the other way around due to the warship's missing landing struts. Another hour elapsed before the droid felt confident enough with the patched-up repairs to leave the shell enclosure and make some low atmosphere flight tests.

chapter 11

Cameron . . .

He started up the old Ford and let it rumble a few moments. It was running a little rougher than usual, but after a short while the engine settled into a smoother sounding idle. He inwardly hoped there wasn't some kind of mechanical issue brewing. Glancing over to Heather, he asked, "Ready?"

She shook her head no.

"Okay . . . how about now?"

"No."

"How about right now?"

Heather almost smiled. "Sure . . . I guess."

Cameron looked out through the cracked windshield where an impatient Loth rocked back and forth. A virtual waterfall of mucus was streaming out both sides of its massive lower jaw. The beast was excited to be back home again, eager to do what it enjoyed doing more than anything else—hunt. Cameron put the truck in reverse and did a backward three-point-turn before easing the vehicle forward down the ship's extended gangway. Once all four tires were on the ground, he goosed the accelerator pedal so the Loth could hurry by them. They watched as the huge creature, still missing several of its tentacles, thumped heavily past them, then continued down the steep slope. The puppy-droid circled high above the Loth's head then briefly disappeared around an outcropping of rocky cliffs before circling back into view.

"Have you come up with a name for it yet?" Cameron asked.

Heather pursed her lips, while watching it play. "How about Whim? You know, for whimsical?"

"Good as any name," Cam said. "Whim it is."

"What's that?" she asked, pointing to an object on his lap.

"A plasma pistol. A parting gift from Alice, just in case we run into some aggressive wildlife."

"That's what I thought the Loth was for . . . to fend off anything that could hurt us."

Cameron slowed as the road narrowed. "Truth is, we probably won't see much of the Loth during the day." He watched her eyes go wide, her foot instinctively stretching forward to brake. "Should you be going so fast down this steep slope?" she asked.

"Sorry, been up and down this road a hundred times. Didn't mean to frighten you."

"I'm not frightened, just concerned." Leaning on one butt cheek sideways, she pulled her iPhone from her back pocket. Entering the passcode, she looked at her most recent texts.

"Not real good cell service around these parts," Cameron said, with a smile

"Ha ha . . . I wish there was a way I could call my dad. I keep seeing his hurt expression. The way I left him, standing on the street his arms reaching out to me."

"I'll talk to Alice when we get back . . . come up with something," Cam said.

"Can we pull over there, get a look at that view?" she asked.

A jutting of rocky cliff cantilevered out over the valley below. Cameron slowed and nosed the truck onto the precarious-looking outcropping. After spending so much time around here, he'd taken for granted just how beautiful this world really was. "Careful getting out," he said.

They opened their side doors and climbed down. There wasn't much room to stand on, on neither side of the truck. Cameron watched Heather climb up onto the hood, then sit with her arms wrapped around her long, drawn-up together, legs. He joined her, leaning back against the windshield. Together, they sat quietly watching undisturbed nature play out within the small Sang-Morang valley below. Looking beyond the cliff side, directly across, was a nearly identical mountain range of the one they were on. Cameron pointed to the tall, aqua-colored woodlands, which covered most of the distant mountainside. "There's a Gleery Beast over there. If you follow that tree line, you'll see it directly across from us."

Heather leaned forward and squinted her eyes. "Yeah, I see something moving around. Can't really tell what it is from here. We're safe, though . . . right?"

"Oh yeah. We're a few miles away. Perfectly safe."

She rested her head on his shoulder and sighed. "Cam . . . it really is amazing. Beautiful. I can't believe I'm here. That I'm actually sitting here with you on an alien planet."

He felt her looking up at him, and smiled. Heather drew in closer and kissed his neck. Then pulled his chin toward her and kissed his mouth. Her lips were soft and sweet. Her tongue found his and in an instant she was on top of him—straddling him. She kissed him again.

"Are we really doing this . . . like right here?" he asked.

"Didn't you say no one else is here to watch us? That we're the only people on the entire planet," she breathlessly whispered, as she kissed, then gently teased and nibbled, his earlobe. He felt a hand working on the buttons of his jeans.

"You're crazy, you know."

Heather said, "Shut up and help me with these stupid buttons."

* * *

The drive down the remainder of the mountainside was slow and blissful. Heather, her elbow out the window, was taking in the beautiful alien vista beyond. A sudden gust of wind caught the bill of her cap, and it flew up and out the open window—airborne in an instant.

"My cap!"

Cameron slowed to a stop and opened his door.

"No, I'll get it," she said, already out, running back up the dirt road. He watched her in the rearview mirror jog toward the speck of red in the distance. She reached the cap, some fifty or sixty yards away, brushed it off, and put it back atop her head. She then turned around, as if she heard something behind her. He remembered his own dire circumstances, on this very stretch of road only a month earlier, when a pack of little Piquet Sprints attacked him. They'd been like ravenous piranhas, capable of stripping the meat off an animal's bones in mere minutes. How could he have let his guard down? What had he been thinking? *Oh my God . . . Heather!*

chapter 12

He was out the door and running toward her—plasma pistol tightly gripped in one hand. "Heather!" he yelled, paralyzing fear increasing with each beat of his racing heart. "Get back here . . . it's not . . . ," then he saw it. Saw what she was staring up at. The same Csillo they'd spotted high in the air earlier. As he ran he tried to remember if these flying serpents were carnivores or herbivores. Heather glanced back at him—uncertainty in her eyes. Behind her, the Csillo was quickly descending, swooping down toward her, something held in the serpent's beak. Something with fur on it—a still-struggling piquet sprint. *Most definitely a carnivore*, Cameron thought, as the Csillo suddenly released it, opting for a much larger prey.

"Get down! Heather, get down!" *Why isn't she listening to me?* She was still thirty yards distance from him. He'd never get to her in time. He stopped, raised the pistol and took aim. He had time for only one shot—*I better make this one count.* He squeezed the trigger. *Fuck!* He'd missed by a mile. He could see that Csillo had extended its two front talons out—its beak opening wider in ready anticipation.

"Cam . . . please . . . help me!" she screamed, her attention fully focused on the predator making its final descent, mere seconds from—

Bonk! The odd sound was straight out of a Saturday morning cartoon—the hollow sound of a metal pipe hitting an empty oil drum. Cameron watched stupefied as Whim circled around overhead—coming in for another strike. *Bonk!* This time Whim struck the Csillo hard enough in the head to knock it unconscious. The serpent dropped like a lifeless toy, landing directly at Heather's feet, its wings and legs still twitching.

By the time Cameron reached her, Heather was already hysterical, bent over, trying to catch her breath. He slowed, then gently placed a hand on her back. All this was entirely his fault; what was he thinking, bringing her here? Her face turned toward him. Reddened cheeks. *Not crying. Not hysterical.* She was laughing!

"Did you see that? Did you see what Whim did?" she asked.

Cameron nodded.

"It saved my life . . . how did it do that?" Breathless, she stood up, a palm placed over her heart. "That was friggin' amazing!" She noticed Cameron was not laughing. That he didn't find anything funny about what had just happened.

"You could have been killed. This place . . . I never should have—"

"Cam, I'm fine! We're both fine," she said, a smile still on her lips. "I chose to come, and yes, I'll have to be more careful.

But . . . God, that was amazing. And the droid, Whim, it saved me. You saw that, right?"

He nodded again, this time allowing a reluctant smile to surface. "We need to go. That body will attract scavengers."

Hurrying back down the slope, Heather was preoccupied, looking up—searching for the droid.

"It's down there, by the truck," Cameron said, pointing.

The black, beer-keg-sized droid was hovering close to the truck's right rear quarter panel. Heather ran the rest of the way down and, upon reaching the mechanical AI, threw her arms around it in an embrace. Whim made several high-pitched, excited-sounding squawks, before wiggling free and jutting off into the air. Laughing, Heather plopped down into the passenger seat, placing her feet up on the dash. Climbing in on the driver side, he closed the door and said, "Heather, we really do need to be more careful."

"I know. Sorry."

Cameron put the truck in gear and together they continued their trek down the mountainside. "I wish I had my own ray gun . . . like yours," she said, staring out the windshield.

"It's a plasma gun, and I'll make you one, once we set up camp."

"Oh, really? You'll just make me one. You have a portable factory somewhere in that mass of stuff back there? Maybe a bunch of little elf workers, too?"

He glanced her way. "I kinda do."

Reaching the bottom of the mountain road, Cameron was relieved to discover the three fast-moving streams hadn't risen too much over the past few days. "Hold on!" he said, driving the truck over the last steep rise then gunning the engine. The big Ford hit the first stream bed with enough force for a tidal wave of water to crash down onto the truck's hood and windshield. Startled, Heather groaned as water began to enter beneath the floorboards and start to pool.

"Are we going to sink?" she asked, studying the makeshift repairs previously made under her feet.

"That's hardened Loth mucus. Practically indestructible . . . impenetrable too."

"Good to know," she said, sounding less than convinced.

As the truck's back section was pulled further downstream by strong currents, Cameron gave the engine a bit more gas. Exchanging a quick glance, he saw Heather's apprehension growing by the second. Then, the rear wheels found purchase, and they were racing up and out of the water and onto the opposite shoreline.

"Show off," she said.

"One more, hold on," he ordered.

"I am holding on!" she replied, her words mostly drowned out by the roar of the accelerating engine. The front of the F-150 plowed into the next, somewhat deeper streambed. This time, water splashed in through the open windows and drenched them both. As the truck swung around, seeming to be carried away down river, Heather didn't give him the satisfaction of looking scared. Instead, she rolled her eyes then casually glanced out the window, as though nothing of interest was taking place.

Up and out and onto the second of the sandy peninsulas, Cameron steered the truck to the approximate middle section and cut the engine. "Home sweet home, sweet cheeks."

Heather, peering down at her sopping wet clothes, stole a quick glance outside then looked again. He could tell by her expression she was struck by the natural beauty of the spot: the surrounding sparking blue waters, the white sands, the nearby forest of towering bright-blue trees. She opened her door and stood. "I think I've just arrived in heaven. Oh, my God, Cam! This is . . . truly magnificent."

Cameron climbed out. Walking around the rear of the truck, he joined her there.

"Is this where you stayed? That last month, were you right here?" she asked.

"Just about. I was up a bit farther." He pointed with an outstretched finger for her eyes to follow, but his expression changed as he took in the distant object. "Now that's a bit odd," he said, his voice just above a whisper. He squinted his eyes against the reflective brightness, coming off the nearby streams. "That's not where I left it."

"Left what?"

"And it's supposed to be upside down."

"What?"

"Do me a favor . . . grab that pistol off the dash. I need to go and check this out." Cam didn't wait for her as he hurried off in the direction of the distant Tangine Shell.

Thirty feet out he focused his attention on the sand surrounding it. Specifically looking for foot impressions made by a large animal—such as the Loth, as it moved past, or even one of the dinosaur-sized Gleery Beasts. But the sand was smooth, unmarred by any larger-type predator that could have recently flipped the shell over, back onto its correct bottom side. Giving the shell a wide berth, he circled around it, to examine it from the opposite side. Then he halted—his forehead creased with worry.

Heather, approaching and noting his expression, pointed the weapon at the Tangine Shell. "What the hell is that thing? Is it dangerous?"

Cameron slowly shook his head. "No, but someone—something—was here."

"How do you know?"

"Because it's been flipped over and . . . somehow repaired."

"How is that possible? You said we're all alone here."

"I know I did. But I was wrong."

chapter 13

Heather...

She joined Cameron along the side of the oblong, approximately ten-foot-high by fifteen-foot-long structure that looked remarkably similar to a giant tortoise shell.

"Still looks pretty beat up. Are those claw marks?" she asked.

"Yeah . . . a Gleery Beast did that. And I was inside there at the time."

"Yet somehow you're still alive to talk about it?" she asked.

"Loth intervened . . . just in time."

"You said it's been repaired?"

"Yeah, the shell's been pried open. Where the beast used its claws trying to get at me. That's been fixed. Look here along this seam, the shell's bent back into alignment. Not a simple task. The thing's practically impregnable. The strength needed to bend it back into shape like this would have to be . . . ," Cameron stopped mid-sentence.

"What is it?" Heather asked.

"I know who . . . what . . . did this. Damn it!"

"That XI droid you told me about? The one you left behind here?"

He nodded. "I thought it was deactivated and beyond repair. Apparently I underestimated it."

Heather looked up, spotting Whim not too far away. "It looks like Whim?"

"Sort of. Somewhere along the line, XI modified itself. Mounted two weird-looking plasma cannons onto each of its sides. If it's at all possible for an artificial intelligence to go crazy, totally whacko, XI fits that bill."

"And it's here. Around here right now?"

Both eyes settled on the dark-gray Tangine Shell, on its elevated panels, each with intricate, swirling designs. Cameron's hand found hers and he took the pistol from her grasp. "The way in is through the hatch over here." Together, they moved around to the front of the shell. To the right of the hatch were a series of indentations.

"Heather, maybe you should stand back, off to the side."

"So only you'll get shot? Leaving me here all alone to deal with a crazy robot and roaming carnivores? No, thank you!"

Cameron placed his palm onto the center indentation, like he had over a month earlier. The hatchway clicked and a moment later it swung inward. Nearly dark inside, muted illumination entered in through a series of one-way windows set around the periphery.

"This is impossible," Heather said, taking a tentative step inside just past the threshold.

"I thought so too when I first entered this thing. Kind of defies physics. I figure it's almost twice the size on the inside as it is on the outside."

"This is way cool," she said, turning about in a circle to take it all in.

Cameron looked about the space, now back to its previous configuration. As if the damage the Gleery Beast caused had never happened. *Maybe some kind of systems reset had occurred?*

Heather ran her hand along the outside of the scaled-down version of an HOD. "It's like what's on the ship in our quarters." Soft light emanating out from the HOD reflected in her bright eyes. "Camping just got a whole lot more palatable . . . more like *glamping*," she said, with a mischievous smile.

He nodded though he was still concerned. More than a little concerned.

Several virtual 3D displays popped up around them. As he'd witnessed before, the nearest one provided a wide variety of diagnostic readings for the Tangine Shell. Its power reserves were at 93%, and the environmental levels were normal for Sang-Morang:

Atmosphere: 75% nitrogen, 23% oxygen, 1.9% argon, and 0.03% carbon dioxide.

He waved a hand in a dismissive gesture and the virtual display reading dissipated away.

"What do all those symbols represent?" Heather asked, gesturing toward the space-age looking control panel of slowly rotating geometric symbols and abstract flashes of light. Cameron knew they were actually high-speed data streams.

Before he could answer her, a new virtual pop-up display appeared.

"Hey Alice," Cameron said.

Alice, full sized, was standing at a terminal on the *Primion's* bridge. Ramen stood right beside her."

Cameron said, "We have a big problem."

"Your Tangine Shell seems to be operational. What is the problem?" she asked.

"Are you serious? It's not like this thing fixed itself. It's not like there's an interstellar repairman wandering around Sang-Morang with a toolbox."

Ramen said, "That's alien Priopax tech. It can reset itself."

"I already know it's Priopax . . . but this thing was far beyond repair. You didn't see what that Gleery Beast did to it. Anyway, I'm talking to Alice right now, not to you."

Ramen shrugged off the comment and stepped away. Alice continued to stare back at him, her face expressionless.

"XI . . . is here. It did this."

"XI was deactivated. Is inoperable," Alice said.

"No. It's the only explanation," he said emphatically.

Her eyes flicked away for a moment, then returned to him. "*Primion's* sensor's do not pickup XI's unique energy signature. It is picking up the other droid. The stupid one you wanted to give to Heather."

"Hey, don't call Whim stupid," Heather objected behind him.

"How difficult would it be for it to change, to shield itself? For an AI such as XI to figure something like this out?" he asked her.

Alice didn't answer right away, then said, "Perhaps it would be best for you to return to the *Primion* now."

"Come on, Cam, we just got here! Aren't there some precautions we can take?" Heather asked.

"Accessing the shell, Alice, can you fix it so only Heather and I can gain access?"

A moment passed. "Done. I've altered the hatch interface to only accept DNA authorization from you and your girlfriend."

"XI is smart . . . will that be enough?"

"I still suggest you return to the *Primion*, where you can be better protected."

Cameron turned to Heather, "Maybe she's right."

"What about the Loth. Can you call it back here?"

Blowing out through puffed cheeks, he thought, *This is getting complicated.* "Okay, we'll try that." Cameron turned back to Alice. "Is there anything you can do? You know, to better detect where XI is now? Maybe figure out what it's up to?"

"I assure you, we are already doing that, Cameron. I will check in with you later this evening, if that is acceptable,"

Alice said, with a slightly raised chin and a formality he hadn't witnessed in her before. *Really? Alice was now acting jealous?*

Cameron nodded, but before he could say anything else, Alice raised a hand and waved him away. He pictured his own virtual pop-up display being casually dismissed—nothing more than a dissipating wisp of smoke on the *Primion's* bridge. He probably deserved it.

"That robot has serious feelings for you," Heather said, making a face.

"That's ridiculous."

"Uh huh . . . answer me this. Is she anatomically female . . . you know, down south?" She lowered her eyes toward her own mid-section.

"What are you talking about?"

"Does she have lady parts? Is there a big hairy robot bush, hiding beneath that tight uniform?"

Cameron laughed out loud. "Shut up! I have no idea and thank you for that mental image. Look, we need to talk safety. If we're going to stay in the wilderness for a few days, there needs to be a few rules."

"Okay."

"No wandering off by yourself. There's too many things that can eat you here . . . eat us. When Piquet Sprints attack there's a whole bevy of them. Smart and dangerous little shits. There're only a few big Greely Beasts in the area. We'll know when one of them is around as the ground shakes. I'm pretty sure that will bring the Loth back to protect us. But that's only a few of the beasts we need to be careful of. I'm going to see if there's something this shell can do to warn us . . . like an alarm, when animals approach."

"That's a good idea. Is the water safe? Anything swimming around in there that can eat us?"

"No . . . water is good to drink and not dangerous at all. There's fish in there."

"So we'll be having that for dinner?" she asked, sliding first one arm free of her shirt and then the other.

"Yeah, I'll make a fire. I have a fishing pole in the truck. What are you doing?"

"Getting undressed." He watched her shimmy out of her tight shorts. "I'm going swimming."

Staring at her, standing there in her panties and bra, he asked, "Who are you, and what have you done with my girlfriend?"

chapter 14

Heather wasn't nearly as immodest, or brave, as she was portraying herself to be to Cam. Perhaps at some level, she figured, he already knew that. But she'd made a commitment—made it in that split second when she could just as easily have stayed back on Earth with her family, with everything familiar to her. *Everything safe.* But she had chosen Cam—running to him; accepting that life from that moment on would be different. *She* would be different. One thing was certain: she'd either become this new person, this audacious risk taker who liked to screw in the open atop the hood of her boyfriend's truck, go skinny-dipping in perilous waters, and argue to remain in a wilderness fraught with innumerable predators—both animal and mechanical—or admit defeat and beg Cameron to take her home. No way. She was a different Heather. She was *Heather 2.0* and there would be no going back, not if she wanted to live with herself with any semblance of self-respect—not to mention, keep the one she loved.

Heather, naked, left her panties and bra lying on the floor within the Tangine Shell. Now, she felt his eyes on her backside as she stood on the shoreline of the largest of the three streams, one that seemed more like a river to her. She glanced back wide-eyed over her shoulder—a portrait of innocence that she knew would leave Cam somewhat weak-kneed. "Now, you're sure . . . that it's safe to go in?"

Standing at the bed of the truck, attempting to find his fishing rod, Cameron nodded. "I'm sure. Or, you can just stand there naked like that . . . works for me," he said.

"Uh huh . . . I bet it does." Heather stepped into the cool water, tempted to nix the idea completely. Heather 2.0 she inwardly repeated to herself like a mantra, then jumped in. The instant chill of the water caught her by surprise—she gasped and unsuccessfully tried to stand upright. The currents were strong and she had to fight not to be dragged downstream. Always a strong swimmer, she began putting that particular skill to good use. She kicked her legs hard while stretching out with her left arm and then her right—long, steady, consistent strokes. She increased her rhythm and soon was back to where she'd first jumped in. Her breathing normalized, she felt strong as the water slid over her bare skin. A full minute later she slowed her pace and flipped over onto her back. The currents swirled and flowed around her, pulling her back downstream. Cam was at the water's edge—his fishing pole grasped loosely in one hand—but he wasn't looking at her, his attention was drawn to something else.

Out of the corner of her eye she saw movement. A dozen undefined dark shapes skittering across the landscape—shapes that were moving fast and drawing closer. She wiped the excess water, dripping down from her wet hair, out of her eyes. Cam dropped his fishing pole, glanced her way, and then back at what looked like a pack of furry beasts. Seeing his nervous expression, Heather quickly scrambled up the embankment of slippery rocks and managed to join him by the truck. She was too concerned with what was heading their way to give her nakedness a second thought.

"We need the pistol!" she said, sending a quick glance into the truck's rear window.

Noticing Cam's expression was far calmer than she'd expected, she realized the approaching beasts weren't dangerous.

"They're the climber animals you told me about?"

"Dalima Climbers. They're peaceful . . . gentle beings."

Cam hadn't looked at her when he spoke, his eyes never leaving the smallest of the beasts.

"Is that Lalik over there?" she asked.

He nodded.

Heather could hear them now—excited sounds of chattering emanating from each one. But it was in their eyes that she noticed their absolute delight at seeing Cam standing there. As he opened his arms wide, the flood of dark-furred creatures came forward to embrace him—to love him.

"Brath!" Cam yelled, as he was lifted high off the ground by the largest of the clan animals. Heather figured this was the leader—perhaps even the father of many of the others. Cameron laughed and she saw wetness in his eyes at being so warmly welcomed back. Somehow ironic, she thought, for the same young man who grew up with such a pitiful amount of love in his life. Parents who died when he was just a small boy, then sent off to live with a criminal, drug-dealing uncle in Texas. And when that uncle met with his own violent end, Cam was sent to live with foster parents, in Larksburg Stand. A glacially cool couple who kept him at arm's length, a good portion of his teen years were spent in near solitude, at least until he met Heather. She watched as the throng of friendly ape-like animals vied for his attention, all speaking their strange language at the same time. The one she was certain was Lalik had climbed up onto his back and was nuzzling the nape of his neck.

Now, somewhat more conscious of her nudity, she side-stepped over to the bed of the truck. Finding her duffle bag, Heather quickly picked out a few things to throw on. Turning back around, she saw they were all staring at her; that same glimmer of amusement in their eyes. It was Lalik who took Heather's hand in hers then pulled her into a mass of furry affection that brought tears to her own eyes. Next, she found Cam and together they laughed. She listened as he introduced each and every one of the creatures to her personally.

Sphial and the one called Lalik, each taking an arm, pulled her along inside the moving huddle. The one called Thilith, a large and older female, was gesturing, communicating with Cam about something—something evidently very important.

At the tree line, Heather glanced back at the truck and the Tangine Shell and wondered if their stuff would be safe, but then realized that no one on this alien world had the slightest interest in anything they possessed. Her eyes searched the sky—the horizon—looking for Whim. She spotted a black speck, far off in the distance. *There you are, little one.* She thought she saw a second tiny black speck moving across the sky, but then it, too, was gone. *Must have been a bird.*

Three or four paces into the tree line, the dappled sunlight shining down from above was quickly obscured by the ever-thickening foliage. Five further steps in, it was so dark she could not see who was next to her. Could not even see her shoes, walking upon the soft ground.

Sphial and Lalik had released her hands and she could no longer hear them; or hear anything at all. "Cam?" she called out—her words sounding flat—absorbed by the dense surroundings. He didn't answer.

She took several more steps forward, her hands extended out before her like a blind person. "Cam!" Heather called out, not caring if fear could be heard in her voice.

Suddenly, she was being pulled up by her arms and into the trees around her. Strong hands grabbed ahold of her wrists then released them to other outstretched hands, which were higher up. Up she went, too surprised—too scared—to make a sound. Then, just as suddenly, she found she was no longer moving, but was perched on a branch. Now more hands were holding her steady. Someone came closer and she felt the tickle of lips at her ear. "You're okay," Cam whispered. "You're completely safe."

Heather nodded into the darkness and, after several deep breaths, felt her quickened heart rate settle down. About to ask Cam what was happening, she saw a light appear some fifty feet away. Almost as if someone had struck a match, a flame now softly flickered in the distance. A moment later, there was another, and then another, the last one much closer. *Not a flickering flame.* She noticed the chest of a nearby Dalima Climber was actually glowing—throbbing a warm, reddish amber of internally generated illumination. With each beat of the creature's pulsing heart, she could make out the outline of internal organs. More and more of the Climbers were exhibiting the same beautiful spectacle. And then came a deep rumbling noise; they were chanting in unison. They were making *music*.

She felt Cameron's arms slip around her waist. He gently kissed her—kissed her where tears had left tracks upon her cheek.

Nestled into his arms, together they rocked back and forth, listening to the chorus of melodic voices. The forest seemed alive—to be one organism. One that they were a part of, were deep inside of. Heather pulled Cam closer and put her lips to his ear: "Thank you for sharing this with me. I'll never forget this moment. Not ever."

chapter 15

Cameron . . .

He had nodded off when he was suddenly awakened by—*something.* Something was *stirring* in the forest. All around him had become ominously quiet. Pitch-black within the forest, he was still perched atop a high-up tree branch, Heather snuggled-in next to him. His arms were still loosely wrapped around her waist.

Then a series of distant, thunderous sounds drew his attention away. He knew that sound. Cameron had a knack for knowing obscure factoids. His foster parents, the Park's, both devout Jehovah Witnesses, had disallowed any access to television programming, or to having a computer, or just about anything that was of interest to a teenage boy. But he had been allowed to read, and reread, then reread again the nearly complete set of well-worn old World Book Encyclopedias. Cameron, with his ridiculously high IQ—an amazing mind he always suspected he'd inherited from his mother—possessed a borderline photographic memory. Now, almost as if having the World Book Encyclopedia, letter **S**, lying on his lap, he mentally flipped to the reference: **Strafing**: *The military practice of attacking ground targets by low-flying aircraft using aircraft-mounted automatic weaponry.* And he knew in that same moment, *Thump, Thump, Thump, Thump,* that something terrible, something unfathomable, was taking place along the distant high ridgeline at the top of the mountain.

"What is it . . . what's happening?" Heather asked, in a sleepy voice.

"The *Primion* . . . it's being attacked. We have to get down from here!" He had no idea how far up in the trees they were, but without help, it would be nearly impossible to traverse safely down. Then, strong hands got ahold of him and he heard Heather utter a startled noise. They were being lowered pretty much the same way they'd been raised up earlier. Only now he was hearing nervous yips and hurried breaths. He didn't know which Dalima Climbers were helping them, but he did know they were terrified. Down they went—twice, he nearly slipped from their hurried grasps.

A tremendously bright blaze of white and yellow suddenly lit up the forest all around them. A split-second later, a nearly deafening explosive concussion nearly shattered Cameron's eardrums. The once beautiful woodlands had been transformed into a fiery hell—all in an instant. And then he was falling. He hit an outstretched branch—careened hard into it—and then was falling again, only to hit the next branch below it even harder. Something whipped across his cheek, perhaps a branch, and he tasted blood as it seeped into his mouth. Falling once more, he heard a scream rise up from below. He hit the ground with enough force to knock the air from his lungs. Lying on his back, fire raged all around them as he tried desperately to inhale a deeper breath. Heather, up on her knees next to him, was coughing. One of her arms was bleeding. Her long hair mostly covered her face. When he finally was able to draw a breath in, it was one full of smoke and ash, which only made him retch and cough more. His lungs were burning—felt on fire—much like the timber all around them.

Cameron had apparently lost consciousness because he next found himself being dragged by his arms. Tree trunks moved past him, one after another. He tried to see who had a firm hold of his wrists. Getting lighter out, he caught a glimpse of long hair the color of wheat. *Heather.* She was pulling him across a floor of pine needles, or whatever Sang-Morang's equivalent of pine needles was. "Let me up . . . I'm okay," he said.

Heather helped him rise to his feet and together they scrambled toward the not so distant tree line. He felt heat on his back and shoulders as the forest continued to blaze. His mind flashed to the Loth. He knew from past experience, the huge creature would often venture into the trees in pursuit of prey. But he couldn't think about that now.

They emerged out of the trees and kept on running. Heather was first to run into the stream, where they crossed it at its shallowest, narrowest, point. They hurried past the Tangine Shell and over to the truck. Out of breath, they stopped and stared. High up along the distant ridgeline, black smoke billowed into the air. Orange flames reached high into the sky, rising up from what was left of the *Primion.*

Honk! . . . *Honk!* . . . *Honk!* Upstream three hundred yards, Cameron saw the unmistakable form of the giant Loth quickly splashing its way down the river toward them. Cameron let out a heavy breath—relieved to see the beast had not been harmed.

Heather, climbing up onto the roof of the truck, was repeatedly waving her hands back and forth over her head. "Loth! Loth! We're over here!" she screamed—now jumping up and down to get its attention.

A loud crackling sound—like a million tiny explosions—suddenly emanated out behind them downstream. Cameron watched as a strange-looking spacecraft of indeterminate size rose up from behind distant boulders. Its powerful thrusters churned up dirt and water from the streams. Heather placed her hands over her ears as the craft zoomed close by overhead—its metallic underbelly an aggregate of hundreds of conduits and all sorts of strange, alien mechanisms. Cameron instinctively ducked as the vessel's shadow momentarily darkened the landscape around them. The alien ship, Cameron figured, was about half the length of the *Primion*—but maybe twice its width. It was *big*.

Expecting the craft to rise up—make its way into the atmosphere now that it had decimated the *Primion*—Cameron watched as it actually slowed and began to descend back down. Heather stared down from where she stood, her face mirroring his confusion.

From where he stood, he could no longer see the Loth, only a series of massively large exhaust cones, protruding out from the aft section of the spaceship. He heard the Loth's repeated honks. Honks that sounded far more desperate.

"Oh my God . . . they're here for the Loth!" Hands balled into white-knuckled fists, legs pumping like diesel pistons, Cameron ran like he'd never run before. The closer he got to the distant ship, the more certain he was who, *what*, was responsible. XI! *Fucking XI.* He ran as fast as he could. His lungs burned and his legs ached. Somewhere behind him he heard Heather call out his name, but stopping now was not an option. He couldn't let them take the Loth. He heard Heather scream out for him then looked up and saw her—above him. *How?*

XI had her grasped within its articulating arms. Heather's legs were flailing and kicking. Cameron stopped running, his mouth open—gasping for breath—and watched as XI, with captive Heather in tow, flew toward the now-reengaged loud crackling sounds of the ship. He heard one last scream, as both Heather and the XI droid disappeared into an open hatch. Thrusters were then powered up and the ship lifted higher into the air. Cameron had to cover his eyes as small rocks and sand swirled all about him. He blinked away the stinging grit and watched as the ominous alien vessel rose ever higher into the air.

It felt like his heart was being ripped from his chest. Heather had been taken. The Loth had been taken.

The vessel turned 180 degrees on its axis and headed down-river. Cameron didn't duck this time as it flew past him close overhead. He turned and watched its progression. A single bright flash emanated out from the ship—a plasma bolt, with precise accuracy, struck the pickup truck. The resulting explosion was barely audible as the alien ship's big engines accelerated the craft up into the atmosphere. Within mere moments, it had become only a speck in the sky. Then it was gone.

chapter 16

For twelve straight hours, Cameron sat mesmerized on the sand while Sang-Morang burned all around him. The forest snapped and crackled—glowing embers drifted up into the soot-filled air. Flames no longer rose above the distant high ridgeline—only smoke—where he imagined the burnt-out superstructure of the *Primion* would be.

His eyes drifted over to his truck—some fifty yards downriver from where he sat. Clearly, there was nothing much left of it. The attacking alien ship had pretty much turned it into ash, even the under frame was gone, melted down under the intense heat of the blast.

Cameron *felt* its creeping approach coming up on him—a dark and heavy thing. It was *sadness*. It was *despair*. He jumped to his feet—spun around—turned right toward it. "No! Get away! You're not going to do this to me! You're not going to win!" He glanced up at the sky where the last few of the nighttime stars still twinkled—tiny reminders of the ever-growing distance between him and Heather. An inner rage coursed through his veins like molten lava. Seething hatred engulfed him. "It may take me a lifetime, twenty lifetimes, but mark my words here today, XI. I will make you pay for this. I will make you suffer."

A metallic sound clanged nearby. Cameron looked for something he could use as a weapon—a stick or a rock— perhaps something he could throw in order to defend himself. Then he saw it. It rolled one way, and then the other. Jerky in its locomotion. it rose into the air several feet then dropped down hard onto the wet sand. Next, it rolled back into the stream, disappearing beneath the surface. Just the sight of it made Cameron want to lash out; to break something. He waited. There was no way he would give it any assistance. At one level he knew it wasn't Whim's fault for looking so similar to the XI droid, but at another level, Cameron blamed their mutually shared alien technology. *If such evil could reside in one of those things, it certainly could reside in all of them.* Seeing that it had been damaged—was barely functional, inspired no intent within Cameron to assist it. "Go ahead and drown in there, you little fucker," he said.

For hours and hours he had tried to think of a way, *some way*, out of this terrible predicament. How he might rescue Heather and the Loth. But the *Primion* was gone. Even his truck was gone. The only real means to defend himself, the plasma pistol, was also gone. Soon the predators would come for him. How long could he survive against a whole pack of a dozen scavenging Piquet Sprints, or against a thirty-foot-tall Greely Beast? *Minutes? Seconds? He shook his head, No . . . I don't have the luxury of feeling sorry for myself. I'm smart. I'm resourceful. And I'm fucking angry. I will get off this planet. Somehow, I will find them.*

Cameron slowly walked toward what remained of his truck. Daylight had crested above the distant horizon, spreading a warm swatch of golden light across the sandy peninsulas and the three streams. He noticed for the first time the Tangine Shell was right where he'd last seen it, a bit farther on. It looked perfectly intact. A momentary spark of hope entered into his consciousness. He'd have a relatively safe place to sleep later on. That, at least, was something. He turned back to the dark stained residue on the sand, where his old F-150 once stood. Taking several steps closer, he marveled at such total destruction, except for an elongated mound of ash right within where the former bed of the truck had been. Cameron continued to stare. Strange, every other aspect of the truck had been completely fried. What was so robust in that mound of ash to still maintain its rough form? Certainly not his bicycle, or his beach umbrella; or his ice chest, or the duffle bag, stuffed with new clothes.

Cameron used the toe of his boot to kick at the mound of blackened ash. *Thump. It was solid.* He knelt down and, mindful of the still rising heat, used his fingers to brush away the top charcoal layer. Something smooth lay beneath. He felt his heart begin to race, even before he consciously comprehended what he was uncovering. *What he was seeing?* Abruptly he stood up, staring down at what he'd uncovered not quite believing his eyes. *Why wasn't it annihilated, like the truck's other contents?* He answered his own question aloud: "Because those Priopax . . . *whoever they were* . . . were fucking geniuses!" Since it was still extremely hot, he used his boot to slide the trinious bundle out from where it lay. Moved it ten feet away so it would cool down more quickly.

Cameron left it there while he returned to the nearby streambed to wash soot from his hands. His inner dialogue was going full-throttle—*Just because the bundle is intact does not mean its contents, all those wonderful alien gadgets, are also intact. They very well might be a congealed, melted, lump of nothingness now.* He stood up and after wiping his wet hands off on his jeans returned to the trinious bundle. Lowering down to one knee, he searched for the nearly imperceptible seam that ran from one end of the bundle to the other. It took a few minutes, but he found it. From past experience he knew exactly how to open it. The Priopax zipper-like seal separated apart as he ran a fingertip along its length. Then, tentatively putting his hand inside, he felt around, finding it surprisingly cool. By sheer touch, he could differentiate the various, oddly shaped, half-dozen objects. He remembered that this collection had been Ramen's—the original organic being, not the creepy, duplicate, cyborg *thing*—who had pilfered the bundle of gadgets from an abandoned, adrift, Priopax spaceship.

One by one, Cameron began removing each dark-gray item and placing it on the sand. He glanced over at the Tangine Shell, which, when fully compressed, had also been a part of this Priopax collection. He took out a circular, dinner-plate-shaped device that was heavy for its size. As with the other devices, a series of small, circular indentations were imbedded upon one side of its surface, along with an intricate, artful, swirling design on its top surface.

Finding the item he was looking for, Cameron flipped the brick-sized device over in his hands until he found an enlarged circular inset. Tapping at it with a forefinger, he waited. It took a moment. Then he heard the familiar old man's voice: "I've missed you, lad. But if you want my two-cents' worth, you're so far up the creek without a paddle, you may not find your way back. Son . . . you need to start using that gray matter between your ears; either that, or . . . you'll soon be a goner."

Cameron was instantly comforted just hearing that familiar Texas twang. He smiled as he looked around. Art liked to find creative ways to make himself visible. And there he was—standing at the water's edge, an ancient-looking fishing pole gripped in one hand. He was dressed as he always was, in a faded red-plaid flannel shirt, worn blue jeans, scuffed leather cowboy boots, and an old Stetson hat with a dark, sweat-stained ring encircling the lower part of its crown. His silvery chin whiskers glistened in the morning sunlight.

Cameron knew that Art wasn't exactly real—was actually *virtual*. But virtual here, using these Priopax devices, was not the same as virtual back on Earth. Art was perfectly capable of interacting with physical matter. Cameron suspected he could, in fact, catch a fish with that old pole of his, if he so intended.

Cameron stood and joined Art near the side of the stream. As they exchanged a quick glance, Art's bright-blue eyes twinkled with good-natured humor. Something tugged at the line of his pole. "Take a seat. I'll build us a fire . . . we need to get something in that belly of yours. Impossible to think clear-headed on an empty stomach."

chapter 17

Heather . . .

S he awoke to a blindingly painful headache. That, and the taste of copper in her mouth—as if she had been sucking on a mouthful of pennies. She opened her eyes into near-total darkness. The deck flooring was icy-cold metal. A distant noise could be heard—a repetitive droning, recycling over and over again—the sound of big powerful engines.

Confusion slowly gave way to recent memories. To the horrific recollection of what had taken place on Sang-Morang. *Oh God . . . Cam.* She envisioned him in her mind's eye—running, calling up to her. Surely, he was dead by now. The droid, *that XI thing*, had told her as much. Heather brought her hands up and buried her eyes into her palms, felt the wetness of tears—tears and blood. She used her fingertip to trace the outline of a recent bloody laceration upon her cheek, which probably caused the taste of copper in her mouth. She wondered what other injuries she may have incurred, too.

Pushing herself up into a sitting position, which only increased the throbbing and pounding in her head, she fought away nausea—swallowing hard. She brought her legs up, hugging them close to her chest. She didn't seem to have any other injuries—nothing more than a few sore muscles, plus some scrapes and bruises. *Nothing catastrophic anyway.* She pushed away thoughts of Cam . . . *oh God.* She inhaled a deep breath, then let it out—attempted to stand, but failed. Falling backward, she landed hard on her rear end and let out a yelp. As nausea returned full force, she leaned over to the side and retched and threw up—the taste of bile replacing the taste of copper in her mouth. She spoke to the acrid, wet puddle of vomit on the deck, "I've been abducted . . . and I'm all alone. I don't even want to imagine what will happen to me . . . what they will do to me." She couldn't help but picture herself being thrown down to the deck by a giant alien—some kind of dirty, disgusting, space pirate. She would become a mere plaything. Probably passed around from one ugly alien to another until they tired of her. Until she was so battered, so used and abused, she'd no longer be of use to them. Then they would kill her. It would be better if she had died back on Sang-Morang, along with Cam. "Maybe it's not too late," she murmured. She would kill herself. Spare herself from what surely was to come. "But how? How does one *off* oneself on an alien spaceship?" she queried aloud.

Heather again attempted to stand, only this time more slowly and more carefully. She nearly lost her balance but this time managed to remain upright. Hands positioned out before her, she took one step forward then another. What little light there was seemed to be coming from somewhere in front of her. She kept moving on, taking one tentative step after another. Soon, light in the area steadily increased, to the point she could make out, at least partially, what was now around her. Metal walls, Cam had told her, on a ship were called bulkheads. These were dull gray and ugly, holding countless numbers of crisscrossing pipes and conduits. Clearly, the aliens onboard were not concerned with visual aesthetics. *Where is everyone—and where is XI?* she wondered.

Disoriented, she veered away from the distant, still undefined, illumination. Her steps became less measured. She wanted to run. Not so much to escape, although that too, but just to have a free, unrestrained feeling—one last time.

"Stop!"

The singular word was yelled out. It sounded more like a thundering broadcast. And she did indeed stop. Two things registered mentally at almost the same instant. First, it was the XI droid who'd issued the ridiculously loud command. It was hovering a good distance away, maybe all the way across to the far side of the vessel. Second, she now could see why the droid had issued the command. Not more than three feet before her was a ledge of sorts. She took a careful step forward and found the steep drop off would have been the end of her. Heather peered down into an open stairwell structure, but one without stairs. Down below, in the murky dark haze, were at least four other decks—probably identical to this one. Heather guessed it was a total of eighty to one hundred feet down—although she couldn't be sure, because she couldn't see the bottom. The fall surely would have been fatal. *But, hey, isn't that what I want?* she asked herself. One more time she pushed any thoughts of Cam away. *Not now . . . I can't.*

Her eyes lifted—locked onto the XI droid, located on the other side of the inter-deck opening. Although motionless, she could feel its gaze steadfast upon her just the same. Could almost sense each intricate circuit calculating what the best course of action would be to keep her from doing what she intended to do. She thought of Cam and felt as if her heart were being clutched within a tight fist—squeezed deep within her chest. *I don't want to live without you, Cam. Not here . . . not like this.* She took a half step forward feeling the edge line of the deck beneath the soles of her shoes as the XI droid rushed forward with astonishing speed.

"Don't!" she yelled, raising a cautionary hand. "I will fucking jump if you so much as twitch."

The droid had advanced its position to the exact middle of the circular opening—was hovered there as if it were the hub on a great wheel. She let her gaze focus downward. It was almost as if the bleak darkness below was calling to her: *Jump, Heather . . . just take that last step.*

Movement.

She looked up. The droid had not moved an inch, but around her, on the other side of the inter-deck opening, other *things* were moving around. Ten feet from where she stood she saw one of them now—relatively close. It had pulled away from the closest bulkhead, as if some of the pipes and conduits had suddenly come alive. It moved with a kind of bipedal, walking locomotion. Skinny stick figures, made of metal pipes, were nearly identical to the intricate latticework she'd noticed on virtually all of the surrounding bulkheads. They were perfectly camouflaged there.

"Stay away from me!" Heather shot sideways, toward the approaching mismatch of angular pipes.

Four feet away, the stick figure halted its progress. Heather now could see it in more detail, that it had two arms and two legs, and even a small head of sorts. Its various joints— elbows, wrists, ankles, knees—were composed of the type of things one would find in the plumbing section of a Home Depot—metal elbow joints, and such fixtures. Its small head was basically a plain metal box.

Then, the boxlike head tilted slightly to one side. Heather watched as two rods emerged—one out the top of the metal box and one out the bottom. Simultaneously, they extended up and down, about a foot in each direction. She never considered she could become even more frightened—but she was. It must be a weapon of sorts, she figured. *This is it.* She was going to be killed, right here and now. *But isn't that what I want?*

What came next was most unexpected. Again, simultaneously, the two rods, which clearly now were not made of metal, began to *unfurl*. Instantly, Heather thought of their similarity to Japanese hand fans. Her best friend back in high school, Donna Sato, had a collection of them mounted onto her bedroom wall. Each was unique. One, Donna's favorite, was hand-painted—decorated with delicate black branches and pink cherry blossoms. Heather had learned that some were made of washi paper, while others, considered more precious, were made of silk. When their unfurling process had completed, the two fans joined together forming a complete circle. Heather marveled at what she now was seeing. Even in the dim light, she could see a design of beautiful iridescent colors, like sunlight reflecting off the wings of a dragonfly.

There were raised edges that cast nearly imperceptible shadows. *I can see it there . . . a face*; one concealed within all the swirls of colors. Two eyes, a nose, and a mouth became more evident as she continued to stare at it.

"What are you?" she asked, without thinking.

"I am not a *what*. I am a who."

"Oh . . . I didn't think there was anyone else alive on this ship."

The very odd pipe-stick figure, with the beautiful fan-like face, smiled. "What is alive, really? Only that which is organic in nature? Perhaps you should broaden your perception of what *alive* really means. Perhaps life is a relative term."

"Fine . . . but I didn't mean anything by it; didn't mean to offend you. I'm not supposed to be here. I don't want to be here."

"Based on present results, you are exactly where you want to be," said the stick figure. "Be where you are . . . be who you are."

Heather continued to keep a close eye on the XI droid as it maintained its hovering position within the center of the deck opening. "Can you tell me your name?" she asked. "Do you have names here? Or do you even think of yourselves that way?"

The question evoked a high-pitched, multi-octave sound that at first startled Heather, then relaxed her. *It was a laugh.* With a quick glance, Heather caught the smile accompanying it.

"I have a name. We all have names. We are not organic in composition, but we are, most assuredly, alive. I'm not sure how we'd get by without having individual names. Interesting thought, though . . . something to think about. Yes, you can call me Balth."

"Balth?"

"Is that not a good name?"

"I don't know . . . I guess it's okay. Where I come from, it would not make for a very good name. No offense." Heather was reconsidering her plan to jump. The diversion of speaking with the alien—or *whatever* it was—gave her fresh pause.

"Can you help me? Protect me from the droid?"

Before the inorganic jumble of pipes could answer her back, Heather heard familiar far-off sounds. Sounds most definitely organic in nature: *Honk! Honk! Honk!*

chapter 18

Cameron . . .

Sitting upon a tree stump in front of a blazing fire, he had a frontier pie pan balanced on his knees, devouring eggs, thick-sliced honey bacon, pan-fried country toast, and black kettle coffee strong enough to strip the paint off a car door. All the while, Art paced back and forth nearby listening to Cameron talk between bites and chewing. Cameron ran down the course of events covering the last few days, although he knew Art was already well aware of everything that had transpired. Art was actually not a single entity, if entity was even the right word for it. Art was a self-described amalgamation—multiple-being consciousness—now represented in this lone interface—this virtual *hick* of an old man, currently picking his teeth with a hay stalk.

"And then the alien ship . . . just took off. Left me here alone with no way to ever leave this damn planet, or have a way to defend myself against predators. I think XI left me here to suffer . . . to die here, with only my thoughts and memories to haunt me till the end."

"Well, you're not dead yet," Art said with a shrug. "And you may be giving the droid more credit than it deserves."

"I didn't say I planned on accommodating him . . . *it*. But I am in a pickle." Cameron gestured toward the distant high ridgeline. "No transportation. No means to defend myself, although food may not be a problem as long as you're around."

Art held up his pacing long enough to scowl down at him.

"What?" Cameron asked.

Art used his hay stalk as a pointer: "That bundle contains everything you'll need to survive. You just need to stop whining long enough to think about it."

Cameron placed the now empty tin pan onto the ground and burped. "Last I looked, there's not an F-150 sitting in there . . . or a spaceship . . . or a plasma pistol. No, I'm pretty much fucked—"

"And you can mind your manners, please. No need for that kind of language."

"Sorry," Cameron said, feeling surprisingly embarrassed at the reprimand. "But come on, Art. As much as I am grateful for your company, your advice, I have to get off this world. I have to find Heather. She didn't sign up for this . . . being abducted by aliens. Who knows what they're doing to her? I don't even want to think about it."

"She's not alone," Art offered.

Cameron thought about that. Art was right. The Loth was with her. A very resourceful Loth that would do everything it could to protect her. Not so much because it had any great affection for her, but because the Loth knew Cameron did.

Art, now standing before the trinious bundle, used a scuffed boot toe to spread the bundle's open gap even farther apart. "Still got that Lox in there, I see."

Cameron let out a defeated breath. "I know I do," he said. He had to admit it had been the most useful, most indispensible, of all the Priopax devices. Akin to a three dimensional Xerox machine, in weeks past he'd made identical duplicates of all kinds of things, including his truck and plasma weapon. "Well . . . it would be great if I wanted to make copies of that Tangine Shell, sitting over there, or maybe this rock," he said, picking a stone up off the ground. "But if you want to copy something—you need to have that original thing here to copy!" He spoke with more anger than he intended. "Sorry, I'm not dealing with any of this all that well. I know you have good intentions, Art, but I've already thought about all this . . . I don't have the things I need for what I have to do."

"Why not?"

"What do you mean why not?"

"Take it out of the bundle."

"The Lox?"

"No, the Statue of Liberty. Of course, the Lox!"

Cameron did as asked, retrieving the dinner-plate-shaped item and placing it on the sand. He glanced up at Art, who was still scowling. "Fine, I'll humor you," Cameron said, placing his fingertips onto the recessed indentations. Within moments the Lox had transformed into its boxy, microwave oven-shaped contours. "There you go . . . the perfect gadget for duplicating this coffee mug." He raised his mug up in a mock toast to Art.

"You've gotten cheeky over the last few days, but I'll let that pass. That there marvel of Priopax ingenuity . . . at its barest minimum . . . has the functionality of one of those smartphones you youngsters are so taken with these days. You can take photographs, yes?"

Cameron nodded, frustrated with Art's tedious way of making a point. Never did he simply tell him what he needed to know. It always had to involve some kind of learning, some self-illumination moment. "Yes, it takes pictures. Even stores them. It's like magic. But I don't . . . ," then it hit him—like a ton of bricks dropped on his head. "No way!"

Art crossed his arms over his chest and waited.

"All those things I've duplicated in the past. . ."

Art's silvery brows arched up in anticipation.

"The truck . . . the pistol . . . other things?"

Art nodded. "Almost as cool as your smartphone, huh?"

Cameron thought about the implications. He placed an open palm over his mouth as his mind continued to race. "Hell, I'll even have clean underwear."

"And not a moment too soon," Art said dryly. "But right now, you need to sleep. You need to get yourself into that Tangine Shell . . . climb into the HOD that's in there and get some rest. I suspect over the next few days you'll have very little time for it. Go on. I'll do the dishes in the meantime."

Cameron watched as Art swiped his hand in front of the still-blazing fire, making it disappear, along with Art, and all the breakfast-making utensils. Now, standing outside all alone—hearing only the pleasant sounds of the babbling brook nearby—he did feel tired. He tried not to think of Heather, or of the Loth. Before heading off to the Tangine Shell, he glanced at the spot where a raging fire had burned only moments before. For a moment he considered, *Had any of it been real? The tree stumps, the blackened coffee kettle, the eggs and bacon?* He burped again, then smiled. *I'm too tired to even care.* Making his way over to the Shell's entrance, he went inside.

chapter 19

Jarred partially upright, Cameron awoke with a start, banging his head hard on the HOD's curved glass interior. He let himself fall back, rubbing the growing knot now on his forehead. He'd had a nightmare, something to do with his uncle. Details of the frightful dream were already slipping away—all he remembered was that it had something to do with that first day—the day he'd met Harley Decker.

Uncle Harley was his father's half-brother. Harley and his father shared the same father. And Harley, short and stocky—with straight brown hair and eyes as dark and lifeless as a rural Texas night sky—looked nothing like Cam's father, who was tall with wavy blond hair. At least, that's what his father looked like in the lone photograph Cameron possessed of both his mother and father. Standing together, their arms around one another in front of a lighthouse somewhere on the East Coast, they looked radiantly happy.

Victoria Hoang, short and petite and of Vietnamese descent, wearing a pink skirt, and a white top, was the social worker assigned to Cameron's case. She took possession of him two days after his parents' fateful car wreck. She accompanied him on the plane ride from LaGuardia Airport in New York to Valley International Airport in Harlingen, Texas. From there, she rented a Chevy Malibu, then drove the twenty-seven miles to where his uncle lived, in Progresso. Cameron remembered most of the details of that day—perhaps because it was the start of a new way of life.

They'd pulled up in front of a ratty-tatty dwelling with a crumbling sidewalk out front. The house, if you could call it that, had gray slump-stone walls. A portion of the house seemed to be collapsing in on itself. A short man, wearing greasy dungarees and a stained wife-beater shirt, was loading something into the back of a plywood camper shell, sitting atop the bed of a run-down pickup truck.

"Stay in the car . . . for just a moment, Cameron. Just while I get a feel for the situation," Victoria Allen said, opening her car door and stepping out into the hot Texas sunlight. Cameron, not quite eight yet, had to squat up on his knees to watch through the car's rear window. He could hear their conversation just fine since the passenger window was wide open.

"Mr. Decker? Hi . . . I'm Victoria Hoang, from Social Services? I called you?"

Cameron watched as his uncle closed and latched the back hatch of the makeshift camper shell. Pulling a rag from a back pocket, he wiped off his hands, then shook hers.

"I remember. Next week . . . the boy comes next week."

"No, sir . . . the boy comes today. As we discussed."

Cameron watched as she gestured toward the car, toward him. "As you can see, he's here now, Mr. Decker."

Cameron gave his uncle a wave. His uncle didn't wave back.

"I'm busy today. Bring him back tomorrow. Better yet, in a few days. I'll have things better situated by then."

Victoria stared at his uncle for a few moments before speaking again. Her next words were spoken softly—*like a whisper*—so Cameron couldn't quite make out what she was saying. But by her expression, it was something threatening. Her eyes narrowed into slits as her lips formed a thin line. Uncle Harley's eyes widened. Eventually, he nodded back in agreement. Together, Victoria Hoang and Harley Decker approached the car. She opened the passenger door and signaled Cameron to climb out. He did as asked. The social worker then reached in and grabbed the black and red Spiderman backpack off the back seat that contained all of Cameron's few possessions. She next took Cameron by the arm, walked three steps to where his uncle stood, and waited for the short man to accept the boy's outraised hand.

"I'm not really a hand-holder," Harley said, shoving his own hands in his pockets.

"No, I suppose you wouldn't be. What you are, Mr. Decker, is a piece of . . . work. A real piece of work."

She turned to Cameron and placed a soft hand on his cheek. "You have a business card of mine in your backpack. Call me if you need anything. Call me if . . . well, just call me if anything bad happens."

Cameron nodded, not understanding why she looked so upset.

"Thanks for bringing me here," Cameron said.

Together, he and his uncle watched as the social worker drove away. Soon after her car had turned the corner, Cameron heard a noise coming from the back of the truck.

"What is that? What'cha got in there?"

"Poultry."

"What's poultry?"

* * *

Cameron had to adjust where he sat in the truck to avoid the rusted metal spring, jutting up into the truck's passenger seat. The cab of the truck was beyond dirty. And the smell was worse than anything Cameron had encountered in his short, seven-and-three-quarter years. They drove down narrow streets into worsening neighborhoods, where soon the roads weren't even paved anymore—were little more than tire tracks in dirt. The sounds coming from the rear camper were growing louder.

"They're anticipating the pit," his uncle said, with an enthusiastic smile.

"Pit?"

His uncle continued on as if Cameron hadn't spoken, ". . . sport goes back to ancient Greece . . . in the time of Themistocles. We're talking five hundred years before Christ, boy. This goes way back, part of an ancient culture."

Cameron nodded thoughtfully, even though he didn't understand anything his uncle was gabbing on about. Two lefts, then a quick right into a narrow alleyway and they apparently had reached their final destination. The truck slowly turned into a gravel lot. He counted five huge structures with corrugated metal siding that were all big and old and frightening-looking. They drove up to the closest one.

"What is this place?" Cameron asked.

"These were factories, of some sort . . . once upon a time. Not now, though."

Cameron could already see that. An abundance of rust, plus a series of small broken windows along the high roofline showed empty neglect. Tumbleweeds cartwheeled across the parking lot.

His uncle pulled right up to the side of the closest building and honked his horn. Two men appeared through an open gap. Chins raised-up in acknowledgement as the two men pushed the big door open. The loud sounds of metal scraping against metal seemed to excite whatever that poultry-thing was in the back of his uncle's truck. Cameron now could hear the frantic battering of wings against the metal cages.

The truck slowly accelerated forward into a vast open space. The door slid back into place behind them. As Cameron's eyes adjusted to the darkness, he noticed there were a lot of other cars and trucks parked along the inner periphery of the building. There were no walls, and the flooring was just uneven, hard-packed dirt. At the center of the football field-sized enclosure was a near-blinding bright swath of light, where the sun shone in through an opening at the top of the building. A crowd of people were there and it seemed as if each and every one of them was yelling out something in Spanish. His uncle backed into a parking space, separated by crudely marked lines spray-painted onto the ground. He turned off the engine.

"Let me see your muscles," he said, holding up his own arm and making a fist to tighten his bicep.

Cameron mimicked the pose, flexing the muscle of his own skinny arm.

"That'll do. Hop on out. It's time we show these boys who's got the meanest, baddest cock in town."

Cameron struggled to carry the smaller of two metal cages. He used both hands, had to walk nearly straight-legged in order to keep the cage from dragging along on the ground. He watched the angry rooster fluttering about within the cage's metal bars.

His uncle waited for Cameron to catch up. "That one there . . . his name is Salvaje. That's 'savage' in Spanish."

"Well, Salvaje really wants out of this cage." Cameron noticed the other rooster was a whole lot calmer than his. "You have a lot nicer bird, Uncle Harley."

"Don't let that fool you. This particular game fowl was named after his famous father, La Parka."

Cameron waited for the rest of it.

"It means 'the grim reaper.'"

When they reached the center area, Cameron could see a lot of men stood in a circle, maybe five or six deep, around an open pit several feet below them. Heads turned in their direction. Cameron didn't understand the exchange of words being yelled at them—but he had a feeling they weren't simply *hellos*.

Stacks of cages, one atop another, formed a near solid wall off to the right. His uncle took both Salvaje's and La Parka's cages and placed them with the others.

A tremendous cheer rose up behind them. Some men sounded happy and excited, while other voices were clearly angry. Cameron watched the back-and-forth exchange of money. Then the crowd separated and two men stepped up and out of the pit, each holding onto a rooster. One was clearly dead—held limply by its claws—every inch of it thick with blood. The other rooster, carried by a far happier-looking fellow, was carried in the crook of one arm. He was stroking its head, like one would a family pet—like a dog or a cat. It, too, was covered in blood, but at least it was alive. It occurred to Cameron that no one here gave too much thought about how horrific a pastime this really was. Not a person was here who didn't absolutely love this—*whatever* it was. *A sport?* Including Uncle Harley.

A giant of a man whose exposed skin was covered in tattoos—the most prominent tattoo, on his neck, showed a bare-chested woman riding a motorcycle, and, Cameron determined later, flipping the bird—barreled through the crowd. He withdrew a rooster, substantially larger than any of the others, and inspected something on its two claws.

Noting Cameron's questioning look, his uncle said, "He's ensuring the spurs are in place."

"What's that?"

"It's like giving these feathery fuckers a knife to defend themselves with."

Cameron glanced over at his uncle's two birds and, sure enough, each had its own set of metal spurs tied just above their claws.

"It's time now for me to go to work, boy," his uncle said, swinging open the gate to La Parka's cage. "Guess you don't need to watch this. Not if you don't want to. Go on back to the truck, if you feel like it."

His uncle checked the surprisingly calm bird's spurs, then placed the rooster within the crook of his arm, much the same way the tattooed man did earlier. Cameron watched as the larger man, carrying his giant rooster, led the way over to the pit. Both men stepped down, were soon out of view as the throng of men closed in around what he would later learn was called the *cockpit*. Cameron debated if he should do as his uncle suggested—go back to the truck. Instead, he wedged himself between four sets of onlooker's legs, then, finding it impossible to proceed any further, got down on his hands and knees and crawled forward the rest of the way. Someone kicked him hard in the ribs, but he didn't cry out. He fought his way through the tightly packed bodies until he was staring down into the open pit. He watched, sickened by the fierce spectacle where both birds fought fearlessly while being shredded in the process. After a while, he wondered how anyone could differentiate one blood-covered rooster from the other. *Oh yeah . . . the size.* Unexpectedly, the nearly eight-year-old Cameron threw-up into the open pit.

chapter 20

By the time Cameron, groggy and wiping sleep from his eyes, emerged from the Tangine Shell, it was morning again—daylight cresting over distant mountain peaks. He saw the trinious bundle with its contents strewn about; still lying on the sand where he'd left them. Annoyed with himself, he shook his head. These devices were his potential ticket off this planet—his means to save Heather and the Loth and he had just left them lying about. An animal, hell, a herd of stampeding Great Plains Bovids could have scattered them off in all directions. Art was right; he did need to start making better use of the gray matter between his ears.

He placed all the items back inside the bundle, except for the brick-sized device. Placing his fingertips within the indentations, he waited for Art to appear. And waited . . . and waited. Three minutes later, Cameron watched as a lone tree branch—a stick—appeared, floating in the air near the shoreline. Moving closer, the tip of the stick began to inscribe something into the wet sand:

Sorry, partner, I'm busy for a spell . . .

Cameron stared at the singular sentence. Then the stick disappeared. The words in the sand also disappeared.

What does that mean? How long is a spell?

Cameron had the feeling this was one of those teaching/learning situations that he'd experienced with Art before. Yet, maybe the 'cowboy consciousness' really was busy doing something more important than helping him out now.

He sat down on the sand and picked up the brick-sized device, which today wasn't gaining him access to Art. Again, placing his fingertips onto its indentations, he asked, "Will you at least tell me what this device is called?"

A different male voice other than Art's answered, "The closest English alternative to Priopax taxonomy, would be Prion Campre."

Cameron placed the Prion Campre back into the trinious bundle then took out the dinner plate-shaped Lox device. He initialized it with his fingertips and waited for it to convert into its larger microwave shape.

"Lox . . . show me previously stored items in the order they most recently were duplicated."

Cameron expected some kind of pop-up menu, like the ones on *Priopax*, but saw instead perfect, albeit small, three-dimensional replications of each of the stored items. They hovered an arm's length distance away from him. Immediately, he recognized his pickup truck and the plasma pistol, but also some things he'd forgotten about. Like a hand-molded bowl, made from still-malleable Loth mucus, that was filled with gasoline for the truck. There were other things too: clothes that he had duplicated, a spark plug, and a replacement inner tube for his bike. His brow furrowed upon noting other items not so recently replicated. "I don't remember these things," he said aloud. He reached for one and took it between his fingers, then brought it even closer for better inspection. *Perhaps it's some kind of measurement tool or meter?* "Lox, what is this thing?"

"That is a food replicator."

"I didn't replicate a food replicator." Then it occurred to him; although he hadn't, maybe the Lox's previous owner had. Perhaps the items were replicated by Ramen, prior to his death.

Cameron jumped to his feet, hearing something clang against the far side of the Tangine Shell. He glanced at the still-hovering Lox items and slowly stepped closer. Pointing to the representation of the plasma pistol, he spoke just above a whisper, "Lox, duplicate this."

"Where would you like it positioned?" the Lox answered back, in an equally hushed voice.

"Can you put it in my hand?"

"That would not be a safe—"

Cameron interrupted, "Just put it on the ground by my feet." Not taking his eyes off the shell, he knelt down as a moving swath of light emanated from the Lox onto the location he'd specified. It took several moments for the Lox unit to complete the task.

Cameron snatched up the weapon, felt its familiar heft in his hand, and breathed somewhat easier now that he was armed. He aimed the pistol up higher and took several side-steps around the Tangine Shell until whomever, or whatever it was, came fully into view. It was Whim.

"What are you doing here?" Cameron asked.

The droid did not answer. It was evident, by the clumsy way it tried to stay aloft, that it had not progressed mechanically much farther than it had the day before.

Cameron turned his back on the droid and went back to the Lox unit. He selected the miniature Ford F-150, and instructed the device to go ahead and make a full-sized duplicate in the same approximate area where the other one had been destroyed.

As he waited for the Lox to do what he asked, Cameron turned back to the Tangine Shell. Deciding that he would no longer leave it here unprotected, he set about condensing it down to its more transportable shape. As the Tangine Shell reduced in size, his F-150 was taking shape twenty-five feet away.

Cameron grabbed the two-foot long, foot wide, eight inch thick compacted Tangine Shell device and stored it within the trinious bundle. He sealed it closed then hefted it up by its strap and placed it atop all the other things heaped within the Ford's bed. Next, he made sure the tarp was well secured over everything. He gave the campsite a quick look around, making sure he hadn't left anything behind. Whim, the droid, was again rolling in and out of the farthest stream. *Pathetic.*

He opened the driver side door, climbed in, and turned the ignition key. The engine came alive. He let the truck idle a few minutes before putting the transmission into drive. He stepped on the gas pedal, cranked the wheel to the right, and drove headlong into the stream. Stealing a quick glance at the rearview mirror, the once-glorious blue forest was no longer there—all that remained were shriveled, blackened remnants of tree trunks with a few attached branches. He thought of the clan of Dalima Climbers and wondered their fate. He preferred to think they had all survived—had moved onto another lush forest location where they had found a new home and were thriving there. He fervently hoped that was true.

In and out of the next stream, Cameron floored the gas pedal and powered the truck up the steep rise that led to the mountain road. He switched the gear selector to four-wheel-drive and felt the tires grip the loose gravel as he steered the truck around several large rocks that had become dislodged overnight. He sat back and drove, letting his mind wander. *How am I going to get off this planet?* He thought of Heather and hoped she was still okay. Like the Dalima Climbers, he suspected she was. Then it struck him like a lightning bolt—he didn't need to guess. There was a way to know exactly how she was doing. He'd done the very same thing just days before, using another one of the Priopax devices. He'd actually been able to spy on Heather back on Earth from up here, far across the Universe. He had also pinpointed exactly where the Griar Loth was hiding, deep within a subterranean vault beneath Larksburg Stand. The inter-dimensional scope was an amazing device. Cameron thought back to one of his and Art's earlier conversations, concerning the basic physics of the device.

"Okay. So what exactly does this inter-dimensional scope-thing do?"

Art sat up straighter, studying him. "You know, of course, that I'm not actually sitting here in front of you, right?"

"Sure . . . of course."

"Where I . . . exist . . . time, specific locations, have little meaning. There's no associated physical construct. But the same technology that allows me to be with you now within this beautiful valley, on this magnificent planet, at this precise moment in time . . . well, it boils down to what you would call the fourth dimension. While the three-dimensional world of physical space is one where you experience the length, width, and height of things, time is the added fourth dimension. Time provides for the variable of direction." Art peered up at Cameron quizzically.

"You can keep going; you're talking pretty basic physics."

"Good. So picture a four-dimensional piece of fabric; we'll call it space-time. Now, when anything with mass plops down on this piece of fabric . . . this space-time . . . it produces a kind of dimple, an actual bending of the fabric . . . of space-time. This bending of space-time-fabric causes objects to move on a measurable curved path. This curvature of space is what we know as—"

"Gravity," Cameron interjected.

"Excellent! So my projected image is sitting here in front of you because there is a specific, four-dimensional, mathematical calculation that allows me . . . as waves of light in this case . . . to interact within your quantum space-time continuum."

Cameron loosely tracked what Art was saying. Recently, he'd learned about similar things, like quantum theory, and how physicists reconcile quantum mechanics with Einstein's general, and specialized, theories of relativity.

"But, hey," Art said, "you really don't need to know any of this. Just know that it is possible to travel, and I am talking virtually now, to other times and places." Already shaking his head, he continued, "Wait, let me rephrase that—to only past or current times and places. The future hasn't happened yet, so let's not go down that road right now. Where would you like to go . . . perhaps someplace back on your home world; back to Earth, maybe?"

Cameron had instantly thought of Heather. He desperately wanted to know if she was okay, but he didn't feel right just suddenly dropping in on her, even virtually. No longer together, he was sure she'd moved on. They both had. Nope. He wasn't about to invade her privacy. "Can you just show me the town I used to live in? Larksburg Stand? The other Loth was there when I left."

Returning to the here and now, Cameron was amazed to find he was already halfway up the mountain road. He thought of the inter-dimensional scope. *Would he be able to operate the thing without Art's assistance?* He didn't think so. It was a complicated piece of technology.

Sorry, partner, I'm busy for a spell . . .

"Crap! How long is a spell, Art?" he asked out loud.

chapter 21

Heather...

Listening, Heather tried to judge the distance of the Loth's far-away honking. She had no idea—couldn't tell if the sound came from either the forward or aft section within the ship. But the simple fact that the beast was still alive—at least to some degree—bolstered her confidence. *I'm not alone here.*

Standing upon the precipice—the deck's central, circular, opening to the rest of the ship below—she felt the sharp edge of its rim beneath the soles of her shoes. It was as if the menacing mechanical bot was taunting her to go ahead—*just go ahead and jump.* Then suddenly, the XI droid was ascending. Moving up to the deck above. A deck she hadn't noticed until right then. Within moments, XI was gone—out of sight.

Relieved, Heather took a step backward. *I don't want to die . . . not here, not now.*

Then, more of the odd-looking pipe beings emerged from their *hidden in plain sight*, cleverly camouflaged positions along various bulkheads. Heather brought her attention back to Balth, the closest stick figure, still exhibiting a beautiful fan-like face. In contrast to its ordinary and unexceptional appearance, it now was something else: a peacock, displaying its true beauty perhaps. "Why do you hide like that? Hide among the pipes on the walls?"

"Unsafe. It was unsafe to be out and about. It is all about being about. We thank you, one and all . . . out and about, all and all, one and all."

"Thank me? What did I do?"

"It is what you will do. Will do soon . . . maybe today . . . maybe tomorrow."

"You've lost me. Look, I don't know why I'm here, other than simply being abducted by that XI droid. But evidently it still wants me alive, at least for the time being. I'm going to need to eat something, and I have to . . . um, use a bathroom. Is that something you can help me out with, or not?"

"Oh yes, we have had organics onboard many times before. You are not the first. Not by any measure. No, no, no, you are not the first."

From the corner of her eye, Heather saw movement. On the far side of the opening was another stick figure. Crawling now on all fours, it was creeping over the edge from below. "You don't have stairs here . . . maybe an elevator?"

"Not here, but yes, here and there . . . here and about. Such impractical things can certainly be found."

"You're just talking in circles," Heather said, frustrated.

"I will take her," a voice announced from behind her.

Heather glanced over her shoulder. Another waif-thin pipe figure was approaching. Its voice held a slightly different characteristic to it than the other one; neither male nor female, just different. Its fan face displayed vibrant colors— more a swirling of hues—reds, yellows, and amber.

"I am Cleop. Balth will be of no help to you . . . too stupid. No, Cleop is the one you are in need of here."

Heather shot Balth an apologetic shrug before offering Cleop her full attention. "Show me the bathroom and I'll be your best friend forever," she said.

"Yes, we will be best friends. I have never had a best friend before, nor any friend, I suppose," Cleop said, in a matter of fact manner. "Follow me; it is not too far, I assure you. Not far at all."

As Heather hurried to catch up to Cleop, she noticed more and more of the stick figures becoming visible. Noticing at least fifty of them milling about, she stopped counting. What once was, not too long ago, a dreary and ugly place, had become transformed, with each unfolding, unique and splendid fan, into a place now colorful and quite beautiful.

"What is it that you, all of you, do here?" she asked.

"Do? Do, do, do, do . . . ? Cleop replied.

Heather realized Cleop was not so different from Balth, after all. There was an enthusiastic nuttiness to these unique beings, who had a way of speaking that reminded her of *Alice in Wonderland's* Mad Hatter, or the Cheshire cat.

"A war vessel such as this one requires only a skeleton crew . . . and a crew of skeletons we truly are."

They were moving toward the bow now and, judging by the increased volume of repetitive *honks*, clearly closer to the Loth, too. Heather felt vibrations rising up through the deck, and then heard several loud thuds. "What is that noise?" she asked.

"We've arrived. We are there . . . now here is there."

"Arrived where? Can you be more specific?"

"Where you can feed and pee . . . feed and pee . . . a world where such uncommon things are commonplace."

Walking together, they crossed through a wide threshold into a massive, cavernous compartment. One that was open and void of individual decks. Each deck, those below and above it, led to individual narrow catwalks that lined the tall bulkheads. Each terminated at a metal spiral staircase, situated off to the left on the starboard side of the vessel.

Below, on the bottom deck, she saw that the Loth was being ushered toward an immense open hatchway. Bound in multiple places—straps securing its tentacles in place and around its torso—each was attached to metal cables.

A repetitive *Honk! Honk! Honk!* rose up, filling the open space. Small flying craft were all about—several tethered to the Loth, via the cables. Others, she saw, were firing off bright electrical charges, clearly used to coax the beast forward.

"They're hurting it! Why are they doing that?" Heather asked, both frustrated and angry, but Cleop was no longer standing at her side. She looked at the closest bulkhead, with its innumerable bending pipes and conduits, and wondered if she was looking right at it—at Cleop? Had it again merged invisibly into the very structure of the ship?

One of the small craft was rising up above the Loth's head then above the other similar craft. Once it had risen all the way up to where she now stood, Heather could see through its marred and dirty windows that XI—within the compact enclosure—was hovering by the controls. The vessel then veered closer to the catwalk on which she stood. The craft, making physical contact, bumped against the walkway. A hatch door on the side of the craft slid to the side.

"Get in, human," the droid said, with neither malice nor pleasantness in its voice. Heather did as told, the hatch securing with a definitive *clack* behind her. No place for her to sit, the craft was foul inside and smelled like grease and something unfamiliar, but repugnant just the same. Rust and drips of brown gunk covered most of the interior surfaces. Eyeing the disgusting confines, she crossed her arms over her chest; made every effort not to come into contact with anything around her. She noticed her white shorts were looking pretty dingy and a blob of something brown and gooey was clinging onto her left thigh. Making a disgusted face, she used an index finger to wipe whatever the stuff was off her leg and onto the closest interior panel.

Descending fast, throwing her off balance, she was forced to reach out a hand to steady herself. She said, "You know . . . there's no reason to torture the Loth like that."

Within seconds the small craft was scooting through the ship's open hatchway and into a tube, or a tunnel, made of some violet-colored, quasi-transparent material. She watched the Loth disappear below and behind them. Outside there were other similar tubes—all leading to a central structure that was so large she couldn't make it all out from her limited vantage point within the small craft. They were on another planet. Heather could make out enough of the outer surroundings to determine that much. It was some kind of depot for arriving spaceships, she surmised.

"Where are you taking me?"

"To your holding pen."

"What will happen to me there? Why did you even abduct me?" she asked.

"Any number of reasons. Humans are uncommon here. Desirable. You will be paired with a strong male. Produce offspring. Replenish dwindling stock levels."

Suddenly, the small craft space seemed to be closing in around her. The stale odor made her want to retch. She turned, hopeful that she could catch a last, fleeting glimpse of the Loth somewhere behind them. But she saw nothing. Turning forward, Heather glared at the hovering black droid.

"I guess I should have jumped when I had the chance."

chapter 22

Cameron . . .

Nearing the last quarter-mile's drive up the mountain, Cameron wasn't sure what his expectations should be when it came to the *Primion*—what would be left of it after yesterday's violent attack? He thought of Alice and was saddened that she, too, was gone from his life. *Just add her to the list*, he thought, discouraged. A list that included Heather and the Loth, the genial clan of Dalima Climbers, and even Art, who was not accessible for an indeterminate amount of time. Cameron contemplated the fact that he was truly alone in this alien world—shipwrecked and alone.

As he cleared the last bend and the remains of the *Primion* came into view, he was surprised to see that not all of the ship was destroyed. Sure, a good ninety percent of it was molten ash, but some of it still appeared to be in one piece.

Cameron braked twenty yards from the still-smoldering vessel. Even inside the cab of his truck, he could feel the heat rising off the nearly incinerated superstructure. It looked as if the drives, the aft hold, as well as the retention area—where the Loth had once been caged—were all that remained. The aft hatchway was wide open, the gangway extended down. He wondered when anyone onboard had the time during such an abrupt and violent attack to manage that.

He shut off the truck's engine and climbed out. That's when he saw them—the bodies. No less than five *Primion* crewmembers' remains were strewn about, mostly lying beneath the aft drive thrusters. With the exception of a few errant charred patches, the cyborgs were void of their flesh-like, epidural layers. Cameron studied their dull metallic carcasses and wondered if they'd suffered in those last frightening moments when the attacking alien ship fired upon them. He found Alice among them, her body leaning back against the aft starboard landing strut. He knelt down next to her. Much of her face was literally melted away; gaps exposed blackened, internal circuitry.

"I'm sorry, Alice," he said, staring off at the distant ridgeline. "This is all my fault. It was my decision to return to Sang-Morang."

"Cam . . . Camer . . . Cameron . . ."

Startled, he abruptly stood up. *How was this even possible?* Then he heard his name spoken aloud again, and it wasn't coming from Alice's lifeless remains. He spun around to see Whim, several paces away, lying on the ground. The droid was attempting to levitate but failing miserably. Still, it had spoken his name.

"You can talk?"

The droid did not answer, suddenly silent."

"Whim . . . I'm listening."

"I . . . am . . . Alice . . ."

Cameron stared at the metallic black canister for several long beats before asking again. "How? How are you Alice?"

"Partial . . . upload . . . seconds . . . before . . ."

"You uploaded from your memory banks? Into Whim?"

The droid managed to rise several feet off the ground, although it was anything but a fluid motion. "Correct."

"What can I do to help?" he asked, watching the droid, in its herky-jerky movements, attempt to ascend the gangway at the rear of the vessel.

"Transfer."

Cameron didn't understand. Perhaps the droid did indeed have Alice's programming—but maybe that too was defective. "I don't think there's much left in there that can help you," he said, coming up the gangway behind the droid. Giving it a little assistance, elevating it higher up, he offered, "Maybe you should just let me carry you." Not waiting for a reply, he wrapped his arms around the droid's circumference and embraced its entire weight. He then carried it the rest of the way up the gangway and into the aft hold.

The compartment was a mess, with all sorts of broken parts scattered about the deck. He felt the droid steering him toward the portside of the hold and accommodated it by moving in that direction. Cameron then became aware of the two remaining non-programmed droids attached to the portside bulkhead, and he understood what Alice meant by *transfer.* To transfer her data, her memories, into a droid that wasn't as damaged as Whim.

"Put . . . down."

He did as asked. "Is there anything else I can do to help you?"

"Yes. Detach from . . . bulkhead."

There were only two droids secured there, so Cameron arbitrarily chose the closest one. Noticing how it was secured to the bulkhead, he unlatched it and grabbed it as it came away from the mounting hardware. He then hefted it over to Alice. The now off-kilter, defective droid lay unmoving on the deck. "Anything else?" he asked.

"No . . . give me . . . time to make . . . the transfer."

Cameron nodded and took a few steps back. He let his eyes roam the aft hold—scanning anything he could possibly use. There were a good number of storage containers strewn about that he could rifle through. Who knew, maybe there was some kind of technology in there that would be of use to him—and then he looked up and saw it; what his eyes had passed right over. He now recalled seeing the thing several times over the last few weeks. A small, winged craft, mounted higher up on the portside bulkhead.

Below it, he saw tiny lights blinking on and off—perhaps communication protocols being established between the two side-by-side droids, lying on the deck. Whatever was going on with them, Cameron didn't want to interrupt. He upended one of the larger containers and pushed it over to the bulkhead, then used it as a makeshift ladder to get a better, closer view of the sleek red craft. It was probably eight or nine feet long, about half that in width. Not high enough up to see into the craft's cockpit, he tried to determine a means of detaching it from where it was securely mounted. Motion caught his eye and he glanced down at the deck to where the two droids were—but only one of them was still there.

"Hello, Cameron."

Off-balance, Cameron nearly tumbled down from the top of the container. The droid was close by, hovering six feet in the air directly behind him. "Give me a warning when you're going to creep up on me like that!" he scolded, steadying himself.

"I apologize. And thank you for your assistance earlier, Cameron."

"So the transfer went okay?" he asked.

"Yes, at least to the extent that a salvaged portion of my AI faculties are operational."

Cameron then recalled seeing the giant, glowing, spheroid-shaped devices, positioned within that dark compartment just aft of the *Primion's* bridge. Referred to as TAM, it was where the *brains* of the AI were housed. TAM and Alice were pretty much one and the same, although he imagined Alice would be operating with a substantially diminished mental capacity now.

"Please move out of the way and I will assist you," Alice said, already rising above his head and moving toward the cockpit section. "This craft was the property of two of the original *Primion* crewmembers. It is *Scalldian* technology from a planet not so unlike this one, or that of Earth."

"Let me guess; one of the two crewmembers was Ramen."

"Correct. Ramen, which, as you know, is not his actual name. The other male gendered individual's name would be equally difficult for you to pronounce. They had only recently absconded with this small craft and they were reprimanded for its misappropriation."

"Absconded? From where? Who?"

"Scalldia Rom Frima. It is a cluster of six planets—you refer to them as the Pegasus arm of the Milky Way. They are primarily a trading and merchant hub for that area of space," Alice said. Having just done something to disengage the small ship's mounting clamps, the droid now was maneuvering the vessel away from the bulkhead and slowly down to the deck.

"So they stole this craft and then got punished for it, right? So did *Primion* crewmembers make a habit of stealing things? I didn't get that impression of Ramen . . . but then again, I only knew him for a short while."

"Your observations were accurate. Ramen was not dishonest . . . was not a thief. But the other one, let us call him Cleft, was far more subject to temptation and even spent time within a *Primion's* retention cell on seven separate occasions. He was, what you would call, a troublemaker."

Cameron stood at the nose of the now-lowered sleek craft, which was just below eye-level, and stared into the darkened cockpit. "I've had friends like that myself . . . always getting into trouble, but sometimes they're the most fun to hang out with. That is until things go awry. Can you open her up?"

Alice hovered at his side, "I believe so. Ramen and Cleft never actually had the opportunity to pilot this craft."

Cameron watched as the little lights on the droid rapidly flashed, he figured some kind of cross-communication was transpiring. "Um . . . Alice?"

"Yes, Cameron."

"Again, I'm sorry about all this. What happened to you, to the *Primion*?"

"Cameron, I am not human. I neither need nor require emotional consoling."

He wondered if that were actually true, but let it go. "So, you wouldn't be interested in regaining a cyborg form . . . something similar to the Alice you resided in before?"

The little blinking lights under the droid's top encircling flange momentarily became steady—then resumed their blinking. "That would not be possible. The *Primion* has been destroyed. Other than that, Sang-Morang does not support the level of technology required—"

"I think I have a way," Cameron interjected.

Now the droid turned toward him, no longer feigning interest in the red spacecraft before them. "Go on."

"Wait here," he said, hurrying from the hold and sprinting down the gangway. He returned several minutes later with his trinious bundle. Placing it down on the deck, he opened it and removed the Priopax Lox device from among its contents. "There's a function this thing has that I only just learned about. There's a virtual catalogue of things in here that Ramen previously stored . . . items that he duplicated. Or replicated in the past, might be a better way to say it."

Cameron, with the Lox now operational, used his hand to physically scroll through the small, three-dimensional items. "Here we go, I noticed this before and meant to ask Art about it when I talked to him again. See here . . . it looks like a person; a Thidion, to be exact. See the membrane ears? But I remember Art telling me that organic life couldn't be replicated. It was dangerous to do so. So this little representative of a person . . . it's a complete cyborgenic being, right?"

"Yes, it is."

"I know it does not look like . . . you know, like you looked before, Alice. But I thought maybe you could still use it somehow?"

The droid lowered and then used one of its articulating arms and mechanical claws to grab onto the small object. "This is unexpected."

Cameron nodded. He watched as the droid tossed the miniature Thidion-looking cyborg farther aft into the hold, then said, "Assimilate selected replicant to indicated location."

Immediately, the Lox unit began doing its job. A swath of light cycled rapidly as the beginnings of a full-sized cyborg, starting at its feet, began to take shape.

"This will take your Priopax device several hours to complete. Highly complex functionality is underway . . . highly complex," the Alice stated.

The hovering droid spun back on its axis toward the winged craft, and Cameron did the same. The cockpit's curved, glass-like canopy was now open and he wondered when that had occurred. Alice, of course, would be highly adept at multitasking.

The cockpit, with its canopy fully retracted, looked surprisingly similar to the open interior of a high-end sports car convertible back home. Two comfortable high back seats were situated behind a dashboard, with a myriad of presently lit-up readouts and indicators that looked complicated, like something you'd see within a fighter jet, requiring years of both classroom, and *real world*, hands-on training to master. "I take it those sets of controls, sticking out there . . . are used for steering?"

"Of course. Controls affect the vessel's attitude, as well as its roll axis and a number of other aspects of manual piloting functionality. This vessel is capable of inter-planetary atmosphere flying, but not well suited for deep space transportation."

"Do you think I can learn how to fly it . . . like on my own?"

"Perhaps. But you should be fully aware that even one piloting misjudgment, one miscalculation, could have catastrophic effects for you. There are auto-piloting modes of operation that should be utilized until you are properly trained.

"Can you pilot this craft?" Cameron asked.

"Yes, I believe so."

chapter 23

While the Alice droid hovered quietly nearby, apparently just observing the slow, methodical, re-creation of the *Primion* cyborgenic being, Cameron busied himself parking the truck closer to what was left of the *Primion*. He then began transferring over various supplies from the truck bed to the far smaller storage space, situated behind the seats of the Scalldian craft. In the process of excavating through the myriad of stuff within the truck bed, things collected through the years, he saw the box. There was nothing out of the ordinary about the simple shipping box that still had the USPS sticker affixed to its top. Several long strips of tape secured the top panels shut. Cameron had never opened the box, not even once. Never opened a flap to take a peek inside. Above the shipping label, written with a black marker in a messy cursive script, was *Cameron Decker*. When the box first arrived at his foster parents' front door not long after he had arrived there—Cameron had recognized his uncle's handwriting. His uncle, a thief and a murderer, was a southern bordertown hoodlum, who, in the end, got what he probably deserved. Eight-year-old Cameron was his only living relative, and vice-versa. His uncle must have had the box stored in a cabinet—maybe in a closet. Whoever had packed up his dead uncle's house had sent the box on to him.

Approximately two feet square in size, faded in color, and its corners crunched, Cameron hesitated on viewing again this stark reminder of his childhood, of the loss of his parents in a New England car wreck, and the disturbing times when he'd witnessed far more than any small child should in that small Texas border town. Was he curious about what his now long-departed uncle had left him? *Just mildly.* Not enough to open what he knew would be a Pandora's box of trouble. He left it where it lay, beneath his bicycle and beach umbrella and another box, holding mostly schoolbooks.

He glanced over to see how progress was moving along, and noticed the cyborg now had most of a head. Clearly female and attractive, she was neither more nor less attractive than the previous Alice cyborg—just different.

"Can I ask you a question?"

The Alice droid spun around to face him.

"Your crew . . . your previous crew. They're all gone now."

"Your point?"

"Did the ship's AI, TAM, have them stored into memory? The same way that the Lox had this cyborg stored by Ramen?"

"Yes."

There's no . . . um . . . like . . . backup of that data anywhere? I'm sure you have something akin to the cloud, like where I have backup of my iPhone data."

"Thidion technology, which the *Primion*, as well as the droids and cyborgs were comprised of, utilizes the arranging of light particles into what is referred to as *flectons*. Flectons do not require physical hardware servers in the same way your media cloud does for storage. So, to answer your question, there are indeed backup flectons. Although flectons are not bound by physical hardware, they do have specific locations. Often, they are arbitrary points, out in deep space . . . and were accessible via the *Primion's* powerful antenna arrays. Why is this of interest to you, Cameron?" the droid asked.

"Was just wondering if you would want to replace your crew? Get things back to where they were . . . you know, before the attack?"

"I will ponder your query, Cameron. For now, it looks as though the Lox processing is nearly complete. And I have an ethical dilemma to work through."

Cameron watched. The blue beams of light, moving at such a high rate of speed, appeared to be one, semi-transparent, cone of illumination. Then, it hit him. This cyborg would not be arriving void of either consciousness or beingness. Alice would need to extricate out *whomever* it was if she wanted to inhabit that body.

"What are you going to do?" he asked.

Instead of answering, the droid approached the now fully constructed cyborg. Smaller than Alice used to be, her hair was dark brown and short. The word cute came to Cameron's mind. The moment came when the cyborg began to blink her eyes, as if new situational awareness was beginning to take place. The cyborg's brow furrowed. There was anger in her eyes as she took in the presence of the Alice droid floating before her—perhaps a momentary battle of wills. Then it was all over.

"The process is complete," said the cyborg—her eyes now on Cameron.

"Alice?"

"Yes."

"And the one in there before? Did you put her into the droid?"

"No. I erased her completely."

As if on cue, the droid began to lose its hovering stability—drifting to the left, it clanged against the bulkhead. Next, it fell hard upon the deck then proceeded to roll down the gangway.

"Remind me to never piss you off," Cameron said.

"Okay, don't ever piss me off, Cameron."

This cyborg woman, who looked to be in her mid-twenties, had a slightly up-turned nose, eyes set a bit farther apart, and full lips, expressed now in an easy smile. Her features did not have the same level of perfection that Alice once possessed. Still, their new formation—her slightly imperfect features—resulted in an even more striking combination. She was beautiful in her own right.

"I guess you found a way to deal with the ethical issue?"

"The earlier Alice was highest among the *Primion's* cyborg hierarchy. I only did what was necessary. What was logical."

Cameron nodded, placing the Lox unit back inside the trinious bundle. After securing it closed, he hefted it up by its strap and deposited it into the Scalldian craft's hold area.

He was aware that Alice, secure within her new form, was watching him. He strode across to the top of the gangway and glanced down at his truck. Earlier, he'd re-secured the tarp over the truck bed and rolled-up the truck's windows, wondering if he'd ever again see this version of the truck again. He didn't think so. Didn't see a need to ever come back; return again to the top of this ridgeline where nothing much of the *Primion* remained.

"You ready to go?" he asked.

"Go?" she asked back.

"Explore some more of this planet. Perhaps come up with a way to get back into space . . . find Heather and the Loth."

"They most likely are on Winforge by now. Incarcerated."

Cameron had mentally fought hard not to think about Heather; about what terrible things she could be dealing with. Feelings of guilt returned. He thought of the Loth and hoped it was still alive to help her.

"And this craft . . . there's no way it could make it to this Winforge place?"

"No. Not as it sits here right now. I will contemplate on the problem, Cameron."

It was the second time she had said such a thing. That she would think, contemplate, on a certain problem. But, clearly, she was incapacitated in that regard—a lack of memory or computing resources. "Fine. How about you show me how to fly this thing."

"I told you, it has auto-navigation functionality. I am also quite adept at piloting—"

"No, Alice! I want to learn. I need to learn. I don't want to be at the mercy of alien technology, unable to get myself out of scrapes on my own." He caught the momentary effect of his choice of words. Inadvertently, he had grouped her in with the term *alien technology*. As though she held little more importance to him than an inanimate thing. Again, he realized she was far more complex than a soulless, preprogramed bot. "Will you teach me? At least, try to teach me? I'm glad you're here with me . . . that I'm not alone on this alien world."

"I will help you. And thank you, Cameron."

"For what? Bringing you back to a world where everything important to you has been destroyed?"

Alice climbed into the right side of the craft. Sitting down, she strapped herself in. "Are you coming? My sensors, as limited as they are, do tell me there is other technology within several hundred miles of our location. Also, a vessel of unknown origin has entered Sang-Morang's upper orbit. I suspect there is a search in progress for their missing spacecraft . . . and its crew."

Cameron looked at her quizzically.

"The spacecraft confiscated by XI . . . the same craft that abducted Heather and the Loth."

"Oh. Yeah, we should get out of here." He moved into the seat next to Alice and watched intently as she began tapping at the controls. "Hey, tell me what you're doing. I have a good memory, so just a quick overview will do fine."

"That will take time. Time we may not have."

"Then you better start talking fast," he said firmly.

chapter 24

Alice piloted the small Scalldian craft out of and away from what was left of the still-smoldering *Primion* ship. Pulling back on the controls, she banked sharply to the starboard side, barely avoiding clipping an outcropping of jagged rock, coming up fast on their port side. The vessel made little sound as their speed steadily increased.

"The controls are sensitive. I mean really sensitive, Cameron."

"Okay, got it."

"Tell me where we're going?" she asked, as she triggered something on the dashboard that made the canopy slide back all the way. Now, like a convertible sports car, wind billowed in—both Cameron's and Alice's hair instantly got wildly tousled. Seeing her like this, she looked more content than he'd seen her in the past—almost childlike.

"You mentioned technology," he said, "that your sensors were picking something up?"

"That would be in Sang-Morang's northeast direction." Alice said, as the zippy little craft suddenly dipped down low within the valley. Following the three streams below them, they were no less than twenty feet off the ground. "Ready?" she asked.

Cameron watched as Alice took her hands off the controls and was looking at him expectantly.

"Like right now?"

She said nothing.

He tentatively took ahold of the identical set of controls on his side of the cockpit and, using care, got a feel for the steering. He nudged the controls ever so slightly to starboard. The vessel angled to the right, slightly off-kilter, though it didn't actually change course. Bringing the ship back in line, he shrugged. "That didn't really work," he said aloud.

Alice pointed: "You have additional means to adjust flight variations, both there and there, on your control unit."

He quickly realized he was afraid of making a mistake—afraid he would crash the small craft, and subsequently dash any chance of ever saving Heather.

"Maybe I should take back the controls," Alice said, reaching for them.

"Wait just a second."

In his mind's eye, he opened up his World Book Encyclopedia to the letter **F**—the book now lying on his virtual lap. He flipped to the reference: **Flight**, and began skimming down the page until he found what he was looking for:

Piloting an aircraft is different than driving a car, or even a boat! Where cars or boats only move in two dimensions, an aircraft can move, unhindered, in three dimensions. Note: Alteration in any one of the three types of motion affects the other two. Roll, pitch, and yaw—Imagine three straight vectors running through an airplane, intersecting at right angles in the airplane's midpoint. Rotation around the front-to-back axis is called roll. Rotation around the side-to-side axis is called pitch. Rotation around the vertical axis is called yaw. . . .

Cameron finished reading the virtual nuances of controlling a small aircraft and, even with this limited additional knowledge, felt somewhat better about his basic understanding of air flight principles. He pushed onto the controls and felt the craft's position alter as the nose crept downward. This time, when he pulled back on the controls—adjusting the pitch upward—he simultaneously used both the *yaw and roll* controls pointed out to him by Alice and the craft banked while turning.

"Nicely done," Cameron. "Just a reminder, the vessel's autopilot mechanism would handle this for you . . . either that, or simply let me do the navigating, the piloting. I am, remember, an artificial intelligence that is more than up to the task."

Not bothering to reply, he'd already made his views clear, about not wanting to be dependent on her, nor on any other technology. At least to the extent he was allowed to be in control.

He maintained piloting control for another thirty to forty minutes, constantly changing things up—getting a real feel for the maneuverable little craft. He found it had an incredible amount of power reserves when he punched the throttle—even to the point he and Alice were pinned hard to the backs of their seats.

"Can I at least show you one more thing . . . something you may find useful?" Alice asked.

"Oh, yeah . . . sorry. I've been hogging things, haven't I?"

"Let go of the controls," she said, retaking them on her side of the craft. "You need to remember something. This craft mimics some of the basic flight controls that airplanes have back on Earth, which you can thank me for. It was my doing through a manipulation of the onboard nav-coding. But this craft is far different than an airplane." She tapped three touch buttons on the dash, one after another, and Cameron watched as both control units altered in shape—and apparently in functionality. She slowed the ship down and used the different finger controls to bring the vessel to a complete stop midair—just as a helicopter is capable of doing—without the typical pounding downwash of wind taking place. The craft's lone engine was just as silent as before, as Alice used another set of finger controls to rotate the Scalldian vessel three hundred-and-sixty degrees on its axis. She glanced over to him with a smile, "Like that?"

"Yeah, I like that; now let me try, okay?"

"Take the controls . . . it's all yours."

And Cameron did exactly that; he spent the next few minutes manipulating the ship's controls like Alice had done, and even more. In the process of practicing, he noticed something outside not associated with piloting the craft. Two hundred yards west, what appeared to be ancient structures had been built into a rocky cliffside. There were hundreds of what looked like rough, hand-hewn doorways and windows.

Outcroppings of timber support beams, and remnants of canopies made from smaller trees—or perhaps saplings—provided shade against the brutal Sang-Morang sunlight.

"I didn't know there was indigenous . . . intelligent life here at one time."

"Perhaps we should just keep to our schedule. Avoid such distractions, Cameron."

Ignoring her, Cameron piloted the ship closer to the cliff. Using the piloting tips Alice had provided him, he brought the craft into a stationary hover—mere feet from one of the window-like openings on the cliff side. He thought about Earth's Mesa Verde cliff-dwelling archeological sites, including the one in Colorado, built in the 1190s. Ancestral Pueblo tribes lived within those protected dwellings for nearly two hundred years—a means of protection from other, often invading, tribes. He briefly wondered whom these people, these aliens, were trying to evade? Goosing the throttle, the ship moved silently along the cliff side, close enough to almost reach out and touch the rock facing. As they passed by another window-like opening—he thought he saw movement within. A dark, undefined, shape—though perhaps it was only a ghostly aberration. A creation possibly of his imagination, he let it go. "Someday, I'd like to come back here—do some exploring."

Before Alice could answer, something whizzed past the craft's windscreen.

"What the . . ."

Three more long projectiles flew past them—two in front, and one close by, just over their heads.

"Arrows!" Cameron yelled, fumbling with the still-unfamiliar controls. "Fuck!" He used the finger levers to pivot the ship starboard the way Alice had shown him earlier, but over-compensated. The ship spun all the way around—to the extent the nose again pointed cliff side. More arrows came fast. He could hear them clattering along the ship's outer hull. "Damn it!" Finally figuring the controls out, he moved the ship away from the clearly not-abandoned ruins. "Crap, that was close! You know, you could have mentioned to me that the ruins were still occupied. Used your sensors . . ."

He stole a quick glance over to her. Stunned, he didn't know what to do—what to think. Alice had a half-buried arrow protruding out the side of her head.

chapter 25

Alice's eyes were open and she blinked several times in rapid succession. She appeared to be contemplating her condition. Cameron took in the intricately made fletching of brightly colored feathers. The arrow was short—maybe two feet long—and had penetrated her left cheek at a downward angle. It protruded out, closer to her jawline, on the right side of her face. The pointed arrow was sharp but, fortunately, didn't have an arrowhead attached to it.

Distant yells carried to them in the wind. Having traveled a suitable distance away from the cliff dwellings and the stealthy natives hiding among them, Cameron spun around in his seat. No less than a dozen dark-skinned figures—indigenous tribes people—that were dressed in what looked like hide loincloths, stood atop various mud walls and timber rooftops.

He turned back to her. "What can I do to help? Can you hear me . . . do you understand what I'm saying?"

Her eyes narrowed. "Of course, I understand what you are saying," Alice replied, her jaw somewhat hindered from working normally. She still hadn't looked at him. "I am a cyborgenic being . . . nothing of importance has been damaged internally."

"Well . . . can I help? You know, pull the thing out?"

"Yes. Please."

"Okay. I should set us down first. Just hold on a minute." Relieved she was not seriously injured, he offered up a confident nod and a crooked smile. "I'm going to move up river some . . . just in case there's more of them around. I still think it's strange that I didn't know, after being here a month, that this planet was inhabited . . . other than by animals. He couldn't specifically remember asking Alice, or even Art, if there were people living here.

"Maybe I'll land over there. That shady spot beneath those outlying trees," he said, piloting the craft low over the water and slowing their speed. A crop of tall trees, lining one side of the three streams, looked similar to big English Oaks back home. The one notable exception was these had dark, aqua-colored foliage—still, they were a remarkably similar tree genus.

Cameron put the craft down on a wide patch of sand, using utmost care not to unduly jostle his injured passenger. They both climbed out from their respective sides.

"I will walk you through what needs to be done," Alice said.

Knowing she wasn't significantly damaged, he allowed himself to relax somewhat. Watching her walk around—pretty much pacing—while an arrow protruded from her head wasn't something he'd seen before, and probably wouldn't see ever again.

She plopped down on the sand. Leaning back on her straightened out arms, she tilted her head so that the shaft of the arrow was nearly vertical with the colorful feathers now pointing up toward the sky. "Get a solid grasp of the shaft. You don't want it slipping through your fingers. And don't twist it as you pull it. Try tugging it out with one continuous pull . . . not with a bunch of small, little tugs. And—"

Cameron pulled the arrow free while she was still talking.

"Hey, I wasn't ready yet! I was going to tell you when to pull!"

"Really? When? All that yammering on . . . I figured you were just nervous so best to rip the Band-Aid off real quick-like."

"It was an arrow, not a Band-Aid. And I don't get nervous."

"Well, then maybe I should shove it back in . . . so we can do it your way," he replied.

With a furrowed brow, her fingertips explored the new small holes on her cheek and jaw. "What are you doing with that?" she asked, gesturing toward the arrow still in his hand.

"Saving it. This is an epic piece of memorabilia." He leaned over the craft's cargo section—his head and shoulders momentarily disappearing from view. After straightening up, he sat down next to her. "You said there was technology here, but you didn't elaborate on that. Was it some kind of ship, or maybe an alien outpost? What do you know about it?"

She looked upstream. "We're about twenty miles out. Definitely it's an outpost of some kind. The spacecraft I detected earlier, in the upper atmosphere, it's there now."

"So, possibly, we have a ride off this planet?"

"Maybe, if you can convince whoever's here to give you that ride. But I find that possibility remote, at best. There is also a good chance we won't be welcomed on our approach."

Based on how the planet's indigenous people welcomed them, she had a good point. But every moment wasted here was time he needed to go find Heather and the Loth. However, cutting corners, he knew, could very well end badly. Which, subsequently, could also end badly for Heather. "Are you thinking we should do a little surveillance . . . maybe wait till dark?"

"I don't believe they are aware of our presence here. I would strongly recommend we keep close to the surface, approach the last few miles on foot."

Back in the small craft, with the canopy now securely closed around them, Alice told Cameron they were twelve miles out. He was flying low, close to the watery surface of the center stream. So close, in fact, several times plumes of spray billowed up behind them like a watery rooster tail. Alice shot him a sideways glance. He hadn't admitted it to himself until just now—knew it was wrong, considering both Heather and the Loth were undoubtedly in dire circumstances—but at least in this moment, he was having fun. He loved piloting the craft, this little flying rocket. How it maneuvered, how it gave him a sense of freedom he'd never experienced before.

He brought the Scalldian ship down on another stretch of sand, then together they exited the craft.

"Even parked now beneath those trees that surround it, it's still more out in the open than I would like," Cameron said, reassessing where he'd landed.

"Agreed," Alice said. She hurried back to the small craft, lifted the nose several feet off the ground then proceeded to drag the vessel another fifteen feet farther into the dense foliage. Something similar to scraggly scrub oaks dominated the under-tree landscape. Cameron helped pile on an additional layer of loose branches to hide the craft even better. Unless one was looking right at it, he was confident that no one passing by would ever notice it. "You lifted the nose of that craft like it weighed nothing. How strong are you?" he asked.

"Strong enough, I suppose," she said. Then added, "Are you really bringing that big thing along?"

Cameron adjusted the strap of the trinious bundle he'd hefted-up onto his back. "I learned my lesson; I don't go anywhere without this thing, which reminds me. . . ." Swinging the bundle down from off his back, he proceeded to open it back up. He fished around inside it until his hand came out, holding onto the plasma pistol. He tucked it into his waistband and, with the trinious bundle now secured and repositioned onto his back, said, "Lead the way . . . I'll be right behind you."

They walked upstream along the sandy shore, keeping beneath the cover of trees, for what to Cameron seemed a long distance—but probably was closer to a mile or two. "Do you ever think about your fellow crewmembers?" Cameron asked.

"Why would I do that?" Alice replied.

"Because they were your crew. Hey, I get it; you're not an organic being. You're a cyborgenic through and through . . . but still. . . ."

"If you're asking me if I have the ability to feel things—like sentimentality, for example—the answer is yes. But that is my choice. I have internal constructs which allow me to adjust my emotional bandwidth parameters. On the *Primion*, I maintained a modest *emotion* setting for both my crew and myself. I have determined that emotions are often counter-productive. They *get in the way*, as you humans would say."

Cameron ducked under a low-hanging branch then quick-ened his pace to catch up with Alice who, unlike him, was neither sweating nor breathing hard. "Sure . . . emotions may, in fact, get in the way, but they also make things worthwhile. Make life worthwhile."

"I suggest you stop talking now. We are approaching our destination."

They walked at least another mile before the landscape around them began to change. The valley had opened up—the parallel towering cliffs they'd passed were now open plains, spreading outward to an undefined distant horizon. Up ahead appeared an immense body of water that he supposed was a lake, though it could pass for an ocean. Cameron next beheld the site where the three streams originated. Hundreds of other streams, also some larger rivers, were spread out in all directions—outflowing moving tributaries. Off to their left were some temporary-looking structures—the alien outpost that Alice had referred to. But none of these were as inter-esting as what he was now witnessing some three hundred yards offshore. There, hovering and skittering across the lake's surface, was a spacecraft. It was ginormous—completely dominating the skyline.

Cameron, staying low, approached the lake's shoreline where Alice joined him. Together, they both knelt down onto one knee. Incoming waves splashed close to their feet. Suddenly, near the ship, something broke free from beneath the lake's surface: *something alive, frantic, and large*. At first, Cameron thought it might be a Loth when perhaps a tentacle breached the lake's churning surface. But no, it was something else. In another, sudden, upward explosion of water more of the creature rose up-up-up-up out of the lake. No, this creature was something quite different from a Loth, and more frightening on a whole other level.

chapter 26

The Loth . . .

The creature didn't understand. Didn't understand why it was there—in such a strange and unnatural environment. It wondered why it was taken from its home—a place where it could hunt Greely Beasts and perhaps, once again, sleep at night near the metal truck and the warming campfire. *Where is my human—where is Cameron?* the beast wondered.

Another bright flash coincided with a burst of excruciating pain. *Honk! Honk! Honk!* One of its tentacles began twitching uncontrollably. Like irritating gnats, no less than four, small, hovering crafts tugged and pulled, sometimes prodding, the Loth. Fury was building-up inside the beast—the need to lash out—retaliate—was increasing by the moment. But the Loth, both bound and secured, could do nothing; was forced to quicken its pace. The hovering crafts wanted it to move faster through the cave. *This was all so wrong.*

The Loth had seen the flying, metal, bug-like, object—the one Cameron called XI. *Why is that metal bug here, in this awful place?* the Loth wondered. It knew that XI was Cameron's enemy—thus, XI was the Loth's enemy too.

After more repeated shocks to prod it along—for what seemed an eternity—the Loth finally entered into a more expansive area. The sounds here were nearly deafening. Wild animal sounds. Close by came a great trumpeting burst. The Loth assessed it and found a surprisingly small, bright-blue creature with floppy ears. Its oversized eyes, for such a small head, stared out through a series of vertical bars. Cages. There were many, many cages in here. Something splattered down from above. Looking up, the Loth could see more cages high overhead, filled with flying creatures. Not only with birds, but with others strange beasts of flight, too.

The Loth, among the very largest of the beasts captured, noticed others here were even larger. Some were becoming highly aggressive as the Loth was slowly paraded past their cages. Angry roars and screeches erupted. Next came an abrupt charging forward of a pair of angry creatures, hindered only by the metal bars keeping them apart. Moving farther into the holding area, the Loth's nasal senses were confronted with an emanation of foul odors—of shit and piss—plus other more subtle animalistic odors, coinciding with the production of various pheromones via glands specific to the various beast types.

Slowing now, the prodding had nearly ceased as the Loth was brought closer to one cage in particular—one kept nearly in the dark. Then, from out of the shadows, came a roar so loud—so thunderously threatening—that the Loth felt the beginnings of something foreign to its nature: *fear.*

The ground shook as the beast stepped out of the darkness. Immense, maybe twice the size of the Loth, its cold calculating eyes were set much too close together behind a long tapered snout. Animals within the other cages went still. Watching, in the now eerie silence, its teeth—far too large for its mouth—cascaded over a bulbous bottom lip that was black and shiny. It made no further sounds to project its dominance like most of the other creatures had done. Clearly, this enormous creature had no need to vocally demonstrate its physical prowess over others. The Loth and the immense beast locked eyes. The Loth could smell the other beast's hot breath. It smelled of death—a recent kill. It was then that the Loth noticed the partial furry arm and claw that protruded limply from the creature's mouth—suspended there at the place where two shiny black lips joined together. A black tongue flickered out—then the clawed arm was gone.

Prodded forward again with multiple, excruciating shocks to its flanks, the Loth noticed a series of smaller cages coming up on the left. These were free of bars, but were made of a clear-sided material instead. Stacked four high along the wall, the Loth saw smaller creatures milling about within them.

"Loth! Oh God . . . Loth! It's me . . . Heather!"

chapter 27

Cameron...

Cameron said, "We need to get onboard that ship."

Alice pursed her lips—seeming to assess his statement, at what surely would be an impossible feat.

"It could be years before another spacecraft comes along . . . hell, it could be never," he added.

The droid merely nodded.

Getting irritated by her continued silence, he asked, "So what do they want with that giant starfish?"

"Starfish?" Alice repeated back.

"Uh huh. Back on Earth we have something similar-looking to that thing. Only it's tiny and doesn't move around much." He turned his attention back to the spacecraft. Continued efforts were being made to affix a harness around the building-sized creature's center mass—a hexagonal area, where a mouth and at least three protruding eyes were positioned. Its five triangular appendages were flailing about half-heartedly as the enormous creature seemed to be losing energy. Even so, the aliens seemed to be having a hard time of it.

"What are you doing now?" Cameron asked.

"I'm querying the vessel's artificial intelligence . . . database records . . . flight logs."

"Cool! You've hacked the alien ship. That's great!"

Alice ignored his enthusiasm, and then her eyes found his. "Same destination."

"As?"

"Winforge . . . this craft has the same mission parameters the *Primion* had, as well as the vessel that absconded with the Loth."

"And Heather," he added with annoyance in his voice.

"Yes, of course, Heather, too."

"Winforge . . . both Art and Ramen spoke to me about that place," Cameron said. "A zoo, of sorts. All kinds of alien creatures brought there."

"Zoo? No, not a zoo."

"Yes . . . a zoo. Why else bring such a diverse assortment of alien wildlife to one location?"

She ignored the question. "The crew on that vessel is comprised primarily of humans." A pop-up display suddenly floated in front of them. Data—various icons and symbols—scrolled past them at a mind-numbingly fast rate of speed.

"It looks as though you've regained more of your previous abilities," he said.

"Sort of . . . I'm *backdooring*-out a miniscule amount of the AI's functionality within the *Albergone*. Won't be noticed."

Cameron raised his brows questioningly.

"*Albergone* is the name the humans have given that ship," the cyborgenic woman said.

"Where are they from? The humanoids?"

Alice looked at him, offering the slightest smile. "Earth."

"Are you going to explain that to me, or force me to keep asking you a ton of questions one at a time?"

"Cameron, there are thousands . . . perhaps millions of humans, living beyond the confines of your small, insignificant planet. Hundreds of thousands of abductions have occurred over the course of a million years. You can do the math, but this particular group . . . all are first and second generation Earth humans. Perhaps abducted as small children, they may have little or no recollection of their life back on your home planet."

"How is it they are here together, capturing animals? Seems far-fetched."

"According to my queries, their captain, a Jeremiah Wilcox, only works alongside other Earth humans. It's a trust issue. He actively recruits all around the universe. That, and he is not adverse to applying his own abduction practices."

"Like back on Earth?"

"Yes, that is his preference."

Cameron shrugged off how ethically wrong that was, and asked, "So, this Captain Wilcox, he might help me? Maybe he's a decent enough guy to assist a fellow humanoid."

"No, Cameron. He is not a decent guy, as you put it. From what I have deciphered via the ship's logs, he is a very bad man. Not to be trusted."

"Hmm . . . anything else you can tell me?"

"Just that their individual, as well as combined, quantifiable intelligence levels are low. Actually, remarkably low. I will attempt to discern why."

"You're telling me they're dumb?"

"I personally do not know many humans to make comparison readings . . . but, based on even your, and Heather's, mental capabilities alone, yes, big dummies."

That evoked a chuckle from Cameron. "I can work with that, okay!" Quiet for a while, he continued to watch as the massive starfish creature was hefted slowly up through a large hatch—and into what, he surmised, was an equally large on-board hold area.

"Okay . . . the vessel has an internal reactor . . . one dedicated to its starboard-most drive," Alice said, bringing up what appeared to be schematics of the ship's aft section on the pop-up display. "Well, I think I know why they are having cognitive issues," she added.

"That leak . . . is it like a radiation thing?"

"No, it's worse than that. It's an escaping antimatter *thing*. Practically undetectable by any of the ship's internal sensors."

"But you caught it . . . that there's a leak?" Cameron asked.

"Deductive reasoning. Something indiscernible by the impaired crew; I'm surprised they can function at all."

"Well, it did take them a long time to capture that creature."

Alice nodded.

"So, I'd be subject to the same affects . . . if I were onboard?"

"Yes, after several days, or weeks, I would need to make necessary repairs." She stood up. "What would you like to do?"

He also stood. "First, answer me this: does Captain Wilcox work for someone else, or is this . . . like, a lone operation going on here?"

"The captain, along with a number of other spaceship captains, works for a consortium entity . . . a large corporation. Capitalism flourishes in deep space, Cameron."

"Okay, so I have an idea. Maybe. Can you help make us look like them? Put us both in some kind of officer's uniforms?"

The cyborg hesitated, taking him in. "I can utilize your Priopax device, the Lox device. But first, I'll need to find an appropriate sample to match us up to . . . within the *Albergone's* database."

* * *

They were moving along at a fast clip, five feet above the surface of the lake. "They're not going to shoot at us?" He asked.

"No," Alice said, piloting the craft. "I've transmitted the appropriate handshaking protocols. I would suspect the Captain and his men are nervously running around now, making the ship presentable for a fleet admiral's unannounced spot inspection."

Cameron closed his eyes and shook his head. "This is a stupid idea. It's not going to work."

"Probably not." Alice agreed.

He glanced over at her—took in her navy-blue uniform pants and jacket, the thin red piping running down the front, on the cuffs, and along the seams of her trousers. His eyes lingered on the shiny gold stars affixed to her collar. She'd done something with her hair too—had parted it more on the side. It looked good. She looked . . . the word *striking* came to mind. "You look good . . . very official."

"The uniform should pass muster," she said. Then added, "You look appropriately dressed as well; as my subordinate . . . my second-in-command."

He caught her intended dig, but didn't take the bait. Cameron didn't care who was in charge—hell, they were playing dress-up and they both were likely to be killed, anyway.

"We've been instructed to enter through sub-hold one's port-side hatchway."

Suddenly, Cameron sat straighter up in his seat. "Shit!"

Alice continued to stare straight ahead.

"This little craft we're in, it's not really a space-worthy ship. So why would we be arriving in it? This is stupid . . . a ridiculous idea!"

"Already thought of that," she said. "We'll tell them we're coming from a larger vessel. One that's stationed off beyond the horizon."

"They'll see that that's a ridiculous lie . . . a ship like theirs has to have incredible sensors . . ."

"I've already taken measures to fool their onboard readings. As far as they are concerned, a fleet command vessel is out of visual sight, but still close. You need to relax. You're sweating profusely and the top of your shirt collar is damp." Alice shot him a disapproving look. "Perhaps I should do most of the talking," she added.

Piloting the small winged craft higher, she then banked left. A large hatch, opening on the hull's port side, loomed black and foreboding before them.

chapter 28

Alice piloted the small craft through the open hatch, into the voluminous confines of the alien ship. It took several moments for Cameron's eyes to adjust from the bright daylight outside to the *Albergone's* dim and murky interior. A steamy brown haze hung heavily within the vessel's hold.

Instinctively, he brought a hand up to cover his nose and mouth. "What the hell is that smell?"

"Grum," Alice shot back. "From that Prinwhin—that's what the ship's manifest has designated the name of that starfish-looking species to be. Grum is its excrement, of which I'm detecting copious amounts, probably due to a strong fear response. All the stress after being so violently captured," Alice said.

Cameron could see they were in a huge, cavernous hold area. Where, sure enough, below them the Prinwhin creature was being secured to a bulkhead—upon which several spotlights were directed. It looked like an elaborate stage prop.

Also illuminated were three raised landing pads—L3, L2, and L1, was stenciled onto each one respectively.

"They want us to land on pad L3," the cyborg said, anticipating his next question.

"Geez, there are quite a few others . . . shackled." Cameron pointed, "Like a beast there . . . and several more over there."

Alice said, "Again, I've seen the manifest. There are twenty-seven captured organics imprisoned here to be exact."

The other creatures, now more visible through the murk, were clearly bound and secured to bulkheads all around the hold. Only then did Cameron become aware of the shrill, constant, high noise level entering in through the canopy. Sorrowful wailing sounds emanated all around them in the gloomy prevailing darkness. He grimaced, hearing multiple species cries of despair. "This is horrible!"

Alice settled the Scalldian craft onto the L3 landing pad. When several more spotlights came on, a connecting transit bridge was illuminated, showing a small contingent of what looked to be humans making their way across it.

"Looks like our welcoming party is en route," he said.

Alice retracted the canopy and the two climbed out. Cameron turned his back on the approaching contingent, shoving the plasma pistol deep into his waistband.

"You know that leaves a bulge . . . anyone can tell you're carrying a weapon," Alice said.

Cameron shrugged. "Still, it's better to have one on than be caught unprepared for the worst." He turned, noting seven

Albergone crewmembers nearing them. He'd assumed his and Alice's new uniforms would look similar enough to what these crewmembers would be wearing, but instead he saw theirs were faded, threadbare, and stained.

Tall and thin, and striding forward with purpose, was a man who looked to be in his mid-sixties. His long silver hair, a bit oily looking, was slicked back and came to his shoulders. And a remarkable-looking mustache, which probably took decades to grow to that length, was elaborately combed back—where it intermingled with equally thick, substantial-looking muttonchops. His high-styled facial hair seemed to be a point of pride for the commanding officer.

Alice stepped forward. "I am Admiral Porter and this is Lieutenant Commander Wright. Captain Wilcox, I presume?"

Coming to a halt, the captain eyed them both questioningly. His scrutinizing appraisal made Cameron a bit uneasy.

"Yes, I am Captain Wilcox," the captain said, narrowing his eyes suspiciously. "Never had an impromptu inspection here before . . . were pretty much left to our own devices . . . to ourselves."

Alice matched his cold stare with one of her own, showing both annoyance and superiority. "I don't care what's gone on in the past here. Things are different now. Profits are down, a lot of graft going on these days . . . certain ship captains skimming a little here and there. It all adds up."

"You make accusations like that, you better be able to back it up, Admiral," Wilcox said, as his back straightened.

Cameron, assessing the six men lurking behind Wilcox, found them to be a motley crew. Clearly, daily bathing practices were optional on this ship. And their half-lidded, watery irises moved slowly within eye sockets as if the lot of them were heavily drugged. They all had long, stringy hair and exhibited the malnourished pallor of a backstreet junky.

Doing a double take, Cameron noticed one man even had his trousers on backward. How he'd managed to zip up—or buckle his belt—would have been a challenge even for one unimpaired. Another crewmember, leering at Alice, was taking her in from head to toe, his heavy breathing sounding more like panting. As moisture accumulated at the corners of his mouth, a continuous saliva stream dripped down his chin. It occurred to Cameron the man was actually drooling, and two thoughts came to him at the same time: one—the physical affects of the reactor leak were indeed real, and two—no way was he going to end up like any of these guys. *No way.* He glanced ahead into the murky haze toward daylight, streaming in through the still-open, distant hatchway. He momentarily contemplated getting back in the Scalldian craft and clearing out of here.

Captain Wilcox said, "In any case, we'll need to make this quick. There are eight potential champions out there, living on three other worlds. We'll need to hunt them down before we head back to Winforge."

Alice shook her head. "Your orders have changed. You'll be heading back immediately. And Lieutenant Commander Wright and I will be heading back with you." Cameron thought it rather strange that the captain referred to those alien creatures as *potential champions*, when Alice continued, "You will have adequate quarters arranged for us immediately." She glanced at Cameron, then back to the captain.

"Your men are smelly; all require thorough bathing . . . and a change of uniform is long overdue."

Captain Wilcox bristled. "Don't you have your own space-craft to return to, Admiral?"

"Already ordered it away," Cameron interjected.

The captain exhaled a long breath, then turned partially around to reassess his men. "Well, we didn't expect company. I'll have your quarters prepared, then get the men to spruce up some. Anything else?" he asked, clearly irritated.

"Yes, you can direct me to the *Albergone's* engineering section. Specifically, to the starboard-side drive unit . . . to the antimatter containment chamber there."

"Ma'am . . . you don't want to go anywhere near that part of the ship. I suspect there's, um . . . issues—"

"Yes, there's an antimatter leak. We detected it from our fleet marauder, from a thousand miles out."

The captain's expression turned from one of irritation to one of confusion. "If there was a leak . . ."

Cameron asked, "Wait, you haven't noticed your crew? That they're getting sick? Have cognitive issues? Just look at them. Hell, that one over there has his pants on backward."

Alice shot Cameron a quick disapproving look. He shrugged at the captain, "But maybe not; I could be wrong."

"You'll instruct your men to evacuate that part of the ship until I issue an all-clear order," Alice said. "Until Lieutenant Commander Wright and I determine the best means to make repairs. Can you assign two men to assist us in that regard?"

Cameron shook his head. "Perhaps it would be best if I got started on the ship's inspection. Maybe start at the bow, then work aft from there."

"No, I'll need you with me, Lieutenant Commander," Alice said.

chapter 29

Heather . . .

S he screamed for the Loth once more, this time waving her
arms over her head to grab its attention. "Loth! It's me,
Heather . . . can you hear me?"

She watched as the tethered, magnificent beast slowly
moved past her. Periodic bright flashes, more like sparks,
emanated from around several small, low-flying, craft. They
were zapping the poor beast to move it along faster. "Leave
the poor thing alone! Assholes!" she shouted.

Honk! Honk! . . . Honk! Honk! Honk! Heth..er! The creature
turned its massive head in her direction and she noted excitement on its face. "Yes, it's me! Heather! Stay strong, Loth . . .
we'll find a way out of this, I promise!" She wiped away fresh
tears, inwardly praying she'd be able to keep that promise.

"Friends with a Minal Loth . . . huh? Impressive."

Heather didn't bother looking toward the towering and muscular female standing upright in the adjacent cage. She'd been ignoring her catcalls for the last ten minutes, ever since XI transferred her into this cage. Her vile, sexually egregious taunts were worse than anything she'd ever heard, or experienced, from men, or anyone, back on Earth.

"That Loth your boyfriend, girly . . . you two do dirty, disgusting things together?"

"Why don't you just shut up for a while? And no, of course not, and stop saying such crude things to me. I have someone in my life. I have a boyfriend."

The brazen woman smiled—exposing a row of top teeth. Chiseled into sharp points, they only exemplified her shark-like cruelty. Her bright red hair was pulled back too tightly into a high ponytail. With her hands on her hips, her bare breasts—full and substantial—pendulumed back-and-forth in unison, as she swayed her hips back and forth suggestively.

"Stop that!" Heather yelled, turning to face her full on. "Why don't you, instead, just tell me where we are? How to escape from this place?"

"Escape?" the giant lesbian laughed out loud, re-exposing the dagger-like teeth in her mouth. "Time for you to face reality, little princess. You have come to your final destination in life. You have arrived at Winforge."

"So what is Winforge, exactly? Why are we all here?" Heather asked.

The woman snickered and grimaced, both at the same time as she glanced around the many cages. Other species—mostly aliens, except for about ten humans—were clustered along their side of the dirt passageway. "Why should I tell you anything? Why should I waste my time on someone who will not survive the week?"

It was then Heather noticed the scars all over her body. *Why had she not spotted them earlier?* Probably because she'd averted her eyes away, not wanting to see her raw nakedness. But now she did look, taking in the full extent of the physical damage the woman had endured—had been subjected to. Her right calf was oddly indented; its red, rough-looking, flesh possibly the result of some vicious bite. *What kind of animal causes bite marks like that?* Heather wondered. The numerous scars on her body, some dark and purple, while others looked fainter, more subtle in appearance, were from years—perhaps even decades—past. A network of scars climbed up her legs, resembling crisscrossing vines. Her flat and muscular tummy had three parallel scars deeply etched across her abdomen. Clearly, she'd been raked over by some very sharp claws.

"You getting a good look, princess? You want to touch them. I have other scars too . . . ones you can't see."

Heather took a few steps closer to her cell, her anger all but gone now, seeing the kind of physical torment the woman must have endured. She asked, "That all happened right here? Here on Winforge?"

A shrug. "Sure. Where else? This is where we fight."

Heather nodded. She'd actually gathered that much; that this place was some kind of alien *fight club*. Perhaps different alien species matched against other species. For sure, some high-stakes betting was going on here, too. Earlier, she'd heard far-off cheers from a distant crowd: A thousand people, maybe more, chanting and yelling indecipherable names. *Is that why I am here?*

"They will start you off with someone easy . . . perhaps someone non-human. Might be a Craing female; they're small, yet scrappy. You need to watch out for those little fuckers."

The woman looked Heather up and down then shook her head. "What do you weigh? One ten, one fifteen?"

"About that; somewhere in there."

"That pretty face of yours won't look that way long . . . scars come with this place. No getting around that. What is your name?"

"I'm Heather."

The woman's wide smile exposed her jagged, fang-like, teeth. "Of course it's Heather. You really are a princess, aren't you?"

"Whatever . . . who are you?"

"My real name? I have no idea. I was abducted away from my family, from Earth, when I was about six. I go by Manny . . . some think I'm manly. Do you think I look like a man, Heather?" Taking ahold of each breast, Manny lifted them up as if they were inanimate—something to be assessed or judged, like two oversized cantaloupes.

Heather shrugged, wanting to change the subject. "Look, I don't know how to fight. I don't want to fight!"

"You'll take a few punches . . . perhaps even a bite or two, but then something miraculous kicks in."

"What's that?"

"Fight or flight instincts. If you're a coward, you'll run around and around and around the arena until you're gasping for breath, till snot's running down your nose, and you're crying like a little bitch. Then, all too quickly you'll be caught . . . and you'll die, just like that. Match over, they'll drag your sorry ass outside and feed it to the Black Snappers, or maybe your Loth friend. But if you have some fight in you . . . some courage, some cunning, you might survive a few matches. It's possible."

"Will they match me against you? In the arena?"

Manny laughed. "You against me? Lord, no! I'd pull your skinny arms free from their sockets then club you to death with them. I'd pull your—"

"Okay! I got it! Not a good match! So . . . can you help me? Teach me some things to help me remain alive."

Manny stared back at her. She licked her lips and moved closer to the bars separating them. "For a price."

Heather shook her head. "No. Not that. But I will help you escape, when the time comes. I promise."

"Oh . . . sure. Like the promise you made to the big Minal Loth. Little you, in your little short-shorts, you're going to help us all escape?"

"Not just me. Cam . . . Cameron is going to do that."

Manny feigned boredom—cleaning something underneath a fingernail.

Heather felt her anger up inside of her. "The Loth . . . it's Cameron's. But you don't have to believe me. You don't have to believe that Cameron survived for over a month on an alien world, one called Sang-Morang, and outwitted the Gleery Beasts roaming there, and scores of vicious little Piquet Sprints. The same guy tamed a Minal Loth, then returned to Earth aboard a ship called the *Primion*. He, well, he pretty much saved Earth. It's what he does. Somehow, he beats the odds; does these amazing things that a kid not yet out of college shouldn't be able to do. But if I tell you he'll be coming for me . . . then you should believe me. You, too, should want to become part of this."

Manny stared back at her with an expression hard to read, then said, "I guess you do have a bit of fight in you after all, princess."

"Don't call me that."

"You know, I did hear something about that *Primion* ship; also about some kind of fight between two monster Loths."

"Mother and son," Heather said.

"Yeah . . . Griar versus Minal . . . that's right, Mother and son. Really a great match?" Manny said, looking truly impressed.

"Cam's Loth is more than just loyal," Heather said back. "It loves Cam."

The warrior lesbian shook her head, "Look . . . nobody ever gets off this planet. Not alive, anyway. You learn that hope is the real enemy here . . . leads you down a dark hole when things turn out badly. Best you make peace with the fact that you can only count on one person here, and that's yourself."

Heather, pursing her lips together, said nothing.

"And maybe . . . maybe I'll watch your back . . . some. Show you a few things . . ."

chapter 30

Cameron . . .

Cameron and Alice followed behind two *Albergone* crewmembers. He noticed both looked skeletal beneath their loose-fitting uniforms. Neither one had spoken. They both appeared to be in a trance-like state as they plodded along several paces in front. They then rode a vertical lift up to another section of the vessel. Apparently, the entire lower section of the ship was dedicated to being the main hold area, along with several smaller ones, while the top portion more resembled the typical ship layout—a bridge, crew quarters, crew mess hall, medical, and engineering.

The two crewmembers slowed then came to a complete stop.

"What's the hold up, fellas?" Cameron asked.

The man on the left teetered a bit unsteadily before placing a palm on a nearby bulkhead for support. The second one started to bend over but then seemed to think otherwise and slowly knelt down instead. The passageway they were in was so poorly illuminated that Cameron was having a hard time making out what the crewmember was doing. At first, he thought he might have stopped to retie a shoelace, but now saw they were wearing laceless boots. Then he saw another pair of legs. The feet were splayed out at a forty-five degree angle. By the look of them—plus the pungent smell of released urine—he was pretty sure it was a dead crewmember lying there.

Alice said, "Leave him. Continue on to engineering."

It was during times like this that Cameron was reminded of just how non-human she actually was. Who knew, maybe these crewmembers had been best buddies; maybe even related to one another. But, in any event, they were moving along the dimly-lit passageway again, and Cameron didn't look down at the dead person lying on the deck. It took them another five minutes to reach the part of the ship clearly dedicated to the ship's propulsion. As the noise level increased, he could see one of the aft towering drive-unit structures.

"Okay . . . good! These are the starboard-side drive components," Alice said. "You two . . . leave us now."

The two skeletal crewmembers looked confused. Either that, or they objected to being told to leave.

Cameron said, "It's okay . . . you can go; we'll tell your captain we ordered you to go."

The two men did as told, and at a glacially slow pace headed back the same way they'd come.

He looked about the large compartment, with its multiple consoles and displays, and had the uncomfortable feeling that this section of the ship should be continuously manned when the vessel was operational, which it now clearly was.

Alice said, "The antimatter containment structure for this drive unit is actually right below us. Purposely positioned in a location that is difficult to get to. Typically, no maintenance, nor upkeep, is necessary for such a sensitive structure." She then hesitated, noticing Cameron's furrowed brow.

Taking a moment to do a quick mental reference, in his mind's eye Cameron opened the hardbound World Book Encyclopedia, the one imprinted with the letter **A**. He mentally flipped forward to the reference: **Antimatter Containment**: *the intricate process whereby antimatter and matter were kept independent from each other by the use of powerful magnetic fields—necessary to prevent the oppositely charged particles from colliding with one another, which would result in the mutual destruction of both matter and antimatter—resulting in a violent and explosive release of pure energy . . .*

"The magnets. What happens when they are out of alignment?" he asked.

"Nothing good," Alice said, striding forward toward a metal staircase.

Cameron stayed where he was. "So maybe the reason the chamber is leaking is due to an alignment issue? And there's a good chance an explosion is . . . like . . . imminent?"

"Very good . . . that's correct," he heard her say as the top of her head disappeared from view. She hurried downward. Then he saw her again, staring up at him. "Over there . . .

on that display. Tell me when you see an error, or a warning start to flash."

"Seriously?"

Already gone out of sight, only the sound of her fading footfalls remained. Cameron took up a position in front of the control panel. The display looked to be off. They all appeared to be off. Then he noticed the faintest flickering on the closest display that could be the blinking *on-and-off* of a cursor prompt. Truth was, this was not the kind of technology he was familiar with. Nothing he'd studied back at Stanford, nor at the ultra-high-tech corporation, HyperCrell, where he'd interned for several years prior to becoming shipwrecked on Sang-Morang had taught him anything like this.

Startled, he saw large red symbols, perhaps an alien word of warning, flashing on the display. He had no idea what was being relayed, but he supposed it was nothing good. Something like *kiss your poor ass goodbye—you're about to be blown to bits*. But then again, it was only one word. He yelled toward the staircase, "Something red is flashing . . . a warning, I think!"

Cameron listened for her reply but instead heard only a distant pounding, like someone using a hammer on a metal pipe. He moved over to the top of the stairs, and shouted down, "Should you be doing that? Banging on things down there?"

He waited there another few minutes, every so often looking back over his shoulder at the still-flashing display, mentally debating about going down the stairs after her. He quickly dismissed the thought, knowing that being even this close to the containment structure was a bad idea. Another check of the display showed the warning symbol had now ceased flashing. When he heard Alice's footsteps on the stairs he took several steps backward. Ascending the top steps, she no longer looked anything like the same Alice as before, although he had seen her in this form before. A form devoid of any Thidion, or human-like traits—such as flesh and hair—Alice was reduced to a basic, cyborgenic form; a reflective metallic understructure that was now more robotic than organic in appearance.

"Christ . . . Alice . . . what happened?"

"It turned out that making necessary modifications required I enter into an intermediary section of the containment area. This is the result of several short radiation blasts."

"Well . . . are you okay?"

"Yes and no. I am not radioactive. And I have repaired this vessel's small antimatter leak."

"But?"

"But I would rather not have lost my epidermis layers."

Cameron nodded, feeling he should say something else—perhaps something consoling. But seeing her shake her head, giving him an annoyed roll of her eyes, he got that it wasn't necessary. She was a cyborg, and although she certainly did express and feel emotions, they weren't human ones.

Alice quickly moved over to the same console Cameron had been standing at moments before. Manipulating an input device, all the surrounding consoles came to life. The high-mounted displays, becoming active, were scrolling out alien characters and symbols. She said, "Earlier power fluctuations resulted in much of this vessel's key systems shutting down. I've got them coming back up. It's really a miracle this ship's still capable of flight since its environmental systems weren't even working. That smell you first noticed was an indication the atmospheric filters were down."

"So . . . will the crew—"

"No. They all will be dead by this time tomorrow."

Cameron stared at her for a long beat. "The ship's captain didn't seem to be that sick."

"Well, he is," she replied, not looking at him as she continued to manipulate the input device—periodically checking the display and making adjustments. "Although he is not as far gone as the others, he is very ill. Apparently, that containment structure began leaking around eight months ago. Oh, but rest assured, your few minutes in this compartment will not adversely affect your own long-term health."

Cameron was relieved to hear that. "So what now? Can we get this ship operational enough to head-off toward Winforge?"

"I'm working on that. But there's another problem . . . perhaps a much bigger problem." She stopped what she was doing on the console and turned to face him. "Captain Wilcox just committed suicide." She tapped something on the console and the display showed a new feed of a dimly lit section of the ship. "This is the captain's quarters. Keep watching."

Cameron leaned in closer. The picture was bluish and fuzzy—super hard to make out much detail. Then he watched as the lanky ship commander, his elaborately styled facial hair making his identification certain, entered the picture. The man wavered back and forth, just as he'd seen some of the other crewmembers do. Captain Wilcox, holding something in his right hand, slowly brought it up to his temple. Then came a bright flash and the captain's head no longer resided upon his neck and shoulders. A brief moment passed before the headless corpse fell lifelessly to the deck.

"I can't believe I just watched that! He knew things would only get worse for him," Cameron said. "I guess that was the problem."

"That wasn't the problem I was referring to," Alice said, as her fingers flew across the input device. All the surrounding displays had become active and were showing feeds from other sections of the ship.

"What am I looking at?"

"Seven different feeds from the hold area," the cyborg said.

"I don't see much of anything," Cameron said.

"Exactly. Prior to late Captain Wilcox's final act, he did something else," Alice said. "He uncoupled all of the containment harnesses."

"Harnesses?"

"Cameron . . . all the beasts are loose. Twenty-seven are free and currently roaming all about the ship. I imagine they are very hungry since they haven't been fed in . . . let me check . . ." her fingers moved quickly upon the input device. "It looks like it's been about eight days."

chapter 31

Heather . . .

"Get your damn hands off me! You touch me again and I'll slap you into next week," she spat.

The others within the passageway chuckled while several laughed out loud. Heather looked over at Manny, who was leaning against the roughly chiseled wall. Arms crossed over her ample breasts, her expression showed neither amusement nor irritation—clearly, she would be zero help in this situation.

Heather instinctively hated the small Craing being who'd continuously accosted her since she'd been brought into this cave-like passageway, which seemed to be some kind of holding area. Eight were waiting before a massive old metal door that easily stood sixty to seventy feet tall. The color of rust, it showed years of wear and tear. She thought some of the darker patches on it might be caked-on dried blood.

She assessed the others who had been ushered there by several armed, hovering droids. Three were human—Heather, Manny, and another young, dark-haired woman who hadn't spoken yet—and two were Thidion females with membrane ears. Another two were some alien species. Frankly, their presence here within this particular group made no sense to her, having both multiple appendages and multiple roving eyes. They spoke gibberish and never seemed to shut up. But it was the small Craing, obviously a male, who demanded her attention. Four feet nothing, the little creep had been around her since being released from his cage. A foul-mouthed, grabby shit who'd tried to feel her up three separate times in the last ten minutes alone.

"That's Phonk," the dark-haired woman said, so softly that Heather almost didn't hear her. "He's always like that: horny and mean. I hate him . . . wish someone would kill him in the arena."

Manny pulled herself up and away from the wall. "Maybe it'll be you, Cleeanne . . . maybe you'll get that wish granted today."

"Try it and I'll beat you into unconsciousness. Then I'll have some fun with that frail limp body of yours," Phonk said, exposing a row of small yellow teeth, that reminded Heather of kernels of corn.

Phonk quietly took a step backward, a half-step behind Heather. Before she had a chance to react, the little monster had a hand cupped around her left breast. He squeezed it so hard her eyes filled with tears. Manny, coming alongside her in two quick strides, backhanded the small Craing so hard he was transported up into the air. He fell in a heap six feet away.

Manny spun around to face Heather, her face tight with anger. "Wake up, princess. We're all here just trying to survive another day . . . not watch over you. That damn Craing is nothing compared to what else you'll be up against while here. That's the last time I'll come to your aid. Next time, I'll simply watch and wait to see who gets the upper hand."

"Fine! I didn't ask for your help, anyway," Heather shot back, her words far more pathetic-sounding than she intended.

But Manny was right. Heather knew she was not cut out for any of this. She wouldn't survive against any of them in a fight, if that was their intention. She felt helpless and frustrated. *Where are you, Cam?*

The Craing man, still on the ground, was staring up at her snickering. All the weekends she'd spent playing on a soccer field as a kid hadn't been for nothing after all—taking a running step, Heather's landed a hard kick to Phonk between his two beady eyes. Yelping in pain, he scurried away from her with a shocked expression.

"That's a start," Manny said, returning to her former position of leaning up against the wall.

What Manny didn't know was that Heather had just broken her big toe. She wanted to cry out—scream and rub the white-hot agonizing pain away—she wanted to throw a tantrum. But she didn't. Instead, she tried to look bored. Tried to look like she went around kicking people in the head on a regular basis.

Clang!

The big metal door slowly opened inward into the passageway. The eight captives moved back several paces to accommodate its swinging open trajectory. For the first time, Heather got a clear view inside the arena. Unlike the door, within lay a brilliant kaleidoscope of bright colors with ultra-modern sports viewing accommodations. Two of the droids were back, now ushering them forward from behind. A bright flash caught Heather's attention when the still-prone Craing was tasered once, then again. Phonk scrambled onto his feet, moving fast to rejoin the others.

Heather spun fully around, taking it all in. Thousands of empty seats were situated around the oval grass field that was two or three times the size of a typical football gridiron. There were giant 3D displays putting the *jumbotrons* back on Earth to shame. High up overhead, two hundred feet or so, a glass-like ceiling strobed a cacophony of various kinds of alien advertisements. High up in the stands, she could see countless concession stands and what could be betting booths. Situated all around the arena, watchful and imposing ornate statues—made either of bronze or some other dark metal—stood fifty feet tall. None were the same. Warriors, muscular aliens, each held some kind of weapon: spears, swords, or other armament that Heather was clueless about.

Honk!

Startled, she hadn't even noticed them out there. In the distance on the playing field were two towering creatures—some two hundred yards away. A reddish-brown dust storm swirled around them as they battled. Heather unconsciously placed a hand over her heart as she watched the Loth, Cam's Loth, in the midst of a desperate battle. Two goliaths now embroiled in a vicious life-and-death struggle. The Loth's tentacles were intertwined around the other beast's neck and torso, while the other giant lobster-looking creature came within inches of the Loth's massive head with its big teeth bared and constantly moving snapping jaws. Heather noticed a long length of a tentacle appendage lying on the ground. To her amazement, it appeared the Loth was on the losing end of things. *How was that possible? Had it lost its will to survive here?* Then she realized why. Cam, the Loth's human, wasn't here. She watched, horrified, as the tentacled Loth was forced down to the ground, another tentacle caught in the creature's clutches.

Honk! Honk! Honk!

Heather heard both despair and misery in the Loth's distant, repeated cries. She had little doubt the Loth would soon be dead as she watched its half-hearted attempt to fend off this most recent attack.

NO! She wasn't going to just stand around and watch that happen. How would she ever explain that to Cam . . . *well, I just watched it happen . . . watched the Loth die. NO!* With no further thought in mind, she was off, racing across the field. Teeth tightly clenched, she put the pain from her broken toe aside, and ran like she'd never run before. Heather heard Manny yelling something behind her, then figured out what she'd shouted out: *The droids are in pursuit, girl!* Legs rhythmically moving like pistons—her arms pumping hard back and forth—she continued to run forward without letting up.

Heather heard them before catching them out of her peripheral vision—two security droids. Bright flashes emanated out from their shocking devices. *They were going to catch her*—they moved faster than she could possibly run. And still at one hundred seventy-five yards out, Cam's Loth was still too far away for her to get its attention.

Oh God. Another droid was now approaching from directly in front of her and would soon cut her off at the proverbial pass, and that would be the end of it. Heather, her lungs now burning— exhaustion overtaking her as she ran ahead of the two pursuing droids—was feeling all her hope dissipate. Her stride faltered.

The droid up ahead was nearly upon her. Bigger than the others, it was black as coal. Then she recognized it—*XI.*

The killer droid veered to the left and fired two quick plasma bursts. She heard one pursuing droid hit the ground hard then roll. Then XI must have circled back behind her. She heard two more blasts then another *thud* as that droid, too, was taken out of action. Heather didn't understand. Why had XI, apparently, helped her? With renewed determination, she sprinted ever closer to the nearly defeated Loth ahead.

"Get up! Get up! Get up! Damn it . . . Loth . . . Get up right NOW!" Breathlessly, she screamed out—to the point she thought her vocal cords might tear apart. But she could run no more, had no energy left. As she fell to her knees, Heather looked up to see if her words had somehow reached the still-distant creature's ears. "Please, Loth . . . don't give up. Don't give up on Cam . . . ," yet she knew she wasn't pleading only to the Loth, but to her own inner self, as well.

chapter 32

The Loth was clearly dead. Through her tears, Heather watched and was sickened by it. She watched as the lobster-like creature dismembered the carcass and began devouring large chunks of it. Her sense of loss was just too heavy—forcing her to face a reality she hadn't wanted to consider until right then. Suppose this was all that was left? That Cameron would never come—killed back on Sang-Morang soon after she and the Loth were abducted. *Is this life even worth surviving?* Heather wondered. Standing on the field, she buried her face in her hands and cried as she inhaled the plastic aroma of artificial turf. She remembered the *red dust cloud*, she looked up and blinked until her vision sufficiently cleared. *Why would there be a red dust cloud when there's no dirt around anywhere?* The lobster-like beast was still feasting away. "Wait . . . that dead Loth has a bluish tint to it," she whispered. "That's not the same Loth; not Cam's Loth!"

Heather slowly rose to her feet and began walking. She didn't even try to hide the need to limp now. The closer she came to the two ginormous beasts—one now partially scavenged—the more apparent it was that something else was wrong. That it wasn't real. Ten paces closer, then fifteen, then twenty, Heather stopped and smiled. "It's a fucking projection," she said aloud. As if on cue, the simulation stopped mid-motion, with the lobster-like beast poised to scarf down another bite of bloodied meat.

Someone was approaching—walking toward her—with the XI droid hovering behind him as if invisibly tethered there. She stopped and waited, letting him cross the remainder of the field. He came to a stop ten feet in front of her. Tall and very good looking, he was neither human nor Thidion but some kind of alien race that held a close proximity to her own. The only obvious differences were the color of his eyes, a deep violet, and an impressive mane of thick hair, which was very lion-like. Dressed in a type of formal business suit, he looked broad-shouldered with a powerful build. He stood tall before her—discerningly taking her in—measuring every aspect of her body, like a seamstress would prior to sewing together a dress or a gown. She saw something else, too. An animalistic, primal hunger there in his gaze.

"My name is Thoran Ginott."

She shrugged, "Good for you."

"It was a mistake to throw you in with the others . . . you are not a combatant."

"Yeah? Well, I might surprise you yet in that regard."

"No, you are . . . simply . . . beyond exquisite." The corners of his mouth turned upward. "I see I'll have to make other, more appropriate, arrangements. Put you to better use. What are you, twenty, twenty-one?"

Heather wasn't about to tell him he'd guessed close. "I would rather die than have you pimp me out as some kind of interstellar whore. I'm serious; I'll find a way to *off myself* before that's going to happen. So screw you and your more 'appropriate' arrangements."

The ever-looming XI droid hovered closer, descending down to eye-level. "You have made an impact on this AI mechanism," Ginott said. "I must tell you, I'm not accustomed to being so mercilessly berated, especially by a non-organic."

"Who are you . . . and what is XI to you?" Heather asked.

"I told you, I am—"

"Yeah, Thoran Ginott, I got that. But why are you here, speaking to me now? What is this place to you . . . and that killer droid?"

He sighed. "You were purposely brought to Winforge, to this world. Yes, it is a horrid place. The sole exception is this expansive facility situated near its northern most pole. Winforge mostly is comprised of a type of igneous rock. Some consider this world to be nothing more than a large, desolate asteroid."

Heather nodded impatiently for him to get on with it.

"I come from a long line of Ginotts. I am the thirteenth Prime Overlord here that covers a span of time close to two hundred of your Earth years."

"So, is that like some kind of family business?"

"Very much so," he said.

"A family business where you, on a continuous basis, abduct beings from their homes . . . from all around the galaxy, I presume. And for what?" She gestured out to the open stands. "To profit from all the misery you've caused?"

"Well . . . the Ginotts have had two centuries to deal with the guilt." He smiled then glanced over to the hovering droid. "As to your other question regarding XI, this AI, in various forms over the years, has proven itself to be uniquely loyal to me and to the enterprise here. The truth is, I'm not entirely sure why XI brought you here. I've had little time to confer with this artificial intelligence. I am aware of one of the reasons, though, and that's self-evident."

Heather raised her brows for him to proceed.

"The Minal Loth, the beast you clearly show affection for, is a prized asset here. One that just may be unrivaled in both strength and tenacity. Loth's have always been a large crowd draw. Betting is fierce with this breed. But a specimen of this size, of this lineage . . . Yes, the exploits of its mother, the Griar Loth, the beast that destroyed much of your home town, not to mention what its surviving spawn are still doing in other areas—"

Heather put a hand up, stopping him mid-sentence: "Spawn? Wait . . . no, the mother Loth's offspring were all killed. Destroyed by a nuclear explosion set beneath the ground. They're all dead, mother and offspring, so you have your facts all wrong."

Ginott shook his head and seemed honestly regretful. "I'm sorry, I do have my facts straight. It is my business to do so. Actually, two Loths survived. You see, there were multiple litters. Deep, deep within the Earth's crust the survivors endured the explosion. Soon interbreeding occurred. Now, many Loths are roaming your planet. Bad for your world, yes, but eventually good business for the Ginotts' family business."

Suddenly, Heather felt light-headed—mentally forced to visualize what was happening back on Earth. She was well aware of the damage just one of the immense creatures was capable of, but many of them? *Oh God . . . it was unimaginable.* She thought of her family—her mother and father. *Were they even still alive?*

Genott, speaking again, said, "So now you can see how important you've become in all this."

"What? I don't . . ."

"The Minal Loth. It cares about you, which is its weakness and also its strength. The promotional media is already abuzz about an upcoming match. The undefeated Minal Loth will be going up against a truly terrible foe: a Tammer."

"I don't know what that is . . . how would I?"

"Tammers are not so different from Loths. Genetically speaking, they are only a bigger brother or sister. Up until this coming event, they've never been matched against anything other than another Tammer. It would have been cruel, and, frankly, uneventful to do otherwise. But your Loth, I imagine, will do just about anything to ensure your safety. And Heather, you, too, will play a very big part in this Tammer versus Loth event."

"Me? You already stated the obvious; I'm not a combatant."

"The betting has already begun. Trillions of *ackneds*—hink of them as denominations of money—being placed on both the Tammer and the Loth. Near even odds, in fact, which is unheard of!" Ginott's features softened some. "You will be here," he gestured to the open field around them. "Your long blonde hair will be worn down and flowing. You'll be dressed in a white silk gown. A vision in white, like a pure-as-snow maiden. A captive virgin. Can you picture it . . . it will be amazing . . . it will be epic."

"Ah . . . no. I won't do that."

Ginott seemed to be transfixed within his own thoughts. "You'll be high up . . . where all can see you and admire your beauty. Of course, you will be chained to a magnificent pillar where you will await your fate. Saved by your loyal Loth, or eaten by the oh-so-vicious Tammer beast. A spectacle that will be spoken of for years . . . maybe generations."

chapter 33

Cameron . . .

He wanted off this wretched tin can. It smelled of death and even though Alice assured him it was relatively safe, he couldn't escape the constant reminder of just how dangerous a place this ship was. Twenty-seven great beasts were moving about the ship. Some found sustenance in devouring-up the ever increasing number of dead *Albergone* crewmembers. But their bodies were scarcely more than racks of bones, not enough to satisfy such immense appetites.

Secured behind what appeared to be a substantial-enough hatchway, Cameron and the cyborg, Alice, sat within the spacious confines of *Albergone's* bridge. Suddenly he got up, and began pacing again.

"Why don't you sit down? Stop that pacing."

He ignored her. "How much longer?" he asked.

"The ship's primary systems are in ill-repair. It's amazing that she's still as operational as she is. Taking her into deep space now would not be prudent."

Cameron stopped moving about to study the nearest bulkhead. He could hear them out there: loud noises, thumping sounds, desperate animalistic cries. "I want them off this ship . . . every last one of them. Open all the external hold hatch doors and let them out."

Alice finally glanced up from what she was doing, her fingers poised over a complicated-looking control panel. Her eyes tracked him as he started pacing again. "Sure, I can do that."

"Then do it."

The words spilled out, more like an order than he'd intended, but it was beginning to feel like she was intentionally stalling, looking for a reason not to head off toward Winforge. "Why are we still in the air . . . hovering above the stupid lake out there? Let's land this thing; let the killer beasts off and get going."

"As I was about to say, I can do that . . . but there would be ramifications. Ones I'd like to discuss with you, before any decisions are made."

There was a time when Alice appeared, more or less, to be a kind of subordinate, just along for the ride—and ever ready to assist him. But now, she wanted their decision-making to be mutual. "There is no logical reason to keep those creatures roaming around this vessel," he told her. "And they definitely are not conducive to my long-term survival. You, they would have no interest in. But me . . . I'm lunch."

"With the exception of the Sang-Morang Prinwhin, the bulk of the creatures inhabiting this ship are from other worlds. Each one of those worlds accommodated its beasts in what most assuredly was a balanced ecosystem. A balance evolved, probably over millions of years. We let any of these beasts roam loose out there—within Sang-Morang's complex, harmonious ecosystem—the results will be devastating. Their whole hierarchical, indigenous life structure would fracture."

Frustrated, Cameron shrugged, offering her an expression back that said . . . *who cares?*

"So, you're okay with the demise of the Great Plains Bovids?" she asked."

"No one ever said life in the wild is easy," he said frankly.

"And the Dalima Climbers? They are a gentle breed who surely won't last long with two dozen additional, and far superior life forms on the food chain, roaming about looking for nourishment."

He thought about the Dalima Climber sisters, Sphial and Shrii, one of which was dead, and the wonderfully affectionate Lalik, who, in her own way, loved him. Then he pictured the tribe being hunted—scared and frantic, picked off one at a time. Would he really be okay with contributing to the extinction of an entire race of primate-type beings? *No, of course he wouldn't.* "So what do you suggest, Alice?"

"I think we should take them along with us," she said.

Cameron plopped down into the seat next to her, then let out a long breath. "I knew you were going to say that."

"And I knew you knew that, too," she said, giving an unnatural-looking smile back.

He continued to stare at her. "You know . . . you're a good friend, Alice."

His comment seemed to make her uneasy. She continued her busy button pushing, then said, "Friendship is an organic—"

He cut her off, "Bullshit."

Alice kept quiet.

"You're far more humanlike when it comes to compassion—plain old goodness of heart—than anyone I've ever met. And you're loyal. I'm very lucky to have you here with me. So I guess I'm just saying thank you. Thank you for being my friend. Even though that's not what you'd call it . . . I would. And I guess that's enough."

Just for a moment her eyes became still. But any introspection was quickly blinked away. "You're welcome, Cameron." She then stood and stared at the nearby bulkhead. "I have an idea. I am not saying it is a good idea, only a possibility."

"Shoot . . . I'm all ears."

"Well, it's clear we cannot do what we need to do without further help. That hatchway won't keep them out long enough for us to reach Winforge."

Cameron, not actually aware of that before, nodded back.

"I want you to look at who's onboard with us."

"The crew? Not many are still alive. I feel bad about that, but I guess their fate was sealed a long time ago . . ."

"Not the crew."

He followed her stare to the nearby bulkhead. "The beasts?"

Alice hurried back to her console and began tapping at the control panel. "Take a look at the display." Now in motion, she'd arranged a repeating few seconds on a loop, revealing one of the creatures Cameron hadn't yet seen.

"This is a Yonk. Twenty-five feet tall . . . lean and mean. And, like all the others, a hungry carnivore. It was selected, as were the others, because it is a ferocious fighter. A perfect combatant for the main arena on Winforge."

Cameron watched the hairy beast, which looked like an art depiction he'd seen of Sasquatch on Earth, only many times larger.

"Certainly a terrific fighter, but dumb as can be. Its intelligence level is low down on the scale for any planet. Next, is another one of our mammoth passengers." This one definitely looked reptilian, or the alien equivalent of reptilian. As tall as the Yonk, but also longer, it had a snake-like torso and extended dangerous-looking claws on each of its four appendages.

"Has a head that's similar to an alligator," Cameron said.

"Shinntoh, it's also a stupid creature. Right now, it's trying to figure out how to maneuver around a two-foot-high pipe. Something it could easily step over."

Cameron was getting the point: each creature onboard the ship was as dumb as a rock. Perhaps that was a good thing.

Alice sent a new feed over to the display. "This strange-looking creature is called a Hengtied Portule."

Cameron tilted his head both left and right, trying to make heads-or-tails of what he was viewing. "It looks like a mound of Loth dung."

"Keep watching," Alice said, now standing by his side.

He waited, about to say something, when the mound moved. It soon became evident—arms and legs, and even a head, were emerging from what appeared to be a fleshy husk of a body.

"When the Hengtied Portule sleeps, it surrounds itself in some kind of organic protective tent. It is now emerging from its slumber period," Alice said.

Cameron watched the fleshy membrane tent deflate. Pulled taut against other parts of the body, like reeled in extra, loose-fitting skin. The creature, now balled into a crouch, looked as if it were ready to do a cannonball jump into a pool. Slowly, it began to rise. Eyes open, it immediately began to dart back and forth, assessing the surrounding environment.

"Not as big as the others," Cameron said.

"No . . . a typical Hengtied stands about fifteen feet tall. This is a male. The females can grow a bit taller . . . and they're stronger too."

The display feed suddenly altered, showing a split screen after Alice had moved back to the control panel. "On the right you can see the creature's cognitive, reasoning capabilities."

The Hengtied feed on the left was again replaying. On the right, a myriad of constantly moving measurement bars showed alien symbols, displayed next to them.

"I can't read that." When the right hand side of the display changed Cameron found he could read the English alphanumeric text, the names of the three new creatures: the Yonk, the Shinntoh, as well as the Hengtied Portule. Next to each name appeared an ever-moving, modulating measurement bar. Similar, they showed little actual range of movement, with the sole exception of the Hengtied Portule creature. Its readings seemed to be off the charts—rapid variations, as its corresponding measurement bar swept back and forth across the display in bright red.

"Yeah, this one's got some major activity readings . . . what's it mean?" The right-hand display changed again. This time, only two name readouts appeared. Then the left-hand video feed changed to include another feed.

"That's me . . . ," Cameron said, watching a repeating few seconds of himself appear that were taken just moments before. On the right were his own intelligence matrices in comparison to those of the Hengtied Portule. They were almost identical.

Cameron had always prided himself on being fairly intelligent. His free-ride scholarship into Stanford and his success as a HyperCrell intern both supported that notion. Added to that, he had a near-photographic memory. Watching the naked, pinkish-hued creature rising up from its crouch, he wasn't sure how to come to terms with the fact that he was not, by any stretch, the smartest organic being onboard the vessel.

"This creature is, as I believe you humans are prone to say, our ticket out of here," Alice said.

chapter 34

"Explain."

Alice replied, "Unless you are okay with simply eliminating the twenty-seven creatures roaming freely around this craft, we will need assistance putting them back into their respective harnesses. Although I have a high ratio of strength to my limited stature, still, it is nowhere near sufficient to corral these beasts."

"Hey, I'm not so weak myself . . . I'd be helping out with all of that."

In response, she gave his slim build a cursory, head-to-toe, sideways glance.

"Okay, fine, I'm not the Incredible Hulk, but there's a lot more to capturing the beasts than just brute force. Maybe we can lure them back," he said.

"May be it can be a combination of both," she added. "In any event, we will need some help. I'm sure you can see the logic in that, Cameron. I will talk to the Hengtied Portule and try to appeal to its higher reasoning."

"I don't think negotiating with a cyborg is the way to go here. If I were in that creature's position, I'd be leery of promises made by a technological-only advanced being. Nope. I should be the one to speak to him," Cameron said.

"Did I neglect to mention to you that this Hengtied is a carnivore? Also a hungry one?"

"I have my weapon . . . if it comes to that. Hello? Hey, are you listening to me?" he asked.

Alice was staring down at Cameron's trinious bundle, laying on the deck nearby. "May I borrow your Lox unit again?"

"Why . . .? It's just us here. I didn't think vanity went hand in hand with someone cyborgenic."

"You're misreading my intentions. The reason I want to maintain a more organic form has nothing to do with such narcissistic behaviors. But you've made a good point. Any interactions I have with organics in upcoming days will benefit us most if I look less like a technologically advanced being, as you so blatantly put it."

That was a rather strange response on her part, Cameron thought. "Go ahead, feel free to use the Lox unit whenever you need it."

* * *

As it turned out, the Hengtied Portule wouldn't be hungry any time soon. Alice had directed Cameron where to head off to. He found the odd-looking creature, currently feasting within the *Albergone's* primary hold area, hunched over the obviously dead Shinntoh. Apparently, the large lizard never figured out how to traverse either up, or around, the two-foot-high pipe.

The Hengtied Portule spun around, observing Cameron's noisy approach. Walking along a narrow, suspended, port-side catwalk within the hold area, Cameron instinctively grimaced, seeing copious amounts of blood oozing out of the creature's mouth and goopy drippings running down its bare chest. What still remained of the Shinntoh was hidden in the shadows, mostly obscured by the huge—now standing erect—irritated-looking Hengtied.

The catwalk wobbled beneath Cameron's feet, forcing him to reach out his hands to grasp onto the waist-high metal railings. It wasn't lost on him how clumsy he must appear right now. He steadied himself and did his best to raise his palms in the lame gesture of *I come in peace.*

"Hey there . . . not here to disrupt anything . . . friend. That Shinntoh carcass is all yours." The Hengtied stared suspiciously back at him. Alice's voice, suddenly loud, echoed around the Hold. Although they'd worked out this part of the plan together, Cameron was still unsure if it was such a good idea. She was speaking in the alien's tongue . . . *Gibberish,* translating his English into the Hengtied Portule's guttural, mostly phonetic groupings of sounds, while he waited.

The creature spoke with a surprisingly soft and pleasant voice. The string of words made no sense to Cameron.

Alice translated what was said over the static-y PA system. "Who are you . . . what do you want of me?"

"Nothing. Well, other than I don't want you to consider me for your second course meal." *Too cute.* He rephrased his response: "Just don't eat me. I'd like to help you, if you'll let me."

Alice translated. The creature responded with a unique hand gesture. Not exactly *flipping the bird* at him, but Cameron was fairly sure its meaning was along those same lines.

He stared at the creature's back, now turned away, but he could tell by the way it rhythmically moved it had resumed feeding. "I'm told you're an intelligent being, that you would be open to reason. If that's true, I'm hoping we can work together. For my part, I'll get you back to wherever you come from. I give you my word on that." *What would that even mean to this beast? Give you my word? Maybe I should have let Alice do the talking after all.* He waited for her to finish translating. This time the creature didn't bother to face him; the same hand gesture thrust out sideways—impatiently. Cameron, somewhat surprised by that, was equally surprised by his own response. He stifled a laugh—then laughed out loud, unable to keep it in, or even muffled with a hand over his mouth.

Another cold stare was sent Cameron's way over the creature's shoulder, followed by an angry glare. It only triggered more laughter. "I'm sorry. I have no idea why I'm laughing. I'm just a stupid human."

Halfway through Alice's translation, the creature's features softened some. In fact, if Cameron was reading things right, the Hengtied Portule, with a bloody face and dripping claws, was now *laughing* too? A series of weird shrieks—its mouth pulled wide in an apparent smile. Cameron figured laughter was pretty recognizable anywhere, no matter who or what was doing it.

Not wanting to press his luck, Cameron decided to slowly sit down. He let his legs hang down off the side of the catwalk. Twenty feet below was a portion of the deck that was roomy enough for both the Hengtied Portule and the mostly devoured Shinntoh. "Can you tell me about your home? Where you come from?"

A few moments passed before the creature spoke. Its gibberish came fast. Cameron found himself trying to decipher the words it uttered even before Alice began to translate. The essence of its response, more or less, was *who gives a rat's ass.* The beast only wanted to know where they were, what this world was, and where it was located in respect to his own planet?

Alice relayed that information back to the creature directly, then told Cameron the Hengtied's home world was four light years distance from Sang-Morang. "The creature says to take it back now and it may let the human one live."

Cameron thought about returning a hand gesture of his own. Suddenly all the humor in him gone. He was tired and something inside of him snapped. *Enough.* "Alice, translate what I say, word-for-word . . ."

"All right."

"Okay, I'm done with all these niceties. Here's what's going to happen. We will be leaving Sang-Morang within the next few hours. Our next stop will be a world called Winforge, which, by the way, was this ship's intended destination in the first place." Alice's rapid translation was keeping up with his words. "There, I will be reunited with another human I care about, also with my pet Loth . . . although I'm sure the Loth thinks it's the other way around. Are you familiar with that particular breed? The Minal Loth? Forty feet tall, hide as thick and tough as a bulkhead, and jaws that can crush—"

The Hengtied excitedly began spewing out words. By the time Alice finished translating, Cameron was up on his feet, striding closer to the beast.

"I know of the Minal and Griar Loths . . . ," Alice translated.

"Good, because I'm going to make you another promise. You either do the right thing here . . . help me . . . help us . . . or I'll make sure the two of you, you and my pet Loth, spend quality time together interred within an undersized confinement cell on Winforge. I'm running out of time. I'm a little punchy 'cause this is taking way too fucking long. So, are you going to help me, or what? Or maybe I should just shoot you in the head instead?" Cameron pulled the plasma pistol free of his waistband and pointed it. He'd never meant to lose his cool like this, but it all had become too much. He knew Heather was in trouble; might be hurt, or even worse. So he'd decided, one way or another, that this greasy, smelly, bucket-of-bolts ship was heading straight into deep space—today! No matter what.

chapter 35

Heather . . .

S he had noticed the way Thoran Ginott looked at her within the confines of the arena. Standing close enough for
her to smell his musky scent, she'd also noticed the growing,
animalistic lust in his eyes.

She looked about her current surroundings. No longer a
captive held behind metal bars, she still was within a cage,
although this particular cage was luxuriously adorned.
Brought here soon after her conversation with Ginott, she
was told that this was one of his private suites of rooms
within the Winforge arena facilities. Once settled in, two
waif-thin alien females attended her, directed her where to
bathe. Then, together, they spent several hours doing things
to her hair, applying facial makeup in such a way that she
looked like a different person—one more sophisticated, yet

more innocent at the same time. Heather was well aware what all the pampering was leading up to.

Why was it some powerful males felt they could just take what they wanted? She thought of Cam. He was truly wonderful. Honest and considerate and always mindful of her feelings—of her needs. But he was also incredibly naïve. Her thoughts flashed back to the HyperCrell Christmas party, held over a year earlier. They'd been geographically separated for some time by then. She was still at home, living a simple life back in Larksburg Stand, mostly working at the Drake Café. Cam, finishing school at Stanford, living in San Jose, California, was interning at one of the world's premiere tech companies. She'd flown out to see him—a spur of the moment thing—hoping that would bring them closer together. She'd needed to see if their waning relationship was worth salvaging.

She'd never worn evening attire like she did that night—exchanging her Nike's for high heels, her skinny jeans and T-shirts for a low-cut, skimpy, little black dress that seemed to attract the attention of virtually every man in close proximity to her. While Cameron was aware of the attention being drawn her way, in no way was he jealous or worried. But he should have been worried and he should have been less trusting. Not of her, but of the one person he'd placed so high up on a pedestal: his boss, the president and CEO of HyperCrell. The flamboyant, handsome, consummate lady's man, Tony Ordell. She had read about him even prior to her visit. The guy dated supermodels and actresses.

The party was everything she had hoped and expected it to be. Cam was acknowledged for his outstanding work, his contributions at HyperCrell. Ordell lavished him with an ultra-expensive gift, some kind of high-end mountain bike. Cam, beyond doubt, was having the best night of his life, so she never was able to tell him of her ordeal there. When she went to the ladies room, Tony Ordell was waiting right outside the door when she exited. He made a move on her that was so surprising, so abrupt, she still, even today, couldn't come to terms with the events that followed. He'd gently grabbed her wrists, guiding her around a corner into an empty hallway. She resisted his advance, nervously laughing off the inappropriate gesture. By no means was this the first time in her life that she needed to push away a man's advances. But this was Tony Ordell, Cam's boss. She laughed along with him and placed a restraining hand against his chest. But he was strong and pulled her closer; pushed her hard up against a wall. Even today, she could still smell the warm whisky on his breath, feel the bristle of his five o'clock shadow when he kissed her mouth. *Why didn't I fight harder? Did I kiss him back?*

Heather honestly didn't know. Or maybe she didn't want to remember. It was only by chance that a young couple ventured into the same hallway at that exact time. Ordell's attention was disrupted enough for her to slip away. Returning to Cam's side, she never mentioned that his boss—the one he so idolized, the one he hoped to emulate—had just made a sexually inappropriate overture to his girlfriend. Tony Ordell was a pig, but she would never tell Cam of the events which transpired within that isolated hallway.

And now there was another *pig* in her life. But this one, at least physically, was far more powerful and threatening. Again, Heather looked about her surroundings, seeking something she could use as a weapon. There were various-sized flower vases, cups and glasses, and flatware in the kitchenette, including butter knives, but no steak knives. Apparently, this alien culture had gone with the spork concept vs. fork. She couldn't see herself doing much damage with one of those. But that was pretty much a moot point anyway, considering a hovering security droid was stationed at the front entrance to the suite. So here she was, all alone and prettied up, wearing what was akin to a negligee. She'd never worn anything like it before. She glanced nervously toward the door for the tenth time in as many minutes. Soon the lion man would come for her.

Heather felt nauseated—guilty that soon, sometime tonight, something would be stolen from her and Cam. Perhaps it was their future together. Her mind raced. "Think, damn it, think!" If only there was some way to call for the Loth. *But the Loth's secured inside some cage, somewhere,* she thought . . . *what's your next stupid idea?*

Aloud Heather said, "Dim the lights!" Something her skinny alien attendees had shown her how to do. That helped—she felt somewhat better. Leaning back into the overstuffed chair, she closed her eyes then heard something. A rustling sound. She peered out through partially opened eyelids.

She gasped—sat up straight. "Who the hell are you? How did you get in here?"

He tipped his hat and nodded and sat down across from her. His boots rose up, their heels taking residency on the low table separating them. "Here we go with that name thing again," he said, in an unmistakably southern, perhaps Texan, drawl. "To be honest, Missy, a single name isn't entirely *fittin'* . . . on account of I'm not one individual so much as a whole herd of mutually inclined, um, essences." He maneuvered a hay stalk from one side of his mouth to the other.

Heather said, "You're Art. You're Cam's Art!" She looked him over. His scuffed and pointy cowboy boots, his gristled chin, and the black Stetson, perched atop his head. His eyes literally twinkled as he offered back a crooked smile. He grabbed a nearby throw, draped over an adjacent couch, and tossed it at her.

"Best you cover yourself, young lady. This here ain't no brothel and I suspect you're too respectable a kind of individual to be dressed as such."

Heather covered herself up, never taking her eyes off Art. "How . . . ?" she searched for the right words. "Cam said you were derived from a contraption, from his trinious bundle *thing*."

"That is correct."

"But . . . ," she fumbled.

Art gestured toward the security droid, no longer stationed at the front entrance to the apartment but merely feet away. It also was 180 degrees upside down. Its little lights were blinking on and off in such a way that it didn't look mechanically sound.

"You're using the droid? Somehow?"

"That I am, little lady, that I am. As to why I am here . . . that is the million-dollar question. It's because I, *we*, have great affection for your young man. That fella is just plain good, through and through. A *friend* not easy to come by . . . you understand? Of course, you understand."

"Yeah . . . he is that. I can't imagine anyone being a better friend than Cam. But you're not actually here . . . not actually real . . . are you?"

"Sure I am, on both accounts."

"Then you can get me out of here? Protect me—"

"Now don't be puttin' the cart before the horse. There are things I can do and things I simply cannot. Or, better stated, things I won't do. Not much into acts of violence, or supporting such acts either. Just not our way, Heather."

She realized that was the first time he'd used her name. "Then how can you help me? To be frank, I'm in real trouble here. Pep talks and good wishes just won't cut it. Sorry if that's a little blunt."

"Blunt works for me. Call it like it is. Yes, straight talk is fine."

Heather waited for something concrete, something she could hang her proverbial hat on.

Art retracted his boots from the table and set them down on the floor. He leaned forward—his expression now serious. "You've got smarts. A good head on those fine shoulders. That's all you will need to get yourself out of this jam, I promise you that."

So this is just a pep talk, Heather thought. Her shoulders visibly slumped.

"Now, don't be doing that. I am here to help you. You can take that to the bank. But it's not our way to intervene. Being here like this breaks a whole slew of rules, but Cam is worth it. I suspect you are too, so listen up. There's a lot I'm going to wing by you and I talk real fast. We don't have a heck of a lot of time before that jackass comes storming through the front door over there."

chapter 36

Cameron . . .

The Hengtied Portule had a strange given name. A name the creature repeated several times in succession before Cameron said, "Come on, that's seven syllables. How 'bout I just call you Joe, for short?"

Alice, standing at Cameron's side—now back to her more Thidion-looking, attractive self—translated. She didn't bother to convey the Hengtied's actual verbal response back—undoubtedly, a crude one.

All twenty-six creatures, running unrestrained within the *Albergone's* vast primary hold area, were, for the most part, weak and ravenous. Luring them back to their respective holding areas using remnants of the Shinntoh carcass as bait was tedious and uneventful work. Cameron was well aware that he and Alice could not have accomplished this feat without Hengtied Joe's help. Big enough to be a physical threat, he was aggressive enough to swipe his lethal claws across any exposed flanks when a rebelling creature resisted or acted up. Although some of the creatures were many times the size of the Hengtied Portule, fight wasn't in them. They only wanted something to eat; to be left alone.

It took them two full days. Each waking hour that passed, Cameron felt his hope of finding Heather unharmed, or even still alive, dwindling. He watched as Joe fastened the last of the oversized harness restraints around the Prinwhin's center mass area. Clenching and unclenching his fists, Cameron shook his head, still thinking about Heather. She wasn't built for this kind of lifestyle. *What on earth was he thinking back then?* If it weren't for his persistence, she would still be on Earth, safe and sound with her family, living in Larksburg Stand. But at least they would be on their way soon. The hiccups and delays certainly had to be over—*I'm coming, Heather. . . .*

Joe stood back and assessed his handiwork. He watched as the Prinwhin finished eating the last of the Shinntoh scraps. Both Cameron and Alice waited on an adjacent catwalk. "Thank you . . . Joe," Cameron said. But before Alice could translate, Joe was speaking—looking even more perturbed than usual.

Cameron looked over at Alice, who was silently listening to what had grown into a long rant and nodding her head. When the creature finally quieted down, Alice turned her eyes to Cameron.

"Joe wants to know which creature we want to sacrifice."

"Sacrifice?"

"Yes."

"Why would I want to sacrifice any of them? Why go to all the trouble of capturing them in the first place?" *Then Cameron suddenly got it.* He watched the Prinwhin take a final, disgusting-sounding swallow. "There's nothing for them to eat?"

Alice nodded her head in assent, while Joe stared up at them from his position in the Prinwhin's holding area below.

"The food replicators? There are a number of them onboard. Food's not great, but—"

Alice cut in, "We'd need one point five tons of food each day to keep this lot alive. There's not a food replicator in existence, that I know of, capable of producing that kind of output."

Joe began speaking and this time Cameron got the gist of what he was saying. In effect, it would have to be Cameron doing the killing. In other words, someone else would need to get their hands dirty.

Cameron said, "One must die, so the rest can live . . . is that what you're saying? That you want me to choose the creature . . . and kill it?"

Joe didn't wait for Alice's translation. The beast simply nodded.

Cameron pointed to the ginormous Prinwhin behind him. "Would the rest of the creatures eat Prinwhin meat?"

Alice was needed to translate the question. Joe then replied that he did not know for sure.

"Well . . . would you? Eat it?" Cameron asked.

Joe smiled back and said, "Yes," in accented English.

Cameron's gaze moved higher as he searched the eyes of the extraordinary starfish-like creature. He wondered if it was aware of what they were saying—what they were discussing? That its very fate was at stake? He was surprised at the level of sadness he now felt. He didn't want to kill this animal.

"Wait here," Cameron said to Alice, moving along the catwalk. He descended the short flight of stairs to where Joe stood. Joe's eyes went to the pistol in his hand.

"I'll kill it," Cameron said. I can then use plasma fire to make manageable portions."

Joe took several steps back as Cameron raised the plasma pistol, taking aim at a point between the Prinwhin's large watery eyes. He stole a quick glance over his shoulder at Alice, whose face was expressionless. *Of course it was.* He turned back to the helpless creature. *Don't look into those eyes,* he told himself—but did anyway. Why is this so difficult? He knew why. The Prinwhin was just one more amazing creature he'd come across—didn't it deserve to live? He began tightening his finger around the trigger.

"Wait!"

Cameron turned back to her.

She said, "We can be at Winforge within two days. I'll need to make further modifications to the propulsion system, but I think I can do it." She turned to Joe and spoke a few words in his language. Joe nodded back, though he didn't look happy.

"What?" Cameron asked.

"I asked him if all the beasts onboard this ship could survive for another two days without sustenance. You saw his response."

Which meant he, too, would go without food for another two days. Cameron only hoped he—the one lone human here—wouldn't become too tempting a sight for Joe over this extended span of time. He lowered his hand. "What can I do to help ready the ship for travel?" he asked, still gazing up at the Prinwhin.

"The bottom of the hold opens . . . large horizontal slats rotate into a vertical position, allowing direct access to the outside world. The accumulated dung within the hold must be dumped, before the atmosphere in here gets any worse. Before the filters get completely clogged."

"That makes sense. This place could use a good airing out," Cameron said.

She continued, "The previous *Albergone* crew manually power-blasted with steam guns all the lower bulkheads and the opened slats. You will find me in engineering, if you have any further questions." She turned and walked toward the closest ascending staircase.

"Where are the controls to open the hold slats?" Cameron yelled after her.

"Three catwalks farther below into the hold. But wear protective overalls. They're on a rack, down there somewhere."

Cameron looked over to Joe. "You're going to just love this next job."

chapter 37

Cameron heard Alice's static-y voice blare overhead through the hold's PA system. "As soon as you're ready, we can attempt to make our ascent."

Cameron, standing with his arms out, his legs wide apart, slowly turned around so Joe could power-spray his reverse side. He was covered from head to toe with dung. Both of them were. The only difference, there weren't any thick, rubber-like overalls—along with a slipover-the-head hood with a green-tinted window to see out of—that were large enough for Joe to wear. Only moments before, Cameron had power-sprayed the constantly complaining creature. He was thankful he had no idea what Joe was saying—what insults were being thrown his way.

Daylight was streaming in from below, through a series of big open slats along the *Albergone's* underbelly. Each louvered slat was now relatively clean and drip-drying in the crisp Sang-Morang breezes billowing in.

Joe turned off the power-sprayer and tossed the contraption, along with its attached water hose, onto the deck. Its technology was fairly basic; just pull the trigger and incredibly hot steam would shoot out of the nozzle end. The simple fact that Joe had no problem figuring out the simple mechanism meant something too. The creature was not barbaric. Putting its eating practices aside, Joe clearly was intelligent—capable of linguistic communication, and also the use of mechanical devices. Cameron wondered what else the highly lethal, fifteen-foot-tall beast was capable of? He reminded himself to be wary whenever he turned his back to Joe; and remember also they were not friends.

Cameron moved across to a series of metal hooks mounted onto a bulkhead. There were six separate sets of hooks holding overalls, which hung like lifeless carcasses, devoid of their muscular and skeletal systems. He removed his hood and draped it onto one of the available hooks. Stepping free of his own oversized overalls, Cameron said, "I'm heading up to the bridge now." He pointed at himself first then upward. "Can you get those slats closed off?" pointing at Joe, then downward where the welcomed fresh air and daylight were entering in. He peppered his question in with a few Hengtied Portule guttural words he'd picked up while conversing with Joe over the last few hours.

Cameron also recognized several of Joe's quick responses; pretty sure they were barbs and insults. But the Hengtied Portule acquiesced just the same, heading off toward a lower platform where the slat controls were located. Cameron debated if he should watch him, make sure he did it correctly. But doing so would be more of an insult than anything he could say to the big alien.

Cameron climbed higher and higher, utilizing the series of interconnecting back-and-forth catwalks and the ascending metal stairways. He listened to the loud, mixed chorus of alien noises, coming at him from all around. The bellowing cries of one creature rising in octaves above the sharp chirps of another creature. Thunderous guttural tones that you'd expect to hear from a ginormous bull frog momentarily eclipsed the others—then came sharp whooping calls you'd expect to come from some kind of jungle bird. Put all together, though, the sounds melded into some kind of primal song not unpleasant to listen to. In fact, it stirred something deep within Cameron. Closing his eyes, he tried to determine just what that was. *Strange, a raw innocence was being conveyed, echoing mournfully throughout the hold.* It occurred to Cameron that he, to some degree, was now responsible for these beasts. Sure, killers—probably each and every one in their own right—but just the same, he couldn't ignore the fact he was responsible, kind of obligated, for their very survival. To what degree, he wasn't entirely sure. He thought of the Loth—a welcome obligation. Soon he would be delivering these desperate souls to what he imagined was a terrible place—to Winforge, where he'd trade the lot of them for Heather and the Loth.

Reaching the final set of stairs leading up out of the hold, Cameron slowed then stopped. Turning around, he observed the cavernous space below from his high-up vantage point. He smiled, as the loud cacophony of animalistic sounds rose up from below. It occurred to Cameron that he'd purposely, albeit unconsciously, avoided scrutinizing the majority of these wild, unique—beyond any doubt—amazing creatures. *Why? You know why. It's because you're about to deliver the whole lot of them to what will undoubtedly end in a long, drawn out, miserable demise.*

"Alice? Can you hear me?"

"I can hear you," she replied.

"Take us up into space as soon as you're ready. I don't need to be in the bridge for you to do that. I'll join you later. First, there's something else I have to do. Something that'll take me a good bit of time." Cameron headed down the stairway—back the way he'd come.

chapter 38

Heather . . .

S he sat alone in the posh, dimly lit, apartment, thinking about all the things Art had mentioned—what she needed to do to survive the next few hours, or maybe days. But the one question that she so needed an answer to, she hadn't even asked him. Perhaps she was too afraid of what the answer might be. *Was Cam okay—was he still alive?*

She tried recalling all Art had said to her. What he'd gone over, and then went over again, for good measure. She soon realized Art's whole *country bumpkin*, Texan drawl thing was an act. *Of course it was!* Art was a technological marvel, created from another realm, was her guess. What he was asking her to do would be highly technical too. Sure, she easily could use an iPhone, a laptop, or program a microwave oven—but what he now was expecting her to do would be near impossible!

Eyes leveled on the entrance to the suite, Heather let her gaze shift toward the droid—now, *seemingly* operating normally; back hovering in a sentry position near the door. She'd learned there was also an identical-looking droid sentry positioned mere feet away, on the other side of the door.

Wrapping her arms around herself, she thought, *No way will I be able to pull this off.* She then thought about Art's parting words: *Some day, maybe soon, maybe years from now, the day will come when you'll catch a glimpse of your own reflection. Tell me . . . will you like who you see standing there?*

In other words, Heather thought—*Buck up, missy, and be brave. Either that, or regret how things went down for the rest of your life.*

* * *

Thoran Ginott entered through the front door, then made his way over to the kitchenette, purposely not acknowledging Heather, still sitting quietly on the couch. He'd had a challenging day having lost one of his most prized and profit-making beasts—a seventy-five-year-old Gonka. He poured himself a stiff drink, studying its dark-amber color, before downing it in one gulp. Only then did he glance at her, making no attempt to hide his contempt for the dour-looking human.

He mentally replayed the day's events as he poured himself another drink. It wasn't even an actual match, only a mere practice session, the readying of the recent arrival of the Minal Loth. He had instructed the Gonka to hold back, get a feel for the other creature. Determine both its strengths and weaknesses so this information could later be conveyed to the *Tammer* prior to their public exhibition match. But the Loth had moved incredibly fast, considering its bulk. It had wasted no time bringing the Gonka down then viciously killing it. A fan favorite, the old Gonka's death meant the loss of many millions of future ackneds. He slammed the glass down onto the counter, frustrated.

Ginott removed his suit jacket and began to unbutton his shirt. He let both the jacket and shirt fall to the floor as he came around the counter. Her eyes were on him—*was that fear in her eyes?* He certainly hoped so. Soon, this young human would experience true terror. Not enough to actually kill her but enough, making the evening ahead somewhat worthwhile for him personally.

He stood before her and took in her natural beauty. "In there . . . to my quarters."

The girl pulled her eyes away from him, staring at the set of closed double doors. She rose to her feet, and hesitated. Staring back at him, she said, "Please . . . don't do this."

Ginott raised the back of his hand high across his chest—threatening a backhand to her face. "Move!" he ordered.

She did as told. He watched her nervously walk toward his sleeping quarters. The sheerness of her garment provided him with a glimpse of her nakedness beneath. She opened the doors then disappeared into the darkness within. Following and now standing in the open doorway, he peered into the dimly lit space, watching as she pulled down the bed covers. Lying down, she slid between the sheets. When she looked up at him, tears were brimming in her eyes. *Good!*

At that moment, Heather—the *real* Heather—watched the course of events unfold from a closet back in the main room. She peered through an inch-wide gap; thankful the slightly open closet door had not been noticed. The security droid had moved, was positioned just outside the bedroom door, and, just like before, it was upside down and askew—its little lights flashing on and off irregularly. Art, it seemed, was still controlling it. He'd also traded his Stetson and cowboy boots attire for a skimpy negligee that now covered a young, human, female body. An exact replica of *Heather's own body*. Having watched this Heather facsimile—first sitting on the couch then nervously striding into the bedroom—was crazy weird. It so easily could have been her. The plan was her projected doppelganger would find a way to keep Thoran Ginott occupied, although never actually letting him lay a hand on *her . . . it*.

Heather silently pushed the closet door open, crept to the bedroom's entrance, then carefully peered in. Six feet away, Ginott was standing in near-total darkness—like one of the towering statues situated within the arena. She could see he was naked—a swath of light exposed his back. His broad shoulders tapered down to narrow hips and round, muscular buttocks—every inch of his skin was covered in a fine layer of light-colored fur. She saw him take a step closer to the bed. All she could see of her look-alike was the reflection of light in her, *its*, eyes.

Heather knew she should already have left the apartment, be making her escape right now. But she was captivated by the situation—by this lion of a beast. She moved, ever so slightly, to gain a better view into the bedroom, then froze. *Why hadn't she given it any thought?* That her mere presence outside could cast a shadow onto the floor inside? She watched Ginott's profile abruptly turn away from the bed. Aware *something* had changed he listened intently. Heather didn't dare move. Didn't even breathe. Ten . . . fifteen . . .

twenty seconds passed before he refocused his attention back on the captive, now lying in his bed.

"I have to . . . um . . . go to the bathroom. Like really bad."

Heather made a face. *Do I really sound like that?* As covers rustled and the fake Heather scurried about the bedroom, Heather slowly backed away, still dressed in the same negligee. Earlier, she'd already looked for her clothes, but they were nowhere to be found in the apartment. Spotting Ginott's jacket lying in a heap on the floor, she grabbed it up. She slid her arms into the sleeves then wrapped the garment around her. It came down to her knees and she had to push the sleeves way up to use her hands. Back inside the bedroom, she heard her body-double moving on to the next step in their plan. She/Art would start acting erratic, all crazy-like. Let him chase *her* around the bedroom—dodge, weaving his advances, as long as he'd participate.

Heather tiptoed to the apartment's front entrance and, taking extra care, opened the door. Slipping out through the door backward and into the corridor, she gently pulled the door shut. *Clank!* Startled by the loud sound of the latch mechanism, she listened intently for other sounds—like Ginott's running footfalls on the other side of the door. But when all remained quiet, she slowly turned away from the door. *Shit!* She barely stifled a scream. The other sentry droid was right there, hovering no more than two feet away. But, similar to its identical-looking companion back inside the apartment, this droid, too, was flipped upside down, not looking fully operational. *Thank you, Art.*

Off and running—Heather's mind was racing equally fast as she tried to remember all that Art had told her, where to go, what to do. She ran past the two intersecting corridors he'd mentioned then made a left down the next, smaller, hallway—one leading to a green painted metal door. A sign was above the door, but she couldn't decipher the alien letters. Once inside, she found she was surrounded by drab-looking concrete in a dimly lit stairwell. Listening hard, she determined there was no one else within these tomb-like confines. Hesitating, she glanced toward the steps leading up and the ones leading down, trying to remember what Art had told her to do at this point. Suddenly a door banged open, several flights up.

chapter 39

The Loth . . .

It listened to the abundant sounds surrounding it within the keep, where there were constant deep inhalations and exhalations, also the stench of different gasses passing. The distant sound of one creature's whimpers undoubtedly derived from a very bad dream. This was the enormous enclosure where all the larger beasts were kept secured, when they weren't being ushered through underground passageways onto one of the arena fields to fight. The Loth did not like this place; he did not like fighting, unless it was a means of survival, or the resulting consequence of a hunt. The Loth missed home, missed hunting near the three streams. Missed sleeping next to the metal vehicle—missed its human. *Where was Cameron?* The Loth thought about the other one: The other human, Cameron's mate, Heather. *She is here . . . somewhere. Will she come for me? Take me to Cameron?*

Blood seeped down from an open wound high up on one of its tentacles. For hours now, the Loth had repeatedly licked the gaping lesion. Only now had the bleeding started to lessen. Hungry, the creature looked about its holding cell for a possible remnant, something left over from its previous day's feedings. It stared at the heaps of dung and the dried saliva mounds, but there was nothing edible to be found.

Other large beasts were caged nearby. One looked like a Greely Beast but was something else. The handlers called it a Thillip. It had been fed today, as well as another large beast, called a Tammer, that filled most of its cage. Directly across from the Loth, it too had been fed. What few bites the Loth had eaten of the old, bitter-tasting Gonka creature back within the arena had left a bad taste in its mouth. If Gonkas lived near the three streams, the Loth would not hunt them. Bitter meat.

A loud noise came from above—like the loudest of thunderstorms at the three streams. The Loth's cage—all the other cages, too—was open to the sky above. The Loth could see and feel the heat radiating from the large daytime star during the day, and witness the brilliance of many stars during the darkness of night. Many space vehicles passed overhead both night and day, but mostly at night. The Loth vaguely comprehended the concept behind spacefaring vehicles, but thinking about such things held little interest for the Minal Loth.

The Loth stopped licking its injury to, once again, survey its surroundings. The other beasts were all sleeping, except for one: the Tammer. The beast that looked so similar to itself, only much larger. The Loth hadn't been led into the arena against the Tammer yet. *Was it even possible to defeat such a gargantuan creature?* Loth did not fear for its own life. It merely contemplated whether the meat on the Tammer would be better tasting than that on the Gonka.

* * *

Heather, nearly out of breath and trying to subdue the sounds of her heavy breathing, took the steps down two at a time. She suspected that whoever it was, now above and behind her, was doing the same thing. *Louder footsteps, so a man not a woman.* It was a race to the bottom. As she came around the last tight bend within the stairwell, she realized it was a race she had won. Reaching the door handle, she pulled. The door didn't budge. She pulled harder—this time planting her feet and using both hands, putting all her weight behind it. The door remained firmly shut in place. *Aren't there universal codes requiring stairwell doors to remain open? Isn't this an egregious safety hazard?* Heather thought. Only then did she remember she wasn't home on Earth. On Winforge, they probably played by a whole different set of rules and regulations. The sounds of approaching footfalls above were getting louder. She glanced about the confined space. No other doors. No *nothing!* There was no escape and in mere seconds, her pursuer would come around the stairs' final bend. *But who could be chasing her?* Definitely not Thoran Ginott, as this person's descent began at least several levels higher than Ginott's suite within the building. Perhaps, though, Ginott contacted one of his people—sent out some 'all-points bulletin' type of thing. But she doubted that, too. Art would find a way to keep the alien boss fully occupied. Heather pictured *lion man*, chasing her body-double around the bed; around the whole damn apartment.

"There you are."

Heather, her back up against the exit door, didn't reply to the tall, extremely muscular young man now standing before her. He was tan and pretty much naked except for a tiny jockstrap type thing just barely covering his privates. He was Hercules incarnate—his every movement caused a further eruption of huge muscles rippling and flexing.

Quickly checking the lower outside pockets of Ginott's jacket, her fingers touched two objects—a wallet, billfold-type of thing, and a thin rectangle. Alien version of a cellphone? Maybe some sort of communication devise? The man watched her. Perplexed, his thin, delicate brows knitted together. She checked the inside breast pocket on the jacket's left side, then the one on the right. She had no idea what she now held in her hand, but she withdrew it anyway, pointing it at the man. "Don't come any closer to me!" she shouted, hearing her voice echo off the concrete walls.

He nodded. "I am not here to harm you . . . just to inform you that Mr. Stillman has requested your immediate presence at the entrance into the arena. And . . . that is a nasty little weapon you found in that pocket. But it just so happens you are holding it all wrong. You would need to flip it around, if you don't want to shoot yourself in the neck."

"You're lying . . . just saying that to save yourself from being shot."

The man shrugged.

Heather stole a glance at the object held tightly within her outstretched hands. *Maybe he was right.* The small opening, perhaps a barrel, was indeed facing right at her. *Why would anyone make a weapon that didn't look anything like a gun?* She next wondered, *Where's the flippin' handle, or the trigger, for that matter?*

"So who are you, again?"

"They call me Perro . . . just Perro. I'm pretty much just a performer in the show." He repeatedly flexed his prominent pectoral muscles, and then smiled down at her. "Years ago, I was abducted from Earth . . . but I do not remember that . . . I was a child. Now I do what I'm told to do, which often involves parading around naked in front of many thousands."

"What's with all the bruises? Your lip is split . . . you have what looks to be the beginnings of black eye."

"Opening show. To get the audience hyped up . . . excited. You know, before the main event with the Tammer? I got a little banged up . . . she surprised me, that's all." He rubbed at his jaw, which was also turning a little purple now that she looked more closely. His reference to his opponent being female left little doubt as to who that 'she' might have been—*Manny.*

"Anyway, I'm due back for my next appearance."

"So you're human? From Earth . . ."

Perro stared back at her blank-faced.

"And who is this Stillman character?" she asked.

"He is not a character . . . everyone here works for him."

"I thought everyone worked for Ginott."

Descending the rest of the stairs, he stood before her. The top of her head barely reached the bottom of his chin. Being this close, she could tell that he was fairly young—perhaps twenty-five.

He smiled. "God, I love being around other humans again . . . I always hoped to go back to Earth someday."

She wondered who was stopping him. He'd said he was a performer—does this Stillman guy own him? "Well, right now might not be the best time for that," she said.

Perro laughed. "I guess you don't know about the Cosmic Axiom," he said.

"What's that?"

"Everyone knows what the Cosmic Axiom is . . . and it doesn't just apply to Earth. Basically, you don't bring advanced alien technology, even the knowledge that there are alien civilizations, to still-developing worlds. It's a death sentence if you do that sort of thing and if you're caught. With what I know . . . I can't go back."

Heather gave him a sideways glance, not sure if he really was leveling with her. Who would know if such a thing ever happened? And who would enforce such a thing? But now was not the right time for such questions. "My name is—"

"Yeah, I know who you are, lady. It's Heather."

"Can you please stop calling me *lady*; we're probably close to the same age, or just about the same age."

"Oh, sorry! You look . . . older." He tilted his head and gestured to the door behind her. "If you stand aside, I'll show you how to open that."

chapter 40

Cameron . . .

He stood before the one-legged creature. Reaching two stories high, as it stood upright it balanced its tremendous girth upon its lone appendage with apparent ease. It apparently moved, when not harnessed to a bulkhead, by hopping—a kind of pogo stick motion.

Joe made an indecipherable comment. Cameron hadn't expected the short-tempered Hengtied Portule to tag along with him as he made his rounds; an attempt to introduce himself to each of the other twenty-six creatures onboard. He could tell that Joe, making his opinion clear, thought the overture was either a waste of time, stupid, or both. What Cameron deeply felt, though there was no way he'd be able to communicate it to Joe, was that they were all in this together. If he didn't take the time, at least attempt to get to know these beasts—convey he wasn't going to harm them—he would be no better than the late Captain Wilcox and his barbarous crew.

"That one, Cameron, is a Bon-Bon . . . from a world about twenty-five light-years distance from here."

Cameron spun around, seeing Alice standing behind him. "Thought you were still on the bridge."

"I'm now tapped into all of the *Albergone's* primary systems. I'm fully capable of multi-tasking, you know."

"Cool. So where are we?"

"I've set a course for Winforge, keeping our speed in check until I know our antimatter containment repairs can withstand the buildup of extended heat levels."

A projected display popped into view in front of the Bon-Bon. Cameron scanned the full range of the species' characteristics, as well as its biological diagnostics. Alice presented the information on the display in English.

"I can't say this one looks all that formidable," Cameron said.

Alice tilted her head. "It can hop up to five times its own height. When it lands on that one single appendage, called a *cleath*, it's like a highly concentrated hammer blow. Quite deadly, I assure you," she added.

"What do you think? Will it be able to understand me? If I talk to it?"

Alice nodded, "Maybe . . . with my assistance, but only to some degree. Keep your sentences short and simplistic."

Cameron took a step closer. Craning his neck, he peered into the Bon-Bon's big brown eyes. "I'm sorry you were taken from your home."

"Simpler than that," Alice instructed.

"We are sorry." He waited for Alice to translate, using a series of strange cawing sounds.

"And we will not hurt you." He asked Alice to translate the sentiment.

"Soon you will be freed." Cameron said and waited for Alice to make the appropriate cawing sounds. The Bon-Bon began to struggle against the harness holding its lone limb in place. Eventually, it made several noises—similar to the ones Alice made—back at her.

She said, "It's going to be the same for all of them. They don't understand why they are here. They are hungry. They want to be freed."

Joe nodded his head then uttered a series of his own strange noises.

Alice, translating again, "He said—"

"I think I know what Joe said," Cameron cut in, "something like, *I told you so.*" Cameron gave the Bon-Bon a half-hearted wave as he headed off toward the next captive creature. It didn't matter that they didn't trust his intentions. Why would they, after the ordeal they had been put through? Humans had already proven they were their enemy. Still, he planned to go ahead. Try just the same.

"This next species is the smallest of all the captured creatures," Alice said.

* * *

By the time Cameron made it back to the bridge two hours later, he had settled into a deep funk. Joe was right, after all; his intent to reassure all the captive creatures was an apparent waste of time. Not one of the captive beasts was receptive to his attempt to communicate, let alone belie their fears. And, to be honest, why should they believe him?

Slumped down in his chair, he used the toe of one foot to keep the swivel chair spinning around and around. He watched his 360 degree view of the *Albergone's* command center pass before his eyes in a constant blur.

"Why don't you stop this self-wallowing and do something constructive?"

"Because I'm a fuckup . . . you don't want a fuckup helping you. It's contagious."

"Self-pity is not contagious," Alice said back, from her station across the compartment.

Cameron made a snarky face at her then dragged his foot, slowing his chair spinning to a stop. "It's not self-pity when there's actual, clear evidence of how one has screwed things up . . . screwed others' lives up."

"Heather is a grown person. She made her own decisions and she knew the risks of life in outer space."

"Let's change the subject," he said. "How 'bout you give me some good news instead. Like you're about to kick this rickety tin can into light-speed."

Alice stopped what she was doing to spin around and face him. "I'm afraid I cannot tell you that. The repairs I made are not holding."

"Oh, come on! Seriously? Can't you go back in . . . do it over again . . . better?"

"Maybe, but not while we're en route. And not while we're in space."

"Where are we . . . relative to Winforge? Can you show me?" he asked, getting up from his chair.

The display directly over Alice's head came alive. A diagram displayed the closest primary star systems.

"We are here." She gestured toward a blinking blip on the left side of the display. "Winforge is there," she said, pointing to a somewhat larger blip on the right side of the display. "We've traversed approximately half the distance."

"To Winforge?"

"No, of course not! Half the distance to the nearest Slip Band."

Cameron already knew it was through Slip Bands that spaceships were able to transmigrate distances, near instantaneously, through deep space. He also knew that in traveling from Earth to Sang-Morang, they would have to pass through four of these spatial anomalies. "How many Slip Band junctures between us and Winforge?"

"Three."

"And we're not even close to the first one?"

"No."

"How long will the repairs take?"

"The longer it takes, the worse the prognosis that effective repairs can be made at all."

Cameron pointed, "What about this star system here? Looks like . . . shit, thirteen exoplanets. Maybe one—"

"None of those worlds orbit their two stars in what your Earth scientists would refer to as the goldilocks zone."

"Uh huh. Got it . . . the circumstellar habitable zone, or CHZ; sometimes referred to as the ecosphere, or even the liquid-water belt."

Alice studied him with renewed interest. "I had forgotten you have an adequate memory, for a biologic."

"So where then?"

"Next system over has several good candidates. I suggest this one, it's the most similar to both Earth and Sang-Morang."

"Great! So what are the drawbacks," he asked.

"There are a few. From my limited database references, this planet is completely uncharted. Undocumented. I do not believe this world has been explored . . . perhaps never visited by extraterrestrial life."

"So we could be going from the frying pan into the fire?"

"That's a stupid analogy. Why don't we say instead it will be very dangerous, that we'll make our time there short?"

He looked at her. Alice, perhaps not realizing it, was becoming more and more human-like with her mannerisms and irreverent, sometimes sarcastic, rhetoric. She must have realized she was being scrutinized. She looked away and busied herself with the control panel before her.

He continued, "Whatever. How long will it take to get there? To this uncharted exoplanet?"

"Five days. But the *Albergone* cannot withstand that timespan."

Frustrated, Cameron simply stared at Alice, his face blank.

"Maybe . . . we can ratchet up our speed . . . to near-light speed," she said. "A short burst that will carry us close to that star system. Then we shut down the antimatter reactor and coast the rest of the way."

"But we could . . . what . . . explode? Like, if your calculations are off?"

"That is always a possibility, but the odds of that happening are very low."

"Of blowing up?"

"Of my calculations being off. Blowing up is a stronger possibility."

"We don't seem to have a lot of options here. I say we go for it."

Alice nodded, showing no sign of trepidation. "Perhaps you should get some rest. The captain's quarters are now free."

He thought about the video feed—the captain blowing his head off in that very compartment. "Yeah, I think I'll find a different one. One more thing, though, before I go."

Alice raised her brows in a most human-like gesture.

"If the *Albergone's* reactor red-lines, or whatever you call it, will there be time to . . . prepare for the worst?"

"Are you serious?"

"Yeah."

"No . . . we'll be . . . all of us . . . everything . . . atomized within the blink of an eye."

chapter 41

Cameron awoke with a start to a loud overhead klaxon blaring. It took him several moments to recall where he was. Then he remembered, he was on the *Albergone*—in a crewmember's quarters. A real pigsty, the crusty bedcovers smelled of sour body odors, while piles of clothes and discarded meal trays were strewn about the deck.

He swung his legs over the side of the bunk, rubbing sleep from his eyes. He was about to call out to Alice, like he did onboard the *Primion*, when he realized where he was. He seriously doubted this relic of a ship would support such a high-tech level of inter-ship communication. He stood and searched for his boots, hidden amongst all the litter on the cluttered deck. At least the bridge was close by, he figured. Pulling one boot on and then the other without tying them, he scurried out from the sleeping quarters. Hurrying now, he headed for the bridge situated at the far end of the corridor he was on. The klaxon continued to blare. There was also another sound, something high-pitched—a kind of squealing. Approaching the bridge, he noticed the hatchway into it was closed. Prior to now, it had always been open. The constant blaring noise was making it difficult to think straight. He used his fist to pound on the hatch. "Hey . . . can you let me in?"

The hatchway slid open.

"Hurry . . . get inside!" Alice shouted.

Cameron did as told, and the hatch quickly slid back in place behind him. "Can you shut that thing off? What the hell is going on?" he asked.

The klaxon noise suddenly stilled, but not the other sounds, like the distant squealing. "I don't like the sound of that. Talk to me."

Alice turned her chair around to face him, dressed in different clothes. At some point in the night she'd exchanged her *Albergone* officer's uniform for more casual, fitted attire. Pants and a white blouse—its sleeves rolled halfway up her forearms, and she'd also brushed out her hair. "The Warg Hammon died three-and-a-half hours ago."

Cameron tried to remember which creature that was. "That the one with feathers?"

"That's right."

"Well, that's unfortunate. But, honestly, did you need to sound a damn klaxon? You could have just told me . . . like when I woke-up later."

"The klaxon is the *Albergone's* auto-response to an emergency; to unforeseeable situations. I don't know what they are called, call them creepers . . . small parasites, that have infiltrated key systems within the ship. The little things eat just about anything, including power lines and couplings placed within bulkheads and consoles, causing all kinds of havoc."

"I don't get the correlation . . . the dead Warg Hammon and the parasites—creepers," Cameron said, mystified.

"My assumption is that they first came onboard hidden beneath the feathers of the Warg Hammon. They didn't want to hang around a now-dead carcass."

Just then, something scurried overhead, scampering from one side of the compartment to the other, and Cameron took note. The unmistakable sound of multiple small claws, clattering against metal, perhaps within an air duct. "Just how serious a situation is this, since things already seemed pretty bad?"

"Worse," she said, hurrying over to another console. Tall and vertical, it stood close to the bridge entrance. She tapped on various touch-sensitive buttons.

"Can we still make it . . . to that unnamed world?"

"Clay."

"What?"

"I've designated its name to be Clay. The ground there, I believe, is comprised of some kind of clay," Alice said.

"Can we make it to Clay?" he asked, not hiding his growing irritation.

"I really don't know. We've already lost functionality of several key systems. One of which you'll soon notice."

"Environmental." Cameron then sighed in exasperation. Alice didn't need to affirm the statement. Air within the bridge already smelled stale. "Stop! Just stop what you're doing for a second." Raising his palms up like a street cop directing traffic, he continued, "I'd rather die fast . . . atomized by an antimatter explosion, than suffocate, or get picked apart by small parasites. You get what I'm saying?"

"I do." Sitting back down, she stared straight ahead—expressionless.

Cameron sat down next to her and waited for her to say something. Eventually, she said, "I can only come up with one possibility for both you and the creatures onboard to survive."

"That sounds promising . . . at least."

Her eyes glistened with moisture. She gazed at him with sadness and spoke softly. "I'll have to go back in, back into the containment area. I'll need to physically hold the structure closed where it's gaping. Hold it in place for an extended acceleration period. This is something I must do myself. Not something a droid would be able to accomplish. Cameron . . . you need to understand . . . there will be nothing left of me . . . afterward."

He heard a break in her voice that took him by surprise. He searched her face, looking for a reason. "I'm sorry, Alice, I know what that means for you. But we have the Lox device. We'll get you back again . . . right?"

She shook her head, so subtly he barely noticed it. "There's no place to put my . . . consciousness. Where to put *me*."

Cameron, not completely following along, suddenly understood—understood she was previously able to store her consciousness, *her beingness*, into the substantial memory banks of the big TAM computer onboard the *Primion*. Or even into a Thidion droid. "You're telling me this ship has nothing even closely adequate to download your memories into?"

"No, that's one of the key systems being infected by the parasites. Power lines to the memory banks have been affected." Alice lowered her head and closed her eyes.

"There has to be *something* we can do. God, anything!" Cameron said.

"Do you think I like any of this?" she asked, clearly angry now. She stood up—her face more animated than he'd ever seen it. "Do you think because I'm not flesh and bone, like you, that I don't have feelings? Real emotions? That I'm not afraid to die?"

Cameron couldn't speak. Didn't know what to say.

"You never had a clue, Cameron. You assumed I was only some kind of impersonal robot. Just a *thing*!"

"No . . . I never—"

"Yes . . . maybe not on purpose, but that is the truth. You never stopped to consider I could have true feelings. Ones, possibly, I shouldn't have. I don't know where, or even how, I acquired them."

"I didn't know, Alice. Honest!"

"There are a lot of things you don't know. Too many things, like the simple fact I love you. Yes, deal with it . . . a robot is in love with you. A robot that knows you're in love with someone else, someone much more suitable for you. Another human. A perfect human."

Cameron hated himself in that moment. He never wanted to hurt Alice, probably his best friend—human or non-human—ever. And he really loved her, too, just not in the same way. Tears filled his eyes; he felt his heart breaking in his chest. "Please just . . . just talk to me a little while longer. We can figure something out. There's other options . . . always other options."

Alice wiped the tears off her cheeks as she backed away from him.

How is it she is crying—do cyborgs cry?

"I've left you detailed directions here within the *Albergone's* limited memory databanks as well as copies you can take with you," she gestured to his trinious bundle lying on the deck. "They're video clips—two hundred and five, to be exact. They are voice-searchable and will explain everything. Landing this ship on Clay; the steps necessary to make all required repairs to this ship. I do so wish I could have done more for you, Cameron. My time was limited."

"Please . . . ," was all he could say, his throat tightening.

"Do not follow me. Do not leave this compartment, for any reason, until the onboard computer queues up my instructions." She then ceased speaking.

He stared at her. Allowed himself to really see her . . . see how beautiful she truly was. He didn't dare say anything in that moment, knowing nothing could be changed. But he did know this moment in time would always be theirs. A moment when they'd forged a connection that went beyond all others, be it human, machine, or anything else made of matter. Something timeless that could never be destroyed.

The hatch door slid open and then she was gone.

chapter 42

Heather . . .

She hurried to keep up with the Adonis of a man. She could smell the rubbed-in oils enhancing his well-defined musculature. She tried to overt her eyes from Perro's fully exposed backside—where a thong-like support strap was buried deep within his round little butt cheeks.

He certainly knows his way around this place, she thought, as he turned right, down one narrow passageway then, abruptly, veered left when they came to a fork in the passageway. This corridor was somewhat narrower than the previous one.

"You sure you know where you're going? Where the large creatures are kept? The Loth?" she yelled ahead. "It seems like we're on too low a level . . . too far underground." Perro didn't answer her. It was becoming a pattern.

Heather hadn't noticed it at first. That this subterranean maze, with its chiseled out rock walls, was vibrating. Slowing down a bit, she heard . . . *something*. A roaring sound, which didn't make sense; *what noise could be so loud it penetrated all the way through solid rock?*

She didn't like the noise and she wasn't so sure she liked Perro. So why was she putting all her trust into someone she instinctively didn't care for? *This is so wrong.* She slowed then came to a complete halt. Watching the little man proceed down the passageway, she considered her options. *What options?* She listened to the strange repetitive sounds, which seemed to come from all around her. *Maybe it's an underground train? A rushing, subterranean river?* Then she knew exactly what it was. *Oh no . . . it's a crowd's chanting and stomping.* She glanced up, listening harder, trying to make out what the many voices were shouting. Surely numbering in the many thousands, they were chanting, *Tammer! Tammer! Tammer!*

She focused her attention back on the winding passageway before her; Perro had stopped and was now waiting for her. "Like a lamb to the slaughter, huh?" Heather said, more to herself than to Perro.

A new sound suddenly invaded the enclosed space. Hearing the familiar *humming* noise, Heather glanced over her shoulder. The hovering black droid was fast approaching. Bright flashes emanated from a cattle prod-type-thing XI grasped within its articulating arms.

Tammer! Tammer! Tammer!

Heather debated which way to go. Forward or back? *Who am I kidding? I don't have a choice . . . I never did,* she thought. She walked toward the waiting young man. When she was close enough, and knew he was within earshot, she said, "Hey Perro. . . I have a question for you."

Perro didn't reply.

"Do you believe in karma?"

She was close enough to register the confusion on his face, which pretty much confirmed one thing anyway—the oversized shit probably wasn't from Earth. Sure, there were some human characteristics, but the whole age thing was wrong. Somehow, he appeared both young and old at the same time. Yeah, definitely something nonhuman about the way he looked. And, now that she thought about it, his voice held undertones of some weird, unearthly accent. She had been too desperate at the time to notice such things; she had been ready to believe someone, a stranger even, would want to help her. *Lesson learned.*

XI was closing in behind her, and she could actually feel heat emanating out from the powerful cattle prod. She didn't look back—didn't acknowledge the droid's presence, now mere feet behind her. Wouldn't give XI the pleasure of seeing the fear on her face.

Perro patiently waited for her. He stepped aside, gestured for her to proceed through an arched entranceway. When in front of him, she said, "Karma, you'll discover, is a real bitch. I hope I'm still alive to witness it."

"I wouldn't count on that," he said, with a patronizing smile. Though he spoke in English, his voice now sounded nothing humanlike.

Heather stepped through the carved rock archway into total mayhem. An immense underground cavern where hundreds of people, mostly aliens, rushed about doing their individual jobs. It reminded her of the behind-the-scenes craziness when she played Sandy in her high school musical production of Grease. But Larksburg High didn't have armed security droids, lining the walls, nor the not too distant noise of captive beasts, vocally expressing their misery. She tried to decipher the Loth's unique honk among the other sounds, but she could not.

The crackling of XI's cattle prod came up right behind her—she tensed, ready for it to make contact with her skin. Instead, the droid said, "Through there, move, go to the left." Glancing sideways, she saw XI hover forward. The large energized weapon it held, crackling with mini bursts of electricity, seemed to have a life of its own.

Heather, doing as told, soon saw Thoran Ginott. Waiting for her beneath one of the hanging overhead lights, he was dressed in different clothes. Wearing a showman's type suit—a shimmering dark-red jacket, paired with snug-fitting black slacks. His blonde mane looked magnificent—like something seen in the Broadway production of The Lion King. As she approached him, his expression turned to one of mild annoyance.

"I was never deceived by your immature ruse, young human. Not for a moment."

She stared up at Ginott defiantly. "Really? So that's what you're going with? Because I was there. I saw you standing in the dark, all naked-like. For a . . . what's it called? Oh yeah, Priopax technology . . . a projection, a mere deception. So tell me, how long did you jump through hoops in that bedroom of yours before you realized you were chasing a ghost—being played? Do you really think I would have let you . . ."

In a blur of motion, his hand was up, wrapped tightly around her throat, cutting off her words. He brought his wide, cat-like face down next to hers. Flushed red, he spoke softly, obviously barely able to control the rage building inside. "I will enjoy watching my Tammer beast devour you. He will start with your limbs . . . pull them from their sockets one at a time.

Heather, struggling to breathe, clawed at his hand to free it from her throat.

He continued, "Tammers like to prolong the suffering of their prey. You'll see what I mean, because soon you'll be experiencing it first-hand. Witnessing that perspective from inside the arena, with the inevitable defeat of that Loth of yours. I imagine it will be quite a disgusting spectacle. But one this crowd has paid handsomely for.

Frantic, desperate, her vision fading within an increasingly narrowing tunnel, Heather knew she was dying. She ceased struggling, felt her arms fall lifeless to her sides as her legs give out beneath her. There was blackness and nothing mattered. Only then did Ginott release her.

She came to, lying on the ground—gasping—desperately trying to fill her lungs with air.

"Deep breaths . . . try to relax . . . take long, deep breaths."

Heather tried to swallow, which only made her cough. Perro, kneeling beside her, said, "That's it. Just try to breathe normally."

Between gasps, she said, "Shut . . . the fuck . . . up!"

When she rose to her knees, massaging her neck with her fingers, Perro was still there. In a raspy voice, she said, "Where is he?"

"He is the Master of Ceremonies . . . lives to be out in front of the crowd. He's out there now, getting them all riled up. Is that the right phrasing, riled up?"

Heather was able to breathe somewhat better. She looked at Perro. "What are you? I know you're not human."

"We really are remarkably close—genetic relatives, for sure. Neighbors, two worlds separated by a mere seven light years distance. I'm a Khommian. From a world of the same name . . . Khomm."

He abruptly stood—gestured them to come forward. "Get her ready . . . make her presentable . . . and hurry!"

They were the same waif-thin females who'd attended her before in Ginott's apartment suite. Perro took several steps back as one of the attendees helped her stand up. Another hustled Ginott's oversized jacket off her shoulders. Weak, barely managing to breathe normally, Heather felt the negligee she wore being lifted, pulled up over her head.

It took Heather a moment to realize she was standing there, among far too many strangers, totally naked. Wrapping one arm across her breasts, the other arm she tried to cover up the nudity below. Perro watched with interest—a spectator to a private showing.

"Get away from me. You're such a creep!" Heather shouted, turning her equally exposed backside toward him.

A moment later the crew of attendees held Heather's arms up while a new garment was drawn over her head, then tugged into place around her torso. "Are you serious? You can practically see right through this flimsy thing!" she fumed.

Next, her arms, one at a time, were directed into another long garment just as sheer as the first one. Open at the front, like a robe, the flowing material was like nothing she had ever seen on Earth. She had to admit it—*it was beautiful.* Underneath the two garments, she felt a tad more covered. Her hair, loosened, was being brushed with long strokes. Her makeup was freshened, and lipstick was applied to her lips.

Perro, again speaking, said, "I'm sorry. I don't like this part of my job. Having to lie, deceive anyone, is . . . well . . . uncomfortable."

"Why are you still here?"

"I work for the Overlord. I'm doing my job . . . that's all."

The three attendees left as quickly as they came. *Was this really happening?* XI was back, along with his crackling torture device. Heather looked from XI to Perro. "Do people really want to watch this? See someone . . . see *me* suffer? I thought space would be different. That . . . alien races would be more evolved. Be better than this."

Perro shrugged. "You should have stayed on Earth. If it's any consolation, I wish you had."

She hadn't realized where she was standing. Streaked with grime and rust, a gigantic metal door, no more than twenty feet away, began to lift. Bright lights and the sounds of the crowd seeped in through the ever-expanding gap. Clickity-clack, clickity-clack, clickity-clack—up, up, up, the immense door rose higher. The sound from the crowd grew to an unimaginably loud level. *Tammer! Tammer! Tammer!*

"Is this really happening to me?" Heather asked aloud. She clasped her hands together—an attempt to control the trembling.

Then, in the distance, she heard a familiar sound—the ferocious call of a Minal Loth. *Honk! Honk! Honk!*

chapter 43

Cameron . . .

He was sitting within the *Albergone's* bridge, in a fog—a mental stupor—when a sudden abrupt acceleration took him by surprise. Cameron, propelled up and out of his seat, reached for something to grasp onto as his body slammed hard into the rear bulkhead. Clearly, the g-force inhibitors were only partially operational. Another key system damaged by the parasites, the creepers, as Alice called had them. Alice . . . *oh God*. The simple fact that the *Albergone* was now rocketing through space meant Alice had indeed traversed into the antimatter containment area. She'd physically secured the leak while remotely piloting the *Albergone* to achieve near-light speed. It also meant, at this moment, there would be little, if anything, left of her.

And then he heard her voice.

". . . there won't be much for you to do. I've isolated what memory banks I could."

Cameron, rising to his feet, steadied himself against increasing g-forces as he made his way back to his seat. Alice's face stared down at him from the overhead display.

"Ship's systems should, at the very least, be normalized by now. And you should continue to receive these Alice feeds as long as there are power reserves available onboard the *Albergone.*"

Her facial expression was passive, unemotional. Just another day in the life of a cyborgenic being—a robot. But he knew that was far from the truth, which only made her sacrifice more meaningful.

"The *Albergone* has initiated a conversation with Slip-Band Alpha-9, which means the light-speed burst, and my attempt to contain the antimatter radiation leak, apparently was a success."

Alice really had thought it all through; had recorded multiple video streams to coincide with variable situations or results. Even knowing she would soon be gone she'd tried to make things easier for him. "Thank you, Alice . . . truly, thank you for everything," Cameron said, sadness in his voice.

Alice's video feed was unresponsive. Her pretty face simply stared back at him emotionless. A robot.

Three new displays came alive at the same time, but it was the feed showing the *Albergone's* relative location in space that most captivated his attention. The ship was fast approaching the Alpha-9 Slip-Band. A thirty-second countdown timer appeared in the lower right corner of the display.

Clang! Clang!

Cameron looked toward the entrance to the bridge.

Clang! Clang!

Moving to the hatch, he yelled, "Hello?"

"Open!" It was Joe . . . his strange alien voice unmistakable.

"No. You're too big!"

"Open!"

Cameron looked back at the rapidly descending countdown. *Fifteen seconds.* He tapped the release control button and the hatch slid open. Joe was there, his strange form totally filling the entrance.

"What do you want?" Cameron asked.

"In."

Cameron, reluctantly, nodded his head and stood aside. "Fine . . . but hurry it up."

Joe literally squeezed through the open hatch. Keeping low and crawling on all fours, he sat down in the middle of the bridge as the hatch slid closed. Cameron, having to sidestep around Joe, took the same seat he had before . . . 09, 08, 07, 06, 05, 04, 03, 02, 01.

The *Albergone's* forward momentum quickly dissipated away. Joe looked about the confined space with a confused expression.

"We're moving into what's called a slip-band . . . a type of black hole. A folding of space that will catapult us far, far away . . . a great distance." Cameron was certain the Hengtied Portule creature had no idea what he was saying, but he didn't mind explaining it, just the same. Noticing Joe watching the overhead display, Cameron spun his seat back around. Already clear of the Slip Band, they soon would be entering what Alice had referred to as an uncharted planetary system. Five exoplanets out from a bright yellow star, he saw it: a tan, blue, and emerald-green world that stood out from all the others. Far less blue and more tan than Earth, evidently Clay possessed smaller oceans and lakes. Just the same, the alien world still appeared strikingly beautiful.

A clattering of little feet scurried past overhead. Joe's attention perked up. He made a deep rumbling sound, a predator's instinctual response.

"Parasites. You understand? Bad. We need to kill them." Cameron pointed up—the sound of little claws scraping against metal.

"Thogna . . . Kill," Joe said.

"Every last one of them. Yes . . . Thogna."

They sat in relative silence for another twenty minutes. Cameron expected a rough landing from what Alice had told him earlier. But not like this. Before the impact, he sat in the bridge, watching the multiple displays feeling totally powerless, like a passenger, no more in control of their destiny than Joe. Then it was lights out.

He had no idea how long he'd lain there unconscious. Coming awake, it felt as though the *Albergone* was listing heavily to starboard. He heard the muffled sounds of the klaxon blaring.

Disoriented, Cameron was fairly certain he was no longer seated at the console. Shifting his weight he realized he was surprisingly comfortable. *But why is it so dark? And what is that God-awful smell?*

As realization set in, he tried sitting upright, freeing himself from the alien's two encircling arms and the membrane shroud that was enveloping him. He heard Joe's deep voice by his ear. The words were nonsensical, alien gibberish.

"I'm fine. You can release me . . . just open this . . . whatever it's called."

Slowly, the Hengtied Portule's arms relaxed their hold around Cameron's chest. The taut, tent-like, skin folded away—first from his head, then from the rest of his body. Cameron glanced up where he found Joe's elongated face just inches from his own. The weird intimacy of the moment prompted Cameron to leap to his feet. He practically jumped out of Joe's all too personal space.

"Um . . . I guess . . . well, thank you. For protecting me like that."

Joe didn't seem to be listening as he crawled toward the hatch.

Cameron squinted toward the high-mounted displays. They were dark. He'd hoped Alice would be there, providing another video clip with further instructions. But the *Albergone*, beyond any doubt, was seriously damaged. Only a few control panel lights around the compartment still glowed. He found the reset control for the klaxon then slapped his hand down upon it with more force than he'd intended. Squeezing by Joe, he opened the hatch door. Just outside on the deck landing, three tiny creatures lay dead; sharp claws and fangs protruding from their little mouths. *Creepers.* Cameron and Joe glanced at each other. Both must have thought the same thing at the same time. *What about all the other creatures onboard?* As if in physical pain, the *Albergone* groaned, like the vessel's very superstructure had twisted out of shape upon impact.

"We need to go check on the creatures!"

Joe, leaving the bridge, moved into the dark recesses beyond. Cameron, about to follow, stopped and scanned the deck behind him. Spotting his trinious bundle wedged beneath one of the bridge consoles, he pulled it free by its strap. He swung the bundle over one shoulder and hurried from the bridge.

Descending the ladder into the lower main hold section of the ship, it occurred to Cameron it was far too light in here. Letting go of the ladder, he let his body fall the last five feet onto the catwalk below. There was no sign of Joe.

Directly across from him a wide fissure in the hull was visible. Easily ten feet wide by thirty feet long it was the source of the daylight streaming in—illuminating everything within the dingy hold. From his still high vantage point, Cameron was able to look down and view most of the individual holding areas. The largest of the beasts, the Prinwhin, lay slumped within its harness ominously still. Others lay just as still. Then, he caught some movement off to the right. Two, no, three of the creatures were actively trying to free themselves from their harnesses . . . *a good sign*. He spotted Joe on a catwalk three levels down, directly beneath him.

"Don't do that!" Cameron yelled.

Joe continued to fiddle with the harness clasps, securing the Bon-Bon's lone appendage.

"We don't want these creatures loose in here! Hey!" but it was too late. The Bon-Bon, now loose, was starting to hop. The strange beast had an amazing sense of balance. Cameron couldn't help but smile, seeing how happy the Bon-Bon was on gaining its freedom. Suddenly, it propelled itself away from the platform, landing on the next one over—then the next, and the next. "It's heading for the light . . . for the gap!" Cameron shouted.

But the Bon-Bon was already shimmying through the hull's ragged breeched opening. "Terrific . . . we haven't been here a full hour and we've already contributed to unbalancing the ecosystem."

He saw Joe staring up at him from below. He was pretty sure Joe was smiling—happy with himself. Cameron halfheartedly smiled and waved back, then looked about the massive hold area. The Prinwhin seemed to be coming around. "I'll probably go straight to hell for this, but let's let them out . . . let them all out!"

chapter 44

The last creature to evacuate through the *Albergone* hull's open fissure was the Prinwhin. It needed some coaxing by both Joe and Cameron—mostly banging on metal pipes, swinging their arms wildly over their heads, and yelling at it to move. Eventually, but in no real hurry, it, too, was outside, exploring the new terrain beyond. Cameron hoped it would find water soon, since he figured it was an amphibian. He remembered the beast being pulled from a large lake back on Sang-Morang.

Cameron purposely kept his distance from the fissure. His immune system was not in any way prepared for what this exoplanet had to offer, just like before when he was exposed to microorganisms and viruses prior to their landing on Sang-Morang all those weeks ago. Back then Alice had instructed him to spend adequate time within a HOD unit.

Now making his way down multiple metal stairways, he crisscrossed back and forth along interconnecting catwalks to reach the platform where he and Alice had last left the little red Scalldian craft. Although it had shifted some, spun halfway around, it appeared to be undisturbed other than that. He let the trinious bundle slide free of his shoulder, setting it down on the deck.

The *Albergone's* hold was ominously quiet. Gone were sounds of the superstructure settling, or any sound of life— the collection of amazing creatures, originally from other worlds, light years away. Apparently, Joe was gone too. *Of course he was.* The Hengtied Portule must be excited to be off exploring a new world; finding something new to hunt. Perhaps it was for the best—Cameron was not in the mood for another goodbye. If meant to be, he'd see the strange alien again . . . someday.

At the bottom of the trinious bundle lay the largest of the Priopax technology devices. He pulled out the two-foot-long, by one-foot-wide, by eight-inches-thick object, and set it down on the deck. He ran his fingertips along the intricately etched surface. Its raised, artistic, swirling edges reminded him of the beauty of these Priopax devices. Placing his fingers over the four, nearly indecipherable indentations—located along the top of the unit—he waited. The object started to grow. Soon, its X, Y, and Z planes began to increase in size at an accelerating rate.

Once the Tangine Shell was back to its full oblong size— about fifteen-feet-long—Cameron moved around to the shell's end, where the entrance was situated. Entering the access code, he stepped inside the cool, technologically-advanced environment with its indirect lighting and scanned the surroundings. He marveled, as he had every time he entered the shell, how it defied physics: so much larger within, space-wise, than it was on the outside. Located in the middle of the compartment was the HOD unit. The multifunctional device was an inducible deep-sleep chamber, as well as a comprehensive bio-health facilitator. It was also a full-body cleansing device. It was within a HOD similar to this one, when back on the *Primion*, that Cameron queried the ship's computer TAM to determine what he would be up against on Sang-Morang.

Placing his palm against the cool-to-the-touch HOD caused both sides of the unit to descend in tandem. Inside, a long cushion, which had an integrated pillow at one end, beckoned him in. Cameron, sitting down, hurriedly unlaced his boots then kicked them off and swung his legs up and over. As he lay back, the sides of the HOD ascended upward. A moment later, he was totally enclosed inside—a soothing, soft-white glow filled the space. Almost immediately, he felt his eyelids growing heavy. He didn't intend to go to sleep right away, still so much to do, but sleep came anyway.

He awoke later, when a sudden flickering of light prompted him to open his eyes. Along the curved, glass-like, surface above him, were multiple information fields suddenly vying for his attention. He hadn't expected the HOD to be functional at this level. *Where's the info coming from?* Cameron wondered. In the past, he figured the TAM computer, with Alice as an interface, supplied the raw information coming into the various HOD units, including this one.

"Rise and shine young man . . . it's time to get a move on . . . we're burning daylight."

"Art?"

"Howdy, young lad . . ."

One of the display fields suddenly grew larger than the rest. Art was there—his cowboy hat pushed back from the crown of his head. Tending to a broken barbed-wire fence, cattle moseyed along in the background behind him.

"Art! You have no idea how good it is to see you," Cameron exclaimed, his thoughts racing. "I wasn't sure I'd ever see you again. Look . . . there's a lot I need to tell you. Um . . . where to begin?" Heather! Oh God, Heather . . . I'm still trying to get to her—"

"Just hold on! Catch your breath, stop your jabbering." Art held up doing what he was doing long enough to send an annoyed glance his way. "Heather is alive."

Cameron tried to make sense of that. "How could you possibly know that?" he asked, realizing it was a stupid question.

Art, back attending to the fence, said, "There is only so much I can do, Cameron. Only so much I can involve myself with in mortal happenstances such as this. Do you understand what I am saying, lad?"

Cameron stared back at the old cowboy. *How could I possibly understand . . . you ridiculous old relic, when I don't know who, or even what, you really are . . . or where you actually are.* But he kept his thoughts to himself. The HOD enclosure was closing in all around him, his breathing sounding more like panting. Art had information about Heather, yet he hadn't been told any of it. "Just tell me, Art. Is she okay?"

"She's in a pickle. I'm not going to lie to you. I won't do that."

"Where is this *pickle* taking place? Can you at least tell me that much?"

"Winforge . . . she and that beast of yours are on Winforge."

Cameron expected as much from his previous discussions with Alice, but it was good to have it confirmed.

"It's a nasty place, that one. Scoundrels and lowlifes there, the whole lot of them."

"But you talked to her? Tell me you at least talked to her," Cameron said.

"I did. And I think I helped her out, to some degree. Not much, mind you, but some."

Cameron let the fact that Heather was still alive sink in, though any relief he felt was short-lived.

"I provided her information. A possible way to escape. But first, she needs to survive what's coming next."

"What's coming next? What does that even mean?"

Art stood up and looked around. The man, or *whatever* he was, looked apprehensive. "Pipe down. There's nothing that either you or I can do to help Heather. She, along with that beast of yours, will have to make the best of a terrible . . . terrible situation. If she survives, if they survive, she'll come to you. Don't go looking for her."

"Hold on! I'm just supposed to wait here on the off-chance she can escape? How will she know where to go? This place is an uncharted fucking planet! Nobody even knows it exists!"

Art's display field blinked before distorting with static.

"No! No! No! Art! Answer me, Art! God . . . just—"

Faint, barely intelligible, Cameron heard Art's fading voice . . . his final words before the signal was completely lost: "I know where you're at, lad . . . I know."

Cameron stared at the spot on the curved glass where Art, the cows, and the broken barbed-wire fence had been visible just moments before. He thought of Heather. *What kind of a pickle was she in?* Suddenly a new information field popped into view that offered new data. Apparently, while he'd slept, his immune system—his physiology—had been bolstered to cope with this world's diverse ecosystem. Scanning the information, he saw he was good to go explore what lay beyond the breeched hull of the *Albergone*.

chapter 45

Heather . . .

"Hey . . . heads up!" Perro shouted, jumping out of the way—saving himself. Heather felt the beast's approach. Turning to see its approach, she was suddenly mesmerized by the sight of the huge creature. Her legs refused to move. Not so different in appearance to the Loth, it was far larger and looked older—more battered. Its hide showed innumerable scars as well as some fresher lacerations. No fewer than five hovering droids, each carrying a stun device, guided what she was certain was the Tammer toward the open entrance into the arena beyond. Syrupy, flowing strings of saliva poured from the creature's gargantuan-sized jaws. Heather took several steps backward—more from the foul smell than a too close proximity.

The awaiting crowd continued their rhythmic chants: *Tammer! Tammer! Tammer!*

A tentacle, thick like the trunk of a sequoia tree, suddenly reached out sideways—directly toward her.

Heather instantly turned away, trying to dodge it. But in the blink of an eye, she felt the tip of an appendage quickly wrap itself around her waist. Once again, she struggled to breathe as she was lifted off the ground—pulled toward the Tammer's wide-open jaws. She tried in vain to free herself. Her desperate screams drowned out by the constant chanting of the crowd. Wide-eyed—frantic—Heather looked around for someone, *something*, to help her. *Was this the end?* Her last moments alive, before being eaten; her flesh and bones turned to pulp—grinded between teeth the size of Cam's pickup truck?

Below her, she saw Perro staring up at her, his face smug. Clearly, the little shit was enjoying this.

The Tammer, not missing a step, moved beneath the now-retracted metal door into the arena. And, strangely enough, Heather was still alive within its grip.

The throngs of onlookers went totally wild. Heather felt their thunderous, deafening cheers vibrating in the air around her. Up, up, up, she went—high over the Tammer's head. She was being touted, exhibited, before the masses of spectators. On looking down—straight into the creature's eyes—she realized this was no dumb beast. Intelligence gleamed within its two steely-gray orbs. Not by accident was she swooped up into the monster's grasp. It was its intention all along.

Heather and the beast, along with the five droids accompanying them, were circling the outer edges of the field, as close to the crazed crowds as physically possible. The Tammer was capable of a fast, trot-like, locomotion. Glimpses of hundreds of different faces sped past her—an assortment of weird, alien features—a wild and diverse cross-section of extraterrestrial life. Completing a full circuit of the arena, the Tammer slowed now out of breath. The beast walked toward the center of the arena. A high, circular, white marble terrace was there, supported by four elaborately carved marble columns. Standing in the center of the terrace was the master of ceremonies, Thoran Ginott. Next to him, a lone vertical pole reached high. Two hanging chains, dangling from above, had shackles affixed to their ends.

Deep and commanding, Ginott's voice filled the arena in all directions. He spoke in a language Heather did not understand. The crowds soon quieted and settled down. Walking the perimeter of the terrace, he gestured toward the field, the crowd, and the approaching Tammer. Ginott, then pointing, used his outstretched hands to focus everyone's attention on Heather. The crowd cheered with exhilarating ferocity—one, Heather was quite certain, boding ill for her longevity.

The Tammer stood erect before the raised supported terrace. Its eyes just about even with Ginott's own. In a voice loud enough for Heather and the Tammer to hear, the master of ceremonies barked off several alien language commands. Heather, feeling the tentacle around her waist constrict, struggled to catch her breath. Ginott repeated his orders, this time even more sternly. Again, the Tammer did not comply. As the five security droids rose higher in the air, electricity crackled from their respective stun weapons.

Heather, focused on the Tammer's eyes, watched it as it contemplated on what it would do next. She noticed a growing hunger in its unwavering stare. Rivers of mucus flowed freely out both corners of its mouth.

XI moved into view—hovered between her and the Tammer's wide-open mouth. With no warning, the droid fired multiple bursts of electricity right into the beast's gaping open maw. Flashes of bright-white light illuminated the disgusting open orifice. Heather was startled to see bits and pieces of meat caught between its teeth—what looked to be an animal's twisted leg and foot.

Heather placed a hand over her mouth, then one over her heart, beating much too fast for much too long. She was certain she would die soon—die of fright. She felt liquid warmth run down her thighs as her bladder released. Salty tears began to run down her cheeks. *Just end this . . . please . . . no more.*

The Tammer loosened its constricting hold around her waist as she was levitated over the terrace. Released, she fell awkwardly down onto her hands and knees, gasping to fill her lungs with air.

A moment later, Ginott was there, kneeling down beside her. When he spoke, there was kindness in his tone. "Soon, this will all come to an end. I have instructed the Tammer, when the time comes, to make it quick . . . not to prolong your suffering."

"How kind of you," she said, her words saturated with hatred.

"For now, though, the crowd demands a good showing. They want to get their money's worth. Betting is heavy this night. Word of your Loth's quick dispatch of my prized Gonka quickly spread—wages are up; way up. Some are even betting on the . . . what do you humans call it? The underdog?"

Ginott stood, pulling Heather up to her feet in the process. Her wet, now even sheerer, coverings clung to her legs. But she felt no embarrassment—no humiliation. There was no one within this arena, or on Winforge, worth a second thought. They were all animals. No—worse than that—they were pond scum, they were excrement. Looking out at the distant faces she screamed at the top of her lungs, "You can all go screw yourselves!"

She hadn't expected her voice to amplify out so loudly. Echoes of her words reverberated around the now-quiet arena, perhaps due to her close proximity to the master of ceremonies—to the small microphone, adhering to his lapel.

Momentarily empowered, she added, "And screw you, too, Ginott! And by the way, that sparkly little costume of yours makes you look like a circus clown . . ."

But her words were drowned out by the returning noise of the crowd. Now on their feet, they chanted, *Tammer! Tammer! Tammer!*

Ginott glanced toward the far end of the arena, where everyone else was looking. Then Heather heard it over the sound of the shouting masses: *Honk! Honk! Honk!*

The Loth was moving closer. Spotlights above illuminated its tentative progress, magnified on the big, jumbotron display. The Loth stopped and regarded the hordes of onlookers.

Heather shook her head. It was as if the creature was— scared? *Oh no.* The Loth wasn't accustomed to this kind of noise—the stomping of feet, the loud chanting. She could see the smaller of the two beasts practically cowering. *Oh God . . . Loth . . . don't show weakness . . . you can't show any weakness . . . not now!*

Thoran Ginott, talking to the crowd again, strolled around the terrace giving everyone the opportunity to see him. Apparently giving them a play-by-play of events, of which, so far, there was little. But Ginott looked animated, excited, repeating his words—looking at her—this time in English.

"Our fair maiden awaits her savior. But I wonder if this timid-looking Minal Loth holds any kind of chance? Any chance at all? Will the Loth rescue our poor maiden, or will the Loth be quickly defeated by the undefeated Tammer?"

"Tammer! Tammer! Tammer! Tammer!"

Heather watched in horror as the Tammer quickly moved off in the direction of the distant Loth. Dual rivers of mucus trailed behind the larger of these two creatures. Only then did the Loth seem to take notice of the approaching beast. She watched as the Loth began to retreat—moving backward. In horror, she knew what everyone else within the arena also knew . . . that the Loth was already defeated. *Cam's Loth is about to die.*

She couldn't watch what was surely about to unfold. If only the Loth knew she was nearby . . . knew what was at stake. Not just its own life—but hers, too.

Motion above caught her eye. The Tammer was attacking—displayed in gruesome detail up on the jumbotron. Sick at heart, she closed her eyes.

Then, feeling one of her wrists lifted, she opened her eyes. XI hovered before her. First one, then the other wrist, was shackled, chained to the vertical post. *Why bother?* Then XI was gone, as quickly as it had arrived. Heather purposely veered her eyes away from the display—from the commotion on the field. The Loth's desperate honks cried out into the night. "I'm sorry, Cam . . . I'm so sorry!" she yelled to the heavens above. With tears in her eyes, she wondered what distant world up there Cam was now on. Her hatred for this place—for what was happening here—consumed her. Again, she screamed, "Loth! I'm so, so sorry!" Falling to her knees she wept. Soon, it all would be over.

The arena became quiet, awaiting the Loth's defeat. Swaying, Heather noticed the entire terrace was moving, rocking back and forth upon the supporting pillars. She reached for the vertical pole with a shackled hand to steady herself.

She screamed, startled. She gawked open-mouthed as the two ginormous beasts suddenly rose before her—their tentacles intertwined—their bloodied, massive jaws snapping and biting. In the midst of a vicious fight to the death, Heather stood, both scared and exhilarated, at their much too close proximity. She screamed up at the smaller of the two huge beasts, "Kill it! Kill the damn thing! Then we can go find Cameron!" The Loth's eyes momentarily found her—where she stood, chained to a post—and showed recognition.

It was all up to the Loth now. Her survival—the Loth's survival—would be determined within the next few minutes.

chapter 46

Cameron . . .

Cameron emerged from the HOD unit thinking about Heather. It was becoming more and more difficult to keep his growing frustration in check. It didn't help any that the only one to blame was himself. He'd brought her into space, arrogantly thought he could protect her.

Tying the laces on his right boot, he forced himself to think about something else. He'd been surprised the HOD had been able to share such a wealth of information about this new world, he wondered where that information, the raw data, had generated from since this world was basically unknown. With TAM and Alice gone, who, or what, had made that data available to the HOD? But then again, wasn't the HOD Priopax technology like the Tangine Shell and the other items he carried around with him within the trinious bundle? He'd probably just have to come to an understanding that there were some things he may never have answers to.

Cameron retrieved the plasma pistol he'd kept next to him while he slept—then pushed himself off the edge of the HOD and stood up. He froze. *Hadn't Art actually confirmed where Heather was? That she was on Winforge?* He glanced about the surrounding Tangine Shell's interior—spotted the trinious bundle right where he'd left it, laying on the floor.

Sitting back down, he hauled the oblong satchel up onto his lap and opened it. He remembered that the Thidion alien, Ramen, had originally pilfered the bundle off an abandoned Priopax ship. Now it was his. Somewhat familiar with the half-dozen items within, all a dark gray and ornately engraved, he had yet to spend an adequate amount of time to gain an understanding of what all of their true functions were. He selected and withdrew a cube-shaped item from the bundle, then placed the object on the floor. Using his fingertips, he located the series of small insets and covered them—one after another.

Immediately, the device began to increase in size. He watched as it expanded out to its full dimensions—about the size of a piece of furniture. Cameron knew it was a highly advanced console—three-and-a-half feet in height, about four feet long, and a couple of feet in width. He'd used this interface before, with its myriad of indicators and inset controls on the top, and multiple rows of touch-sensitive buttons.

Cameron glanced toward the bundle again, spotting the circular, dinner plate sized object lying inside. It was how he'd originally, like Aladdin with his magic lamp, called Art forth. But at the moment, he didn't want Art's help. He'd come to realize the old cowboy, as instrumental to his own survival as he, or *it,* had been in the past, was also undependable. If he couldn't count on Art to be there when he needed him, best to go it alone. No, the one thing Cameron had going for himself was his own near-photographic memory.

Getting to his feet, there was scarcely enough room for him to squeeze between the HOD and the Priopax console within the confines of the Tangine Shell. But now, standing before the complex-looking control panel, he closed his eyes. Mentally replaying the course of events over the past weeks when he and Art configured the thing's coordinates to the proper time/space settings in conformity to Earth's location within the galaxy. They had fine-tuned the controls, eventually able to view Cameron's hometown on Earth—Larksburg Stand. To his utter discouragement, he had found the small mountain hamlet decimated by a Griar Loth—his Loth's mother.

Now Cameron began manipulating the controls, his eyes roving back and forth between the control board and the 3D virtual display. Only deep space, with innumerable twinkling stars, was visible. He entered Winforge's relative spatial coordinates, something he'd queried Alice about weeks before and still remembered. While adjusting the visual perspective to a specific point in space, he went about the fine-tuning process, similar to what Art had performed weeks prior. "Crap!" The display continued to show space and stars and vast blackness. Then, suddenly, he realized the perspective of this particular view of space had indeed changed. Slapping his forehead with the palm of his hand, he muttered, "Of course!" He'd neglected to manipulate the level of the four detail sliders. By delicately adjusting them, in unison, the zoom level could be reconfigured. He'd actually been looking at the associated planetary system already. It was larger than anything else in the surrounding space. Beyond doubt, Winforge was there too, among the other worlds now orbiting the bright star at the center of that system.

It took another few minutes before Winforge's image filled the virtual display. Cameron made a face. It was an ugly planet—colorless, cold, and looking inhospitable. He thought of Heather, of her being there, and checked the time/space settings. If he'd set the controls correctly, he was looking at things in real-time. The exoplanet, although not nearly as large as Earth, still had one hundred twenty million square miles of surface space he'd need to survey. Pursing his lips, he ran his fingers through his unkempt mop of brown hair. "Okay . . . now to find the proverbial needle in the haystack," he said aloud.

Ten minutes later, Cameron was ready to pull his hair out by the fistful. As it turned out, the exoplanet basically was a cold, uninhabitable, cluster of jagged and mountainous igneous rock. The only population center, a large complex, was situated within the warmest region, along Winforge's midline equator. He located the sprawling complex, which had a number of associated buildings. Various landing pads and runways, and an airport of some kind for space vehicles were situated to the north. From what his readings were telling him, there were subterranean levels to the site as well. But the brightly lit arena was what captured his attention. Something *big* was going on there. He readjusted the level of detail sliders again, having gained a better expertise of how sensitive the controls were at this level of detail.

"Wow! This place is packed to the gills . . . ," he said, letting a brief smile pull at the corners of his lips. "Look at them sitting there!" The ultra-high resolution visuals were amazing. As if he, personally, was right there, overlooking the stands—like the computer-controlled, stabilized, cable-suspended camera systems used by the NFL. "Skycams," he said aloud, remembering the name. His eyes scanned back and forth over the control board. "So how is the audio controlled on this thing?" The words no sooner left his lips, before he spotted the section on the board dedicated to that function. He tapped the inset button.

Tammer! Tammer! Tammer!

Up until that moment, Cameron almost enjoyed the deductive process of finding Winforge and finding the one location where Heather might be kept. But now, seeing two giant creatures in the midst of a life-and-death battle, all he felt was sick. Even covered with streaks of blood, he recognized the Loth—his Loth—immediately. The other creature, perhaps some kind of Loth too, was far larger.

Tammer! Tammer! Tammer!

The chanting crowd angered him. If the amazing console possessed the capability of dropping a bomb upon their freaky, alien heads, he'd gladly do so. Push the button right now, and watch them all be obliterated.

In a flash Cameron's thoughts transported him back to another time—to another place. Back to a different kind of arena, one with a dirt floor. Where the acrid, bloody smell of copper hung heavy in the humid air inside an abandoned factory. Where his eight-year-old self learned to enjoy that number one Progresso, Texas pastime. Hadn't he watched his Uncle Harley's prized fighting cocks literally claw and rip opposing roosters to shreds? Hadn't he cheered with the rest of them? Young Cameron would position himself, down on his hands and knees, at the front line. How many times did he return home with the dried splattering of blood and guts on his cheeks?

What now was happening on Winforge, was it really all that different? Cameron didn't know. Back when he was eight, he was trying to connect with the only living relative he had left in the world. If he could do it all over again, could change the past, he would. But these chanting aliens were not children, and the two large creatures fighting for their lives were not simple roosters. This was different—wasn't it? He continued to watch them go at it. Neither seemed to be getting the upper hand.

"Come on, Loth . . . do what you do better than any other living beast."

The dueling creatures moved closer to the center of the arena, where some kind of ornate platform was erected. Stunned, Cameron heard a voice coming over the arena's PA system, "Kill it! Kill the damn thing! Then we can go find Cameron!"

With his heart practically leaping out of his chest, Cameron clumsily fumbled with the controls, re-centering his point of view to include the entire platform. And there she was! Long blond hair, cascading over her shoulders, surrounded her beautiful face. Shackled to a pole, she was practically naked. *Why? Why are they doing this to you, Heather?* He shook his head in disbelief. Had he actually found her—only to witness her immanent death? With clenched fists, he glared up—an angry, ugly snarl distorting his face. "God . . . if you've brought me this far . . . this close . . . only to see her die . . ."

The noise from the cheering crowd pulled his attention back to the virtual display. To Heather, standing there alone.

He leaned in closer, his brows knitting into one. He'd seen that same expression on her face a thousand times before. *Indignation.*

Cameron forced himself to become calm, to slow down his breathing. Heather hadn't given up the fight yet, and neither would he.

chapter 47

Heather . . .

Oh, how she wished Cameron was there to witness this spectacle. The longer the two goliaths battled, the more evident it was that Cam's Loth was going to defeat the far larger beast. It was hard to watch the amount of physical damage these two were inflicting upon one another. But now, clearly, the larger of the two beasts—the Tammer—would not survive the ordeal. Heather watched with stunned disbelief as the Loth systematically ripped away one tentacle after another until only two remained. Two weren't adequate for the Tammer to shuffle away from its relentless pursuer.

Heather turned her attention to the master of ceremonies, Thoran Ginott. He, too, was in a state of shock, no longer delivering a play-by-play account to the hushed crowd. When he momentarily glanced in her direction, she had little illusion her life would be spared simply because the Tammer had been defeated. *But at least I won't be eaten alive*, she thought pragmatically. But then again, maybe she had more going for her than just that. She leveled her eyes on Ginott. *All this was his, wasn't it? Didn't everyone answer to him?* She shot a glance over to the Loth. It was close by and had moved onto the reaping of rewards aspect of the battle. She watched as the Loth tossed a Volkswagen-sized chunk of Tammer meat into its mouth.

Thoran Ginott began broadcasting again, his voice's effect on the crowd was nearly instantaneous. "My friends . . . a new champion has emerged, right before your very eyes!"

Heather moved as close to the Loth as her restraints allowed. From this new vantage point she could view the Tammer's partially eaten carcass. When she spoke, her voice was strong, held a level of authority she didn't know she possessed. "Loth! Can you hear me, Loth?"

The beast, continuing to chew, raised its massive head high enough to see over the edge of the terrace.

"Do you want to see Cameron again, Loth? Do you want to get away from here . . . from this place?"

Ginott ceased with the hyperbole, the droning on and on, not quite grasping what Heather was up to.

"Loth! I need your help. Can you help me? Can you do that . . . right now?" She knew the creature understood certain words, even short sentences. But would the Loth understand what she was saying to it now?

Although the Loth had lost a tentacle of its own during the battle, it moved sufficiently well to come closer to the terrace. Still chewing, the beast's large eyes stared down at her, unmoving for an entire moment. From the corner of her eye, Heather saw them coming. The high-hovering security droids, arranged in a net V formation, XI in the lead. *Oh my God . . . why did I think the Loth would have any sense of loyalty to me? I'm not Cameron.*

One of the Loth's still-intact tentacles suddenly appeared over the edge of the terrace. Snake-like, it slithered across to her. The tentacle's tip, rising to eye-level, gently stroked one side of Heather's face several times. Her fear quickly turned to streaming tears of gratitude. "These chains . . . can you break them?"

But the security droids were already upon them—surrounding the Loth like a swarm of angry bees. Bright flashes from their Taser weapons came alive. XI kept its distance—perhaps communicating orders silently from relative safety.

The Loth honked as painful shockwaves coursed through its body. Thoran Ginott smiled and stepped close enough for Heather to hear him.

"All this . . . well, it just makes for splendid drama. In the end, pretty human, both you and the beast will live for another day. Another exposition. The Loth, our new champion, and you, the young maiden it is willing to fight for . . . even die for."

Heather was only half-listening to him. She watched as the Loth batted away one, two, then three of the apparently too slow to get out of the way droids. Then another tentacle appeared over the edge of the terrace, right behind Thoran Ginott, wrapping around his waist. Raising him high in the air, the Loth opened its massive jaws in anticipation.

"No!" Heather yelled. "Not yet . . . don't eat him . . . we need him alive!"

Ginott struggled helplessly to free himself. He yelled to XI. "Don't just hover there, you stupid machine . . . help me!"

The remaining security droids were taking their toll on the Loth, weakened by the constant jolts of electricity and the exhaustive battle that took place with the Tammer.

"Free me, Loth. Can you do that right now?"

The Loth did as told, repurposing one tentacle away from swatting at droids to helping her. Heather marveled at the creature's ability to multitask: hold Ginott aloft in one tentacle, swat at Taser-yielding droids with another, and use the tip of another tentacle to first probe at, then yank the individual chains away from where they were fastened onto the vertical pole.

Finally freed, Heather collected up the excess lengths of chains and wrapped them around her hands. Hurrying over to Ginott above her, still struggling to free himself, she said, "Listen to me, Ginott . . . do as I say and you will live. Don't listen to me and I'll instruct the Loth to bite your head off. Have I made myself clear?"

Ginott stopped his struggling. "Anything! Tell me what you want."

"Instruct the droids to back off . . . that includes XI."

Ginott stared down at her for several long beats, then at the remaining droids and over to XI. He spoke quickly in a language she didn't understand. Immediately, all flashes from the droids' Taser weapons ceased.

The Loth slumped to one side, exhaling a long foul breath—exhausted.

Heather kept her eyes glued on XI. That wretched tin can was the cause of all of their misery. Under orders, which it never seemed to disobey, it had kidnapped both her and the Loth. And before that, it made Cam's life a living hell. She asked, "Who does XI ultimately take its orders from? Have allegiance to?"

Ginott looked both irritated and confused. "Who cares? The thing did as it was told. Now tell the beast to let me go."

"Not going to happen. You may as well get comfortable up there. So who is it XI ultimately answers to?" she asked again.

"The corporation lays out the instructions for the remote AI's."

She narrowed her eyes.

"Fine . . . me! I was the one who dispatched it to that other vessel . . . whatever it was called . . ."

"The *Primion*?" she asked.

"Sure . . . whatever . . . the *Primion*. Like a thousand similar droids I sent onto a hundred other spaceships . . . to ensure that we acquired the necessary livestock for this arena. Although I must say, this particular droid seems to be more driven . . . like, on a whole other level."

Tell me about it, she thought. "Tell XI that it now gives its total allegiance to me. That it does only what I command it to do. Only me. That my survival and the Loth's are its new directive. Tell XI in English . . . I know it'll understand. Do it!"

Ginott spoke to the droid in English, while including strings of various numbers and characters—like access codes, she assumed.

"Okay . . . it's done. You have yourself one crazy loyal droid. May you both be happy together. Now let me go!" Ginott yelled.

"Not so fast. Next, I want you to place me in charge of this place. Transfer all your authority over to me. Make me the boss."

Ginott began to struggle again. "No. That's never going to happen."

Heather turned to the Loth, who seemed to be dozing. Gazing now up at XI, she ordered, "XI . . . remove Thoran Ginott's left ear."

The hovering black droid didn't hesitate, moving down from its present location over to Ginott, gripped firmly within the Loth's tentacle, and raised one of its articulating, clawed, arms. Ginott thrashed about—jerking his head this way and that. It took several tries before XI's claw found purchase on Ginott's left ear. Ginott screamed. His continued wailing amplified out to the stands—to the many thousands of mesmerized onlookers.

"Okay, okay! I'll do it! I'll do it . . . just tell it to stop, please! It's pulling my ear off!"

"XI . . . stop pulling on his ear."

XI did as told.

Heather smiled. That was a good test. She didn't trust the evil droid as far as she could throw it, but at least this was a step in the right direction.

Ginott continued to dab at his damaged ear with his fingers, his once proud blond mane now matted with saturated blood on the left side of his head. "You have to understand . . . changing the ownership is a complicated procedure. There are shareholders, and boards of directors, and official deeds that need to be generated and signed . . ."

She turned her gaze to XI and nodded. "Take his ear."

"Wait! Just wait a second. I need to think. How I can do this, transfer the title so quickly."

She watched him go deep in thought—perhaps contemplating if it would be easier to just have his ear ripped off. Ginott spoke quickly, mostly in English, but also in another alien language. She could only grasp bits and pieces. When he finished, XI had no less than ten questions and requested more access codes, which Ginott quickly answered.

Ginott said, "It's done."

Heather raised a brow toward XI. "Is he telling the truth? Do I now own this facility . . . have complete control over what happens here?"

"Yes. The new deed of ownership has been filed. All necessary parties have been notified. Legalities have been properly complied with," the droid replied.

"Good. Now tell them to leave," she said to Ginott.

"Who? Tell whom to leave?" he asked.

"Them . . . the spectators," she said, gesturing to the stands. "Tell them the show is over, and that they are no longer welcome here. Tell them Winforge is closed . . . indefinitely."

Ginott stared down at her with contempt in his eyes. "I can't do that."

"You can and you will."

"There are still outstanding wagers . . . financial dealings that must be—"

"Go ahead and pull his ear off, XI."

This time she didn't halt the droid from completing its task.

chapter 48

Cameron . . .

He couldn't have been more surprised—or more impressed. Cameron had feared he was about to watch something beyond terrible happen to Heather, when, instead, she somehow, miraculously, turned things around.

He continued to stare unblinkingly at the virtual display from his cramped position within the Tangine Shell as he watched the course of events taking place within that colossal arena on Winforge, light years away. More than a little relieved, he let a smile cross over his lips. He always knew Heather was amazing and that she just needed to realize what everyone else already knew—that more than just beautiful, she was also smart, resourceful, and ridiculously competitive.

And he shouldn't have been that surprised by the Loth's conquest over the far larger *Tammer* beast. Cameron felt something akin to pride at the Loth's victory—then unconsciously grimaced, mentally flashing back to that abandoned factory in Texas and his uncle Harley, standing there, encircled by all the other cheering cockfighters, his own flapping, bloodied rooster raised high above his head in triumph. *Am I so different?*

Cameron let that disturbing mental image pass as he focused on the display. He could imagine the wheels turning inside Heather's head as she puzzled over what to do next, and how to get herself out of the mess she was in. He couldn't wait to see what that was. A glimmer of hope sparked deep within him—*just maybe they would see each other again. Hopefully soon. Unfortunately, based on the condition of the Albergone, it may have to be Heather that comes to him, instead of the other way around.*

A loud series of noises caught his attention. Cameron tilted his head to better determine their origin. *Maybe the creepers were back?* No, these sounds were much too loud, far too forceful for those small, rodent-like critters to make. Suddenly, everything turned sideways. Violently thrown off his feet into the Tangine Shell's closest interior wall, Cameron reached out for something, anything, to grasp onto. But the shell was already being upended in the opposite direction. His head smacked against the ceiling as he was catapulted over the HOD unit, careening him into the opposite wall. Dazed, he managed to find his footing, rise onto to his feet and stagger around to the end of the HOD. The Priopax console had retracted into its original, small brick-sized contours, perhaps due to some kind of built-in safeguard measure that avoided the damaging of electronics.

One thing was certain, he needed to exit this shell—get far away from whatever was outside now trying to get in. He scooped the small Priopax device up off the floor and shoved it into the still-open trinious bundle. Securing the bundle closed, he swung it over one shoulder.

He moved closer to the wall and squinted his eyes. The heavily tinted interior windows provided little help in viewing what was going on outside. The darkness within the *Albergone's* hold area meant insufficient daylight streaming in through the hold's open gap. *It was night. Perhaps some kind of large nighttime scavenger had entered the hold—maybe even more than one.*

Cameron remembered being in a situation like this once before when he was almost killed by a hungry and persistent Greely Beast back on Sang-Morang. It ripped and clawed at the Tangine Shell, sufficient enough to pry open a gap. But now was different. This time he was armed with a plasma pistol. Whoever, *whatever*, was out there was about to meet its maker.

As the shell continued to be jostled about, although somewhat less violently now, Cameron staggered toward the entrance. Spreading his legs and steadying himself, he took a deep breath and raised his weapon. With his other hand, he opened the hatch.

His finger poised on the pistol's trigger, he stepped out into relative darkness and immediately spun left then right. Seeing nothing, he looked over the top of the oblong shell's surface but found nothing there. *Whatever* was tossing the Tangine Shell around, as if it were a child's toy, it was nowhere to be seen. Cameron figured it had to be at the other end of the shell, hiding.

Sidestepping slowly, he cautiously proceeded forward. In the darkness, he spotted the outline of the little Scalldian craft, off to his left. It looked precariously close to falling off the far edge of the platform. The Tangine Shell was no longer moving about as he continued to slowly sidestep ahead. He figured in three steps he'd be able to see around the far end. He took the next step and still saw nothing. Quickly taking another two steps, he tightened his finger around the trigger. His breath caught in his chest. Something was there; something standing in the darkness, keeping perfectly still.

"Don't move!" Cameron rolled his eyes at his own ridiculous command. Whatever was out there was already standing still as could be. *So . . . what now?*

He pointed the pistol slightly away from the dark figure and pulled, holding the trigger down. A continuous beam of bright-blue plasma shot across the hold, hitting the opposite bulkhead, and illuminating the contours of the figure.

About Cameron's height, six feet tall, it was a robot. Nothing like Alice, nowhere near that level of cyborgenic technology. This one was a true-to-form, mostly mechanical-looking, robot. With the weapon becoming hot in his hand, Cameron's finger relaxed its hold on the trigger.

As his eyes adjusted in the near-total darkness, he asked, "Can you understand me? Can you communicate?"

Aware of subtle whirling sounds emanating from the robot, he pulled the trigger again for a sustained ten-second period. This time, he concentrated on details. The robot was old. Rusted metal, like something you'd find in a scrapyard back on Earth. Made in the image of a bipedal organism—it had two arms, two legs, and a head. Its metal face had two eyes, a nose, a mouth.

Reluctant to continue using his plasma pistol as a flashlight, Cameron had no idea how many times he could pull the trigger before it was spent and had exhausted its supply of generated plasma. But then again, it might be inexhaustible. He had no way of knowing.

Clicking sounds—more like ratcheting sounds made from a ratchet wrench—indicated the robot was moving.

"Hey! Stay where you are!" Cameron commanded, pointing the pistol at its head. He watched an arm move, then stay like that—elevated. *Fuck!* He averted his aim and pulled the trigger once more. The short burst was enough to see where the robot was pointing. Pointing its mechanical, digit-like finger.

Cameron glanced back over his shoulder into total darkness. Bozo the clown could be doing twirling pirouettes behind him and he wouldn't be able to tell. He turned back to the mechanical figure frustrated and shrugged. "You'll have to do better than that . . . what are you pointing at? Already more than a little freaked out, the robot's silent pointing was giving off a weird, grim reaper, vibe.

Apparently, the rickety old robot had a headlight. Situated on the top of its head, it suddenly came on. Dim, it didn't give off much light, just enough to illuminate the nearby hold surroundings in a soft-yellowish glow. Cameron noticed the robot's arm was a confluence of various-sized gears; two long piston-looking things; and an assortment of metal rods and bands. And still it was pointing. *Of course it was.* Reluctantly, and very slowly, Cameron looked back over his shoulder.

Shit.

chapter 49

"Shit," he said again.

Twelve robots stood huddled together. Ancient looking, they were in various states of disrepair, no two exactly the same. Unblinking, the eclectic band of robots stared back at him. The lone headlight, emanating from the mechanical man still behind Cameron, cast misshapen shadows, making the lot of them look like a scene from a scary movie.

Clearly, Alice had been wrong about this planet. It may have been some time ago, but evidently this world, Clay, was once inhabited by intelligent life. He scanned the sorry lot. One robot, short in stature and barrel-chested, grasped a mechanical leg with an attached foot in one of its articulating claws. Cameron noticed it belonged to the robot right next to it, the oldest, most rusted one of them all. Off-kilter, it leaned to one side. Another robot started to twitch. The twitching proceeded to get worse and worse, to the point two other robots had to reach out with mechanical arms to help steady it.

One of the robots moved out from the back of the pack. Three lower leg appendages, attached to three revolving tread mechanisms, reminding Cameron of oversized belt-sanders, were its method of mobility. Two stubby mechanical arms teeter-tottered up and down as it moved, similar to how a tightrope walker, striving to keep his balance, would extend his arms out to keep himself steady on the rope.

One of the tread mechanisms made a loud grinding noise. One or more of the internal bearings was shot.

"Shit . . . shit . . . shit . . . ," the robot repeated, as it rolled to a stop five feet in front of Cameron. "You are a human from the planet Earth. The English word *shit*, in origin, is most probably Germanic . . . a derivative of the word *scheissen*, which is a verb. Shit can be used as a noun, referring to fecal matter. Humans produce consistent amounts of fecal matter as it pertains to their relative body mass. As a verb, shit refers to defecating. Will you be defecating now? Are you communicating this to us for a reason? Perhaps you need assistance?"

Cameron didn't answer right away. "Um . . . no, I don't need assistance. And the word shit is also used as a slang term, or as an expression of surprise, or annoyance. Sometimes in anger."

"Which of those human emotions are you experiencing now?"

"I don't know. I just said it, because I felt like saying it."

Cameron noticed the four-foot-tall, tri-legged robot had a perfectly round head. What would be considered its face, its eyes, nose, and mouth, were faded—all but gone now. Perhaps, at one time, they'd been painted, or stenciled on, but over time had worn away. What primarily remained were a series of small slits. Slits, Cameron suspected, were openings associated to electronic sensors for sight, smell, and speech. He leaned sideways to get a better look at one side of the volleyball-sized head. Again, a faded discoloration revealed a stenciled-on ear. But, mostly, only a series of tiny slits remained.

"What are you doing here? What do you want?" Cameron asked, peering down at the robot before him, then at the others patiently standing in their same huddled group.

"You will make repairs. It has been far too long since anyone has landed on this world. Far too long since our mechanisms have been properly serviced."

"You can't do that yourself?" Cameron asked.

"Yes, many repairs already made. Many still required. We wait for new organic . . . one with adequate finger dexterity . . . to make further, needed repairs."

"You're telling me you've been waiting here on the off-chance an organic life form would arrive on this planet? Arrive right here? Would make the necessary repairs for you? Cameron looked over to the robot, holding onto another robot's leg. "You there, how long have you been lugging that thing around with you?"

Volleyball-head answered for it: "Using your method of time-keeping . . . years, months, weeks, days, hours, minutes, seconds . . . it would be eighteen years, five months, three weeks—"

"Okay, okay . . . I got it. A long time. A ridiculously long time." Cameron scratched the stubble on his chin. He wondered if these broken-down assemblages of machinery had simply been left behind—too broken to be of further use. "So what do I call you?"

"165430009341111100000 GOHHHM THACK 54."

"That's a really long name. How about I just call you Thack. Would that be okay?"

The robot's head bobbled a bit, and then spun around to face the others. For the first time, Cameron heard the others communicate—a series of electronic squawks and beeps and several pings. Thack's head spun back around, then indicated its assent giving a nodding motion. "Each of us will provide you with abbreviated nomenclature, if so desired."

"Sure . . . later, maybe. Right now, I wonder if you can tell me a few things. Are there others here . . . on this world . . . like me? Human? Or maybe some other alien intelligent life?"

"Oh yes. There is much organic life here. A diverse ecosystem. Some not so intelligent."

Cameron figured as much. "How about another ship . . . a spacecraft, like this one? I need to leave. I need to be on my way as soon as possible."

Volleyball-head spun back around. More sounds were exchanged between the robots. "Repairs first. Must make repairs to non-organic constructs first."

"So there is a ship?"

"Repairs first."

Cameron leaned over and stared at the one he'd named Thack and did a quick, off-the-cuff assessment of the broken-down machine's various appendages. Thack seemed to be in better repair than many of the others—he glanced at the rest of them. Straightening up, he looked about the dark hold. The *Albergone's* overhead lights, typically on, were out. The ship was basically dead. No power.

"Look . . . this ship doesn't even have power. I'll need light to see what I'm doing. So that means waiting till tomorrow morning." He reached out with both hands and manually swiveled Thack's elbow joint back and forth. He shook his head. "That's not too bad. I may be able to replicate still-operational parts of functioning robots . . . utilize them on others. I have the means of doing that . . . replicating things," he said, considering how he could use the Lox Priopax device. Cameron moved back to the entrance of the trinious bundle and, using his fingertips, initiated the shell to begin its retraction process. Once back to its smaller, rectangular contours, he picked it up and placed it within the bundle. During this process, he realized he'd not only tucked his plasma pistol into his jeans' waistband, he'd also unconsciously turned his back to the robots. Foolish. He had no idea if they were dangerous—if one or more of them intended him any harm.

When he turned around to face them, nary a one had even moved an inch.

"There may be radiation issues on this ship. So I'm going to set up camp, somewhere out there." He gestured to the hold's open gap. "Any recommendations? Somewhere where the wildlife will leave me alone?" He moved toward the Scalldian craft. The nose of the little ship, hanging over the side of the platform, looked as if the slightest nudge would send it over the edge. He stared down into the darkness below. The fall would surely damage it beyond repair.

"Wildlife . . . there is much wildlife here. Large carnivores that can eat you. Large omnivores that can step on you. Many varieties of parasites, both small and large. And there are the Morpars."

Cameron, only half listening to Thack, set the trinious bundle down and opened it. Removing the Lox device, he placed it fifteen feet away from the small craft and made the necessary configuration settings to scan it into memory. Soon, a bright swath of light became visible and rapidly began its cycling back and forth. Confident things were proceeding properly, he mentally replayed back Thack's last words—something about Morpars.

chapter 50

Heather . . .

Ginott continued to scream and writhe, holding the side of his head where once his ear had been attached, while blood trickled out between his fingers. The Loth was awakened by the loud commotion and raised Ginott's still tightly grasped body several feet higher from where it had drifted lower.

Heather gazed out toward the stands where thousands of unhappy spectators were now shuffling out of the arena. Soon, the skies above would be filled with their departing spacecraft.

She, too, wanted to be gone from here, away from this place, along with the Loth, on their way to find Cameron at Sang-Morang where she'd left him stranded. She looked over at XI. "Does Ginott own a large spaceship?"

"No . . ."

She could see a pinkish wad of flesh peeking through one of the droid's pincer claws. "That seems highly unlikely," she said, shaking her head. "How would he travel—"

But XI, still speaking, added, "All physical Winforge assets have been transferred to new corporate ownership."

She thought about that. *Physical Winforge assets?* "What does that even mean, basically?"

"That you own everything . . . the whole fucking planet!" Ginott spat.

I own a planet? Heather never owned anything. Even her Volkswagen bug was in her father's name. She didn't have a credit card in her name, yet she now owned a planet!

"You can put him down, Loth."

The Loth did as asked, releasing its tentacled hold from around Ginott's waist. Ginott dropped ten feet down onto the terrace. She heard the sound of a bone, or maybe multiple bones, *crack*. She hadn't meant for the Loth to just drop him like that.

He cried out and reached for one leg. The guy was a ruthless pig, but she didn't want him to suffer. She stepped closer. "I'm sorry . . . I didn't—"

Ginott looked up at her, his face full of venom. "I will make it my life's purpose to see you suffer, human." Panting through the pain—gasping—he said, "But there again . . . you have far bigger problems to worry about than me . . . for now."

Heather waited for him to continue.

"This facility . . . it's highly leveraged—recent unre-strained-spending. The debts are staggering . . . billions and billions of ackneds . . . so, it won't be long before the creditors, a vicious lot, will be coming for both you and their assets. You've actually done me an immense favor, missy." He attempted a smile, but it came out more like a grimace.

"Assets?" she repeated. Not a businessperson, she had little concept of what running a business might entail.

"All that you see around us. Even more important, all the creatures . . . the beasts those spectators paid dearly to watch in this arena."

She felt sick; she didn't like the thought of strange beings, aliens coming here, looking for her. Pressuring her to keep this awful place going. She wondered how much time she had. Perhaps they were already en route to Winforge. If so, she needed to leave quickly. *But outer space is so huge—vast. They couldn't possibly find me . . . could they?* But first she needed to do something—what Cam, she was certain, would want her to do.

"XI, I have more work for you. Um . . . listen carefully." Heather closed her eyes, trying to think clearly. "Right away, we need to return these creatures to their home planets, back from where they were originally abducted. Do those records exist? Can you make that happen?"

"There are currently three hundred-and-ninety-seven organics confined on Winforge, at this facility, and in two smaller ones nearby."

"Okay . . ."

"There are incomplete database records for twenty-three of these organics. Their indigenous habitats are unknown."

"Fine! So you can return the other three hundred and . . ."

"Three hundred-and-seventy four," XI said. "There are insufficient means of transport for carrying out this objective."

The sound of the Loth's chewing, combined with the wafting-up smell from the Tammer's reeking carcass were making Heather nauseated. That, and she could smell herself, too— the urine on her gown. Ginott was attempting to crawl away, but she wasn't sure where he'd go. Making poor progress, he often stopped to cradle his injured leg spewing unintelligible comments back her way.

I can't do this myself. I need help. But first, I need a shower!

"Come up with a plan to return all these creatures, XI. Perhaps certain ships will have to make multiple trips. I don't know, but come up with something. Right now, though, I need to shower and I need different clothes. Get me back to Ginott's quarters."

She noticed movement at the far end of the arena. A small inbound transport sled was being piloted by a droid. "Also . . . I want Manny and Cleeanne released immediately. Let them bathe, give them clean clothes, then have them brought to Ginott's quarters . . . actually, *my* quarters now."

The droid turned to leave when Heather made one more request. "And get Ginott to a hospital . . . a medical bay. There must be one here, right?"

XI did not answer. Speeding up and away, it soon was hovering high above the field.

* * *

Heather stepped out from the hot, still-steaming bathroom into Ginott's bedroom, pulling a large comb through the remaining tangles in her wet hair. Lying on the bed before her were the clothes she'd asked for. They were her own: her own bra and panties, her white shorts and tank top, all meticulously cleaned. Brand-new, black high-top boots rested on the floor in place of her old, undoubtedly too thrashed to do anything with, shoes. After getting dressed, she opened the door to the rest of the suite. Cleeanne was sitting on the couch. Behind her, milling around in the kitchen, was Manny. Both wore generic-looking blue overalls. They looked clean and healthy.

"This place is an insult to my sensibilities. A blatant attempt at bribery!"

Heather hadn't noticed Phonk. The small, nasty Craing was also in the kitchen. Only the top of his head showed partially above the level of the counter.

Manny, apparently able to read her expression, laughed and said, "Hey, the little bastard can be relentless . . . he wouldn't shut up, insisted he could help. I gave in, okay?—My bad."

Cleeanne, continuing to sit quietly on the couch, offered up a shy smile.

Manny, her mouth full of something that crunched loudly, said, "You did it. You did the impossible, girl. Single-handedly brought down this dreadful place. Long live the queen . . . long live the queen of Winforge!" She bowed, lowering her head in a dramatic gesture.

Cleeanne made small, mini-clapping motions with her hands that made no sound. "You saved us, Heather. You saved all of us. I will love you forever!"

"You can thank the Loth . . . all I did was take advantage of the situation."

Phonk began to climb the shelves of an open cabinet like they were a ladder. He pulled various items out as he went, inspected the contents then quickly discarded them onto the floor below. Obviously, he was not finding what he was looking for.

"Can you stop doing that?" Heather asked, remembering how much she hated the little troll.

"I need meat. Have you seen my teeth? They're sharp as little knives for a good reason."

Manny opened what was akin to a refrigerator. Cold air billowed out from the lit, locker-like appliance. "There's all kinds of meat in here . . . but you're cleaning up that mess before you get anything else."

Phonk jumped down from his high perch. Ignoring her, he made a beeline for the locker. Manny quickly grabbed ahold of him by the nape of his collar, lifting him up to eye-level. "I already want to strangle you. I want to watch your eyes pop out of your little head. No one will stop me. Now go sit down and be good and I'll find you something to eat. But say one word, and you're a dead dwarf." As Manny deposited him down on the couch, Cleeanne scooted farther away.

"I want to get all of you back to where you came from . . . to your home planets. And I want to do so just as soon as I can. Things are already in process, I think. But I'm going to need your help. This is bigger than me . . . of what I'm even marginally capable of handling. I need help from someone I can trust . . . besides the Loth. I'm hoping that it's you guys. Will you help me?"

Phonk said, "Phlork shin!"

Heather stared down at him with a blank look.

Cleeanne, her voice meek, barely audible, said, "That means F-you . . . I think."

"No kidding," Manny said to Cleeanne sarcastically. "Yeah, Heather, we'll help you. You've saved our lives. Saved us from the arena. Speaking for myself, and for Cleeanne too, I'm sure, you've earned a lifetime of help."

Heather nodded, feeling somewhat better, then looked over to Phonk who said, "Fine . . . but I need to eat. And you need to keep that one away from me." He stared at Manny.

Heather, about to reply, was interrupted by the sudden opening of the front door. XI, followed by three security droids, hovered into the room.

chapter 51

Cameron . . .

Cameron waited for the last of the slow-moving geriatric robots to pass through the gap in the *Albergone's* hull. He found himself getting impatient—he wanted to see what the world here was like. If the *Albergone* was still leaking radiation, he also wanted to be a good distance away from the ship as quickly as possible. Finally, bringing up the rear, it was now his turn to exit. He glanced back over his shoulder and thought of Alice. What was left of her, if anything, was still here. Would remain, be part of the *Albergone* in its final resting place. "I'm sorry, Alice," he said as he hurried out into the warm early morning air.

He'd only experienced two other worlds to make a comparison to Clay—Earth and Sang-Morang. Planet Clay, as it turned out, was similar to those worlds, yet quite different, too. The first thing he noticed was the God-awful humidity.

Already, his shirt was clinging to his back and his thick hair was dampening. Huge jungle-like large green palm fronds obscured any clear view of the sky above. Dew dripped down from the leaves—a continuous dribble noise coming from all around.

"Just how far away is this place we're headed to?" he asked the tall robot, the same one responsible for upending the Tangine Shell within the hold. Silent until now, the robot said, "Not far."

Relative to what? Cameron thought. But there was plenty enough around to keep his mind, his thoughts, busy. So many things were new, different from anything he was used to. The ground, mostly light gray in color, though sometimes white, had a clay-like consistency. And the jungle-like fauna was unlike the jungles of the Amazon in South America because virtually all the plant life here was covered in tiny hairs, like a layer of fur. Perhaps an evolutionary leap took place here that hadn't occurred on Earth, or on Sang-Morang? A genetic leap, perhaps, uniting both plant and animal life? In his mind's eye, he opened up his World Book Encyclopedia to the letter **P**, the book laying on his virtual lap. He flipped to the reference: **Plant**, and began skimming down the page until he found what he was looking for:

Plants are primarily multicellular, predominantly photosynthetic eukaryotes of the kingdom, Plantae. They form the clade Viridiplantae which is Latin for "green plants" . . . these include all the flowering plants, conifers and other gymnosperms, including ferns, hornworts, clubmosses, mosses, liverworts, and even green algae.

Little of that info seemed to fit with the environment he was now witnessing. Strange, much of what he'd previously learned from Alice about this place, as well as during his recent time within the HOD, did not match—did not correspond to his present eyewitness account. It was almost like this was a completely different world. Cameron stopped to inspect a waist-high, diamond-shaped leaf. He'd been brushing up against such leaves for close to ten minutes. Leaning in, he noticed the abundance of fur on the leaf's surface. "Huh . . . truth is, this doesn't look too much like a plant at all." He took in its cool swirling design, not that different from what you'd find on the wings of a butterfly. He tapped on the broad leaf with a finger. Startled, he immediately jumped back, "I saw an eye! The plant . . . it . . . it . . . blinked!"

The tall robot, several paces ahead, stopped and turned to look at him. "That is not a plant. Be mindful of its mouth . . . or mouths. They bite."

As the robot turned back forward, slowly resuming its lemming-like pursuit of its fellow mechanical brethren, Cameron was hesitant to move forward. He scanned the surrounding jungle foliage, quickly realizing this might be a very dangerous place for a human. Why didn't he notice them before? All the blinking eyes—and yes, mouths too—indentations, where the ever-present moisture had accumulated. He called ahead, "Are there teeth in those mouths?" The tall robot, now twenty paces ahead, did not turn around—did not answer.

Cameron swung the trinious bundle from his shoulder and held it sideways, across his mid-section, where it extended a foot or so beyond his body on either side. At least this way there would be something, other than himself, making direct contact with these surroundings. He hurried to catch up to the procession of robots.

Cameron figured they'd traversed close to ten miles before stopping. Covered in sweat, he felt drained—exhausted. He leaned sideways, hoping to get a better view of what lay ahead. "Are we there yet?" he yelled. The sound of his loud voice within such a quiet environment caused a reaction, not from the robots, but from the surrounding fauna. It was then he noticed something else: a disturbing revelation. He'd assumed the animal-like plants had sprouted up from the clay soil on not so thick stems. But now he could see they weren't stems at all. They were spindly legs. The abrupt sound of his voice caused the closest of the animal- plants to fall back in what he considered to be a reflexive response. Such a response required some semblance of a brain. Cameron was quickly coming to the conclusion that he was not going to like this new world.

He first heard, then spotted Thack moving down the line of robots coming his way. "We have arrived. I found a place for you that is safe from roaming carnivores."

Cameron glanced about. "Looks pretty much the same here as the last few miles we've been walking."

"Come . . . I will show you." Thack began heading back in the direction it had come from, only suddenly to dramatically slow down again. The grinding noise had increased; smoke billowed out from the robot's faulty tread mechanism. A nearby robot came forward—used its metal claw to hammer down on top of the tread. That seemed to do the trick. Thack was off and running again at a fast clip. Cameron sidestepped around the other robots to hurry after Thack. He only had to worry about the animal plants on his left side, since the other robots formed a barrier on the right.

Reaching the front of the line at the top of a steep grade, things started to make more sense. Coming to a halt, Thack rocked and swayed. Cameron and the robot stood, gazing across the distant open plains, several thousand feet in elevation below. Their high-up perch offered Cameron enough information. Now he could make several simple deductions. Beyond lay a large spacecraft. One, ordinarily, that would be both tall and wide—if it hadn't crashed into the ground nose first. It looked relatively new, similar to an advanced Apollo lunar lander, with its three landing struts and disk-like pad assemblies. Currently, all were facing skyward instead of providing the necessary landing support. The ground around the crumpled ship was covered in green, more of those same animal-plants. The plants looked to have originated from, and expanded out from, the ship in a wide circumference of many miles. The further away from the ship the fewer animal-plants there were. It seemed clear these plant-creatures, or whatever they were, were quickly making this world their own.

"How long . . . has that crashed ship been there?" Cameron asked, wishing the robot had mentioned earlier that there actually could be other intelligent life forms around. He wondered if anyone, conceivably, lived through such a crash.

"Maybe several days. Maybe several weeks," Thack said.

Cameron felt something brush against the back of his neck and quickly jerked away. One of the animal-plants had crept right up on him. "Just how dangerous are these things . . . like to organics?"

Thack's head spun around then, tilting upward to look at him. "Did you not notice the Morpar?"

"You never really told me what that was. I wouldn't have known what to look for." Thack pointed a mechanical arm in the direction just over Cameron's left shoulder. He turned and saw nothing out of the ordinary, just more of the same damn animal-plants along a tall rock ridgeline. A ridgeline, now that he scrutinized it, not made of rock. An obviously large dead animal was lying prone on the ground. He could make out a head and the contours of a dinosaur-like body. Much of its flesh still remained. Exposed bones on its wide-framed ribcage were totally infiltrated with the animal plants, which were moving, scurrying about, pecking at the mountain of a carcass. Even in this furnace-like environment, Cameron felt a chill run up his spine.

"How long has that animal, that Morpar been here?"

"Indeterminate. Perhaps a day."

"And they killed it, killed this Morpar?"

"No. The intruders, that is what we call them . . . are scavengers. They could not bring down a full-sized Morpar. Not bring down any organic animal on their own. Intruders are scavengers . . . not predators."

"Then who or what killed it?" Cameron asked, and then remembered the creatures aboard the *Albergone* that had escaped through the open gap in the hull. *Would any of those beasts be capable of this? Probably.*

chapter 52

Thack proceeded ahead over the crest of the overlooking rise and headed down a steep, albeit wide, path. Cameron hadn't noticed this back-and-forth switchback trail descending below until right then. From what he could see, the animal-plants had yet to infiltrate this part of the landscape. Following behind Thack, he soon was right behind the little robot again. Without looking back, Cameron could hear the other robots not too far behind.

"Where are you taking me? Not to that ship, I hope."

"Taking you to Bunker 250. Safe there."

"Can you tell me . . . how you and the other robots came to this planet?"

"Repairs. You will make repairs within Bunker 250."

"How far is it? This bunker?"

"Close to our current location. Fifteen miles. Need to keep moving. Best not to delay."

Cameron didn't like the idea of walking that far, especially with so many potentially hidden dangers lurking along the way. "Just stop for a minute."

Thack, doing as directed, spun its head around.

"I may be able to get us there faster. This trail . . . does it stay this wide the rest of the way?"

"Wide?"

"Yeah. Does it get any narrower?"

"A trail is a trail is a trail . . ."

Cameron huffed out a frustrated breath. Even the Loth was easier to talk to than this robot. He swung the trinious bundle free from his back and set it down onto the ground.

It took a few moments to get things set up, but soon a familiar low hum droning sound emanated from the Lox unit. A moment later, a bright cone-shaped beam of light began to perform back-and-forth swiping motions. It took twelve of such cycles to complete the perfect replica of his 2004 Ford V8 F150. Seeing his old, beat-to-shit pickup again was like meeting an old friend.

The thirteen robots now gathered around—were watching with rapt fascination. They'd become far chattier of late, perhaps becoming more comfortable around him. They mostly conversed amongst themselves, in various beeps, pops, and squawks. But it seemed to Cameron that the conversing, as of late, was turning more to a kind of squabbling. He found it distracting. Rubbing his temple, he felt a headache coming on.

"One down, three more to go," he said to no one in particular. With each completed reproduction of his truck, he had to pick up the Lox unit and move it farther down the incline. He then repeated the re-materializing process.

Soon, four identical pickup trucks stood ready to go on the clay, inclined trail. Each had a set of keys dangling in the ignition. The robots moved in closer and began inspecting the vehicles.

"I guess I'll need to show all of you how to operate such a vehicle, huh?"

Thack, first to figure out how to open the door, lifted itself up then onto the first truck's passenger seat. Cameron hurried around to the driver's side and climbed in behind the wheel. "Gather around everyone . . . pay attention."

He had to go through the basics of driving a Ford pickup truck several times. How to start the truck by turning the ignition key, explain the automatic transmission selector lever, and when to use the park, drive, and reverse settings. How to steer, and where the accelerator and braking pedals were. That last aspect became a hot point of contention. Some of the robots weren't anatomically suited to sit on the seat and still reach the pedals. More bickering started. Cameron, afraid an out-and-out brawl would soon erupt, struggled to keep his temper in check. It occurred to him they were like the seven little dwarfs—only there were thirteen—and there wasn't a Happy dwarf amongst the lot.

It took a full hour before an assigned driver robot was allocated for each truck. The others would find a place to position themselves—either on the passenger seat, or sitting in the truck's bed atop the tarp covering all the personal crap stored beneath it.

Cameron returned to sitting behind the wheel of the lead truck, with Thack sitting beside him riding shotgun. He turned the key and the engine rumbled to life. Letting the big V8 idle a minute, he glanced in the rearview mirror and watched the robot drivers get their respective vehicles started up. He saw a commotion-taking place in each of the three trailing vehicles—saw rapid mechanical arm movements and heard more bickering. Shaking his head, he glanced over at Thack, who had at some point secured the passenger-side seatbelt into place. A horn blasted from behind them, then another, and then another. "I don't suppose we can just leave them here?"

Thack didn't reply.

Cameron, about to put the truck in gear, both heard and felt the truck directly behind them collide into their rear bumper. "What was I thinking? This'll never work."

Thack raised up a mechanical arm in a *let's get going* gesture, so he put the truck in gear and goosed the accelerator. He avoided looking in the mirror. *If they make it, they make it—if they don't, they don't.*

They made their way down, traversing from one steep switchback over to the next. It was slow going. Putting the truck into low gear while riding the brake, he went back to checking in the rearview mirror—concerned one of the farther back trucks might have veered off the trail. *Shit.* He dreaded the idea of having to go back to check. Three-quarters of the way down the mesa path they were traversing, Cameron hit the brakes. The truck swerved and skidded to a stop. Up ahead, standing tall in the middle of the trail was a lone figure.

"This isn't possible . . ."

chapter 53

Heather . . .

S he stayed quiet as XI and the three security droids moved farther into the apartment suite. Approaching the seating area where she, Cleeanne, and Phonk were situated, they slowed to a stop—hovering in place. Each security droid was armed with a Taser—sparking and crackling. Heather found it hard to pull her eyes away from the pain-inflicting devices. The mere presence of the four droids was frightening. At any moment, she half-expected, along with the others, to be shackled and quickly herded below ground to the confinement cages. And that everything transpiring earlier—primarily the transfer of power from Ginott over to herself—would be irrevocably reversed. Part of her wouldn't be surprised in the least. She was way, way out of her league here, a girl barely out of her teens. Hell, just hours earlier, she'd literally peed herself from fright—did so in front of thousands of onlookers.

"I think you're supposed to . . . like . . . tell them something, or ask them something, Heather," Manny said, eyeing the droids.

Heather nodded. "I already know that. I'm just . . . thinking things through."

Phonk, on the couch, said, "You don't look like you're thinking. You look like you're lost."

Ignoring him, Heather said, "What is it you want, XI?"

"The transfer of livestock onto available transport vessels has commenced."

"That's good. When will they, um . . . depart? Get on their way?"

Phonk rolled his eyes.

"Within the hour," XI replied succinctly.

"Okay . . . well, what else do you need from me right now? Is there something else?"

"The Loth. We have loaded the Loth onto a transport. I am unclear which planet you wish it delivered to. DA Corean 5, where the breed originates, or Sang-Morang, or Earth?"

She hadn't expected the Loth to already be loaded onto a spacecraft. Why would they do that? Without the Loth's protection, she feared she'd be no safer than anyone else here—she'd be powerless. More importantly, without the Loth, Cam's Loth, her sole remaining, physical connection to Cam would be gone.

"The Loth stays with me!" she said with conviction. "Don't make assumptions. If I wanted the beast loaded onto a spacecraft I would have said so."

The menacing-looking black droid did not respond. She looked over to Manny, and then Cleeanne, inwardly chiding herself. The whole prospect of where to deliver the Loth reminded her of something else. Something that was very important—something crucial. "XI . . . will you answer me truthfully. Any question that I have?"

"There is no reason to deceive you."

Heather took that as a yes. "That little weasel, Ginott, told me that Earth was in grave trouble, infested now with killer Loths, and that earlier attempts to eradicate the Griar Loth's offspring had actually failed. He said that Earth was being overrun. Is there any truth to that? Is Earth really in trouble?"

"Ginott spoke the truth. Yes, Earth is in trouble."

Earth is in trouble. She replayed XI's words in her mind. Four words that changed everything. She knew she could no longer leave here to search for Cam back on Sang-Morang. She needed to return to Earth; try to do *something* to help the people, *her people*, back home. She thought of Cameron waiting for her—all alone. But he knew that world. He loved it there and he'd find a way to survive and could do so even without the Loth by his side. She'd find a way to get to him eventually. She remembered how incredibly resourceful Cam could be. *What if, by then, he'd already gone or was gone now?* She thought about that—the unlikely prospect that he had found a way off that world already. If so, he would do everything he could to come after her. *Is he headed here to Winforge to rescue her?* But not seeing how that could be possible, she mentally let that prospect go.

"There's a change of plan, XI. Actually, more like the plan has expanded." Again, she glanced over to Cleeanne, Manny, then Phonk.

"XI, I still want you to continue transporting and resettling the creatures on Winforge back to their home worlds. But the highest priority now will be Earth. Saving Earth."

"Why even bother?" Phonk asked.

Both Cleeanne and Manny looked concerned. Clearly, they had not heard the news of what was happening to their home planet Earth.

"How many more of you . . . security droids, and such . . . are there here?" Heather asked.

"There are two-hundred-twenty-nine activated units."

Heather considered that amount. Not many, considering the overwhelming task at hand.

XI continued, "Eight-thousand-two-hundred-and-ninety-five inactive units are contained within subterranean storage depots eight, nine, and thirteen."

Manny asked, "What would it take to get them out of storage, up and running like the four of you?"

XI remained quiet.

"Go ahead . . . you can answer her question," Heather said.

"Twenty-four-hours time should be adequate."

"And you can arm them . . . give them weapons suitable to attack something like a Loth?" Heather asked.

"There is no weapon within our armory that would be sufficient for such a task."

Heather should have expected that answer. Griar and Minal Loths were impervious to most weapons, even big bombs. "Let me make myself perfectly clear, XI. You are tasked with saving Earth from the Griar Loths. You will go to war with the Loths if need be. Activate your army of droids, then arm them with the largest, most powerful weapons you have. I don't know much about such things, but I'm assuming you do."

"Yeah, and you don't want to disappoint her . . . ," Manny added.

"That ship, the one you loaded the Loth onto. It's big, right?"

"That is correct, the largest vessel—"

Excited now, Heather continued speaking over the droid, "Large enough to transport your entire army of activated droids?"

"No. That would require four additional such vessels."

"Okay. Change of plan again. I guess the transfer of some of the creatures here on Winforge will just have to wait. First, we save Earth. You are to divert the necessary spacecraft required for that. Can you do that for me?"

"Yes."

Some part of Heather wondered how long XI would stay this accommodating. She still expected it to revert back to its evil self at any moment. Being able to bark off orders like she was some kind of military general seemed far too easy, especially since she had no idea what she was doing. But she would continue to play this role, just like she played Sandy Olsson, in that high school production of Grease. She turned to the others. "This actually might work. Oh, and we, too, will be on that transport. Ensure accommodations are made for us, X1."

"No. Forget it! I'm not going to Earth. Why would I want to go to Earth?" Phonk asked.

Manny shrugged, "Good question. Your little cage is probably still waiting for you . . . underground," gesturing with her chin toward the floor. "Hey, if you're lucky, no one will forget about you, forget to feed you that slop you're so fond of."

Phonk looked to be reconsidering his position.

"Well, what are you waiting for? Haven't I given you enough to do, XI? We're wheels up in twenty-four hours!" Heather briefly wondered if that was the right expression, but seeing XI and the three security droids hurrying toward the door was certainly encouraging.

"Wheels up?" Phonk repeated.

"Oh, shut up," Manny said back.

Cleeanne asked, "So . . . we're going home? We're really going home?"

Heather nodded. "Yeah, whatever's still left of it."

chapter 54

Cameron . . .

T*his isn't possible . . .* Cameron repeated the same words over and over in his head. He forced himself to look away from the tall figure standing some thirty feet away on the incline. He closed his eyes—squeezed his eyelids tightly shut. Perhaps unaware of it, he had been bitten by one of these animal-plants—the invaders—and right now hallucinogenic psychoactive agents were coursing through his veins. Perhaps that was the reason he'd totally lost his grip on reality. *It made sense.*

He glanced up, squinted through the F-150's cracked and bug-splattered windshield, then opened the driver-side door and slowly got out.

"It's me . . . I promise, your eyes aren't playing tricks on you, son."

"Sheriff?"

Still wearing his official Larksburg Stand khaki-colored police uniform, Sheriff Bart Christy looked as intimidating as ever. With his shiny domed pate, his penetrating blue eyes, even here on an alien world he seemed bigger than life.

"Sheriff Christy, that really you?"

Hearing his title spoken, the older man squared his shoulders and nodded. Three other individuals slowly walked into view too—stood to the right of Heather's father. One was Deputy Kirk, whom Cameron was not particularly happy to see, another was an alien male of undeterminable origin. Next to him stood a pale *Plain Jane* female, possibly a Thidion. The alien male wore something around his neck—a device of some kind.

"I can explain . . . both how . . . and why I am here," the sheriff said.

Cameron gestured to the still-visible crashed craft off in the distance. "I assume you arrived in that upside-down ship out there."

The sheriff didn't try to hide his annoyance at the Thidion, standing next to him. *Perhaps he was the pilot,* Cameron thought.

"The important thing is we found you." But he looked concerned as his eyes scrutinized the small caravan of replicated trucks. "Cameron, where is Heather?"

Cameron held up a steadying hand. "Look, we got temporarily separated, but as far as I know she's still alive . . . and doing well. He felt his face grow hot—the weight of heavy guilt upon him telling a father he hadn't kept his promise—hadn't kept his little girl safe from harm.

"Where the hell is she?" Deputy Kirk asked accusingly.

"She was abducted . . . while we were on Sang-Morang. That's another world. I know where she is now . . . I was actually headed there when we got waylaid here while en route. It's a long and convoluted story. I promise, I'll tell you all about it."

The sheriff and his deputy didn't appear remotely satisfied with his answer. Cameron took several steps closer. "Can you tell me how you found me? How you're even standing here, light years from Earth?"

The sheriff looked reluctant to move past the subject of Heather, and understandably so. His chest expanded as he took a deep breath in then let it out. "With the help of this here . . . individual, we tracked and found the *Primion*—found what was left of the ship up on a ridgeline, there on . . ."

"Sang-Morang," the Thidion male volunteered.

His words sounded tinny—computer generated. The thing around his neck was some kind of translation device, Cameron figured.

"And who are you?" Cameron asked, studying the alien male, who was of average height and wearing some kind of black and gray uniform.

"Rand. That's what we call him," the sheriff said, answering for him. "His actual name is too hard to pronounce. Cameron, understand that soon after you left other spaceships began arriving on Earth from outer space. All alien, of course, but fortunately friendly. Something about a Cosmic Axiom no longer enforceable, no longer restricting visits to Earth by alien species."

"So Rand here just happened to show up on Earth? And . . . like offered you a lift into space?" Cameron asked.

Rand sounded irritated with Cameron's questioning skepticism. "We did not accidentally happen . . . to land there, in L a r k s b u . . ."

Cameron, the sheriff, and Deputy Kirk all in unison said, "Larksburg Stand."

Rand's tinny voice was already getting on Cameron's nerves. He suspected the others had come to the same conclusion a while ago.

"Yes, Larksburg Stand, thank you," Rand said. "It is common knowledge, the recent troubles on Earth, the infestation of Loths. I am a Cheffdf . . ." He looked to the female on his right, questioningly. She murmured something unintelligible back to him. "I apologize, some words in my language do not directly translate into yours. I am a *scientist*. I collect biological samples. Study them." Rand gestured toward a cluster of hundreds of invader animal-plants nearby. "Those are just one of the biological sample genomes I collected . . . that were contained on my vessel."

Obviously not contained very well, Cameron thought to himself.

The sheriff's patience with the alien seemed to be running thin. "Look, son, Earth is in big trouble. There are many more of them. More of those same creatures . . . like yours."

"Loths," Rand interjected unnecessarily.

"More Loths?"

The sheriff nodded. "I guess some, maybe a few, survived the underground nuclear explosion. There was another nest, one farther down into the Earth's crust. It wasn't long before they began reproducing amongst themselves. Within days after your departure with Heather, they started coming up out of the ground. The only silver lining to any of this, if there even is one, is that they all quickly moved away from Larksburg Stand."

"How many—"

"There's close to a hundred now," Kirk said. "Loss of life is estimated to be in the hundreds of thousands. Other townships are being ravaged. They are progressively moving toward New York City. Attempts to kill them by the military haven't been successful."

Cameron tried to imagine one hundred Loths, like his Loth, freely roaming the Earth. What devastation they would bring to a huge population center like Manhattan. These enormous creatures were already at the top of the food chain—how long would it take before mankind was totally wiped out?

The sheriff put hands on hips. "We've come here looking for you, Cameron. For you and that Loth of yours. To bring you and Heather and the Loth back to Earth." He scanned the surrounding landscape.

"The Loth was taken too, along with Heather on Sang-Mo-rang. Again, I'm going to find both her and the Loth, I promise. But I don't understand, why do you need my Loth? Why bring it back to Earth."

Deputy Kirk, joining the sheriff's side, said, "The way Rand explained it to us is that Loths, by their very nature when there are a good number of them . . . like what's happening now, back on Earth . . . tend to run in packs . . . called swalls.

They'll follow a particular leader, typically an older, more dominant Loth that is routinely tested to see if it will defend its dominance."

"I still don't understand why bringing—"

The sheriff briefly placed a hand on Kirk's shoulder before closing the space between him and Cameron. "The Loths that are ravaging Earth, our home world, will follow a strong leader. The strongest leader."

Rand's device crackled, "One more thing. The Loths roaming on your home planet are somewhat smaller than the typical Loths, due to the interbreeding aspect. They are referred to as Bantam Loths."

"Again, basically, they'll follow after the biggest and badest leader," Kyle said, his brows raised high.

Now it makes perfect sense, Cameron thought. His Loth had already proven itself to be a total badass, most assuredly dominant in battles. "But even if these packs, or Swalls, as you call them, are of a smaller size, my Loth would never survive going up against—"

Rand shook his head. "Your Loth would only need to show its dominance several times. Prove it cannot be defeated."

"So then what? So my Loth proves its dominance?"

Thidion female spoke, "Then they will be herded off to a specific holding area. There, they will be euthanized. Poisoned."

Cameron took note of her near-perfect English. What she said made sense. A decent plan, but one now moot. "Well, that ship of yours isn't going anywhere soon. You're as ship-wrecked here as I am," Cameron said.

"Communications equipment onboard Rand's ship is still functional. He's already dispatched another ship to meet us here. It'll be another day or two," the sheriff said. He looked over at Cameron and waited.

"Getting to Heather, of course, is my top priority, but yeah, sounds like a solid plan, sheriff."

As if a weight had been lifted from the big man's shoulders, the sheriff said, "Good . . . I just hope we make it back to Earth in time."

A loud screeching noise came from behind—startling everyone. Cameron turned around to see Thack, with its smoking tread assembly, moving closer. The other robots, forming a semi-circle in front of the caravan of trucks, were keeping their distance.

Cameron asked, "You . . . Rand, you have tools on that ship of yours?"

chapter 55

"I think getting back onboard that ship would be . . . problematic," the sheriff said, giving the alien another sideways glance. "Those plants can bite and they're all over the ship inside."

Deputy Kirk added, "Several of the plants escaped midway during the voyage. It didn't take long before the whole ship was infested . . . crawling with them. Eventually, they got onto the bridge."

Cameron glanced over at Rand, who'd been pretty much scratching at his left knee nonstop. "It was a matter of unfortunate timing."

Cameron had already assumed that the alien pilot was bitten just as he was landing the craft. In truth, it didn't really matter now. "What's the ETA on your rescue ship?"

All eyes turned to Rand. He looked up, as if the ship would suddenly appear out of the sky at any moment. "I do not know, for sure. "Today . . . tomorrow, maybe the next day."

"Can we go back to the ship you arrived on, Cameron? Wait there?" the sheriff asked.

"I suspect there's been a radiation leak. Since all the onboard systems failed a while back and then the power went completely out, I had no way to test things. But I don't think it's safe there."

"Where were you headed?" the Thidion woman asked in perfect English, pointing down the incline.

"To some kind of bunker," Cameron said. "Where all these robots have been holing up for a number of years. I promised I'd try to get needed repairs done to them. It's a promise I'd like to keep."

Deputy Kirk made a face. "To a bunch of broken-down robots? Who gives a shit? And what's with so many identical-looking jalopy trucks?"

Ignoring him, Cameron said, "I suggest we take refuge in the bunker. Until your ship arrives."

"You have room . . . for us and the robots?"

"I think so, Sheriff. Just need to shuffle the bots around a bit."

After conferring with Thack and the other robots, they had no problem redistributing themselves within the three trailing vehicles. "Uh, why don't you sit up front with me, Sheriff? "You don't mind sitting in back, do you deputy?"

Deputy Kirk eyed the tarp-covered truck bed. "There's no room in that bed."

"Just sit on top of it. You can't really hurt anything in there."

"And you have the same exact load of crap in all four of your trucks?" Kirk asked, making an overly dramatic wave of his hand.

"That's right. I have a way of making duplicates of the things that are needed."

With a smirk, the deputy moved to the back of the truck, found the release latch, then lowered the tailgate. Without any hesitation, he began pulling items out and tossing them haphazardly off to the side of the trail: An old suitcase with assorted clothes inside; the beach umbrella; his mountain bike that cost more than anything else he owned; his plastic ice chest, which still made the sound of water sloshing about; and the still-unopened cardboard box, sent to him by his now long dead Uncle Hardy. Strangely, it was seeing the box tossed so roughly onto the ground—no regard for what might be inside—that was the last straw for Cameron.

"Stop!" Coming around the rear of the truck, he stood between the deputy and the now half-empty truck bed. "I don't want you treating my things like that."

"It's a bunch of crap. I've known derelict hoarders with better possessions. And . . . you've got three more truckloads carrying this same shit!"

"I said I don't like my things being disrespected!" Cameron repeated, several notches louder, getting right into the deputy's face.

"There's plenty of room in there to sit," the sheriff interjected. "And he's right, you didn't need to disrespect his things like that, deputy. Now, get in the truck . . . let's get moving before those plants creep up on us."

Kirk huffed a bit, then shrugged, and climbed onto what still remained of the mess. Both Rand and the woman also climbed in and found places to sit. On his way back to the driver's side door, Cameron spotted the cardboard box. One side of it had split apart, exposing the inner contents. He unintentionally gasped. Hesitating for a moment, he continued to stare.

"Christ, man . . . you want me to say I'm sorry? That I'll tape your little box back together for you?"

"No, Kirk. What I want you to do is shut the fuck up," Cameron said. Climbing in behind the wheel, he started the engine.

"I don't approve of language like that, son. I know my deputy can be a—"

"Sheriff, we're not in Larksburg Stand right now and you're not my boss. And sometimes there's just no better word to use than the word *fuck*."

Cameron was angry but he shouldn't be taking it out on Heather's father. He needed to get past what he'd seen in the box. Checking the rearview mirror, he found the other trucks had edged closer with everyone ready to get moving.

The trek down the trail was slow going. The switchback turns were getting fairly tight and approaching the next one, Cameron was forced to come to a complete stop and put the truck in reverse. He then drove forward at a better angle. Cameron knew there was no way the robots would be able to handle that kind of maneuvering. Without saying anything, the sheriff hopped out of the truck. In the mirror, he saw Rand and Deputy Kyle jump down from the truck's bed and hurry back to assist the clearly overwhelmed driver robots.

With the caravan moving again, the three displaced robots were sitting in the back of Cameron's lead truck. The Thidion woman, Cameron still didn't know her name, had joined him in the cab and was now sitting in the passenger seat.

He shot her a glance. "You know, you remind me of someone . . ."

She continued to stare out the windshield but nodded.

"What's your name? Is it something I'd be able to pronounce? Thidion names are—"

"You assumed I am Thidion, but I am not. My name is Sanu Sre Cahl . . . please, just call me Sanu."

"So what's your deal with Rand?" Cameron could see the corners of her mouth turning up.

"I was . . . ," she paused in thought. "I think the term is hitching a ride from him."

Cameron nodded. There was a lot he wanted to ask her and could easily bombard her with a hundred questions. "Your English . . ."

"You'll find speaking non-native languages is hardly a problem for those capable of intergalactic travel. If you think about the innumerable races of people, on so many worlds throughout the galaxy, advanced technology would be needed in order to bridge the communications barriers. Some use intuitive cranial implants, some use what you would consider a type of smart nanoparticles, while others use older tech, like what Rand utilizes."

"And you?"

"I am an android, Cameron. That capability is pretty much standard equipment issued from the factory."

"You've been to Earth . . . lived there. To say something like that, that it's standard equipment . . ."

"That's right. The sheriff and his deputy weren't the only ones catching a ride away from Earth."

"And you're an android. That's different than a cyborg, I suppose?"

"Tomatoes, to-mat-oes . . . it's the degree or the prevalence of organic composition that is involved within our makeup."

"You have more than . . ."

"Than Alice had?" she asked, looking at him for the first time.

"How would you know that name?"

"The sheriff told you that we went to Sang-Morang looking for you and his daughter, right? And we found the nearly destroyed ship, the *Primion*, up on a ridgeline. I was able to mill around for a while. Discovered the ship's AI was a TAM unit. Highly advanced. The actual AI was caput, of course; completely destroyed. But there were several chard nodes, or droids, not sure what they were, that I was able to run mem-paps on."

"Mem-paps?"

"Think of it as a quick memory scan. Residing residual energy still organized into quasi-functional states. It fascinates me . . . like doing an archeological dig. Gaining important anthropological data. I am a student of such things. Organic or machine, no matter, it's all fascinating. It's about learning what makes an individual tick."

Cameron thought of Alice. He wondered how much information about her Sanu was able to glean from what little residual energy she'd discovered.

"You would be able to detect a radiation leak . . . from the *Albergone*. Why didn't you say something back there?"

"I prefer to keep such things to myself."

He slowed coming up to another hairpin turn.

"But I didn't detect any such leak. Keep in mind, I'm mostly organic, not that similar to Alice. From what I've picked up, it was an amazing piece of technology."

"She."

Sanu glanced over at him with a questioning expression.

"Alice is, or *was*, a she . . . I'm just saying."

"I stand corrected. And I apologize if I've upset you."

"I'm not upset . . . not about that. I'm just more frustrated than anything else. Those I most care about are in grave trouble light years from here. Being stuck on this planet is really starting to weigh on my nerves."

Sanu nodded back.

"Can Rand be trusted?" he asked. "Something cagey about that guy."

chapter 56

Heather . . .

It was two days before the droids returned to Ginott's apartment suite. Two days she had to endure not knowing what was going on with the Loth—not knowing if all her demands were, in fact, being followed. *Demands . . .* the mere notion that she actually had any kind of authority still seemed ridiculous to her.

Now dusk, she, Manny, Cleeanne, and Phonk were currently being escorted to an awaiting spacecraft. It supposedly was located just beyond the surrounding modern complex of tall glass structures. It felt good to be outside, breathe in the chilled Winforge air. They proceeded along a sidewalk that wound around ornate garden islands filled with flowering plants and lush trees of a variety she had never seen before. XI earlier conveyed that the Loth was there and had not been mistreated. Heather still didn't trust XI any farther than she could throw the menacing droid, but what choice did she have? She needed to get back to Earth—whatever it took to do that would be well worth it. She thought of her mother and father, then of the nearly destroyed hamlet town of Larksburg Stand. That presently, more of those same beasts were destroying her homeland. There might be nothing that she, and primarily the Loth, could do to help but she had to try. Her heart sank as she thought of Cam—shipwrecked again and all alone back on Sang-Morang. That he was waiting for her there. The guilt she was feeling served no purpose, so, for the hundredth time, she pushed such thoughts away.

"Look at them . . . disgusting . . . revolting," Phonk said.

Heather, suddenly pulled back from her thoughts, looked down at the unpleasant Craing man. She followed his scornful gaze to Manny and Cleeanne, walking together several paces ahead. "What? What's wrong now?"

Phonk continued to glower at the twosome.

"Is it that they're holding hands? That they're a couple? You need to get over yourself . . . we're all in this together. We need to watch out for each other. Can you do that? Think of someone else other than yourself?"

The only impact her words seemed to have on Phonk was to provoke an even nastier snarl. Heather quickened her pace to move further away from him.

The same three armed-security droids, as well as XI, hovered enough of a distance away for them to know they were there, yet not close enough to be tempted into swatting them away. Path lights were now coming on—bright spotlights illuminated the trunks of trees. Heather, gazing across the manicured landscape, had to admit the complex was beautiful. In the distance, she could see the towering outline of the arena. It remained dark—looked deserted—a good sign.

Up ahead, she could see some kind of airfield. She hadn't known what to expect, but this was far beyond anything she had ever imagined, easily stretching a mile wide by two miles long. Rising in varying sizes and heights above the ground were hundreds of large metal platforms. *Landing pads.* Near several of the largest landing pads were long enclosed structures, similar to jet-ways at an airport. With the exception of only a single huge spacecraft, the enormous airfield seemed deserted. Heather imagined days earlier—the battle between the Loth and the Tammer—when this same lot was completely filled with a variety of private spaceships.

The vessel that awaited them now was sleek, yet tall and wide-bodied. A bright white color, this was no old clunker of a spaceship. The four of them closed ranks. As they moved closer, the sheer size of the vessel became even harder to fathom. *A hundred Loths could fit inside that craft,* Heather figured.

"This what you expected?" Manny asked.

Heather shook her head. "I didn't know what to expect, but it wasn't this." The four droids moved in closer to them.

"Proceed forward . . . to beneath the craft's superstructure," XI ordered.

The group did as XI instructed, where a set of stairs gave access to the top of the landing pad. Once up there, they stared in wonder at the spaceship's wide underbelly, easily five hundred feet above their heads. Suddenly, up there on what was the ship's smooth contours, new seams and widening gaps appeared—the outline of a protruding square.

"It's some kind of elevator lift," Manny said. "I think we need to step back out of the way." Earlier, Manny had torn the sleeves free from her top, revealing arms as muscular as those on a lumberjack. At that moment she was using those big arms to push everyone out of the path of the quickly descending lift.

"Keep your hands off me!" Phonk protested as he stumbled backward.

The lift settled onto the pad with a definitive *thump*. The size of a small house, the cube-like lift was completely see-through as if made of glass.

"Oh shit . . . ," Manny said.

"Oh no . . . ," Heather said.

Phonk and Cleeanne remained quiet.

Standing inside the lift were two passengers—one tall and well dressed, the other short and rumpled looking. Doors quietly slid to one side, and the two passengers stepped out onto the landing pad.

"Good evening, my young friends," Thoran Ginott said. He looked squarely at them, one at a time, giving each a polite nod of his head. "You all look well. Rested."

Heather stared up at him, taking in his perfectly tailored suit and that gorgeous mane of blond hair. And at an ear where there shouldn't have been one. He looked at ease, healthy, and confident.

"For those of you who have not yet met my superior . . . the primary shareholder of the Winforge holdings, this is Mr. Stillman."

The *weasel-looking* man smiled at Heather, ignoring the others. He was short and balding. Really, really short— Michael J. Fox short. But in no way as good looking. She took in the way he was dressed—rumpled slacks and some sort of dress jacket—a smaller version of Ginott's. A potbelly hung over his synched-too-tight belt.

"So that was what, Ginott . . . all a ruse? A trick from the very start?" Heather asked.

"Yes and no. We did not anticipate your resourcefulness. I did not anticipate your influence with that wonderful Loth, and I certainly did not anticipate losing an ear in the process."

Heather shrugged, not having a clue what to say. She felt foolish—like an immature child, which she basically still was.

"It is amazing how quickly a perfect DNA-matched ear can be grown then attached these days. Broken bones repaired in minutes." His lighthearted expression quickly changed. "But I assure you . . . the excruciating pain I had to withstand through that ordeal . . . was real. Something I will not soon forget."

"It is time to leave," Stillman said, seeming bored with the conversation.

"We're not going anywhere with you," Heather said. "Tell me . . . this place . . . it's still operational, isn't it? And not a single creature has been relocated back to where you took it from."

Ginott, with a patronizing smirk, shook his head. "In fact, we foresee exponential growth of the Winforge complex in the not too distant future."

Heather felt sick. She wanted to run and hide, but of course XI was there. She could see the droid hovering nearby in her peripheral vision. Turning her head, she glared directly at it. "I suppose there's no honor amongst any of you. Well, I promise someday I'll have the pleasure of watching you all get what you deserve. And that one . . . hovering over there, will get stomped on . . . get crushed like a used tin can."

"Uh huh, those are certainly harsh words, missy. But right now it is time for us to leave."

"She's already told you, we're not going anywhere," Manny said, taking a step closer to Ginott.

As XI quickly approached them, Ginott held up a restraining hand. "No need for violence, XI. I think once our friends learn where we are going, they will be more than happy to come aboard. If not, you can kill them. All but our pretty young maiden."

Heather eyed him with suspicion.

"We are taking you home . . . just as you requested. You see, I am honorable after all."

She could find no reason for him to lie. But what were their ulterior motives? She didn't understand.

The Craing man said, "You don't get it, stupid human. Stupid, naïve . . ."

Heather contemplated kicking Phonk in the face. Instead, she directed an impatient stare at him.

"Think . . . what is it they want? Simple. They need to fill the arena with spectators. And what is it that Earth at this moment in time has an abundance of?" Phonk stared back at her, as if defying her to figure it out.

Heather had no idea. She glanced back over her shoulder in the direction the arena then looked at Ginott and Stillman. Then she got it. Champions! They needed the ultimate killer combatants to attract bigger crowds. To maximize the betting, they needed Loths! And right now, Earth had plenty of them.

Ginott gestured toward the lift where Stillman was already waiting. "Heather, you are important to us. Essential even. These others," his gaze turned to Manny, Cleeanne, and Phonk, "are not. I will not hesitate to eliminate one or all of them if you do not do exactly what I ask of you going forward. So let's make this an . . . *enjoyable* journey, shall we?"

chapter 57

Cameron . . .

When he'd first stepped out of the *Albergone* earlier that morning, Cameron felt more alone than he'd ever been in his life. With the alien creature, Joe, gone—off to who knew where—he was having doubts whether he'd ever again make contact with another intelligent being on planet Clay. Strange, though, how quickly things could change. Now, a total of eighteen, including the robots, were trudging along together. Five miles back, it became apparent they'd need to continue the rest of the way on foot. The trail had become too narrow, with too many obstacles in the way: trees, boulders, and, strangely enough, another Morpar carcass—this one still relatively fresh and only partially devoured. They'd left the trucks parked back there, keys still in the ignitions.

Now with Thack at the front of the line, they were slowly making progress through an area that had yet to be infested with the invader animal-plants. Cameron and the sheriff walked side-by-side, although neither one spoke much along the way. Their only common interest was Heather, and Cameron could sense the sheriff's continuing resentment, even though he didn't come right out and say anything in that regard.

Thack's broken tread unit began screeching so Cameron hurried forward and gave it a couple of whacks with a rock. That did the trick as Thack sped away and disappeared into the trees. Up ahead, he heard the robot exclaim, "We have arrived!"

Cameron readjusted the strap of the trinious bundle, draped across his back, and gave the plasma pistol, tucked into his waistband and hidden beneath his shirt, a couple of quick reassuring pats. He then hurried ahead of the others.

He found Thack beyond the tree line, waiting within a circular clearing. Both time and the elements had taken their toll on the entrance into the bunker. Made from some kind of metal, two angled, ten-foot-high, walls acted as an entrance. Functionally, they gave protection to the descending ramp. As Cameron approached, he could see all the way below to the lower landing, which he guessed was about thirty feet down. Recessed within the shadows was what appeared to be a substantial metal door.

"This is it . . . the bunker? Where you've been living?"

Thack's round head tilted to one side.

"Where you've been residing all these years?" Cameron clarified.

"That is correct," Thack said, and proceeded to descend the ramp as the others arrived within the clearing. The robots moved directly toward the ramp, leading down into the bunker, while the others drew together—clearly, no one wanted to head down the ramp without at least some discussion.

Rand was the first one to speak: "On approach, when onboard my ship, there was very little information available about this world. Like what kind of, if any, previous explorations had taken place here. Or if there were mining operations, which would explain there being a bunker and worker bots. . . ." He turned to Cameron, "Have any of these robots explained what it was they were doing here . . . in years past?"

"Not really. I found the whole lot of them to be barely functional. Not only in physical disrepair, which is obvious, but the way they process information. I don't know, they're all messed up. I've yet to get a straight answer out of any of them. The one I call Thack is the most communicative of all, but even that's like speaking with a three-year-old child."

"Any idea what we'll find down there . . . in that bunker? Is it safe?" the sheriff asked.

Deputy Kirk broke off from the group and stood at the top of the ramp. "I'll go down. No sense we all take a risk." He pulled his service weapon out from its holster.

"If anyone's going down there it will be me," the sheriff said.

"Um, can we just hold up a minute?" Cameron asked. He stared at Sanu Sre Cahl for several seconds then raised his eyebrows.

She shrugged, "What?"

"Don't you have internal sensors? Better resistance to things that the rest of us don't have?"

"What's he talking about," the sheriff asked, looking at her.

Sanu ignored the sheriff's question. "True enough, I should be the one to go down there first," she said, stepping around Kirk and heading down the ramp.

The sheriff looked confused. "She's not . . ."

Rand said, "She's an *arliogaff . . . gaff for short.* What you'd refer to as some kind of android, or cyborgenic being, but she's also different than either of those concepts. Comprised of both organic and inorganic materials, where she comes from . . . her world . . . everyone is a gaff. Yes, she's the best choice to go down first. Investigate, before the rest of us go on down, perhaps jeopardizing our lives."

Now Cameron felt like a total ass. *Why should she be the sacrificial lamb?* He'd made the assumption, since she wasn't one hundred percent organic, was part machine, that her life was somehow less important. A mistake similar to what he'd made with Alice.

"Hold on, Sanu!" he yelled, as he hurried around the corner of the wall, though she was already three-quarters of the way down the ramp. "I'm coming with you." As he ran down the slope, he pulled the plasma pistol free from beneath his shirt. Catching up with her, he said, "That was a totally dick move back there on my part. Sorry. How about we check out the bunker together?"

Sanu nodded indifferently. "That's fine. But I think you and the others are making this a bigger deal than it needs to be."

"Maybe so." He reached the tall metal door and looked for a latch—some way to open the thing.

Sanu, reaching around him, rapped her knuckles three times on the door. "Sometimes the simplest solution is best."

Almost immediately the door noisily began to roll open, disappearing within the bunker's left-side wall. Cameron took a step back, covering his mouth and nose with one hand. He had to fight against the urge to gag. "Don't you smell that?"

"Oh yeah . . . I smell it. Unpleasant, even to a gaff like me. But it won't kill you, if you can tolerate it."

He nodded, reluctantly proceeding forward into the semi-darkness. It took nearly a minute for his eyes to adjust to the oppressive gloom—barely able to discern the dimly lit silhouetted forms moving about around them. A large space, Cameron had the feeling there must be other rooms or compartments beyond this one. Robots within the space were working—plodding along, probably doing the same repetitive functions they'd been doing for many years. He wondered what the various machines were that they were working at.

"Can you see what it is they're doing in here? It's too dark. And this smoky haze . . ."

"Cameron, I think you should leave. Tell the others not to come down here."

"Why not? What is it? Your sensors picking up something."

"Forget my sensors! I can see it with my own eyes. Just look, Cameron . . . it's there . . . right there in front of you!"

He squinted into the murk then finally saw it. Desperately wishing he hadn't, his breath caught in his chest—the beating of his heart a kettledrum in his ears.

Different sounds now, of loud voices echoing into the chamber behind him. The others had followed them and were entering into the bunker. *Oh God . . .* he had to warn them—tell them to run!

Unfortunately, it was already too late for that. Revealed within the foul mist was a chamber that was much, much, bigger space than Cameron first assumed. They were all there—the creatures from the *Albergone*. At least, what was left of them. And something else.

chapter 58

At first Cameron thought they were simply other, much larger, robots. But these were no robots. He guessed they were about twelve feet tall and, most assuredly, beneath their armored spacesuits were organic alien beings. Alien beings that were now pointing the muzzles of their energy weapons directly at them.

Five of them, moving about the space like armed sentries, were overseeing that the operation continued on without a hitch.

Cameron and the others raised their hands. He felt the plasma pistol pulled from his fingers. Looking up, he saw another, a sixth sentry, standing directly behind where he stood—his helmeted head six feet above his own. Behind a series of narrow slits two alien eyes stared down at him.

Both the sheriff's and the deputy's service weapons were also confiscated.

Cameron had assumed the thirteen robots were here all alone; had based that conclusion mostly on Alice's early assessment—that this planet was uninhabited. Again, clearly it wasn't. Had she deliberately lied to him, or had her own internal processing become severely compromised, perhaps from direct contact with too much radiation? He chose to believe the latter.

"It's some kind of meat processing plant," Sheriff Christy said.

Cameron watched, sickened by what he was witnessing, as the assembly line operation continued—robots going about their individual, methodical, functions. A large conveyor belt assembly snaked its way from one robot station to the next. First, the meat was butchered at the far end of the chamber. Cameron could make out what little remained of the large, starfish-looking Prinwhin beast, that only the day before was held captive within the *Albergone*. Generous slabs of its meat moved along the conveyor belt to another station, where a robot used a steam nozzle of sorts to spray it down. Next, the now-cleaned meat was transferred into some kind of vacuum-wrapping packaging process. There, an awaiting robot transferred the package onto a different conveyor belt, where it entered the mouth of another machine. Seconds later, it emerged as a frozen square block. On and on, the same factory-like processing continued.

"Fascinating," Sanu said, "but the question arises . . . who would, or could, consume such an immense amount of flesh?"

At the moment, Cameron was more concerned whether they too would become cuts of meat soon, albeit much smaller ones, making their way through this maze of processing functions.

A deep, digitized, voice thundered down from above, "Follow the guardian."

One of the sentries momentarily signaled with a raised arm then turned and headed away.

"I guess we should follow him . . . do as they say," Rand said.

"So I can be chopped up and made into a frozen Big Mac or a Quarter Pounder? I don't think so," Deputy Kirk said defiantly.

"This is not the time for heroics, Kirk," the sheriff said. "Let's just see how this plays out."

Cameron agreed with the sheriff. They were led deeper into the subterranean chamber, then through a wide opening in a wall and into another chamber, this one smaller than the first. More meat processing was going on in here. Cameron watched as several familiar robots, now stationed within this area, went about stacking frozen meat packs onto flatbed trolleys, which were then rolled away, presumably off to some ginormous-sized storage locker, or a freezer somewhere.

The leading guardian made a sharp left turn into a corridor that barely provided him enough headroom. Cameron stole a glance backward, checking to see if the others were following behind him. Another armed sentry was bringing up the rear.

"Where are you taking us?" Cameron asked, staring up at some kind of breathing apparatus on the guardian's broad back. He noticed a multitude of semi-transparent hoses— some entering into and some exiting a flat section on the back of the sentry's angular headgear. Viscous liquids, globules, could be seen coursing through the tubing. Added to that, a disgusting slurping sound was audible as the alien breathed in and out. Cameron was just fine never seeing what lay beneath any of their helmets. His question, where they were being taken, was now moot, since they'd apparently arrived.

He saw Thack up ahead, in a slightly better lit area, waiting for them there. The guardian stepped to one side of the corridor, signaling everyone to move on past him.

"They don't like the light," Sanu commented from behind him. "These aliens' physiology is consistent with those of deep-ground dwellers."

"You can determine that, even though they're wearing those heavy suits?"

This time it was Rand who spoke up: "The narrow slits in their headgear . . . the avoidance of well-lit areas. She's right. Ground dwellers. More common within the universe than you would think."

"Follow me," Thack said, hurrying through another tall opening. "You can get started right away, everything you need is here. Yes, get started right away."

It was a workroom of sorts. Floor-to-ceiling shelves lined two of the four walls. Odd pieces of equipment were visible here and there on the shelves, though they were empty for the most part. Two long workbenches were strewn with assorted robot subassemblies—a leg, several arms, and three heads.

"What's all this? Kirk asked, looking about.

"It's where they make repairs to the robots. At least their intentions were truthful," Cameron said, moving over to the first workbench. "So Kirk, you won't be made into a Big Mac, at least not in the foreseeable future."

"I don't know. It might not be such a good idea to help them," the sheriff said. "Best not to become some kind of indentured servant . . . slave labor. And you saw what they're doing back there. It's retched."

Cameron picked up a leg assembly. The mechanical knee joint was completely seized-up. "Sheriff, if you think about it, back on Earth our own meat packing plants are not much different. Although I've never actually been inside one of those factories, I guess it would be just as disgusting. Maybe worse. People have to eat. Aliens have to eat. So, as long as there are carnivores around, lower life forms will be sacrificed for the appetite of higher life forms."

"I suppose." The sheriff moved over to Cameron's side and scrutinized the robotic leg Cameron now had standing upright. "So you told them . . . the robots . . . you can help them? Can repair those in disrepair?" he asked.

"I did. I know the necessary engineering principles from school. During my intern job at HyperCrell, I often had to repair a variety of mechanical prototypes, including robots.

"I can help," Sanu said.

"Good. First of all, let's get all the tools rounded up, they're scattered all over the place. Let's see what we're working with. Everyone, let's stack them up over there, on the other bench."

"Looks like we have incoming . . . ," Rand said.

A line had formed at the entrance into the workroom, Thack out front.

"We'll set up like we're in a medical triage situation. Sheriff, and you, too, Deputy, find out what each robot's problem areas are and then jot it down. Find something to write with."

"We carry a notepad and pen . . . all cops do," he said.

Cameron swung the trinious bundle from his back. "Rand, we need to clear the area over here. Let's make this into our parts reproduction operation. I'll show you how to use a Priopax Lox unit."

They worked as a team and started with Thack, who'd been lifted up onto the workbench. His forward tread mechanism was removed, along with his left one, then that one was scanned and entered into the Lox unit's memory banks. A copy was then regenerated for use as the forward tread replacement. On and on it went. Cameron directed the others on what needed to be done until no further direction was necessary. Sanu turned out to be an essential asset.

Back at HyperCrell, Cameron had all sorts of electrical test equipment available, with their various probes and clips, but Sanu—simply by a fingertip touch—was able to provide detailed verbal cues as to what the precise energy levels were at specific component locations. Since these robots did not use DC or AC electricity, or electric components, per se, Cameron had to pick up the alien design concepts and power implementations as he went along. It both fascinated, as well as frustrated, him. There was only so much he could learn this way; only so much he was able to do. Not every robot could be fixed back to one hundred percent functional proficiency. But as the day wore on, he was getting better and better at making repairs.

Four hours into the operation, Thack and one of the now-repaired robots returned with trays of hot meals, some kind of meat covered in brown gravy. Cameron first wondered if this meat belonged to a recently killed, processed

Prinwhin, but found he really didn't care. He was starving and it smelled fantastic.

They ate together, sitting in a circle on the floor. Suddenly, as the lights dimmed, everyone stopped eating and glanced about. Something was happening.

A sentry entered the workroom, followed by another similarly outfitted tall alien, only this one wore a more personalized armored spacesuit. Still old and worn, it had distinct decorative areas—reflective, like once well-polished chrome.

The seated group in unison wore similar disgusted expressions on their faces. For Cameron, the gurgling sounds, emitted from this alien's respirator unit, were enough to make his stomach lurch.

The alien wearing the fancier spacesuit and the defective respirator unit, gestured with a wave of his hand for the sentry to move aside. Cameron noticed fancy suit had only three fingers on that hand. Actually, on both of his hands. A quick look to the sentry and he saw he, too, was limited to just three fingers per hand. And in the sentry's case, his gloves had clearly been modified—as if there had, at one time, been two more digits there. Digits now removed. Cameron suspected they all were handicapped in this way. A punishment? It certainly explained the lack of dexterity that would be needed to repair the robots.

Fancy suit looked down at Cameron, and said, "You will now repair my clogged breathing apparatus." A wheezing slurp accentuated his directive.

Deputy Kirk tossed his plate of half-eaten mystery meat onto the floor then raised his hands in mock surrender. "I'm done."

Cameron stared up at the looming alien, the sheriff's cautionary words replaying in his head: *"Best not to become some kind of indentured servant . . . slave labor."*

He thought of Heather. Wondered if he would ever be free of this mess—if he would ever see her again.

chapter 59

Heather . . .

Once again, one of the same three waif-thin attendees dragged a comb through Heather's wet hair. She'd been thoroughly washed clean, then the same primping had ensued. Sitting naked upon an ornate duvet, she let them do whatever they wanted to her. Makeup was applied to her face, as well as to certain parts of her body. Highlights and accents.

"Raise your arms over your head," one of the attendees ordered in a monotone, heavily accented voice. Heather did as asked, letting her mind wander. Over and over, she ran through the course of events that occurred within the arena. There was a brief time when XI was under her control, she was certain of that, and Ginott lost an ear in the process. If it happened once, maybe it could again. Maybe there was a way to make it permanent this time—*but how?* Without the help of XI, she may be doomed. She then thought about Art—his earlier fortuitous visit. The old cowboy—*that strange aberration*—seemed apprehensive at the time—was clearly going out on a limb to help her. She wouldn't hold her breath for a repeat showing.

Heather looked about the luxurious suite, what Ginott called *the stateroom*. These were his quarters and the primping being done this time were not meant for the benefit of an arena full of spectators. The only spectator would be Ginott himself. He'd made it real clear what he expected from her this night. And what would happen to the three others if she did not comply with his every demand.

Upon stepping out of the lift, Manny, Cleeanne, and Phonk had been whisked away by a security droid—off to parts of the ship unknown. Heather had been on three spacecraft in her short life: The *Primion*, then another older vessel that she didn't remember the name of, and now this one, the *Ginott 3*. The second she'd stepped out from the lift she knew this craft was something extraordinary. Everything was white and so clean it glistened. Even the air was fresh. And huge—the spaceship was colossal. As Ginott and Stillman escorted her forward along the wide corridors, similar to the ones on the *Primion*, she noticed there were a variety of 3D pop-up displays. They actually seemed more customized for Stillman's taste than Ginott's. That was when she had the first clue this was probably Stillman's vessel, or maybe had once been his before it became Ginott's. Maybe they had a fleet of such vessels.

"Stand and slowly turn as I spray."

Heather, pulled from her thoughts, wasn't sure she'd heard her right. "Spray? Spray what?"

The three female attendees gently, but firmly, pulled her to her feet. One held some kind of appliance in her hand. She gestured, making a spinning motion with her arm, then said. "Slowly turn in circles. And close your eyes."

Heather did as asked and felt something cool being sprayed onto her naked skin. *Are they painting me?*

"Keep turning . . . around and around."

She complied, bewildered.

When they finished Heather opened her eyes, then padded over to a full-length mirror and gasped. Every inch of her body was covered with a delicate layer of blonde fur. There was something animalistic about it, as well as *erotic*. Oh, she knew exactly why she was festooned in this way—to better match her physiology to that of her captor Ginott. Although the intended reasons for her altered appearance disgusted her, now taking in her reflection, it was quite captivating. In the mirror, she caught the eye of the attendee holding the appliance, who offered her a devilish smile before turning away to stow the spray unit.

Heather asked, "How long . . . will this stay on my skin? Will it wash off?"

They ignored her question so she asked again, only louder this time.

"A long while . . . no, it will not easily wash off."

Twenty minutes later she was alone in the stateroom, back sitting on the same duvet, a pink, practically see-through wrap draped over her shoulders. She pulled it closed across her chest as she glanced toward the entrance hatch for the hundredth time. "I won't be able to overpower him, or fend off his advances," she mused aloud. There was nothing she could do. Sometime soon, she was going to be taken forcibly by him. Her hatred for the beast man was only trumped by a deep sorrow—what was to come would, most assuredly, impact her relationship with Cam. If she even survived that long. *There has to be something I can do.* One thought kept nudging to be acknowledged from the depths of her consciousness. She pursed her lips. Then she remembered. It was when they'd escorted her here—Ginott and Stillman. The way the rumpled little alien had looked at her. Had placed a possessive hand on the small of her back as they proceeded along. She'd seen visible distaste reflected in Ginott's face. The jealousy there.

She jumped as the hatchway slid open and Ginott stepped inside. He stood there a moment until his eyes found hers. Seeing the hunger in his stare scared her.

No, don't show fear . . . that will ruin it, she quickly thought to herself. If this had any chance of working, she needed to convey a completely different vibe—one of indifference.

He approached, a bemused expression on his face as he took in her nakedness—her fur.

Heather looked back at him, playing up her inner actress, with a weary, tired expression, said, "Okay . . . here we go again. Round two."

Only blank confusion showed on his face.

"You'll want me to take a shower. You know . . . since he just left."

"Since who just left?"

She smirked, offering up a sarcastic snicker. "As if you didn't know. On Earth they call it a tag team. But again, you'll want me to take a few minutes in the shower." She stood, turned away from him, and headed toward the adjacent bathroom—she inwardly prayed he was buying her act.

"Tell me! Tell me now, human tramp!"

She glanced back at him over her shoulder. "Stillman, of course . . . He just left minutes before you got here." She pointed to the bed. To the covers thrown haphazardly onto the floor. "Just tell me he's not coming back."

Sure, she'd expected a reaction. Expected anger. But what she was seeing in Ginott's eyes now was pure unadulterated fury. A death glare that left little doubt what he wanted to do to her. In that moment, Heather knew she had taken things too far. Had paved the way for an early demise. Staring at his two balled, white-knuckled fists—fists twice the size of any man's—she only hoped her end would come quick.

From deep within his chest came a rumbling growl—a growl that vibrated the air, her skin, even her bones. And then he was moving. Not toward her but out through the entrance hatch. His distant running footfalls echoed until they no longer could be heard. Heather continued to stare at the open hatch, waiting for it to slide close like it did only minutes before when Ginott arrived. But it remained open.

Swallowing hard, she tried to think. *I need to get out of here. I need to get to the Loth.* Heather dashed toward the bedding heap, lying on the floor near the bed, and snatched up the ruby-red bedcover. She swung the thick fabric over her shoulders and, without missing a beat, scrambled through the still-open hatchway. Trying to remember which way the lift was, she had another thought. *What would Ginott do to the unsuspecting Stillman?* Then, pulling the bedcover close around herself, she ran for her life.

chapter 60

Only now did Heather become self-conscious about her lack of clothing beneath the bedcover—of her exposed legs and bare feet. She turned a corner at the end of the corridor only to be greeted by another annoying pop-up display. Ignoring it, she felt her heart sink. She'd already been discovered. *Of course I have,* she inwardly chided herself. A spaceship like this one had so much ultra-modern technology. No way to sneak around and not be observed. She proceeded on anyway, not completely sure if she was heading in the right direction. *Why didn't I pay more attention before?* Up ahead, she noticed three uniformed male crewmembers approaching. Laughing, they hadn't noticed her presence. She looked about her for an intersecting corridor to turn into—nothing. Raising her chin, she tried to appear normal, though there was nothing normal about a practically naked girl hurrying along a ship's corridor. The three slowed and Heather spotted matched expressions of confusion on their faces. Not surprisingly, their puzzled expressions quickly turned to varying degrees of apprehension.

Heather slowed. Unable to think of anything else to do, she took on a haughty air of privilege. "What's your problem?"

The alien male in the middle spoke in a language she didn't understand.

"I don't understand you," she said.

Looking somewhat baffled, the one on the right touched his ear, waited a moment then asked in perfect English, "Who are you . . . and why are you—"

Impatient, she cut him off, "Which one of you can guide me to the lower decks? To where . . . ," she tried to think of an excuse for visiting the Loth. "I need to check on the livestock."

The three exchanged quizzical looks.

"I'm here with Thoran Ginott. Tell me . . . is it your intention to embarrass me? Shall I tell him of the ill-treatment three of his crew provided one of his special guests?" She let the bedcover fall open just enough to expose a bit more cleavage.

"No . . . I apologize. We apologize. I would be happy to escort you," a now eager crewmember volunteered.

She watched as his eyes roved from her chest, then up to her face, then down to her exposed feet and inwardly thanked the three attendees for the convincing layer of animal fur that covered every inch of her body. Animal fur so similar to what covered Ginott's body.

She nodded, "Please . . . lead the way," and hurried behind the lone crewmember. She guessed he was about her same age. He looked back—checking to see if she was keeping up. "We need to descend to the containment deck. It's this way to the lifts."

They turned a corner where up ahead were four big windows, two on either side of a vestibule, or waiting area.

A pop-up display appeared as they approached. The crew-member spoke up in English, which Heather suspected was for her benefit: "Containment area . . . level two."

"Prepare for lift arrival," the pop-up display cordially responded back and then disappeared.

A clear, cube-like lift descended into view behind one of the windows. As the door slid open, they stepped in together and the door closed. Immediately, the cube began its descent. Heather looked out as they flew past one level after another, seeing curious crewmembers turn their heads to observe who was within the fishbowl-like lift. *Hey, it's only a beasty-looking female, sporting a red bedcover. No big deal!*

The lift slowed and came to a stop. When the door opened the crewmember gestured for her to exit first.

"Thank you. If you will just direct me, I can make my way from here."

"Are you sure? It is no trouble."

"I'm positive. The larger animals, where are they kept?"

"Keep going straight down this corridor. They are all there . . . down that way. But you'll—"

"Thank you. Um, you can go, be on your way. I am fine." She stepped from the lift and hurried off, hearing the lift door *swoosh* close behind her.

Any moment now, she was certain, alarms would sound. Dispatched security droids were probably already on their way. She picked up her pace.

A pop-up display appeared directly in front of her. "You are entering a level four secured area. Please prepare to be bio-scanned."

"Damn!" Why on earth did I tell him to leave?

Just ahead, a familiar looking bank of windows—more elevator lifts. As she passed them, she noticed a cube lift rapidly descending. Within eyeshot were two sets of legs coming into view. She started to run.

Swoosh.

"Stop!" It was Ginott's unmistakable, commanding voice.

She stole a glance over her shoulder, almost stumbling over the dragging bedcover.

"Heather, stop! Stop now!"

Stillman was with him. His face clearly had been badly beaten. On his collar, down the front of his shirt, were drips and splotches of blood. *Good!* She gathered up the ends of the bedcover higher, sure her backside was fully exposed. Not caring, she ran as fast as her legs could carry her.

One after another, a flurry of new pop-up displays accosted her senses as she ran straight through them. One of them, she recalled an instant later, had the symbol of a hat. *A Stetson.* She tried to remember the text written beneath it. Ginott's hurried footsteps were getting louder—closer. There was no way she'd be able to outrun him. Letting loose of the bedcover, she felt lighter—freer to lengthen her stride and to pump her arms.

Up ahead, a clear hatch door spanned the corridor. It was closed. Distorted by the thick glass, she noted no movement inside. Gasping—out of breath—sheer exhaustion was catching up with her. Undoubtedly, Ginott must be experiencing it, too.

Happy trails young lady . . . she remembered the pop-up's four words written beneath the Stetson.

Slowing to a jog, her chest heaving, Heather had no strength left. As she approached the closed glass hatchway, she saw Ginott's reflection behind her, walking fast and looking out of breath.

"Move it! Get her!" Ginott yelled.

She heard a distant buzzing sound—in the glass's reflection were five security droids, coming up fast behind her. The hatch suddenly slid open. A pleasant voice said, "Bio-scan approved." Then another voice, one with a distinct Texan accent, said, "Good luck, young lassie."

"Thank you, Art . . . wherever you are." Gulping in a lungful of air, Heather staggered forward through the opening hearing the hatch slide shut behind her. Within seconds the sounds of fists pounding on the glass could be heard. *With luck, Art will keep the hatch secured for a good while,* she thought.

The fresh smell that pervaded the upper floors was gone down here. By the cacophony of loud and wild sounds, she knew she was in the right place, surrounded on either side by holding cells. More like jail cells, with vertical iron bars and latched gates.

"Heather?" A familiar face peered out five cells away. "Is that really you?"

Heather hurried over to her and reached a hand in through the bars. "Manny, oh God . . . I'm so glad I found you." She could see Manny's sudden reluctance—the odd expression on her face.

"It's me, Heather . . . what's wrong? Why . . . ?"

"You're covered in hair."

"It's not hair, its fur," she snapped back defensively. "It's not like I had a choice in the matter."

Manny offered up a half-smile. "And you're naked."

"Thank you, I'm happy to see you, too. Where are the others?" Heather asked, feeling Manny's eyes scanning her from head to toe. "Where are the others!"

"Right behind you . . . Cleeanne is there, and Phonk is five or six cages beyond her. And hey, I'm sorry! I am so glad to see you." Smiling, she asked, "Can you get us out of here?"

"With what? It's a miracle I made it this far. I need to get to the Loth. Have you heard it? Any honking?"

Oh yeah . . . it's down there . . . somewhere. And by the sound of it, it's not happy."

Heather nodded. "Hang tight, I'll be back as soon as I can." She gave Manny's hand a quick squeeze and retrieved her arm. The pounding on the hatch door behind her had ceased. She wasn't sure if that was a good sign or a bad sign. She heard Phonk make a lewd comment, but ignored it as she hurried toward the sounds of wild creatures in the near distance. For the most part, the cages were empty, only an occasional lone creature stared out at her as she passed by. She finally saw the Loth, huddled within a back corner of one of the larger cages. As she approached the thick bars she momentarily hesitated. *Suppose the Loth doesn't recognize me?*

"Loth?"

The creature didn't move.

"Loth . . . it's me, Heather. I've come for you. It's time we go find Cameron. Can you look at me . . . Loth?"

A full minute passed and she wondered if waiting there was a waste of time. Looking back toward the distant hatchway, she knew it was only a matter of minutes before they would find some way inside. Then she caught movement out the corner of her eye. *The Loth was stirring.*

chapter 61

Cameron . . .

"We told you getting involved with this would be a bad idea," Deputy Kirk said, pacing back and forth behind him. "We're stuck in here . . . and that smell! I for one can't take it much longer."

Cameron couldn't argue with anything Kirk said. For six straight hours, he, along with the help of Sanu by his side, had been cleaning, doing minor repairs to respirator units on no fewer than two dozen clogged alien helmets. Nasty, disgusting work, the only upside was a better understanding of the aliens physiology. Perhaps slightly different from humans, they clearly did not breathe the same air found on Earth, mostly nitrogen and oxygen. On their home planet, a different ratio of gasses existed, maybe more argon and carbon dioxide.

And these creatures really liked the dark. Holding one of the heavy helmets in his hands, Cameron took in the elaborate measures they used to protect their sensitive optic nerves. The slats covered their eyes from direct light, and the micro-jet sprayers within the cavity would keep their eyes doused with a special solution, or ointment. The helmets also had an elaborate array of coms functionality built in to them.

"Can you tell me what's going on with Earth, like . . . going back to when I left?"

Sanu handed him one of the long narrow brushes used for evacuating the intake lines. "You wouldn't recognize Earth. Sure, due to the Loths' destruction of much of the upper eastern coast of the United States, and well beyond . . . but also by the recent presence of what you would call extraterrestrials. Alien spacecraft descended onto the world in droves."

"Really?"

"Remember, the Cosmic Axiom is real. Terrestrial beings cannot bring advanced technology, or even share knowledge of alien civilizations, to still-developing worlds. The death sentence for doing such is also quite real."

Cameron wondered who it was that would enforce such a thing, but let Sanu continue on uninterrupted.

"With the Axiom now basically moot, or in question, visits to Earth by alien vessels have pretty much been non-stop. By beings like myself," she said. "You have no idea how many cultures had been waiting for the Axiom to be removed. There are very few worlds as beautiful or as pristine as that of Earth. So much wonderful water . . . everywhere! But now, for better or worse, Cameron, your world will never be the same."

"And the Loths . . . no one can stop them?"

Sanu shook her head. "Not so far, but not for lack of trying."

Cameron was aware both the sheriff and Rand had been huddled close together in conversation, at the far end of the workroom, for some time now. The sheriff's baritone voice suddenly rose in volume several octaves, ". . . and you didn't think it important enough to tell me any of this at the time?"

Cameron and Sanu exchanged a glance. "What do you think that's all about," Cameron asked her.

"Rand is just now informing the sheriff that the rescue ship didn't actually commit to rescuing us. That if they are in our vicinity within the next few weeks they may make a flyby."

"Weeks not days?" Cameron asked, no longer speaking in low tones either. "You sure you're hearing them right?"

"My hearing is on a whole different level than that of humans," she said. "I'm hearing them just fine."

Cameron dropped the alien helmet he was working on onto the workbench and charged over to where the sheriff and Rand were standing. As their heads turned—noticing his approach—Cameron let loose with a roundhouse punch to Rand's left cheek, putting his weight behind it. The alien pilot's head snapped back, and his legs wobbled before giving out beneath him. Crumpled to the floor—it was lights-out-time for Rand.

The sheriff stood still, seeming surprised but not angry. He stared at Cameron and said, "You literally beat me to the punch, young man."

"Is it true? That there's no spaceship coming for us? We're stuck here?"

The sheriff looked down at Rand's body, heaped on the floor. When he spoke it was just above a whisper: "I've screwed this up from the start . . . I failed. I just wanted to help . . . help Earth. That and make sure my little girl was safe. I've done neither."

Cameron looked about the room, but nobody else spoke up. Even Deputy Kirk was silent. "I may have an idea," Cameron said.

He hurried to the closed door and pounded on it with a fist. Several moments passed before he heard the door unlatch and then swing open.

Thack looked up at him. "Ready for another helmet?"

Cameron said, "No . . . I want you to take me to your leader . . ."

* * *

Cameron was being escorted through a maze of narrow, yet high-ceilinged, passageways. The little robot was hesitant at first to do what was asked of it, until Cameron simply asked it how its replaced front tread unit was doing, the not so subtle reminder that the robot owed him a favor worked.

He would not have been able to make the long trek on his own. It was too dark and there were too many left and right turns, no clear difference between one tunnel-like passage and another.

"We have arrived!" Thack announced.

"Down there?" Cameron asked, peering down a descending staircase into total blackness. "You can't show me . . . take me any farther than this?"

"Do not do well with stairs. Turn right at bottom of stairs." With that, Thack was off, scooting back the way they'd just come.

Cameron tried not to let his imagination run wild, what waited in the darkness below. He took the stairs two at a time then, as instructed, made a right turn when he reached the bottom. Although dark, it was still possible to make out the surroundings somewhat.

"Hello? Anyone down here?" He stopped and listened.

"Come this way, human."

Cameron would have complied quickly, but he didn't know exactly where the voice emanated from. It seemed to echo all around him.

"Walk straight ahead . . . I am here." The voice was weak, had an out-of- breath quality to it.

Then movement in the hazy darkness and the outline of a figure stood ten feet before him. "I'm Cameron . . . are you the leader here? The one in charge?"

"I am Lapths. I have been responsible for this outpost, for those that work here, for . . . a long time."

"Do you never leave? Do you not have transportation?"

"No."

Cameron peered through the deep murk and realized the alien before him was not wearing headgear. He then understood why the large helmets he'd been working on for much of the day had such a strange shape to them. In the semi-darkness, he caught the outline of Lapth's long snout. *Lizard-like.* "No, you cannot leave here, or no, you don't have transportation out?"

"Those that are stationed here will remain here for the entirety of their lives. Mine included. It is our punishment. Although . . . perhaps things will change now."

Cameron thought about that. This outpost was some kind of working prison. He heard footsteps coming down the stairs behind him. A moment later, one of the sentry guardians brushed past him. In the near-darkness, he watched the sentry kneel, holding something out with his outstretched hands. Next came an exchange of words Cameron did not understand. Squinting to see, he watched as Lapth took the item then brought it up to his head. No, not to his head . . . but *over* his head. It was a helmet. He heard the alien leader take a long, deep breath inward. Gone suddenly were the sickening sounds of clogged respiration intake lines. Obviously, Lapth was wearing one of the helmets he and Sanu had repaired earlier.

"I have not been able to breath . . . sufficiently for . . . I cannot even remember when, it has been that long." Lapth's voice was stronger and clearer.

"You, human, the one who calls himself Cameron . . . you have changed . . . you have changed everything here."

Cameron wasn't sure what that meant, whether it was a good thing or not. He thought about the invading animal-plants, currently ravaging the outside landscape, and cringed. "I don't know what to say . . ."

Lapth continued, "We have hunted and killed the oversized creatures you brought to this world. Such a plentiful supply of fresh flesh for us to process, food-stuffs that will feed our hungry world."

"This world?"

"Our home world . . . two light years distance from here. A rare meat surplus, like none other from this outpost . . . or any other outposts, from any of the worlds within the Poshnak Empire."

"That is your home . . . this Poshnak Empire place?" Cameron thought he saw the alien nod his head.

"You have repaired our mechanical workers. You have repaired our harsh environment suits. And you have given us something even more important. *Hope.* Hope that our life-sentences will, someday, be commuted. That someday we may be allowed to return to our homes."

Since Larth put it like that, Cameron didn't mind making the next request. "Will you help us get off this world?"

"I would if that were possible. I am sorry, we possess no transport vessel here."

Cameron's heart sank. To be shipwrecked here, possibly forever, was becoming a reality that he needed to face. He pushed away all thoughts of Heather. "Wait . . . this food surplus you now have won't find its way to the Poshnak Empire on its own."

"No, of course not. A squab-lift is scheduled for pickup soon."

Cameron didn't know what a squab-lift was, and frankly he didn't care. "When is *soon?*"

"Today . . . when it becomes dark outside."

chapter 62

Heather . . .

Behind her, she heard the hatch door open farther down the corridor. She kept her eyes locked onto the Loth. It looked so different. Now sallow grey in color, it bore a poor resemblance to the former, powerful creature it once was. Clearly, it had been broken, beaten, into this cowering— pathetic—beast. Just moments before, the Loth had been her one and only hope of survival here. But now, seeing the creature's eyes—its apathetic, half-lidded stare—she knew the Loth had lost its will to fight, its will to live. Letting her eyes drift downward to the creature's lower torso—she understood. Multiple crimson stubs oozed a viscous gore. All but one of its tentacles had been severed off close to its body. It didn't make any sense. Of what use would this beast be to them in its present condition?

Heather heard XI's distinctive sound coming up behind her. Also sounds of running footsteps—*Ginott and Stillman*. Suddenly aware of her near-nakedness, her vulnerability, she offered the Loth the only thing she could do in that brief moment—an apologetic nod and, "I'm so sorry."

She knew XI was right behind her. Felt its presence. Finally, turning to face the diabolical machine, she found the stun gun was no longer clutched within its mechanical claws, although it still had the two odd, jury-rigged plasma guns affixed to either side of its canister-like housing. The guns, she figured, were the source of the Loth's terrible injuries. "Why would you do such a thing? To what end?" she asked. "I thought you needed the Loth on Earth."

Thirty yards away, Ginott and Stillman, out of breath, were walking fast—both huffing and puffing after their long chase.

"What is your command?"

"Look at it . . . look what you've done!" she said.

"What is your command?" XI repeated.

"Why don't you just kill me and get it over with?"

"Is that your command?"

Heather stared back at the hovering menace. *What the hell?* "No . . . what I want is to be freed. To be safe—"

Arriving, Ginott spoke over her: "Kill her . . . we'll manage without the human."

Had she detected the slightest hint of desperation in his tone? *Strange*, since he was the one with all the power.

Stillman joined the party—his face bloodied, his nose, unmistakably broken, was pointed a little off-center. Hatred seethed from his bloodshot eyes. "You heard him . . . kill her!"

In that moment she thought of Cam. He'd probably never know how she'd tried to make things right. That she died thinking of him.

Honk . . .

"I order you, destroy the human!" Stillman commanded.

Honk . . . Honk.

Heather tore her eyes away from the droid's two plasma weapons, looking instead farther down the corridor—hearing the far off *honks*. Confusion registered on her face.

Stillman and Ginott exchanged a concerned look. At that moment, Heather *got* it. She felt stupid, having missed it, and wondered if Cam would have figured it out before now. *Of course, he would!* The droid indeed had been reconfigured to follow her commands back in the arena. Ginott losing an ear was proof of that. But somehow, desperate while within the clutches of the Loth, Ginott cleverly made sure that he, too, maintained some control over the droid. *But not exclusively.* She hadn't even thought to test if she still had control over XI too.

Honk! . . . Honk! . . . Honk!

And this pathetic creature huddled in the cage behind her was not Cam's Loth. She felt both instant relief and exhilaration, and inwardly thanked Cam for befriending such an amazing creature. Again, she looked farther down the corridor and wondered if she really did have control over the droid. "Release the other Loth . . . release Cameron's Loth. Do as I say, XI . . . I order you . . . do it now!"

"No. Ignore her," Ginott commanded. "I own you . . . I—" his words trailed off as XI quickly moved away from them.

"Do something!" Stillman yelled. "You said you still had control over that damn machine."

"Be quiet! I do . . . ," Ginott barked, as he continued on down the corridor. "Unfortunately, we both do," he added quietly. Ginott slowed to a stop, "XI, I order you to get back here!"

Heather saw XI come to a halt farther on in the distance and then heard the sounds of metal latches being released.

The punch caught Heather totally by surprise. Stillman's knuckle blow to her cheek staggered her backward and she saw stars—her sense of balance disrupted. His next punch caught her in the jaw and she collapsed downward onto her knees, desperately trying to protect her face with her arms and hands. She tried to speak—yell out for the Loth to help her—but Stillman's next attack came with a kick to her exposed belly.

She could only hope that what she was seeing behind Stillman was real. Everything was blurry—out of focus. *Was that really the towering Loth there now, nearly filling the corridor?* She tried to make eye contact with the beast, but wasn't sure if she actually had. Her head was killing her—everything was spinning.

In a blur of thumping, noisy, tentacles, the Loth was scrambling to get to her. *Honk! Honk!*

Running to get out of the way, but clearly not running fast enough, Ginott was catapulted off his feet and thrown hard, sideways, into the bulkhead with one casual swipe of the Loth's tentacles. His now limp, unconscious body fell to the deck where it lay motionless. The Loth, without stopping, used a trailing tentacle to scoop up Ginott's inert body.

On the verge of losing consciousness, she realized she was no longer the one being attacked—the Loth, honking and looking furious, also had Stillman already wrapped tightly within one of its tentacles. Mucus flowed freely from both sides of the beast's open mouth. Stillman was moments away from being devoured.

"Stop!" she muttered. "Loth . . . I need him alive. Do you understand me?"

The creature brought the petrified, struggling Stillman even closer to its mouth, but did nothing further.

Heather, battered from too many punches to the head, fought to stay conscious. "Where is XI . . . where is the droid?"

Surprisingly, it was Stillman himself, desperate now to help, who said, "Right there . . . up higher than you're looking. Please . . . tell the creature to let me go. I'll do anything you ask. I swear."

The hovering droid came into focus. "Tell me, XI," she said ". . . who is it that really commands you?"

XI slowly began to descend. Its digitized voice filled the corridor. "Within the arena, the one you refer to as Ginott initiated a programming redirect. One that provided for a parallel level command hierarchy."

"But just now you did as I asked . . . you released the Loth. You ignored Ginott."

XI did not reply.

"And who owns Winforge . . . controls the facility?"

"Stillman."

She looked over to him; his head now mere inches from the Loth's mouth. "Give it to me, Stillman . . . all of it. Complete control and ownership. I'm not going to let you torture so many people and all those animals any longer. Do it!"

It took several minutes for Stillman to do as was asked of him. This time she had the killer droid repeat back what was happening. Had it verify that she indeed did have the full control of the Winforge facility. She struggled to keep her eyes open, well aware she was suffering from the effects of a concussion. She stared at Stillman's defeated face. Her vision blurred, then suddenly his face was gone. *No!* she gasped. *Not just his face*—his whole upper torso had disappeared into the Loth's mouth. *Oops.*

Now, as she no longer could fight to stay conscious, she thought she heard the Loth's triumphal call, *Honk! Honk! Honk!*

* * *

Heather awoke to the sounds of hushed voices, and where the light was muted. Lying on her side, her head rested on a hard pillow. Someone's gentle fingers were moving stray hairs away from her eyes.

"She's awake."

Heather realized she wasn't lying on a pillow. Her head lay in someone's lap.

Manny leaned over and spoke just above a whisper, "Welcome back, girl."

She tried to swallow. "Water," she croaked.

"Do you want to try to sit up?"

She tried to nod her assent only to regret the motion. Taking a shallow breath in, she prepared for what would come next as she raised herself up. As excruciating pain enveloped her, a moan escaped through her lips.

Several pairs of hands assisted in bringing her into a seated position. She saw Cleeanne and sour-faced Phonk, standing nearby. "Where am I?" She peered around, noticing the metal decking. Nearby, lay a monumental mound of Loth mucus.

"The Loth brought you back to its cage. Then it wouldn't let us move you."

Heather glanced around her surroundings then noticed the tip of a tentacle still wrapped around one of her ankles. Although it hurt to move even a little bit, she turned just enough to see the Loth resting mere feet from her. Its eyes were closed—its breathing deep and loud. The creature, even asleep, exuded immense raw power and vitality. *How did I ever confuse the two Loths?* Her eyes widened. "Ginott?"

"My guess is you're right next to him," Phonk said.

Heather tried to move her head to better see.

"He's being crude," Cleeanne said. "The beast ate him, too." She pointed toward the Loth's massive midsection.

Heather examined both their faces to see if they were serious. *They were.* "And XI . . . where is the droid?"

Manny said, "For the last three hours it kept—"

Heather cut her off, "I've been out that long?"

"Longer, actually. Anyway, the droid hovered around you like a bee. Constantly repeating the same thing over and over again: What's your command? I think something's wrong with it. Definitely defective."

"So where is it?"

"You woke up a few times earlier . . . guess you don't remember."

Heather shook her head.

"You told it where you wanted us to go. Where our heading should be once we take off."

Heather thought of Cam. How she'd never needed anyone more than she needed him right then. "Did I say Sang-Morang?"

Both Manny and Cleanne shook their heads no.

Phonk said, "You said Earth . . . insisted upon it. Why you get to decide our fate I don't get. Don't we, don't I get a vote? My home world is closer."

"Shut up, Phonk," Manny said. "She wants to save her home planet . . . our home planet. And we're going to help her . . . isn't that right? She glared back at the small Craing man.

Phonk looked away, not committing.

Heather felt herself slipping back into unconsciousness. Her head was killing her and her vision was screwy.

"Stay awake, girl. There's a top-notch medical bay onboard this ship. You need to tell that Loth creature to let loose of you for a while. Can you do that?"

Heather nodded, "Yeah . . . I'll try."

chapter 63

Cameron...

Having been escorted back to the workroom, Cameron handed back both Sheriff Christy and Deputy Kyle's service weapons. His own plasma pistol was already tucked into his trousers' waistband beneath his shirt.

"Apparently, we're no longer considered a threat," Cameron said. "That and they want us to leave . . . like soon . . . at daybreak. They're open to helping us. But their leader, someone named Lapth, has a few conditions before that happens."

"And what. We're just supposed to trust him?" Rand asked.

Cameron had avoided looking at Rand for one simple reason—he hated the smug alien. Now, returning an equally distasteful stare back, he said, "Up to now, Lapth has neither lied nor misrepresented himself to me in any way. Can we say the same thing about you?"

The sheriff finished checking the magazine of his weapon then shoved the gun into the holster on his hip. "Let's not have any further altercations between you two, okay?" The big man crossed his arms over his chest and asked, "So what is the plan?"

"A squab-lift is scheduled to land sometime in the morning hours. Lapth has made it clear that nothing, in no way, can hinder the delivery of their most recent windfall of fresh meat to the Poshnak Empire. Nor can any of them within Bunker 250 be tied to anything nefarious that we might do . . . such as an abduction of a Poshnak Empire vessel."

Rand asked, "How are we supposed to get around those restrictions? Sounds impossible. You've made promises that can't be kept . . . made things a whole lot worse for us in the long run."

"Lapth wants us to negotiate with the captain of the squab-lift when they land here," Cameron said.

"What if he, or she, says no?" Kyle asked. "We just say okay and live the rest of our lives cleaning snot out of alien helmets?"

"There's another alternative," Sanu said, and everyone turned in her direction. Sitting in front of the same work-bench, she added, "We could sneak ourselves onboard."

"You must have read my mind," Cameron said. "We make ourselves blend in with the meat delivery. Hide ourselves within the cargo."

"How would that even work?" the sheriff asked, raising a brow. "There's still the issue of not abducting one of their vessels."

"It's a stupid idea," Rand added.

Kyle shrugged then nodded. "Look, I'm sorry if there could be negative repercussions for you and your new BFF, this Lapth guy, Cameron. But we're talking about trying to save Earth. What's more important to you . . . a few meals delivered to this Poshnak Empire, or saving Earth? Our primary mission has been to find the Loth as well as Heather, but since you haven't been able to accomplish either, I guess you have to ask yourself, what's more important to you at this point?"

Kyle was right, of course. Cameron knew that. But purposely misleading— hell, outright deceiving the outpost's leader was a hard pill to swallow.

Sanu, rising from her stool, headed for the door. She opened it and looked out. "There's no one standing guard. If we're going to do something, now's the time."

"It's not going to work . . . we can't simply hide within the cargo. Lapth is expecting us, or rather me, to negotiate with the squab-lift captain." Cameron glanced around the work-room, biting the inside of his lip as he thought about their dilemma. His eyes then refocused on his trinious bundle, lying on the floor. "Okay . . . I may have an idea. Not a very good one . . . but it'll have to do." He turned to Rand. "You're sneaky. Do you think you can take those here, get them into a cargo container unnoticed?"

"I think so. You're not coming with us?" he asked, not bothering to conceal his delight at the prospect.

"No . . . I'll stay behind. Make a pretense of negotiating with the lift captain. Tell him and Lapth that the rest of you already went back to your crashed vessel to get supplies for the trip . . . something like that. Though thinking about it, I can't see the captain agreeing to our request for a ride. Why would he?"

"What then?" the sheriff asked, looking concerned. "We'll be locked into a cargo bin, while you're stuck here on this alien world?"

"Remember that I had duplicated my old truck?"

The sheriff nodded back.

"I have a small flying craft that is supposed to be capable of space travel. Not something that could get me all the way to Winforge, mind you, but at least up into orbit . . . probably. I'll need to follow the squab-lift, where it intersects with the mother ship."

"You have a ship in that satchel thing of yours, yet you didn't think to mention it?" Rand asked.

"It's a tiny, two-man craft. I wouldn't go so far as to call it a ship. No way could we all squeeze into it."

"I'll go with you," Sanu said. "You'll need my AI capabilities."

The sheriff and Kyle glanced at Sanu with some skepticism.

"Rand . . . you need to go. Get everyone safely hid within a cargo container. Hurry, yet be mindful of their roving guardians. Don't get caught. I'll take care of things on my end."

No one moved until the sheriff extended his hand out.

Cameron put his own hand out, too. Firmly shaking hands, he said, "We'll get Heather back, sir. I promise. You have to know, there is nothing more important to me . . . nothing." Releasing the sheriff's hand, he hurried over to the workbench and retrieved the Lox unit.

As the others began to file out the door, Rand held up. Turning back toward Cameron and Sanu, he said, "Don't screw this up for us, human." With that, he, too, was gone.

Cameron returned the Lox unit to the trinious bundle and sealed it closed. When he stood back up, he found Sanu studying him. "You don't have to stay with me," he told her. "I'd manage just fine—"

"Oh, stop," she interjected. "Navigating a craft, especially a small one in open space, is no simple task. And the thought of being cloistered within a cargo container for who knows how many hours sounds dreadful to me. Anyway, this will give me time to ask you about that all important box of yours."

Cameron stared at Sanu Sre Cahl for several long beats before asking, "What makes you say that?"

"I saw the way you looked at it, at the ready to spill out contents. I told you, I am a student of sorts. Humans fascinate me. How they think . . . what makes them tick, as your kind would say. Your expression was one of concern, and of surprise too. So, tell me about the box."

"Now's not the proper time, if there ever will be one," Cameron said, lifting the bundle up by its strap and swinging it over one shoulder. "Let's head out . . . we can wait in the clearing topside." He noticed a flicker of disappointment cross her face before it returned to her standard expression of mild bemusement.

With Sanu in the lead, they made their way through the dark maze of tall passageways. Climbing up the stairs, they made no attempt to hide their presence. In fact, Cameron thought it a good idea to bring as much attention toward themselves as possible. They passed two patrolling guardians on their way out. Cameron gave them each a casual wave. The robots were nowhere to be seen. The machines were off—the conveyor belt still. With the exception of the two roving guards, the processing plant seemed deserted.

By the time they reached the clearing at the top of the stairs, sunlight was filtering through branches of the surrounding trees. Unshouldering the bundle, he placed it against the metal wall, feeling completely exhausted. *When was the last time I slept?* Cameron wondered. "We have some time . . . before the squab-lift shows up. I'm going to grab some sleep." He sat down, leaning his back against the wall, and let his eyes close. "I just need a few minutes . . . ," he was asleep without finishing the sentence.

The abrupt sound of landing thrusters jarred him wide-awake. Dust was swirling all around them and the thunderous noise was nearly deafening. Rising to his feet, Cameron saw Sanu standing nearby—her face turned away from the wind and grit. Grabbing up the trinious bundle, he moved closer to Sanu, noticing it was now bright daylight outside. "How long was I asleep?"

"A few hours."

Next came a series of loud metallic clangs. A section of the ground near them, now partially cleared of dirt and dust, suddenly exposed previously unseen large metal doors that swung both upward and open. The first cargo containers were being raised from below. Cameron wondered which of the containers held the hiding stowaways.

Not knowing what to expect—what the squab-lift looked like—seeing it now it looked like a no-frills basic cargo transport. Eight sturdy-looking landing struts supported a hexagonal-shaped superstructure atop them. No windows, and no features considered aesthetic, it was purely a functional spacecraft. A center section of the fuselage began to lower down—an elevator platform. Cameron could see several aliens, dressed in similarly harsh environmental suits to those worn by the aliens present within the bunker. Oblong helmets turned in their direction as the aliens took notice of them. Cameron waved, tried to appear friendly.

Sanu waved too. "You know . . . this *really* was a stupid idea."

He kept his smile in place, "Oh, I already know that."

Another handful of aliens appeared on the descending platform. All of a sudden, familiar robots, including Thack, began milling about, assisting with the hefting of cargo containers from below. Aliens inside the bunker were also seen exiting the stairwell. Hand waves were exchanged with the new arrivals as they stepped off the lowered lift platform. It seemed to be a happy reunion.

Cameron, surprised, noticed Lapth's sudden presence at his side.

"Where are your companions? On the way out, I noticed the workshop was empty."

"Headed out early to retrieve much needed supplies . . . from the crashed ship. Should be back any minute now." Cameron hated lying; knew he wasn't very good at it. Studying the alien leader—he wondered if he believed him?

"Ah . . . there is the captain now. I wish luck for you and for your friends in your endeavor to find passage. His name is Captain Morth. Come, I'll introduce you."

Cameron exchanged a quick glance with Sanu before heading after the alien leader. The clearing was a mass of activity, and he had to stop several times to let robots and aliens, dressed in environmental suits, pass by him. By the time he reached Lapth and Captain Morth, he could see things weren't going great. The captain was shaking his head, gesturing toward his ship with abrupt motions of his hands.

Well, that's not entirely unexpected, Cameron thought to himself. He and Sanu would make their way into space using the small Scalldian craft.

A sudden commotion stopped Cameron in his tracks. Apparently, judging by the simple fact that most everyone had turned in that direction, something had emerged from the tree line. One of the containers, being hoisted up onto the lift platform, blocked his view as raised voices quickly turned to screams. Cameron, hurrying now to better see what was happening, didn't immediately register what he was seeing. *Joe?*

The fifteen-foot-tall Hengtied Portule moved through the clearing with astonishing speed. *Oh no . . .* He was like some kind of vicious overgrown bat. Cameron watched in horror as one after another were struck by Joe's fast moving, extended claws. Actually, it was more like they were being shredded. Only a few of the Bunker 250 guardians were armed, and they either were too slow on the draw, or too caught by surprise to react quickly enough.

"Stop!" he heard himself say—but it was too late.

"We have to run!" Sanu yelled.

Cameron turned, seeing Sanu wide-eyed—terrified—standing behind him. She tugged on his arm, trying to drag him away from the horrendous carnage now taking place.

"Running wouldn't do us any good, Sanu. Look at it . . . the beast is too fast. But I don't think we're in danger."

"Are you fucking crazy? Just look around!" she said.

"Don't run! I promise you, I know him . . . it," Cameron said, turning back just in time to see both the squab-lift captain and Lapth being struck down. He suddenly felt sick to his stomach. *Perhaps Sanu was right.* Maybe they should have made a run for the trees after all. But it was too late for that now. Joe stood motionless within the clearing, calmly surveying his butchery. With the sole exception of Sanu and himself, all others were dead.

The creature's attention next fell solely on Cameron. *We should have run . . .* Joe approached slowly, his odd-shaped body now moving more normally.

Somewhat clumsy still, but nothing like during that torrent of terror he'd waged just moments before.

Cameron felt Sanu pressing in behind him—felt her trembling there. For an android, she sure acted more like an organic sometimes. When five feet away, Joe came to a stop—towering over them.

"Cameron," the creature said in his strange alien accent, "I have missed you." The beast's quasi-transparent, sack-like extra flesh—like a protective cape—extended outward as he raised his arms, blocking the morning daylight.

"Oh God . . . we're going to die," Sanu's muffled voice sobbed behind him.

Then Joe was upon them—enveloping them.

chapter 64

Initially, Cameron had his eyes closed—had stopped breathing while he waited for the end to come. But the end didn't come. Now cocooned within the darkness, he thought of all those who had senselessly died here today. He thought of Heather—and the growing mess he'd made of everything. He also thought of Earth and how his home world would never be the same; from both the ravaging Loths and the recent alien activity. He was both saddened and angered. And then he thought of the nondescript shipping box. His near-photographic memory replayed the image of it laying split open on the ground near one of the old Ford truck replicas. New truths were revealed—what its simple contents told. Folded neatly were an infant's tiny clothes, and tiny shoes, with their laces tied together to keep them from being separated. And a framed photograph of his mother and father standing together—she in a wedding dress, and he in an ill-fitting suit.

But it was not his father, at least not the father he thought he had. Instead, it was none other than Uncle Harley.

Cameron let himself consider the implications of that for the first time. That he wasn't the son of Carl and Mandy Decker, but actually was the son of Harley and Mandy Decker. He didn't even attempt to figure out the course of events that would lead his mother to leave one brother for the other. Harley was a lowlife criminal, while Carl, from what he remembered and had been told, was a wonderful, kind man. *So who am I?* Does knowing I'm the spawn of such a man as Harley, that criminal deviant, make any difference? Change things? Is his deviancy somehow inbred in me too—deep down in some part of my DNA?

"Uh . . . so what's happening?" Sanu asked within their shrouded darkness.

"I don't really know for sure. I think . . . maybe . . . we're now in some kind of a hug."

"Well, I can't breathe well in here. And that awful smell!"

Cameron could hear the beating of Joe's heart—slow and steady—the warmth of Joe's body, pressed against his face. Strangely, there was something comforting about his embrace, yet peculiar, too. Mental images of the recent slaughter were still sickly fresh in his mind. But Joe, clearly, did not mean them any personal harm and that, at least, was something. Feeling the fleshy cloak around them withdraw, he blinked into the morning light.

Cameron looked up, meeting the Hengtied Portule's serious stare. "Why? Why kill them all, Joe? They were not violent . . ."

"Poshnaks!"

"Yeah . . . so what?"

"Hunters. They come to . . . my home. Eaters of our flesh."

Cameron felt Sanu move into view from behind him. Joe stared down at the petite android woman.

"Please don't hurt me," she said. Tentatively, she reached a hand up and touched Joe. "You're a Hengtied Portule." She glanced at Cameron and said, "There are very few of them still in existence."

A low growl emanated up from within Joe's chest.

"And he's right . . . his kind have been mercilessly hunted for centuries. By the Poshnak Empire, also by others. Their meat is considered a rare delicacy." She looked up at Joe with compassionate eyes. "There never were many of his kind on . . . ," she stared away in thought.

"Fawn Lore," Joe said.

Sanu nodded, "Fawn Lore . . . that's right. His kind's were hunted to near extinction. And because they are so hard to kill," she gestured to the surrounding carnage, "any hunter's successful quarry is that much more prized."

Cameron remembered Alice telling him of Joe's world, of Fawn Lore, that it was a mere four light-years away from Sang-Morang. "I'm sorry, Joe. I didn't know." He tore his eyes away from the dead aliens, spread about them wearing their harsh environment suits.

Steam hissed loudly from the squab-lift's thruster cones. "Sanu . . . this vessel, can it get us to Winforge on its own? Do we even need to bother with the mother ship?"

She furrowed her brow, considering his question. "I'll need to go onboard, too many unknowns. Like its fuel reserves. What velocity can be achieved in deep space?"

Joe suddenly turned his head—looking behind him as though he'd heard something.

Then Cameron heard it too. "That's the others . . . hiding in one of those containers. They're my friends, Joe. You won't hurt them." He'd said it as a statement, not a question. "Let's get them out of there. Sanu, how about you go check out the squab-lift. Find out what we're working with there. See if it can make it to Winforge, relatively quick."

Only then did Cameron notice the robots. Now exiting out from where they'd found hiding places, from behind the tall metal stairwell walls, behind cargo containers, and from behind the landing struts of the squab-lift. They looked lost and confused. He wondered what they would do now, no longer having an instructed purpose to fulfill.

chapter 65

Heather . . .

She needed help walking. Fortunately, Manny was there to support much of her weight. Wearing someone's uniform shirt, she didn't remember whose it was, or even how she'd gotten into it. As they stepped out of the lift, two individuals were waiting for them. Heather stopped short, shocked to see him there. It was the medic from the *Primion*. The cyborg was unmistakable—had a very unique face. "You're Lutous Bright 953 . . . you were on the *Primion*," she asked.

The cyborg smiled kindly. "Same model, but different cyborg. My name is Radiant 211. If you haven't noticed, this vessel incorporates much of the same Thidion technology as found on that older spacecraft. And *Ginott 3* has a TAM AI, like that of the *Primion*, as well as other high-end technology—"

The older uniformed man, standing to the cyborg's right, cleared his throat. "Excuse me, I am Captain Peel, the commander of this vessel . . . of the *Ginott 3*."

Heather inwardly shuddered hearing that dreadful name again. *How could they name such a beautiful vessel after such a shit of a being?*

"I understand *Ginott 3* has undergone a holdings transfer," he said.

Radiant 211, the Lutous Bright 953 look-a-like, moved to Heather's other side, taking ahold of her arm then assisting their forward progress down the corridor.

The captain's demeanor seemed to be growing more and more tense as each moment passed. "Okay . . . I'm not sure what that means, but I'll take your word for it," Heather said.

"Ownership of the *Ginott 3*!" The ship's captain stayed motionless where he stood—making a stand, apparently.

"Yes, I got that. The ship has a new owner now," Heather replied, back over her shoulder.

"And that is you? You . . . one and the same?" he asked.

"I don't know. Maybe . . . I guess so. I don't feel well. Can we talk about this later, please?" She heard the captain fast walking in order to catch up with them.

"I have been the captain of this vessel for . . . in human terms . . . four years. If there is to be a change of crew personnel, of executive-level—"

"Captain . . ."

"Peel," Manny said.

"Captain Peel, I don't think your job, nor anyone else's, is going to change in the near future. And if you do work for me, of which I'm not at all certain, your first order of business will be to change the name of the ship. I don't ever want to hear, or see, the name *Ginott 3* again." She glanced up in time to notice they'd arrived. On the pristine, glass-like hatchway was etched:

Ginott 3

Juvinate Plastron

The hatch quietly slid to one side. Heather winced in pain as the cyborg attendant, along with Manny's help, maneuvered her inside then onto one of the unoccupied medical platforms. After taking in all the high-tech medical devices surrounding them, Heather noticed the captain was still lurking nearby.

"What . . . what else do you need from me? I really don't feel very well."

"A destination. Hasn't the droid XI already requested this information from you?"

Radiant 211, after helping her to lean back, quickly placed a small device on each of her temples. She then felt him positioning more devices on other areas of her body. *Where should we go? Earth? That was the plan, wasn't it?* That the Loth, Cam's Loth, could do something . . . could somehow help. And there were the army of security droids that supposedly were onboard this ship. She was feeling drowsy, something the cyborg did to her, probably. It was hard to think—hard to make such important decisions when everything was so mentally foggy.

"Hey, Captain, you need to back off a while. Let the poor girl recover from the beatings your former bosses gave her. You got that? You understand me?"

Heather put a restraining hand on Manny's arm. "It's all right." As her eyes closed, her voice just above a whisper, she murmured, "Captain . . . set a course for Sang-Morang."

"You sure, girl?" Manny sounded concerned. "Not Earth?"

Heather had barely the strength to nod her head. Swallowing, "I need Cam. The Loth . . . will listen to him . . . not me. We need Cam." She then drifted off to sleep.

chapter 66

Cameron...

The squab-lift could barely accommodate the five of them, let alone the addition of a large Hengtied Portule, and one of the robots, Thack, who'd requested to come along with them.

Although Sanu seemed quite competent for piloting the small cargo craft, Rand insisted he was far more qualified for performing such a task. "Do you really want a half-breed robot at the helm, performing such an important function?" he asked, with no consideration for her feelings. Fortunately, Sanu did not seem to mind the slight, but tasked herself to conforming the craft's internal atmospheric environment to one suitable for humans. Within the hour, everyone was either strapped in, or holding tight to the nearest bulkhead, as Rand lifted the vessel off from exoplanet Clay.

Pretty much just a single, bare-bones compartment existed above the larger cargo area below. Cameron was seated next to Deputy Kyle and the sheriff. As the squab-lift cleared the atmosphere and entered what was akin to Earth's stratosphere, the little craft began to vibrate, then buck and shudder violently.

"This bucket of bolts even going to make it up into space?" Kyle asked, clearly trying not to show his nervousness.

The sheriff, who also seemed concerned, turned to Cameron, brows raised. Apparently Cameron's limited time in space, although in a number of different crafts over the past few months, made him an expert.

"It's fine. We'll move past all this turbulence soon." Catching Sanu's eye across the compartment, she nodded back in approval.

"We'll be entering low orbit momentarily," Rand announced, over the loud, obviously straining propulsion system. "Next stop, Winforge . . . if this thing holds together that long."

A repetitive tone, along with a synchronized, blinking indicator light positioned on the control board, suddenly brought a concerned expression onto Rand's face. "It's the Mothership!"

Cameron had all but forgotten about that aspect. Of course, that ship would be tracking her own cargo vessel. Probably had tried repeatedly to establish contact with the crew.

Rand began tapping on buttons, with not too much rhyme or reason behind it, until a display blinked several times before coming fully to life.

"I don't like the looks of that!" the sheriff exclaimed.

No one else spoke for several seconds. Cameron assessed the vessel. The Mothership was huge! And it looked—not coming up with a better word for it—dangerous.

Rand shook his head. "That's a re-commissioned war cutter. Heavily armed, also fast. Sorry, folks, but we need to acknowledge their hail and do whatever they tell us to do."

"They'll kill us," Cameron said. "Or did you forget the little matter of their dead crew, splayed back there on the ground?"

"That was the fault of that . . . *thing*, you brought along. Not me . . . not us."

Cameron shot a glance toward Joe. Fortunately, the creature was still wrapped up within its protective fleshy cloak.

"Make a run for it! Do whatever you have to do . . . you will not surrender this vessel!" Everyone glanced up at the now-standing sheriff. His service pistol was drawn, and, by the look on his face, no one doubted his conviction to pull the trigger.

Rand stared into the muzzle of the gun for several beats before turning back to the console. The squab-lift suddenly accelerated forward fast, throwing the sheriff back into his seat.

"Just so you know . . . we're all going to die," Rand said.

"Head for the closest slip-band!" Cameron yelled. "It's not far . . ."

"Already on it. But we're burning fuel . . . lots of it. We won't have a lot of options once we're beyond it."

"I know a place," Cameron said. "I know the perfect place."

"They're firing on us!" Rand said, his voice surprisingly calm. "We've been hit . . . twice."

Everyone peered about the cramped space.

"Cargo hold . . . not in here," Rand added. "We're entering the slip-band." He leaned back, expelling a long breath.

"Are they following us?" the sheriff asked.

Rand shook his head. "They don't appear to be. Last I looked, the Mothership was circling back toward the planet. I'm sure they've gone to check on their unresponsive crew."

* * *

Having to conserve what little fuel remained, it took eight full days before they reached Sang-Morang's upper orbit.

"We need to land . . . and fast. Any preference?" Rand asked.

Cameron then recalled that Rand and the others had actually been here before. They'd come looking for Heather and him and found what was left of the *Primion*. "Yes. Um, can you put us down close to the *Primion*?"

"Sure, why not?"

Now what? Cameron thought to himself. He was right back where he'd started. He mentally began working on a new plan of attack, one that would get them to Winforge. Surely, there was still some fuel left in the tank. He could use the Lox device to make more. It would take some time, but somehow they would—"

Rand turned to face him "Sorry . . . but it looks as though your parking space is already taken."

Cameron didn't understand. Then he did. "Just set us down behind it," he said, now remembering he'd left one of his replicated F-150 trucks parked there just days before.

"There is no room behind that huge spacecraft, none at all. I'll have to set us down above the ridgeline, up on the plateau. We're just about out of fuel . . . so we're landing, no matter what. The bigger question is, will whoever they are be friendly?"

Huge spacecraft? Cameron got up to take a better look at the video feed on the display. Sure enough, there was a big spaceship there, one that landed, apparently, right on top of the *Primion* and his old truck. *Who in hell would land a big vessel like that there?* He didn't know whether he should be angry or thrilled now that there potentially was another way off this planet.

"Maybe we should rethink this," Rand said. "I may have just enough fuel to fly us a few miles away."

Cameron stared at the display with disbelief. *Did I really just see that?* "No! Land this thing and get that hatch open!"

Rand shrugged, but then did as told. The landing struts had no sooner touched ground when Cameron was already out, climbing down the outer side of the craft. Not waiting for the slow-moving cargo lift, he ran toward the ridgeline and the magnificent white ship now towering above it. He then saw movement again, the upper section of a forty-five-foot-tall Loth, and heard repeating honking sounds. Reaching the ridge, Cameron focused his attention on the path, winding its way downward to the beautiful valley below where three bright-blue streams coursed their way north.

The Loth was already a quarter of the way down the grade when Cameron, cupping both hands around his mouth, yelled out, "LOTH!"

The ginormous beast slowed—using its tree-trunk-sized tentacles to come to a halt. A thick dust cloud formed around the beast; to the point it could no longer be seen. Then he did. The Loth was looking back toward the rise—studying from where the voice had come from. Cameron waved a hand and smiled. Blinking away the tears forming in his eyes, he yelled again, "Get up here, Loth . . . get on up here!"

Honk! . . . Honk! . . . Honk!

It would take the Loth a few minutes. Turning his attention back to the huge white ship, he could see someone climbing the steep ridge, and doing a terrible job of it. With all the loose dirt cascading down beneath his feet, the guy was not making very good headway. Cameron stared intently. *Wait.* That's not a he—that's a *she.* A hundred yards away, down below, he could now see her. Her hair was pulled up into a tight ponytail. He began walking toward her, not daring to hope it actually, impossibly, could really be her.

"Cam!"

He stopped in his tracks, staring.

"Damn it, Cam . . . come help me!"

He heard her laugh—that wonderful, frustrated sounding, laugh. *I love that laugh.* Running toward the ridge, he saw that she'd already managed to climb to the top. She looked out of breath as she stood there with her hands on her knees breathing hard.

He ran to her and then stopped several paces away. She looked different. Very different. Then he saw her welcoming smile—and the tears glistening in her eyes. He stepped into her now open arms and they melded into one. He held her tight and breathed her in. Then, hungrily, desperately, they kissed. All the longing he had felt for her and had tried to suppress—for so long—he could now, finally, express.

"I love you, Cam . . . I love you, I love you, I love you." Her hands cradled both sides of his face as she kissed his cheeks, his chin, and then his lips. "Don't you *ever* leave me again!" she said, seeming angry.

"I won't . . . I promise. But just to clarify, you left me."

"Oh, just shut up and kiss me."

He did, then held her an arm's length away. "Heather . . . why are you—"

"Furry?"

Cameron nodded, taking her in more fully, carefully scrutinizing her altered appearance.

"You hate it . . . you hate the way I look. I'm like an animal, that's what you're thinking."

He laughed out loud, but then found she saw no humor in the situation. Continuing to gaze at her, he said, "I love it . . . you're more beautiful than ever. And it's . . . kind of sexy."

"No, it's not."

"Yes, it is."

The smile returned to her lips. "I think it is, too . . . but keep in mind, it's only temporary and will fade away over time. Oh, Cam . . . there's so much I have to tell you! Earth is in trouble, like *big* trouble. More Loths . . . and Winforge . . . oh God, let me tell you, it's no zoo—"

Next, with no warning, Cameron was propelled high into the air. As a tentacle wrapped around his chest, he barely had the time to cover his head with his arms and hands before the Loth's massive tongue began licking him. Soon, gobs of sticky mucus covered his entire body from head to toe. "I missed you too, Loth. Put me down now, okay?"

His feet back on firm ground, he turned toward Heather. "I need a shower, fast, before this shit turns to stone on me." But Heather wasn't looking at him. She was staring behind him, in the direction of the squab-lift.

"Dad?"

chapter 67

Cameron turned around, following Heather's gaze toward the others in his party who'd just now come into view behind them.

"Is that Kyle?" she asked, seeming even more confused.

"Yup. I'm sure you can imagine how excited I was seeing him again . . . ," but Heather was already running off.

"Dad! Oh my God . . . I can't believe it's really you!" Heather ran into her father's open arms, where she was swept up into his tight embrace.

Hearing the sounds of footsteps coming behind him, Cameron turned and found three strangers: a brawny, muscular-looking woman; a slender, a more demure-like woman; and a rather small male, an alien, with an unpleasant expression on his face.

"My name is Manny . . . you must be Cam."

"That I am. I'd really like to meet the three of you . . . but if I don't wash this Loth mucus shit off me, like right now, I'll be in big trouble. Is there a shower on board that big beautiful ship of yours?"

"Um . . . probably, but it's not my ship. It's hers," Manny said, gesturing toward Heather. She was with the others in his crew, as introductions all around were being made.

Cameron smiled. *And I was worried she'd never survive in outer space.*

* * *

Two hours later, Heather and Cameron, holding hands, walked along the shore of the familiar, center-most, Sang-Mo-rang valley stream. In the distance, the Loth splashed and played—clearly happy to be back home.

Sharing their respective, albeit harrowing adventures, both listened carefully, saving any questions until the other finished speaking.

Cameron stopped to pull Heather close in his arms, something he'd already done a number of times. He just couldn't get enough of her. "I'm sorry. It was selfish of me, dragging you away from your home. Practically getting you killed . . . what sounds like over and over again."

A few moments passed before she looked up. Tears in her eyes, she said, "Truth is, I was more than a little angry with you. I wanted to punch you in your *stupid* face. Even fantasized about it. Me, this sheltered hostess from the Drake Café, was ill-prepared for so many intergalactic, death-defying adventures."

"I'm so sorry—"

She interrupted his apology, adding, "But somewhere along the way, I stopped blaming you. I recognized my own place in all the craziness. How I might actually make my own small impact. That I could actually make real changes . . . little ol' me! Not only to a deplorable place like Winforge, but also in here . . . within myself." Placing a palm over her heart, she added, "It's all because of you, Cam . . . the belief you put in me . . . to be more than just that simple girl from Larksburg Stand. I can never go back to being . . . to being the old me."

"Okay, then I'm not all that sorry," Cameron said, grinning.

"The question now is, what's next?" she asked.

Still smiling, he said, "Earth, of course! We all climb into that ginormous spaceship of yours and go save fucking Earth . . . somehow."

The End

Thank you for reading Ship Wrecked II. Book III in the series is on the way.

If you enjoyed this book, PLEASE leave a review on Amazon.com—it really helps!

To be notified the moment all future books are released—please join my mailing list. I hate spam and will never, ever, share your information. Jump to this link to sign up:

http://eepurl.com/bs7M9r

Acknowledgments

First and foremost, I am grateful to the fans of my writing and the ongoing support for all my books. I'd like to thank my wife, Kim, she's my rock and is a crucial, loving, component of my publishing business. I'd like to thank my mother, Lura Genz, for her tireless work as my first-phase creative editor and a staunch cheerleader of my writing. I'd also like to thank Kimberly Peticolas for her amazing detailed editing work. Others who provided fantastic support include Lura and James Fischer, Stuart Church, and Eric Sundius.

Check out the other available titles by Mark Wayne McGinnis on the following page.

Other Books By MWM

Ship Wrecked Series
Ship Wrecked
Ship Wrecked II

Scrapyard Ship Series
Scrapyard Ship
HAB 12
Space Vengeance
Realms of Time
Craing Dominion
The Great Space
Call to Battle

Tapped In Series
Mad Powers
Deadly Powers

Lone Star Renegades Series
Lone Star Renegades (also called Jacked)

Star Watch Series
Star Watch
Ricket
Boomer
Glory for Sea and Space
Space Chase
Scrapyard LEGACY

The Simpleton Series
The Simpleton
The Simpleton Quest

Galaxy Man Series
Galaxy Man

Boy Gone Series
Boy Gone

Made in the USA
Coppell, TX
01 August 2022

80761131R00270